Cowboy Rising

A novel by Linda Ellison

Book three in *The Cutter* series

© Linda Ellison 2019

Linda Ellison asserts the moral right to be identified as the author of
'Cowboy Rising'

Cover photography by Linda Ellison

Design and typeset by Green Avenue Design

Published by Cilento Publishing, Sydney Australia

ISBN Paperback: 978-0-6487566-1-3

ISBN Australian Paperback: 978-0-6487566-0-6

ISBN Kindle: 978-0-6487566-2-0

This novel is entirely a work of fiction. Any resemblance to actual persons, living or dead, is entirely coincidental.

Instagram: lindaellison.author

For
Anders, Logan & Chanel

There is a special place in my heart that is yours alone
I am your teacher, your protector, your friend
When you fail, I promise to pick you up
When your heart breaks, my heart breaks for you
You will do a lot of stupid things, but tell no lies and keep no secrets from me
At times you will disappoint me, crush me, and hurt me, but you are
already forgiven
I will walk to the ends of the earth for you and give you my last breath
There is no one in this world that will love and care for you more,
because I am, and always will be,
your Momma
xxx

Chapter One

It's dark. The lights are out and the arena is deathly silent, in a state of complete blackness.

There is an atmosphere. A pause. A whistle. It's enough to start up the crowd who are anxious for the last ride of the night and they begin to shout and stomp their feet, all spurring on the last cowboy. The sound from the stands of five thousand pairs of boots drumming the floor is deafening. A lone spotlight highlights the chute and the applause goes over the top. The music thumps to the beat of a very fired up audience and the arena is lit up with a spectacular burst of sparks that shoot up high into the air. Colors of red, white and blue reach for the overhead lighting and fall gracefully, disappearing before they hit the ground, as the announcer fills the empty space with his voice to introduce the last courageous rider.

Raylee hates this. Wishing that she wasn't there, she desperately wanted it over.

Rodeos had been a big part of her life growing up and had never bothered her before, until Cutter was hurt by a rogue bull that chased him down and slammed him hard against the rails, knocking him out cold and breaking his arm. Even though that was how they came to be together, she'd never look at rodeo in the same way and tonight was certainly no exception.

She couldn't take her eyes off the chute and as she slipped her hand into Cutter's and gripped it tight, she held her breath and was tempted to look away. Her stomach turned over and her fear came up into her throat, making her swallow hard, while her feet were now restless and her sweaty hands were shaking violently.

"Don't look," Cutter said.

"I can't. I have to look," she replied in a trembling voice, and Cutter put his arm around the back of her chair and pulled her in close to help settle her.

It was the longest wait of her life and added to the sickly feeling that was sitting silently in her heart. An explosion of colored lights filled the arena and the music hit an all time high when the cowboy gave a nod and the chute was pulled open. The bull launched forward. He was big, aggressive, and when he felt those spurs in his sides, his eyes widened and he went ballistic.

The cowboy was young and held on tight, as he sat high on the bull's back with no less than two thousand pounds between his legs. Balancing with his arm thrown back, the cowboy was being spun around in tight circles with every thrust of the bull's ferocious buck and twist. It was fast and perfectly in time to Raylee's heartbeat, and when Cutter felt her hand squeeze his, he was sure it was cutting off the circulation to his fingers.

The crowd were cheering him on as the seconds raced on the clock. The cowboy was hanging on for his life, feeling the full adrenalin charge of the bull who was now totally pissed at the rider on his back. He was unleashing every bit of fury he had in him to get that rider off, with an untamed strength of power and an eye that was deadly.

All eyes were on the cowboy, but when the timer reached the six second mark, the bull gave a vicious twist that caught the cowboy off balance, spitting him to the dirt.

It was done. He had given it his best shot, although tonight his best was not good enough. Landing on his knees, clear of the bull, the cowboy immediately stood up and ran in the opposite direction away from danger as the bull was now being distracted by the two bullfighters, who were spectacularly encouraging him towards the gate.

Everyone in the stands rose to their feet to applaud him, even though he put his head down as he walked back to the chute, annoyed at himself and disappointed in that ride. Raylee released Cutter's hand and she stood up to join everyone in an applause that was long and drawn out.

The night was now finally over.

"Wooo," Cutter said loudly. He was pumped up and was applauding too. "That was insane," he said, pleased for the young cowboy even though he didn't reach his eight second target.

Raylee agreed with him. "Insane is right. In more ways than one," she added seriously.

The crowd remained standing, waiting for the official results to hit the big screen while the announcer was dramatically filling in the time with rambling commentary. Cutter and Raylee didn't need to see the results to know that it was another ride and another unsuccessful rodeo for Colton Jones.

"I'm so pleased it's over," Raylee stated, feeling the relief that her son had walked away in one piece. "That was way too close for my liking."

Cutter picked up on her relief. "Hey, you can start breathing now," he said, to help ease her mind.

It had been an intense night and now that it was over, Raylee turned to Johnny and Emma O'Brien, who had made the trip to Nashville with them. Their daughter, Avery, had tagged along with Colton and his sister, Dakota, for their first road trip together out of state.

Johnny reached over and grabbed Cutter on the shoulder. "He's still got a lot of work to do," he said in an honest but supportive way, and Cutter couldn't disagree with him, much to the complete disapproval of Raylee, who would rather her son rode cutting horses like his father instead of bulls.

When the presentation was done and the music had died down, the crowd dispersed slowly through the many exits and the bright lights of the arena came back on. The officials came in with tractors to prepare the sand while others packed down the extra rails and the presentation stand. Cutter and Raylee didn't rush. They were staying in town for the weekend and were there to surprise their son. After the crowd had thinned out, they made their way out of the arena to the competitor car park where they were sure to give Colton and the two girls a shock they weren't expecting.

They found his truck easily enough. It didn't take long, as Cutter had lent them his father's old blue truck for their first trip away and it stood out among all the other late models. It was only when his father had passed away over twenty years ago that Cutter had taken it out of the garage and started to drive it. He'd looked after it for all those years and it held a personal value that couldn't be replaced.

Cutter pulled on the handle. It was locked and neither Colton nor the girls were anywhere to be seen. He asked around and nobody had seen them. The heads-up was that many of the riders from the rodeo were in the big tent out the back, and as the four of them made their way to the other side of the arena to look for their kids, when they neared, they could hear the music from the live band thumping out a song.

It was dark and late, and as they entered the makeshift club, it was full of drunk and disorderly cowboys and cowgirls, celebrating the success of the night or drowning their disappointing results. Everyone seemed to be having a good time on the dance floor, as it was packed to capacity. The lights were dim and it was smoky, with only a few colored spotlights that helped them to see.

Cutter picked up Raylee's hand and unintentionally squeezed it. He never went to the bar after a show. He hadn't been to a bar for nearly thirty years since he knew that was where all trouble begins and ends. It was an unwritten law in their house and it was the last place he ever expected to see his son. They looked around. Everyone was wearing the same thing. Jeans, boots and hats, and it made looking for their kids and Avery a little difficult in the seedy dark room.

"I can't see them," Raylee said loudly in Cutter's ear so that he could hear. He didn't answer and he kept walking around anyway, just to make sure.

They split up. Johnny and Emma went over to the bar while Cutter and Raylee walked around the outside of the dance floor. "Maybe they're back at the truck now," Raylee said, only as a suggestion, as it seemed unlikely they would find them in this loose crowd of party goers. "Let's go back and look again," she added, although it was more so they could leave.

He didn't answer again and was beginning to think that Raylee was right. This wasn't where they were going to find their kids. It was more likely they had missed them in passing and that they were already back at the hotel.

Feeling uncomfortable about being there, they turned around and were heading towards the door to leave when Raylee stopped still, stunned by what she was looking at. Cutter pulled her by the hand to move and when she didn't, he looked up. He was completely floored.

On the dance floor was their daughter; up close and very personal with a cowboy who had his hands all over her, touching her provocatively while he had his face buried in her neck. Dakota was clearly loving every minute of it, as she held her arms up high and rocked to the band while shouting out the words to the song as if it was hers.

Cutter and Raylee stood watching, unsure of what to do next. Should they turn around and walk away? Should they break it up? The reality of what they were looking at hadn't sunk in and their confusion was only added to when they saw Colton dancing next to her, beer bottle in the air with Avery hanging off him, throwing back a whiskey. They were well on their way to being drunk and their public display of dirty dance moves looked more appropriate for a private dance party for two, behind closed doors.

No, this can't be happening, Cutter thought. Colton and Avery, both drunk? Dakota, dancing with some sleazy cowboy, allowing him to touch her that way?

Whatever level of crazy thoughts were going through Cutter's mind as to how this was happening, was only taking less priority over what he was going to do about it. His son didn't drink, let alone party. His daughter wasn't some cheap and easy flirt. His thoughts snapped back to the dance floor and as they were making their way through the crowd towards them, Dakota saw her parents coming and she froze. She stopped still. It was enough to put the fear in her while the others kept dancing, unaware that their party had just been seriously crashed. Cutter pushed through the crowd and had almost reached them when a fist came from nowhere and took his son to the floor.

Cutter looked up. It was Johnny who was standing over Colton. He had just laid Colton out with a fistful of anger that landed him on the ground. While Cutter thought his son may have deserved it and it had crossed his mind to do the same thing, it was his instincts that took over when he landed one in return on Johnny's cheek in Colton's defense. There was a scuffle on the dance floor and when all the cowgirls scattered to clear a way, a dozen fights broke out and no one knew who was fighting who and for what reason.

Emma grabbed Avery and pulled her to the side while Raylee took Dakota by the hand and led her away. The four girls stood watching helplessly and screamed at the boys to stop fighting, while the band didn't miss a beat and the bar was still in full swing, fuelling up the crowd for the long night ahead.

It was more of a wild brawl and every cowboy seemed to be more than willing to get involved. The security team was quick to the center of the dance floor and pulled everyone apart, and when they had Johnny restrained, Cutter leaned down to his son who was still lying on the floor, slowly coming around.

"Wake up," Cutter said forcefully, while he was slapping Colton on the side of his face.

Colton was on his back and moving. He had a gash across his cheekbone and the outside of his eye was glowing red. He lifted his head and rested back on his elbows, looking up into his father's face. He tried to focus but didn't speak, and he gave him a drunken smug grin that made Cutter fume, before another fist came from over the top of Cutter's shoulder and knocked Colton out again.

It was lights out.

"What the hell were you thinking?"

It was the question thrown to Colton from both his parents when they were back in the hotel room later that night.

His mother was looking closely at the cut on his face, assessing the need for stitches while his father was pacing around the room, ready to explode. Cutter was now tired, stressed and totally pissed off.

"And you," Cutter said aggressively when he pointed directly at his daughter. "I have no words for what I saw you doing tonight." Cutter was angry at the behavior of both his children and he let them know it. "And as for you drinking, you're both underage," he stated. "I don't understand where that's come from."

"I wasn't drinking," Dakota threw back quickly, knowing that both her parents disapproved.

Cutter looked into her face. She was teary and had been sobbing all the way back to the hotel, and while he hated making girls cry, it didn't soften him this time. He could have easily unleashed more fury on her and reeled off what exactly was on his mind, except that he turned to his son instead. "You disappointed me tonight," Cutter told Colton in simple, straight forward terms. He was still fired up, though would try to tone it down and tackle the situation more diplomatically.

Colton was quick to fire it back. "Disappoint you? That's all I've ever done, isn't it?" he said sharply, and he stood up and threw some weight behind his words. "You're the legendary Cutter Jones. The best horse trainer in the entire country and I've had to live up to your name my whole life. Everyone expects me to stand in your boots and go on to train the best horses and win the big shows. Just like you. Well I'm sorry I couldn't do that. And I'm sorry that disappoints you."

Cutter was deeply cut. He'd never heard this from his son before and it surprised him in the most saddened kind of way. "You think that because you don't train cutting horses, that I look at you as if you're a failure?" he asked.

"It's West that's gonna carry on your name in the cutting world. Not me," he said. "I know it, and everyone else knows it too. So what's the point of even trying?"

Westyn Jones had already made a good name for himself in the cutting horse industry, even though he was still riding in the junior ranks. He'd already trained two of his own horses and was on a successful path. As the younger brother, he was nothing like Colton and it was clear from tonight that there was a jealousy that had never been openly admitted before.

"You don't need to compare yourself to your brother. Why would you do that? He's good at what he does," Cutter said in support of his youngest son. "It is what it is."

"I can't even ride a bull as long as you could," Colton yelled. "How do you think that makes me feel?"

Cutter looked at him. All he wanted to do was reach out now and show his son just how much he loved him. But this was tough love. This wasn't the time to back down. "Do you know what you've done here tonight? With Avery? With Johnny?" he asked, and before Colton could answer, he explained. "Johnny's been my best friend my whole life and we've never argued once, and tonight, you changed that."

While Cutter could only agree with Johnny, he still didn't feel it was right to lay his son out like that. It was still unclear just how close the friendship between their two kids had become and Cutter wanted some answers. "So what's going on with you and Avery?" he asked, since they had all grown up together and no one was suspecting that they had advanced to anything more than just friends.

It was something that Colton was less committed to answering. He didn't want to bring Avery into their argument and he remained silent about her. Tonight was not about her. As far as Colton was concerned, this was all about him and his father.

Cutter looked to his daughter. "Kotie... How long's this been going on?" he asked, expecting Dakota to give him an honest answer.

Dakota looked to her brother. He gave her the silent eyes and she said nothing.

Cutter didn't say anymore. It was clear that neither of his children were spilling the details and looking at his son's bruised eye and cut face, Cutter decided that he'd copped enough for one night. The beer seemed to be taking the immediate pain away and he knew that by tomorrow morning, Colton would be feeling the worst of it.

"I'll be back," Cutter said, and he left the room.

Raylee was most upset. They had planned the weekend away with the O'Briens and thought it would be a nice surprise for Colton to know that he had his parents' full support in the rodeo. They had left their ranches in good hands with both their boys. Jake O'Brien and Westyn Jones were taking care of everything back home for a couple of days, giving both parents the chance to get away and think of something else for a change, instead of cattle, horses and housework.

They had only flown in that afternoon and were planning on having a nice relaxing weekend. They were on course to having a good time and instead, they were now at the center of a family and friends' dispute with their son being the cause of it all.

When Cutter knocked on his neighbor's door, Johnny was quick to answer it. They were staying in the next room and when Johnny stepped out into the corridor, he pulled the door closed behind him.

"Hit me," Cutter said, standing close to Johnny without any sign of defense.

Johnny stood straight. He was only an inch taller than Cutter and only looked down at him from a near level. "I'm not gonna hit you. Why would I do that?" he asked.

"Because I deserve it... And it will make us even." Cutter was sorry for striking his best friend like that, though he couldn't take it back now. "I'm sorry. I don't know what happened back there and I can't believe I hit you."

Johnny put his hand on Cutter's shoulder and looked into his eyes. "Bro... It's not you I'm gonna hit," he said, making it clear that this was far from over.

"How's Avery? Has she said anything?"

"She hasn't said much. But I'll let her mother talk to her. Maybe Em will have more luck than me," he said. "She's drunk, Cutter," he stated, letting his disappointment be known.

"I can't tell you how sorry I am. I never saw this coming." Cutter was as shocked as everyone else and while it wasn't his fault, he still felt partially responsible.

"I don't know what to tell you," Johnny began to say, before he felt the need to give it to him straight. "But if you don't get some control over Colton now, he's gonna get a whole lot worse."

Chapter Two

The next couple of days were a little strained to say the least.

Avery left Nashville on the plane with her parents, while Cutter drove Colton home in the truck. Little was said on the eleven hour drive, although it wasn't from a lack of trying. Cutter tried to get to the bottom of all the issues that had been thrown his way in the last twelve hours, after Colton had unleashed all his anger and blame towards his father for everything that had ever gone wrong in his life.

While Colton's bull ride at the rodeo only got one mention the entire trip, it turned out that it was his father's fault too.

There were stretches of highway where the silence was just as boring as the road. Not letting Avery get mixed up in what Colton thought was the more important issue at hand; he remained tight lipped about their relationship, leaving his father second guessing.

When Cutter looked to his passenger, he could see that Colton's ego was as bruised as his face and his head was hurting. Nothing said hangover quite like his bloodshot eyes that he had trouble keeping open, although it was nothing compared to the uneasy feeling in his gut from the several shots of whiskey that had been chased down by a beer. Colton hadn't been a drinker until he hit the rodeo circuit and he didn't need to drink much to wipe himself out.

Cutter was in deep thought. He was nothing like his son and was now having a difficult time finding a connection. Wanting him to take full responsibility for his actions and mistakes, Cutter knew that with every mile they travelled, it was less likely he was going to hear an apology, especially when Colton spent more time looking out the window and was thinking more about the consequences that were heading his way when they arrived home.

Growing up, Colton had been Cutter's blue-eyed boy. Very quiet, though quite mischievous at times, yet always following his father everywhere he went. He couldn't wait to fit into his father's boots one day and showed promising signs early on that he was talented on a horse. His work on the ranch was very thorough and he knew everything there was to know about cattle and the land.

Trailing behind him was his younger brother, Westyn, who looked up to Colton and admired everything that he was. Together the two boys made the barn and the sand yard their life, before and after school each day. Every ride across the ranch and every training session with the horses, they did it together and for the best part of their lives, they were inseparable.

Since Colton had left school and gone to work for his father full-time on the ranch, things had changed.

Their friendly challenge to each other to fully train a young horse and show it at the biggest event on the national calendar, turned out to be not so friendly when Westyn was thrown into the spotlight by winning a gold buckle. It was the beginning of the end for the two boys, and their closeness slowly drifted to an intolerance that was almost unfamily.

When the truck pulled up in front of the barn, Raylee came out of the kitchen and stood on the porch, watching them grab their bags from the backseat and walk to the house. Colton, with his sunken shoulders, didn't speak when he walked up the steps, but gave her a kiss on the cheek and went inside while Cutter put his bag down and gave her a hug with a squeeze that came from his need to feel her close.

"How was your trip?" she asked.

"It totally sucked," he replied, giving her an honest and quick description. "What about yours?"

"It was awkward," Raylee admitted. "I'm so glad you're home," she said and from the looks of him, so was he.

"Hey, you wanna go for a ride?"

"What for?" she asked. "You only just got home."

He looked at her. She had forgotten. She racked her brain, looking at his face as if she should know. It was clear to Cutter, although with everything that had happened over the messed up weekend, nothing else was playing on Raylee's mind except for Nashville.

"It's Marnie's birthday," he announced. She didn't need to respond, as the look on her face said a thousand words. "I'll just take my bags upstairs and change my shirt. Then I need to get some fresh air."

Raylee needed some fresh air too. They had arrived home earlier that same afternoon and had only beaten the boys by four hours. The mood in the house was a little flat, especially when Westyn noticed his sister was home in his father's place and he asked how their weekend was, followed by a hundred questions.

Yet today was Marnie's birthday and since they were both home now, Cutter and Raylee put Nashville behind them to pay her a visit.

When he came back downstairs a short while later, he had his work hat on and a fresh clean shirt. "You ready?" he asked.

As they walked to the barn, Raylee gave Cutter a rundown about her trip home. "Emma's made it quite clear, there's to be no contact between Colt and Avery, so you may want to tell him to lay low until everything cools down," she said.

He put his hand on the back of her neck. "From the way Johnny was last night, I don't think it's gonna cool down in a hurry," Cutter stated, and he could hardly blame him. He was just as furious and disappointed that his son had behaved so inappropriately with his best friend's daughter. Added in was the fact that Colton was drunk and had both girls in his care; this tormented Cutter even more.

It was supposed to be a friends' road trip. Cutter didn't want Colton going to Nashville on his own and had only agreed if his sister went along with him. When Avery heard of their plans, she'd booked her position in the backseat of the truck after she'd convinced her parents to let her go.

Looking back, that was their first mistake.

Dakota and Avery had grown up together and were best friends. While Colton always looked at them both like his sisters, it wasn't until a few months ago that he'd noticed Avery in a different way. She had grown up and had filled out in all the right places, and Colton took a liking to her. Once it was returned, it was secretly on between them and they did all they could to sneak around and hide their attraction to one another. Even though the trip was planned out well, it still made both parents a little nervous that their kids were going away for a weekend of country music festivals and the rodeo. Only to ease their concerns, they'd planned to fly in for a couple of days, just to make sure there were no problems and to join them as a family for a good time.

As it turned out, that was their second mistake.

Cutter slid the barn door open. There were only a couple of horses inside and he pulled out a nice young mare that he had trained a few years ago and had won a tidy sum of money on. She was not a champion like their stallion, Midnight, was and had only been retired to ranch work in the last six months.

Raylee, on the other hand, went to the small day yards next to the barn and brought her horse in, tying her up outside the tack room.

She was out of the blue roan mare and had been sired by Midnight. Cutter had trained her and ridden her through all her aged events, while Raylee had added another three buckles to her collection over the years. She was twelve years old now and since Raylee had slowed down in the cutting pen, she didn't have a need to replace her. Riding her on the ranch was something that she liked to do each week. Keeping herself in the saddle and in touch with the progress of the cattle, and spending time with the boys, Raylee took the edge off everyone when they were busy.

They rode out the gate, side by side. Looking back, the view hadn't changed in over twenty years and when they looked to the barn and the house, it was still the same.

"I can't believe we raised three kids here," Raylee stated, although it was more to comment on the years that had flashed by them.

"And I can't believe that after everything we taught them, the way they were raised, that Colt has let me down like that." Cutter was still cut that his son had gone against everything he'd taught him. Against everything he believed in.

"But he is right in one way," Raylee said in her son's defense, and Cutter looked at her.

"I'm sorry, but I don't see anything right about what happened last night."

"I mean about living in your boots," she explained. "He's right. Everyone in the cutting world would be expecting him to live up to your name. He just wants to be his own person. Do his own thing and be successful doing what he loves. Not what everyone else expects him to be."

"And what is that exactly? Because I'm not real sure what that is."

"I don't know," she agreed. "It's always been cutting in this family. Maybe he thought that he didn't have a choice to do anything else."

"Well I'm sorry, but everyone has a choice in this world. I never expected him to go on and train horses like me if he didn't want to. He's making his own decisions."

The afternoon sun was cooling down and riding through the shadows of the trees was a little cold. The ranch had seen many cattle come and go over the years and had provided a good steady flow of numbers through the training process, then turned into good profit when they were finished off. The land was safe and they had survived the worst of times. A couple of major droughts and one out of control fire that tore through the back pasture, narrowly missing the resting place but taking out miles of fencing in its path, while the occasional flood had cut them off from town a few times. It had always come back though, and this season had a good body of feed that ensured the cattle would reach their targeted weight in the least amount of time. Double J Ranch was having a very good season.

On their way to the resting place, they stopped by the field of flowers and Raylee leaned down to pick a bunch for the graves. They hadn't been to the grave site together for some time and when they arrived, it was noticeably quiet. They tied the horses to the fence and walked through the gate.

It always made Raylee emotional when she went there and even though Marnie had been laid to rest five years ago, it still brought the tears out of her on every visit. She knelt in front of her grave and read it, then placed the flowers in Marnie's special floral teacup that sat on the ground in front of her headstone. They didn't need to say anything, just knowing that Marnie was a big part of both their lives and they missed her greatly.

Cutter stood up. "I'm so pleased she's not here to see what's going on in this family. She would be disappointed too," he said, being so sure of what Marnie's reaction would be.

"Or maybe she'd know exactly what to do," Raylee added. She stood up and put her arms around his waist as they looked over to Macca and Mary-Ann's graves.

Cutter rubbed his face. He was tired from the long drive home and stressed from the events of the rodeo. Looking at his parents' graves only added to the family pain. It was Raylee who was more forgiving than Cutter. "Do you remember when my parents caught us together?" she asked, not letting him forget that pivotal moment in their relationship.

He smiled. "That's something I'll never forget," he said. "I don't really know what would've happened if your dad's aim had been better," he stated.

She laughed, totally agreeing with him. "Just don't forget what it was like all those years ago, when all we wanted was to be together against my parents' demands to end it."

"I'm so pleased you didn't listen to them."

"And so am I," she agreed. "And maybe Colt and Avery will be the same. Maybe one day they'll look back at this time in their life and laugh at everything that happened this weekend and so will we."

They didn't need to be there long and they left the resting place once again with a little peace adding much needed calm to their very stressful weekend.

The mood on the ranch was a little unsettled since Nashville. Dakota was going out of her way to make up for her recent behavior, doing everything to please everyone and making herself useful. She was going that extra mile. Cutter had thrown himself into his work and was going through his normal daily routine in the barn and yards with Westyn by his side, before and after he finished school. Colton was avoiding his father as much as he could, leaving Raylee to be the one stuck in the middle. It kept everyone on edge, especially at meal times when Colton weighed the table down with his sombre mood and negative attitude towards everything. It was a different story at the O'Brien ranch. Avery was being closely guarded by both her parents. She was expected to pick up more of the workload to keep herself busy while her parents were monitoring her phone for any messages from Colton. He was banned from having any contact with her and she easily played along to please her father. She figured out quickly that the more sorry and cooperative she was, the sooner she would be released from their clutches.

The Jones' ranch was having less success. Everything that had happened made Colton spiral into a closed up book, where he wouldn't surface until after ten o'clock each day. Mostly it was not to work but because he was hungry. It would annoy his father when Colton wandered into the barn each afternoon and was uninterested in riding the ranch or doing any sort of cattle work with him.

It made Cutter pour out his frustrations into his training, and he tried everything to work with his son whenever there was an opportunity. Late of an afternoon when he should have been finishing up and winding everything down in the barn, he was saddling up and looking for extra work instead, just to include Colton in part of his day. Nothing was helping.

It had been a couple of weeks since the rodeo and no one from either ranch had crossed paths either out riding or in town picking up supplies. There had been no phone calls and no messages. There were no get togethers between the two families for dinners that were regularly classed as normal, and no team work when there were huge cattle numbers to get through the yards.

The Joneses and the O'Briens were simply not talking.

The blackened eye that Colton had been sporting had disappeared, although there were a few times when Cutter liked it better when it was there to remind his son that he had completely stuffed things up. It was Dakota who didn't want reminding. To keep out of trouble, she had been looking for a job and managed to pick up a few shifts at the diner in town. On her days off, she would help on the ranch wherever she was needed. Avery, on the other hand, was still looking for work and filled in her time babysitting for a couple of neighbouring families occasionally. Both girls had finished school and were taking time out to decide on their future, as they weren't wanting to rush into such an important decision without careful consideration.

Cutter could now see that the girls had a little too much time on their hands as of late, and he was thankful that they were now spending some time apart and were more focussed on work.

If only he could say the same about his son.

"I need you to go to town and pick up some feed," Cutter said to Colton when he came down to the barn one afternoon. It was getting late and he was still in the pen working with a young horse and didn't want to take the time out to do it himself. After all, he was looking for something that Colton could do instead of moping around feeling sorry for himself.

Colton agreed without giving his father any grief and he went into the feed room to work out exactly what was needed. He grabbed the keys to Macca's truck and left without any further discussion. It suited Colton just fine. He didn't want to be around for the rest of the day and he was beyond bored. It was making him agitated just hanging around and the thought of leaving the ranch was enough to brighten him up.

Macca's truck was used as the old work truck now. Cutter didn't drive it very often, but when he did, he always felt close to his father. It had been a heartbreaking decision to replace it, since it had taken the family everywhere and had done some serious miles over the years.

With the need to be away from the ranch, Colton was happy to drive to town, taking his time and listening to the radio. He turned it up when his favorite song came on, giving him an instant lift. The time was irrelevant to him as long as he was there before closing, as the feed wouldn't be needed until early the next morning. He parked out the front and went inside, placing his order at the counter and had a look around while he waited.

A new set of spurs caught his attention and he picked them up and looked at the detail. He held onto them and looked through the tack. There was nothing there that he didn't love, yet his head was everywhere else except ranching.

"Your order's ready, Colt," the store owner called out. "I'll put it on your dad's account," he added, while he was writing everything down the old fashioned way.

Colton threw the new set of spurs and straps on the counter. "Just add those to it," he said, as if it was his given right to have anything he wanted at the expense of his father.

When he threw the feed into the back and started the truck, he wound down the window to put his elbow out while he waited for the cars to pass by. A bang on the passenger window startled him. He looked over and was about to throw some choice words in that direction when he saw Avery. She opened the door and climbed in with a huge smile on her face.

"What're you doing?" Colton asked in a panic, and he started to look around to see who was watching them or if they had been set up. When he knew they were clear, he looked happy to see her.

"I can't help it if we just ran into each other like this," she defended, and she reached over and planted a kiss on the side of his mouth. He closed his eyes when she did and put his hand behind her head to hold her there longer, letting her kiss linger. He'd missed her touch and immediately fell for her all over again.

"I've only got an hour," she said, pulling away and making it clear that she was game if he was.

When there was a break in the flow of traffic, Colton pulled the truck out. "Put your head down," he requested, so that no one would see them in the truck together and she did, lying across the front seat while they talked.

"What did your dad say?" he asked of Nashville.

"You don't want to know. He's still not over it," she said, making it clear that Johnny was still wound up by it all.

"What about your mom?" he asked.

She had her head in his lap and was looking up into his face, keeping out of sight while he kept driving. "They're both not happy... I didn't tell them everything, but what I didn't tell them they guessed anyway. What about your parents?"

"Same. Although they're not unhappy with you. It's me they're really pissed at," he said. "Especially my dad."

They left town, driving out onto some country winding roads that Colton rarely went on. It was quite pretty on the other side of town, as the trees on either side of the road cast shadows across the truck as they drove through them. They were happy to be together, and headed towards a secluded and abandoned barn that was well known to the kids from school as a place to park and hang out on a Friday night. A place where the boys earned their bragging rights and the girls fell in love for the first time. Both of which had already been accomplished without going there for that reason.

Colton looked down at Avery and touched her face. She was beautiful. Her dark brown hair lay across his legs and her strawberry colored lips highlighted her smile. But it was the sparkle in her eyes that told him she felt the same way as he did.

"You can sit up now," he said, when he looked into the mirrors and found they were alone on the isolated road. "We'll be there soon."

She didn't sit up or reply, though she did unbuckle his belt and unzipped his jeans. His heart pumped fast, surprised that this could be happening before they got there. He didn't question her, and just sat back in the driver's seat and gripped the steering wheel tight, taking the corners like a race car driver on a winning drive.

He wanted to close his eyes and couldn't, feeling stirred up by her touches and wet kisses, while staring down at the lines on the road. She released his seatbelt and pulled up his shirt, touching his skin all over. To Colton, it felt so good and he'd just fallen in love with her all over again.

The lines on the road disappeared when they were close to the turn off, as it narrowed slightly and the bends sharpened up. He didn't slow down though, since his head was all over the other journey he was on and was taking his mind to another place. He was wanting this to never end, and could have driven all the way to San Francisco and back again with the in-drive entertainment this good. His breathing caught up to his heartbeat and when he looked down and watched her, his fingers dug into the steering wheel and the intensity took him to a whole new level. This had only been a distant thought for the last couple of weeks. A wish. A dream. A late night fantasy. Not thinking it could actually happen, and a few more turns in the winding road would see them both arrive at their destination.

When he took a blind bend still at full speed, he came across a small mob of cattle standing idle in the shadows in the middle of the road. He swerved to miss the first one and collected the second cow with the rear of the truck. The sound was of metal crunching and tires screeching and as he overcorrected the turning of the wheel, he was all over the road to miss the rest of the mob and ran into a ditch on the roadside, crashing into a tree. The truck came to a sudden stop and rested on its side.

The automatic doors opened for Cutter and Raylee as they ran towards the entrance at the hospital. The woman at the front desk only pointed down the corridor, knowing exactly what they were there for. It was a nurse in a pale blue uniform holding a clipboard who looked up and saw them coming in her direction, that slowed them both down.

"He's alright," she assured them straight away. "The doctor's in the room with him now, but when he's done, I'm sure you'll be able to go in."

"Does he have anything broken?" Raylee asked and they both looked to the nurse, wanting to hear only good news.

"No ma'am, there doesn't appear to be. He's got a few scrapes and a cut to his hand, and he's a bit shaken. But from what I hear, he'll be going home today." The nurse turned away to finish filling out her paperwork.

They stood outside the room. Cutter leaned against the wall, feeling relieved. They had passed the tow truck on their way to the hospital, taking Macca's banged up piece of blue metal to a holding yard in town. It was a devastating sight to see his father's truck totally smashed up like that, yet Cutter was pleased that his son had walked away with only a few minor scratches.

When the doctor opened the door, he had their immediate attention.

"Can we go in?" Cutter asked, almost pushing his way past, desperate to see his son.

The doctor stopped him. "Not yet. Just give him a few minutes. He's getting dressed," he advised them both. "Actually, I need to speak to you first... Alone if you don't mind," he added, as he looked at Raylee, expecting that she would walk away so they could talk in private.

Raylee hesitated, then turned and looked up to see Johnny almost on their heels. It surprised them both, since he was the last person they expected to see after what happened in Nashville.

"Hey, thanks for coming," Cutter said, thankful for his friend's support. "But how did you hear?" he asked.

Johnny returned a look that was a cross between anger and confusion. "What do you mean, how did I hear? They called me," he replied sharply.

It was now Cutter that looked confused. "Well why would they do that?" he asked.

"Maybe you should ask Colton. Maybe he'll explain to us all what he was doing with my daughter in your truck?" he said explosively, when his level of calm had just become enraged.

"What?" Cutter and Raylee said at the same time.

"Yeah, she's down the hall in another room with a neck brace on and cuts all over her face," Johnny stated. "And I hope you tested that son of a bitch for driving while drunk?" he said to the doctor, although it was more of a demand.

It had shocked Raylee the most to hear that her son and Avery were together, although not as much as when Johnny tried to go into Colton's room. Both the doctor and Cutter stopped him with force and when they looked at his face, they could see that he was furious.

"I wouldn't do that if I was you," Cutter warned, and he made it clear that he would lay another one on him if he pushed his way in.

The doctor stood in the doorway and blocked him, and requested that the nurse call security.

Johnny looked at his best friend. He took a deep breath and controlled his anger before he got up in Cutter's face and pointed to him. "If you don't deal with him, then I will," he threatened quietly.

Johnny walked away. Cutter watched him and he rubbed his face, taking in Johnny's reaction. He knew that if it was Dakota, he'd react in exactly the same way. They had no idea that Avery was in the truck with Colton and it was enough to raise the fire in Cutter too.

"Before you go in, you might want to look at the statement from the officer who was first at the scene," the doctor said, and he handed Cutter the folder.

"Was he drinking?" he asked, expecting the worst before he read the details.

"No sir, he wasn't drinking," the doctor confirmed, and both Cutter and Raylee were instantly relieved. "But read it anyway. It might give you some of the answers you're looking for. The full report will follow," he said, and he walked away.

Cutter opened the folder and read the brief that had been prepared quickly. He started at the top and read fast down the page.

"No," Cutter said loudly to himself while he was pacing, reading the report. "No," he said again, making Raylee curious.

"What is it?" she asked, though he didn't reply or look at her.

He paced faster, read faster and fired up some more.

"Stay here," Cutter demanded of Raylee, and he went into the room and closed the door hard behind him, shutting her out.

Colton was sitting on the side of the bed. He was buttoning up his shirt with his lightly bandaged hand when he looked up and saw his father. Cutter looked at him and paced some more, hoping that it would spark the right thing to say. The words were not coming easily and Colton sat there wondering if he should get in first with an apology.

"What the hell were you thinking?" Cutter asked aggressively, for the second time in as many weeks.

Colton knew his father was angry. "I'm sorry," he said as his only defense.

Cutter looked at him. "Well sorry isn't gonna cut it this time... Do you know what you've done?" he asked, and without waiting for a reply, he followed on with another question that had a deep tone that he rarely used. "How could you?" he asked.

It was one of those deep shit moments and Colton could only look at him, reserved to speak for fear of not knowing exactly what his father knew.

"Just tell me how Avery came to be in the truck with you, when you're not supposed to be anywhere near her?" Cutter's heart was racing fast and an explosion of words followed. He was not so silent when he delivered the next blow. "And I know that you were screwing around in the front seat with her and now my dad's truck is a wreck because of that and she's down the hall with her face all cut and a neck brace on."

Colton sat in silence and knew that his father was aware of everything. There was no hiding any of the facts; he knew the details and there was no chance of lying his way out of it.

What did surprise him though, was when his father grabbed him by the shirt. "I gave you one job to do. One simple job and you couldn't even do it right."

"I can't do anything right in your eyes, can I?" Colton threw at him. "I'm good at nothing."

They were only a few inches apart and the fury was all one sided. "Well you're good at screwing everything up. In fact, you're great at it. And if it were a contest, you'd win the first damn prize for sure." When Cutter saw his son's eyes fill up, he released his shirt. "And you're lucky that Johnny didn't get in here first, because I'm not sure what he would've done if he did."

Cutter opened the door to let Raylee in. She came in cautiously and looked at her son, then threw her arms around his neck and Colton let go with a huge sob, feeling his mother's care. He always felt that she loved him unconditionally. Then again, she didn't know all the details just yet.

"When we get back to the ranch, I want you to pack your bags," Cutter demanded, as he leaned on the rail at the end of the bed and watched them. They both looked to him for an explanation. "Tomorrow, I want you to take Colt to your mom and dad's," he said to Raylee, and she looked at him as to why that was necessary and thought it was a little over the top. "Stay for a week and get him set up, then he's on his own. Allan can deal with him after that."

"No. I'm not going to Australia," Colton intervened.

Cutter ignored him. "I'll call them tonight and make the arrangements."

"You can't do that," Colton said, protesting hard.

Ignoring him again, Cutter was giving Raylee more instructions. "I'll drop you at the airport for the first flight out in the morning."

"I'm not going," Colton said abruptly, although he was mostly pleading.

It was at that point, Colton became part of the conversation. "Oh yes you are going," his father said. "And if you don't go, then I'll be letting Johnny O'Brien in here to deal with you and I promise you one thing... You won't walk out of here when he's finished with you."

Colton would rather deal with his father than Avery's. He wasn't a big enough man yet to be able to stand up to Johnny and own up to his foolish and stupid mistakes. His father's eyes and the tone in his voice told Colton that he meant every word. There would be no persuading and no argument. It was not open for further discussion. Nothing he could have said in his own defense would change his father's decision so he shut his mouth and backed down, wanting to get out of there as soon as possible.

Chapter Three

Raylee always loved the thought of going home to Australia. In those early years, since making her life in Texas, they had tried to visit as often as they could. Yet with two ranches to take care of, more horses in training and three kids in school, it made the years in between visits stretch out longer than what she would have liked.

Colton was no stranger to the vineyard. He had been there six times in his life while his grandparents, Allan and Evelyn, had been consistent in their travels to Texas, only slowing down in the last couple of years due to health reasons.

They were getting on in age now, although Allan would still try to get on a horse at least once a week. Raylee wasn't sure if it was to show her mother that there was still some cowboy left in him, or if he genuinely had the need to ride. Either way, her parents were as strong as ever since they'd remarried after their short separation all those years ago, and the vineyard and horse complex ran along like it always did. Perhaps even a little better.

When Raylee put the window down at the front gate, she punched in the magic number. The code hadn't changed in thirty years and it made her smile when she watched the high black gates open up slowly. She drove along the tree-lined driveway, looking either side into the horse yards and at the rows of vines.

She was home.

The last thing Cutter said to her at the airport when he dropped her off, was to make sure she felt homesick for Texas. When she drove up to the house, it made her feel homesick for her family home. The house she grew up in. It didn't matter how many years she'd spent away, there was an undeniable feeling of connection that she had to her family and to the vineyard.

Her mother was waiting at the front door when Raylee pulled the hire car around the roundabout and parked as close as she could to the path. When they got out of the car, the welcome party had expanded to include her father.

"How did you know we were here?" Raylee asked, as they walked up to the front door.

Everyone was excited to exchange the long awaited greetings, and warm hugs and kisses were shared around.

"We changed the security system over the whole property. Everything's under camera now. We could see you smiling at the front gate," Allan said to his daughter.

"Have you had some trouble here?" she asked.

"No. But I have to keep finding new things to spend my money on," he stated, making Colton laugh at how wealthy his grandparents were.

Colton had grown up very comfortably, having everything the family ever needed. They had lived in the same house on the ranch that his father had grown up in, and the only changes were a new kitchen added some years ago when Cutter felt that it was time for an update, and a repaint throughout to freshen it up. They always went on family holidays every year and upgraded their trucks and cars when needed. It was the barn where no expense was spared. Cutter made sure they only had the best horses and tack, and the best trucks and trailers, making the working side of the ranch a priority. But Colton's home life was overshadowed by the way his grandparents lived.

When Raylee walked into her family home, it was so familiar. It was as if no time had passed at all, as everything was still the same. Right down to the old brown leather sofa.

"Well, you could spend your money on a new couch," Raylee suggested. "It's a bit outdated don't you think?"

"But it's so comfortable. I like my couch," Allan defended. "You know you can't buy a good couch like you used to."

Evelyn put the kettle on and Raylee went to the overhead cupboards, straight for the cups where they were always kept. As she began to settle into the idea of being home again, Colton decided to excuse himself, as he didn't have the need to sit through the boredom of playing family catch-ups.

"I'm going to the barn," Colton said. "Can I take the car?" he asked his mom.

Allan cut in before she could answer. "Take your mom's car. It's in the garage," he said, and Raylee looked at him without adding words. "What? He's got to have a car while he's here and you haven't driven it for two years." He looked at his grandson. "You know where the keys are."

"Thanks… I won't be long," he said, and he went straight to the key board in the hallway and found the keys to his mother's car.

It had been parked in the garage, only coming out when they visited or if Allan thought to take it for a run to keep the battery charged. It was quite extravagant for such a rare visit, except that Allan wanted the family to feel that he catered for them whenever they did manage the trip over. This time, it was short notice and very unexpected.

Colton drove back down the driveway, branching off onto the gravel road that led to the complex. Nothing had changed. Everything looked exactly the same as he remembered, except that the horses had been turned over or had reproduced over the years and the workers had moved on, replaced by a full time trainer, separate from the vineyard staff.

It was Allan's idea to take the complex side of the property forward, instead of letting it slow down and fade out after Raylee had left for Texas. He was keen to kickstart a new line of Midnight progeny and had been the exclusive breeder in the country. No one in Australia was able to breed directly from the stallion and it made the foals they produced at the property worth a lot of money. It really put their name up in lights, as many of the top horses now had Midnight bloodlines that came directly from him. And with a professional trainer dedicated to the property, he had been responsible for the ongoing success of the stud. It was a profitable business and it didn't look like slowing down anytime soon.

Colton pulled the car up at the entrance to the barn. The doors were open and he walked through the breezeway, looking everywhere for the trainer. He couldn't find him and when he made his way towards the arena, he could hear the music playing quietly from the speakers and the mechanical cow zipping up and down the wire to a routine that was slow and steady.

Standing on the bottom rail, Colton watched the trainer work the horse, both concentrating on the black and white leather bag that sort of resembled a cow. The trainer knew exactly what he was doing as he corrected the filly's mistakes and made her respond immediately, getting her head on the job. After another few minutes, he pulled up the reins and switched off the program, then ran her through a few warm down exercises in the middle of the arena before he headed back to the gate.

Still not noticing that anyone had been watching, Colton called out to him. "Hey, Uncle Jesse?" he said loudly, to alert him to the fact he had an audience.

Jesse looked up. "Hey, Colt. When did you get here?" he asked, happy to see him again. He rode over and went to foot, meeting on the sand.

"Just now," Colton said, and the way Jesse pulled him close to his shoulder, it was clear that Colton was one of his favorites. "Where's Aims?" he asked.

"She's picking the girls up from school," Jesse said, and they led the horse back towards the barn. "I didn't tell Aimee you were coming. I thought it would be a good surprise."

"She'll be expecting to see my dad."

Jesse didn't know the reason for the visit. He'd only found out yesterday from Allan and was spared of any details. All he knew was that Colton was arriving with Raylee for an unknown time.

"Couldn't he get away?" Jesse asked.

"No sir, I don't think he wanted to. Mom's only here for the week then she's going home," Colton explained.

Jesse tied the horse up outside the tack room. He took the saddle off then led her to the wash bay. "And you're staying on?"

"For a while," Colton said, without explaining why.

Jesse sensed there was something going on within the family and he didn't need it spilled out to him in the first ten minutes. After all, Colton was there indefinitely and there would be time for that later.

"Aimee will be back soon. You may wanna get outta here so you don't ruin your grandma's surprise dinner party she's got planned for tonight."

Colton agreed. He was excited to see his aunty and cousins, but had to wait just that bit longer. He made his way back to the house, hoping that his mother had already dished out all the drama over the last few weeks so that he didn't have to sit through it all over again.

He settled into the guest bedroom downstairs, while Raylee took her room upstairs. It hadn't changed in all the years she had been gone, except for the new quilt and bedside lamps added just recently. Evelyn always made sure she had something new to surprise her daughter with every time she returned home.

To keep busy until dinner that evening, Colton unpacked his bag and hung everything up in the wardrobe. He figured that he was going to be there for some time even though no set dates had been mentioned. A couple of weeks. A few max. Definitely no more than a month. However long it was going to be, he didn't want to live out of his suitcase so he made himself at home, complete with a framed picture of Avery that he sat next to the bed on the side table.

When he was done, he lay back on the pillow and crossed his legs, looking at the photo. It was taken on their trip to Nashville before the untimely end to what had been a great weekend. She had posed for the camera, pouting her lips and pulling her hat down low over her sexy eyes.

It drew him in.

When he stared at her and remembered how he felt when they were together, he was sure that he was in love with her, making his heart ache and his head go crazy. It was the only explanation as to why he was so lost without her.

He hated his father for sending him away. He hated Johnny for not understanding that he loved Avery. She could have done a lot worse. At least he didn't want her for just a bit of fun. He actually cared for her and was devastated when he heard of her injuries in the crash. All he could do now, was rely on his sister to keep him updated. She was the only one who could get close to Avery since he was to have no contact with her, and his only hope was that Dakota would keep them distantly connected.

He put the photo down, deciding to take a shower so he didn't fall into an unconscious sleep after the long flight, and to get himself ready for the surprise dinner, where he couldn't wait to see the look on Aimee's face.

In Colton's younger years, Jesse and Aimee had lived in Texas, next door on the ranch that Allan had bought. Jesse had become a cutting horse trainer in his own right, learning all he could about cattle from the land, while Cutter had taught him everything he needed to know in the cutting pen. It had still taken a good three years to build up his skills to where he was able to stand alone and take on his own clients, and he and Cutter had shared the pen and practice sessions which worked out quite well for the both of them.

It was an offer from Allan that changed the course Jesse was on. He wanted to bring Jesse and Aimee over to Australia and give Midnight a boost to his name. Aimee agreed to go for a couple of years to get the stud working well again. Ten years on, they were still there. Their girls had made good friends at school and at the local pony club, and didn't want to leave. They were almost Australian. While Aimee had only been home once in that time, her regular Texan visitors came over often enough to keep her satisfied.

As the night was closing in, a loud knock on the door was the announcement that the McCallister family had arrived. Jesse was the first one in the door so that he could stand back and watch his wife's reaction.

"Raylee?" Aimee screamed, and she ran to her and threw her arms around Raylee's neck, squeezing her tight. "What are you doing here? I didn't know you were coming," she said enthusiastically.

"It's a long story," Raylee replied, and she was equally excited to see her, though not excited to tell her the reason.

Aimee immediately looked around for her brother. "Where is he?"

"Who, Cutter?" Raylee asked.

"Yes ma'am. Where's he hiding?" Aimee was now anticipating the next surprise and she wandered through the house, looking for him, expecting that he was going to pop out from behind a closed door.

It was Colton who came out of the guest room and gave her another shock. "Colt," Aimee screamed all over again, pleased to see him. "Haven't you grown up," she stated, as it had been a few years since she'd last seen him. She hugged him also.

"Hey Aims," Colton said happily, squeezing her in return.

When Aimee's excitement had finally settled, she was a little disappointed to learn that her brother hadn't made the trip too. That would have really been the cherry on top of the surprise cake for her, and after Raylee and Colton made a fuss over the two girls at how much they had grown, they all took a seat at the table.

Jesse and Aimee's oldest daughter, Lucy, was just fourteen, while Paige was three years younger. Both girls looked just like their mom with many of their father's traits. They had been riding since they could walk, but had only just started cutting last year.

Allan made sure that everyone had their glasses full while Evelyn was serving the dinner. They all listened to the two sister-in-laws catch up on everything that was going on at home, without anyone else getting a word in. Cutter was the hot topic, much to the very silent annoyance of Colton.

"So, you haven't said," Jesse interrupted, wanting to switch subjects just as dinner was placed in front of him. "What are you here for?"

There was a hesitation, before Raylee felt the need to just come right out and say it. "We had some trouble at home and Cutter thought it was best to get Colt out of town for a while."

"Must have been some kind of trouble?" Aimee asked. She was totally intrigued, thinking that he could have easily gone to Dallas to stay at his other grandparents' place instead.

LINDA ELLISON

"It's not as bad as they're all making it out to be," Colton said, playing it down. "I've just been seeing Avery for a while and everyone freaked out about it when they found out."

"As in O'Brien? You've been seeing Avery O'Brien?" Aimee was sounding pleased for him. She was all for it.

"Yes ma'am. Just for the past few months. But now Johnny wants to kill me and dad's having a major mental breakdown over it."

Aimee laughed. "Oh, I know exactly what you mean. When Jesse and I first got together, your dad had a meltdown like you wouldn't believe."

"Really?" Colton asked. He was pleased to hear that he had someone in his corner who understood what he was going through.

"Yes sir, he did. He didn't cope with it at all and now look at us. Been married for eighteen years this September." Aimee touched Jesse on the leg under the table, remembering those early days.

Colton looked at everyone around the table. Their silence told him that they all knew about his father's irrational overreaction to something that was first time news to him.

Aimee continued. "And let's not forget that your father did the same thing with your mom," she blurted out. "And it was Allan who freaked out."

Colton was loving this. He'd never heard any of these stories before and the young girls both giggled along with him, all wanting to hear more.

"It's not the same thing," Raylee said to let them down gently.

Colton wouldn't allow it. "Granddad, you freaked out? I can't imagine that," he said with a smug look.

Aimee was having so much fun and was pushing the boundaries of secrecy a little too far. "You should ask him how he nearly shot your father when he found them in bed together."

"You're kidding me?"

"Alright. That's enough," Allan said firmly, deciding that Aimee had spilled one too many family secrets that had been laid to rest more than twenty years ago. "You're not helping," he stated with a frown that Aimee had seen many times before.

Aimee thought it was funny that Colton was going through exactly the same kind of situation that his parents had endured. Her laughter was very contagious and was beginning to lighten everyone's mood as the picture was unfolding. While at the time it had been quite serious, recalling some of those

32

memories from years gone by now seemed so entertaining, yet highly inappropriate at the family dinner table, especially in front of the two young girls who couldn't stop giggling.

"Yes sir. Happened right there in that room," Aimee said, and she pointed to the guest bedroom door. "Probably the same bed you're sleeping in tonight," she teased, and she laughed some more.

Colton was stunned and looked at his mother. "Is that right?" he asked, with an ugly distorted face.

It was too late to deny anything. Aimee had let the cat out of the bag and putting it back in would be impossible now. "I'll bet if you look above your head at the ceiling tonight, you can see where the bullet went through. I don't think they patched it up that well," Aimee added.

Raylee slowly unwound and began to relax about it. "You're lucky your granddad's not a very good shot, or you wouldn't be here," she said to Colton, then looked at her father.

Everyone had now joined in on the fun.

"Did you know any of this?" Colton asked Jesse.

They all looked to him. Jesse had been standing at the end of the bed taking the rifle out of Allan's hands when the shot was fired. When he thought about how close it was, it made him twitch. "Your dad owes me big time," he said.

The laughter carried on for a while. Colton had not felt this happy around his family for quite some time. He loved his uncle and aunty, and spending time with them wasn't going to be so bad. Perhaps there was more to learn about his family than he'd thought.

"Anyway," Raylee said, to divert the focus away from herself. "a few things happened back home and we thought it would be in Colt's best interest if he came to see his grandparents for a while."

"How long are you staying?" Aimee asked, after hearing the serious tone in Raylee's voice.

"Long enough to live. Short enough to get my life back," he said.

"So you're here to work?" Jesse asked.

"Work?" Colton repeated, and was quick to set the record straight. "Who said anything about work? I'm just here to lay low for a while until Johnny pulls his head out of his..."

"Colton," Raylee said abruptly to cut him off. "Not in front of the girls," she said in her motherly voice.

"Or in front of your grandma," Allan added, touching Evelyn gently on the hand.

Jesse was beginning to see how everything had unfolded. He was good at reading between the lines without the unnecessary details. It was clear to him that Colton had crossed a boundary that was unacceptable to Johnny. He didn't need to know what his nephew had done, to know that he needed to be out of the country and out of harm's way. Out of reach.

"Or by the sounds of it," Jesse said. "I'd say that Johnny would think it's the other way around."

That pissed Colton off somewhat. He didn't let it openly bother him and he put on a tough front.

By the end of the night, when they'd finished with a warming coffee, it was Raylee who was beginning to feel tired from the long day. She had been on a high to see her family again, and now that they had caught up on plenty, it was time she turned in.

The two girls had fallen asleep on the couch and Evelyn had thrown a blanket over them, while Aimee was still overwhelmed by the surprise. It would be an early start for Jesse and he needed to get home. Besides, Raylee and Aimee had a full week to spend together and had already been making plans as to what they were going to do to fill in the rest of their time.

When Colton went to bed that night, he was tired. He picked up the photo of Avery and stared at it. She consumed him. It twisted his thoughts and tormented him that he couldn't see her and to make it worse, he couldn't speak to her either.

He looked above his head. He scanned the ceiling and eventually found the patched up hole where the bullet had gone through. To think that his grandfather had walked in and found his mom and dad together in this very bed and tried to shoot him, gave Colton an insight that his parents and family weren't as perfect as he had always thought. That there was drama and a family scandal that had been very well hidden over the years, and it made him smile.

He reached over and switched out the light, drifting into Avery's world.

When Colton wandered into the kitchen the next morning, Evelyn had his plate set at the breakfast bar.

"Where is everyone?" he asked.

"Well good morning," Evelyn said. "Your mom and Aimee have gone to the day spa, your grandfather has gone to the office and I'm guessing that Jesse is at the barn, working," she said. "You do know it's eleven o'clock, don't you?" she asked.

"Yes ma'am. But I just woke up," he stated, and from the look of him, it was obvious that he had.

"Well you could always go to the barn and help Jesse if you're looking for something to do," she suggested kindly.

Evelyn pulled out the cereal and milk and placed it on the counter in front of him. "Toast?" she asked.

"No thanks," he said, and he began to fill his bowl. "It's a nice day. I thought I might go for a swim. Do you have a towel I can use?"

It was clear to Evelyn that her grandson was not there to work. This was a holiday as far as he was concerned and he was going to make the most of it.

After breakfast, Colton made himself comfortable by the pool. Taking up a sun lounge with his towel laid out, he began to work on catching some rays. Since he wore jeans and boots every day on the ranch, his feet were now enjoying the freedom and the warmth of the sun. Even though he had not been long out of bed, he yawned, as he lay back and closed his eyes.

"What's for lunch?" Colton asked his grandmother, when he went into the kitchen a couple of hours later.

"You can have whatever you like. Anything you can find in the fridge is yours." Evelyn decided that as much as she loved her grandson, she was not about to wait on him hand and foot like he was expecting. He diverted to the fruit bowl and grabbed an apple instead, being an easy fix to his cravings.

The afternoon was spent lazing around the house. He wandered through the different rooms, looking at everything. He picked up some framed photos from the side table. There were eight grandchildren in total, plus the two girls that Allan and Evelyn treated as their own, since they were a long way from home.

There was no favoritism, and each of his cousins had the same amount of photos as the others.

Out on the side deck, he leaned against the post, watching the workers in the vineyard. After only a few short minutes it began to bore him. There was nothing to do. This amazing property should keep anyone busy with the complex, swimming pool and tennis court, not to mention the billiard table, theatre room, gym and sauna. Colton had always enjoyed his holidays at the vineyard with his family, yet he was there alone in the house and on his second day, he was completely at a loss for something to do. He went for a shower, just to fill in the time. Lying on the bed, he looked at Avery's photo again. He'd already stared at it a dozen times since he arrived and it wasn't helping with taking the pain away.

The patched up ceiling caught his eye. His father was not as perfect as he had always thought. His father had screwed things up too and only for Aimee sharing some insights into the past, Colton was beginning to see that the road had not been easy riding for his parents.

It was a knock on the door that changed the direction of his thinking.

"Come in," he said loudly, as the doors were quite heavy and the walls were almost sound proof.

Raylee only came into the room after she was invited. "I bought you something while I was out," she said, waving a paper bag at him, hoping it would cheer him up.

That wouldn't take much, Colton thought. "What is it?" he asked.

"Just some of the best country baked cookies that I used to love when I was young," she said, and she sat down on the side of the bed and gave him the bag. She and Aimee had been to the day spa, courtesy of Allan, and had dined out for lunch in an exclusive boutique restaurant in the heart of The Valley.

He put it down on the side table next to the photo of Avery. It was the first time that Raylee had seen the photo. "She's beautiful, isn't she?" Raylee said.

"Yes ma'am. She sure is," he agreed. "But you should already know that."

Raylee did. Avery had just about grown up in their house, just like Dakota had spent equal amounts of time at the O'Brien ranch. The two girls were always together, sitting next to each other on the school bus and in class. Of a weekend, they'd sleepover and share their clothes and makeup, while styling each other's hair and talking about which boys they liked and which ones they didn't. If they weren't sitting at the same dinner table, then they were out riding the ranches together. Dakota and Avery were as close as two friends could get.

"I do know that," she said. "And that's why you should understand that your relationship caught everyone by surprise."

"But not as much as yours and dads?" he was quick to add.

Raylee couldn't dispute it. "Aimee shouldn't have told you that," she said, so that he didn't get the two situations confused. "That was a long time ago and it has nothing to do with you and Avery."

"It has everything to do with me and Avery." Colton was wanting to mix the two up to prove that his parents' love affair was no different to theirs.

Raylee was always softened by her son and she felt for him. "You know, it would have been so different if you had just asked Johnny if it was okay to date Avery. Then it would have been all out in the open. No hiding or sneaking around. No pretending to be somewhere when you're not, and take it slow. No fooling around so quickly."

"Is that what Dad did?" Colton asked. "Did he ask Granddad's permission to date you? Because it sounds to me like you were sneaking around and got caught too."

Colton wasn't far wrong.

"Except that we weren't sneaking around," she defended.

"But you still stayed together, even after Granddad tried to shoot Dad." Colton was smart. He knew that this was no different.

"Whatever happened between me and your father has nothing to do with Johnny. He's annoyed at you and he has every right to be."

"I still don't know what the big deal is. We were only having a couple of drinks and having some fun. Dancing's not against the law now, is it?"

It didn't matter what angle Raylee came from, she was up against someone who was going to dig his heels in and bend all the rules to suit his own needs, holding onto anything he could to make his own situation better than it was.

"If it wasn't as bad as you say, then why didn't you go to Johnny and apologize?" she said smartly.

She had him stumped.

"Because he'd probably lay me out again for no good reason."

"And that's the difference between you and your father. He was at least willing to face my dad and apologize. He was big enough to know that he screwed up and he wanted to make things right."

"And what did Granddad say?"

Raylee was not so committed to answering that. "Well, maybe while you've got all the time in the world to do nothing over the next while, you should ask him." She touched him on the leg. "I'm meeting Aimee at the barn. You want to come?"

"It sure beats sitting around here all afternoon."

After a quick change, Colton came out of the room with his jeans on and his boots in his hands. He was at least smart enough to know not to wear board shorts to the barn. Raylee was sitting at the kitchen counter and had to take a double look when Colton walked out of the room looking just like his father. With his blue tee shirt and his brown hat on, it reminded her of the first time Cutter came to the vineyard and she stared at her son, lost in those far gone memories.

"You ready? Let's go," he said, just like his father would say.

They drove to the complex. Raylee kept the conversation clear from the events of the last few weeks as well as the details on what happened at the vineyard all those years ago with Cutter. Instead, she shared stories of her years growing up with her brothers on the property. When they pulled up outside the complex, it was clear that Aimee had taken her exclusive parking position next to the barn door. The place where Raylee always parked her car. It was the first time she'd been to the barn and when they went in, Jesse was coming back to the stall with a young horse he had in training.

"What do you think?" Jesse asked, when he tied him to the rail.

"Wow. He looks just like Midnight," Raylee stated, and she began to rub him down.

"He's one of his last lines. He's going okay. I've still got a couple of months to get him ready for the show and he'll need every bit of it," Jesse said, as if he wasn't sure he'd be ready in time. "He can be quite lazy at times."

"Well he's got the best bloodlines running through him," Raylee said proudly. She had studied up on every foal they had produced and had followed their progress.

Raylee looked to Colton. "What do you think?" she asked, trying to raise some interest out of him.

"He's nice," Colton replied.

"Nice?" she said harshly. "He's more than nice. He's impressive."

"But if he can't cut for shit, it won't matter what blood runs through his veins or how impressive he looks," Colton stated.

Well that was true. He just didn't need to put it that way.

"And I'll be down here every morning working him if you wanna help," Jesse added, to let Colton know that he was more than welcome to join him.

Jesse and Aimee gave them a tour of the stalls and yards, pointing out each horse and going through the details of how old they were and which mare they were out of. They seemed to have the program working well, with Lucy and Paige helping out after school each day. It was the extra outside help they got on the weekends and in the school holidays that allowed them to go away as a family to the shows.

It was another day done and Raylee went to bed that night missing Cutter and feeling the emptiness of her bed where he should have been lying next to her. There was no feeling in the world like being home, although she felt incomplete without the rest of her family there. She was missing them all and after only two days, she began to feel homesick for the ranch.

Under normal circumstances, a week would fly by for Raylee, yet this week seemed to drag on and on. She spent her days with Aimee and loved every minute of it. Going shopping and visiting all her favorite cafes. In her time spent at the barn, Jesse had her on a couple of well trained cutting horses, giving her a run on the mechanical cow, then they'd sit down together after a ride to review the new breeding program. With Midnight now gone, they looked at his progeny, making some decisions on where to take the business next.

The evenings around the dinner table were filled with family fun, with her brothers and their wives joining them for a barbecue one evening. It was nice to catch up with them, although their children had all grown up and were now living from one side of the country to the other.

Her late night cups of coffee sitting on the back deck with her parents gave her a sense of security. At the suggestion of retirement, her father made it quite clear that he had no intention of sitting around the house all day and growing old. Raylee pointed out that he had already reached that milestone and should at least consider slowing down. Although nothing she said was convincing enough to make Allan even think about it.

As much as Raylee was having a good time with everyone and had used the week productively, after six days, she was more than ready to go home.

At the same time every night, Cutter would call to give her an update from home. Since it was just the three of them at the ranch, it had been very quiet and Raylee hadn't missed much over the week that she was away.

"I miss you all," she said seriously, while she was tucked up in bed, talking on the phone.

"And I can't wait for you to get home," Cutter agreed. "I think Kotie needs some lessons in the kitchen."

"Oh, is that why you want me to come home?" she laughed.

"Yes ma'am, it's one of the reasons," he admitted. "The other reason is because the washing is piling up and I can't find the floor," he teased.

Raylee laughed some more. "I'm so glad you're missing me."

"Actually... I'm missing you more than you know and when you get home, I'm gonna show you just how much."

They played along and flirted some more before it was time to hang up. "I can't believe I'm coming home tomorrow," she stated.

"And I'll be there to pick you up," he confirmed. "I'll be the one in the truck, wearing the hat."

Raylee laughed and was very quick to point out the obvious. "You do know you're in Texas, don't you?"

He knew. "I can't wait to see you," he said, winding up their half hour conversation.

"And I can't wait to see you," she replied. "I love you."

"And I love you too."

Chapter Four

Driving down the long narrow driveway of Double J Ranch, the trees were rustling in the breeze. Tiny buds were swirling in the air and were landing on the windscreen, then settled on the wiper blades. Raylee looked into the yards on either side and gave a big yawn. The long flight was starting to take its toll. If it wasn't for Allan upgrading her to business class on the way home, then she would have felt completely wiped out.

She expected her children to be standing on the porch, anxious to see her, or popping their heads out of the barn, dropping their chores and rushing over to welcome her home and help with her bags, yet Dakota and Westyn were nowhere to be seen.

When Cutter pulled the truck up at the side of the barn, it was Millie that met Raylee at the door when she stepped out. She gave a playful bark and was wagging her tail, fully excited to see her home.

"Well I'm pleased to see that someone missed me," she said, and she bent down, giving Millie's face a rub with both hands.

Cutter came around the front of the truck and closed her door, then grabbed her bags off the backseat. They started to walk to the house when Raylee stopped in her tracks.

"Oh Cutter," she said, like her last breath had just blown away in a puff of wind.

Macca's truck was back at the ranch. It was parked along the fence out of the way and when Raylee walked up to it, her eyes filled with tears.

Cutter was silently gutted. There was nothing he could do to change the outcome and he wasn't sure exactly what to do with it now that it was parked in clear view as a constant reminder. Raylee walked around it, looking at the panels that were pushed in and dented badly. The roof had been crushed in on one side and the glass was all but gone on every window. It was a mess.

"It's beyond repair," he said disappointingly, and that was enough for Raylee to fully let go and she started to cry. Cutter put his arm around her shoulder and pulled her close.

"I can't believe it," she said, after she wiped the tears away.

Raylee still remembered the first time she ever saw Macca's truck. Every drive to town, every show they went to and bringing Colton home from the hospital when he was born. The truck held memories and was as much a part of their lives as their children and horses were. It was part of the ranch and part of the family. It had done the miles and after all this time, the only real value was sentimental.

Cutter put his hand around the back of her neck for comfort. They walked up the front steps of the house and stood on the porch.

"Where's the kids?" Raylee asked.

"I don't know. Probably out the back, checking the heifers," he presumed. "Kotie was on strict instructions not to leave her brother's side while I was away, so where ever they are, they'll be together."

Cutter and Raylee couldn't have had three more different children. The two boys were extreme opposites. Colton was rebellious and outspoken, and had started to show signs of not owning up to his responsibilities. Westyn, on the other hand, was quiet and hard working, only speaking if it was worthy of being said, and taking full pride in his work and achievements. He was very respectful. Dakota was somewhere in the middle. She knew right from wrong and was quite head strong. Right now, her father had her bluffed and she was not stepping one foot out of line.

They went inside the house. It was exactly how Raylee had left it, clean and tidy, except when she looked at the sink, she could see a pile of dirty dishes that looked as if it was her welcome home gift.

Cutter rushed over and blocked her. "Don't worry about it. I'll do it while you have a shower," he said, and he more or less pushed her up the stairs then turned around and cursed the kids for leaving their mess unattended to.

It didn't take long for Raylee to feel at ease after taking a quick shower and changing into her ranch jeans. When she made her way downstairs a short time later, Cutter had the coffee brewed. He could always read her mind and knew what she wanted, though it was their close connection that enabled him to know exactly what she needed.

They went out onto the porch and sat together on the swing and began to talk. They'd had many private and important conversations on that swing, some of which were life changing. Should they purchase the blue roan mare to add an outside line to their already impressive list of horses? Would it be a good idea to train Jesse in the cutting pen and go up against him in competition? Did they really want to have a third baby?

Most of the big decisions in their life were decided on that swing and there was not one decision that they regretted making.

"How was Colt when you left?" It was the first time in a week that Cutter had mentioned his son's name.

"It's difficult to say. He seems alright, but he thinks he's only on holiday and is coming home soon," she said. "Have you talked to Johnny this week?"

"Nah. I thought it was best to give him some space for a while."

The coffee was going down nicely. The swing was swaying ever so slightly, making Raylee feel relaxed.

"Your sister told Colton everything that happened all those years ago when my dad nearly shot you," she explained.

"What? Why would she do that?" he asked.

"I don't know. Maybe because she thought it was funny that he didn't know. And now Colton doesn't see the difference between what happened to us and what's happening to him."

Cutter laughed a little. "It was funny when you think about it," he said, remembering Allan standing at the end of the bed with his rifle pointed at him.

"And maybe we'll be laughing at Colt and Avery in years to come," she said, stepping lightly, hoping to soften him.

He looked at her. "I don't think so," he disagreed. "I just can't get it out of my head what they were doing in my dad's truck, and now look at it."

Raylee looked over at the truck. It was a sad and sorry sight. "It's not all his fault. Avery is as much to blame," she pointed out.

"And that's why he shouldn't have allowed her to get in with him."

"Well you can hardly blame him. He loves her."

This was news to Cutter. As far as he was concerned, Colton and Avery were just good friends. Good friends, with extra special benefits and he was surprised by this sudden announcement. "He does?"

"That's what he told me," Raylee confirmed.

"Well he's too young to know what love is, and he's old enough to know better than to put my dad's truck at risk like that." Cutter was still very unforgiving.

She looked at him and ran her hand through the back of his hair below his hat, while she flashed her loving eyes his way. "And if it was me wanting to do that to you in the front seat of your truck, would you have said no?" she flirted.

He knew he was cornered. "Hell no," he stated. "Not a chance," he said for sure and certain. He stood up and pulled her to her feet and headed for the steps.

"Where are we going?" she asked, laughing.

"My truck. Let's go and find out."

She pulled him to a sudden stop, still laughing together and they settled against the rail, looking out at the barn. He put his arms around her and squeezed her. "I'm so pleased you're home. I really missed you this week."

Raylee loved that after more than twenty years together, Cutter could barely survive a week without her. More importantly, he let her know it.

In the distance they could hear cattle on the move. Looking up, they could see a small mob being pushed through the last gate. Westyn took control of them from behind while Dakota applied the pressure from the side to direct them towards the yards.

Raylee instantly lit up with another smile. "What're they doing?"

"I have no idea. But no doubt they're up to something."

They stood silently on the porch and watched their kids bring the mob in. Neither of them were out of position or lost control of the situation. They had done this their whole life and it was second nature to them. Although Cutter was curious, he didn't go to the yards to find out. He was content just watching from the porch and let them do their thing.

He crossed his arms when he leaned on the rail. "Raylee. I've made a decision," he said with a sudden change in his tone that told her to start worrying.

"That sounds serious?"

That sparkle in his eyes was gone and he looked tense. Not the way he was when he'd picked her up from the airport, and not the way he had been while sitting together on the swing. He had changed.

"You made it without me?" she asked disappointingly, since they always discussed everything first before settling on a decision.

"Yes ma'am, I had to. Because I knew you'd talk me out of it."

She was now deeply worried. "Well it sounds to me like it's final. That no matter what I say, I won't change your mind."

"You won't," he confirmed. "But what I do want, is for you to understand and support me on this one."

She would not commit to that. Not without hearing it first. It could have been a thousand things that he had decided on and not one was coming to her mind.

"I'm quitting," he announced.

"Quitting what?"

"Cutting and training... I'm quitting it all."

"What?" she retaliated quickly. Raylee was shocked by his sudden irrational decision to end his career. "You can't. Why would you do that?" she asked. "You can still do this for years and you're still at the top."

Cutter looked at the kids pushing the cattle into the yards. Westyn launched himself off the horse and tied it to the rail then closed the gate. It reminded Cutter of himself at the same age. Their son was only fifteen and could easily run the ranch on his own. He had a passion for the land and a love for the horses, with a healthy respect for both. It ran freely through his veins. Whenever Cutter looked at his son, he saw himself. It was like looking at his own reflection. "They're the reason," he said.

For Raylee, that didn't make any sense. Their kids should have been every reason to keep going, not end it all.

"I'm not sure I get it," she said, wanting a full explanation.

"When I went cutting with my dad, I thought it was the greatest thing ever. It was something we could do together. But when we started competing against each other, he knew it was time to step aside. He was with me every day in training and never missed a show and he always had my back, helping me in the stables and preparing the horses to ride. I needed him. Without him behind me, I couldn't have done what I did."

Raylee just listened. It was clear that he'd given this a lot of thought over the last week while she was away.

"I never thought about stepping aside for them until Colt made it quite clear that he could never live up to my name."

"That wasn't fair and you know it." Raylee disagreed with Colton laying all the blame on his father.

"But it's true. He doesn't wanna be in this game if I'm still riding, and the only way he thinks he'll be any good is if I'm not in it anymore. Same goes for

West. He doesn't wanna go up against me. It'll be better if I'm working for them, not riding against them."

Raylee was beginning to understand his logic, although the thought of Cutter giving it all up was devastating to her. The only reason she was prepared to support him, was in order to advance their kids' careers.

Cutter took Raylee by the hand and they wandered over to the yards. Dakota came out of the barn with a bale of hay and she dropped it on the ground when she saw her mom.

"How was your trip?" Dakota asked, after she gave her mom a warm hug.

"It was good, but I missed everyone," Raylee said in return.

"Not as much as we missed you. It's been bootcamp here," she stated, looking at her father with a frown.

Raylee looked at Cutter.

"Hey. It's not my job to pick up after them," he explained.

When Westyn came out of the barn leading a couple of saddled horses, he handed one to his sister before he kissed his mom on the cheek as if he'd only seen her yesterday.

"What're you two doing?" Raylee asked.

"Dakota wants to learn to cut," Westyn said, as if it was no big deal.

"What?" both parents said at the same time.

"Come into the pen with us," he added, to invite them both into a training session.

It was something they couldn't resist. Dakota had grown up on a horse and had ridden the ranch all her life. She knew everything there was to know about horses and cattle, while never once showing an interest in the cutting pen. She'd always left that to her father and brothers.

By the time they had their horses saddled, the kids had gone through some warm up exercises. Westyn let the cows into the pen and they stood on the back wall, huddled close together.

When Raylee and Cutter took a corner each and Dakota sat out in front to push on them, Westyn began making his way into the mob. He walked through steadily while talking to his sister, explaining everything he was doing and what he was looking for. He didn't stop talking and Cutter sat there silently and just listened, and couldn't be anything but impressed.

His technique and comments were spot on, and while there were a few things Cutter would have explained differently, it wasn't wrong, so he didn't interfere. He knew that his son had listened to everything he'd said over the years, even adapting his own thoughts and language. They were all having a great time, laughing and throwing funny remarks around at each other in between some serious moments working the cows.

Dakota had tried different events growing up, with barrels being her strongest and favorite discipline, though she never seemed interested in pursuing it any further than the local rodeo days. Cutting, on the other hand, was something that everyone else on the ranch did, and so much time was devoted to it that there was never enough time for her to give it a go. She'd sat in the corners and helped out more often than not, though she was more dedicated to her school books, and her social life became a priority in her high school years.

Raylee sat in the corner and watched her family. Together they were the perfect team. With Colton being away, Raylee knew their perfect team was incomplete, in the house and in the cutting pen, and she wished he was there.

"Grab me that lead," Jesse said to Colton, when he pulled the colt up outside the barn late one afternoon.

He did, without offering any more help.

"What're you doing down here?" Jesse asked, curious as to why he was hanging around.

"I'm bored," Colton replied truthfully.

"Well you could always give me a hand whenever you want." It was only a suggestion that Jesse threw his way.

Colton didn't think much of the offer. As far as he was concerned, he was still on break and spending time with the horses was work whichever way he looked at it.

"How's he coming along?" Colton asked while he stood next to the colt, rubbing his front and feeling the warmth.

"Not as good as I expected. He's still got a lot of work to do and not much time to do it before the show." Jesse sounded disgruntled in the colt's training. "I had high expectations of this horse and so did his owner. If he doesn't pick up soon, I'll quit him."

Jesse had a lot on his schedule. He was training three young horses, handling another couple of babies as well as keeping the Derby and Classic horses up to speed. With the new breeding program building momentum again, he was more than busy, while trying to stay on top of the maintenance in the barn and around the yards. Whatever time he had leftover, it was spent on the cattle. With Aimee and Allan's help, they were just managing. Then again, Jesse had been trained by the best teacher and he was as thorough in the training process as what Cutter was, with great results and quite a few buckles on his trophy wall now.

It was his regular five o'clock start times that got him through his workday, and when Colton showed up at all hours of the afternoon, Jesse was just about finished and was closing the barn down for the night.

Every day was the same. Jesse would be going about the night feeds when his nephew would turn up at the barn, always looking for something to do. While Jesse didn't pressure him, it was clear that as the weeks rolled on, Colton was becoming lazier. It wasn't until he turned up at the barn at three o'clock on a Friday afternoon that he saw Jesse loading the horses into the float. Aimee was throwing their saddles in and the girls were already sitting in the backseat.

"Where're you going?" Colton asked.

"To a show," Jesse answered quickly, without detail.

It was Aimee who filled in the gaps. "We'll be gone for a week," she informed him.

Colton was jealous. "Why didn't you ask me to go? I could have gone with you," he said, disappointed that he had to stay at the vineyard now, alone.

Aimee went to answer him, before Jesse got in first. "Because we're going away for work. And you're still on holiday," he said abruptly.

"So you're expecting me to look after the barn while you're away?"

"Nah mate. You're still on break. You take it easy," Jesse threw straight back at him. "It's all taken care of. Our friend George will be here in the morning... Have a good week," Jesse added, before he climbed into the driver's seat. He started the engine, giving Aimee the hurry-up.

Aimee gave Colton a quick kiss on the cheek, then she too climbed in, her door barely closed as Jesse started to move out. The girls waved to him out the window, disappointed that their cousin was being left behind.

Colton stood in the car park outside the barn, watching them leave with three horses onboard, going to a show. He really felt alone now. That sucked.

He looked around. The barn was closed down and the horses were all out, rugged and feeding as the afternoon sun was making its way down. There was nothing to do and he went for a drive around the property, just to fill in the long night ahead.

Lying in bed that night, he picked up Avery's photo. He couldn't wait to see her again and he wondered how her injuries were healing. Was she scarred for life? Did she still have to wear the neck brace? More importantly to Colton, was she missing him as much as he was missing her? They were his last thoughts before he fell asleep in the early hours of the morning.

After another long session by the pool, Colton went for a shower then stood in front of the mirror, drying himself off while admiring his suntan. He pulled on a pair of jeans and went out into the kitchen. Evelyn had made lunch and since they had already eaten, she left his plate sitting under a cover. Now he had to eat his lunch alone too.

"Why don't you go to the barn for me and see how everything is?" Evelyn asked.

It was the least Colton could do for his grandmother, and he wasn't rude enough to tell her no.

"Has my dad called?" he asked, wanting to hear some good news that it was safe to go home.

"Not yet," she said gently. "But I wouldn't be holding my breath if I was you."

"Well they can't keep me here forever."

"No they can't," she agreed. "But while you're here, you should make yourself useful."

"Alright, I'll go and take a look around... After I finish my lunch." Colton was letting his grandmother know his priorities.

Allan walked into the room when Colton was placing his empty plate into the sink. "And if you want, you can take the quad bike," Allan offered. "You know where the keys are."

It brightened him up immediately. Colton had seen the quad sitting in the garage and wasn't game enough to touch it. But with his grandfather's permission, he was now keen to give it a blast. It wasn't very old and Allan had bought it so that he could get around the property easily without taking his new BMW off track.

"Hey," Allan said sharply to get his grandson's attention, as he'd already started walking towards the key board in the hall. Colton turned around. "It's not a race track," he said firmly. "Just remember that."

He found the keys and went to the garage, pressing the automatic door. He threw his leg over the quad and put the key in. It was the biggest, meanest, fastest four wheel bike on the market and was only six months old. Allan didn't need it for its size or speed, but he did want it because it was the best that money could buy.

Finding reverse, he backed out of the garage carefully. Shuffling the lever into drive position, he applied the throttle steadily to gauge how powerful it was. It didn't take him long to find out, as a quick burst saw him back off and grab his hat after he nearly lost it, and it made him feel good for the first time in weeks.

Leaving the road, he made his way to the barn through every gully and creek crossing, through the rows of vines and when he rode past the horses, he gave it another blast, just to watch them run. Everywhere that he couldn't go in his mother's car, he took the quad. It was the first taste of something fun since Avery's show of affection in the front seat of the truck, and he was feeling uplifted again.

He pulled up outside the barn. It was open and a car was parked out front in Aimee's position. He turned the quad off and walked into the breezeway with a feeling of temporary contentment. There was no one to be seen and he followed the sound of music playing, out to the arena.

Someone was in the arena, more than likely working a horse, and when he put his boot onto the rail and pulled himself up, he could see a practice session was taking place.

There were three barrels set up and when he looked for the rider, she had just started her run. She was fast when she took that first barrel and charged across the pen towards the second, clipping it slightly as she kept it tight before digging her spurs in and racing for the third and final barrel. It was her accelerated sprint for the finish line that told Colton that she was good. It was over and done and without hesitating, he put his hands together and gave her an applause.

She pulled the horse up quickly and looked over to the gate, not knowing she had an audience. She rode over to the young cowboy, and Colton threw his leg over and met her in the sand.

"That was awesome," he said, very impressed.

"I didn't know anyone was here," she said. "I might have tried a bit harder if I'd known." She put her hand out to meet him. "Hi... I'm Georgie," she said in a very upfront and forward manner.

"Georgie?" Colton asked. "You're George?"

"Yes," she said.

"I'm sorry, but I thought you were a guy."

She looked down towards her boots then back up again. "Not the last time I looked," she said with a friendly smile.

He tried to correct himself. "I'm sorry," he said again. "I just meant... Never mind. Hey, that was fast. Do you compete?"

She began to lead the horse back to the barn. "Whenever I can. If I'm not studying or working then I try to get around to a few events."

"Well you're pretty good," he complimented, and when he looked at the oversized buckle she was wearing, he knew that she didn't need telling.

"And that's not all I'm good at," she said, smiling at him some more.

Colton looked at her. Was she flirting with him?

"Do you want some help with that?" he asked, when she began to take off the saddle.

"Sure," she said, willing to let him help.

He was a little nervous. "Do I need to ask what else you're good at?" He was bordering on the line between flirting back and just being polite.

She laughed at him. "I'm studying to be a vet nurse."

"Oh, that's really great. I'm sure you'll be really good at it."

"Well how would you know? You don't even know me," she stated in a teasing way. "Anyway, I don't even know your name," she added.

"It's Colton."

"And let me guess... With that Texan accent, you must have something to do with Aimee?"

"Yes ma'am. She's my aunty."

"Right... Colt... I've heard all about you. But I thought you were just a little kid."

He looked down towards his boots and back up again. "Well, it looks like I've grown up," he said, giving her a fun smile in return.

She laughed. It was clear to Georgie that he was still quite young even though he was more grown up than anything she had ever heard of him. He opened the gate of the wash bay and tied the horse up. Colton immediately went for the hose and turned the tap on. Getting the temperature right, he sprayed the horse with warm water while she went for the products.

It was the first time since he arrived that he felt the need to help out in the barn. They talked and laughed, and when the horse was finished, Georgie tied him up out the front to dry off in the sun. It was now well into the afternoon and she went into the feed room to prepare the feeds for the night.

"Let me help you," Colton offered, and he began to mix up the individual buckets of feed for each horse.

It was faster with the two of them working side by side and they loaded them into the trolley and walked out to the yards, giving each horse their mix. After a quick clean up in the barn and everything was put away in the feed room, Colton sat on a bale of hay.

"You want a beer?" Georgie asked, when she came in holding two bottles, handing one to Colton.

It was at that point that he should have said no.

"Thanks," he said, as he willingly took it and cracked the top open.

She sat down on a bale next to him and they talked. Georgie asked lots of questions about where he was from and how he was connected to the Tremayne family, while Colton wanted to know more about who she was and her barrel racing success. As it turned out, she was nine years older than him yet when they talked, Colton put that age difference aside.

The beer was ice cold and went down well, although a little too quickly. When they finished, they brought the horse into the barn and threw a rug over him before they put him into a stall for the night. The afternoon was now gone.

"So I guess I'll see you tomorrow?" she asked, standing beside her car.

"Yes ma'am. You bet," he agreed, keen to finally spend some time with someone else other than family. "And thanks for the beer," he added.

They said their goodbyes and he watched her drive out of the property, closing each gate behind her as she left. Colton threw his leg over the quad and started it up. He rode back towards the house, finding every diversion he could, pushing the quad to its limits as if he was on a race track. He felt content and as he rode home the only thing on his mind, was what might be on the program for tomorrow.

Chapter Five

"Have you talked to your brother?" Raylee asked the kids at breakfast.

"Not for a few weeks," Dakota replied, then she looked to Westyn.

"Hey, don't look at me. I haven't talked to him since he left," he said. "Come to think of it, I don't think I've talked to him in the last six months."

The phone calls and messages between Raylee and her parents had slowed down over the last few weeks, and without picking up the phone to call her mother for another disappointing update, Raylee felt that it was best to wait until Colton had a desperate need to contact her. He needed this time to reflect on what had happened, and to understand how it had impacted on everyone else involved.

With Colton in Australia, the house was now pleasant to be in. There were no mood swings, arguments or drama unfolding from behaving inappropriately. The family worked well together and the cattle work was up to date with the added help from Raylee and Dakota. She was more settled without her brother leading her astray, and was focusing each day on the ranch and spending time with the horses. She spent endless hours in the cutting pen with Westyn and was beginning to show promising signs of being a good cutter. Then again, she came from good bloodlines and had some well trained, high profile horses underneath her, as well as the best teachers in her corner.

Raylee had given up on the idea of talking Cutter out of quitting. Over the last few weeks, she had tried every angle she could for him to reconsider his decision, yet he was sticking to it. Personally, she thought that he'd had enough of the pressures that went with competition and was wanting to sit on the rails for a while, where he could enjoy watching the kids show their talent.

His devotion to the ranch and the cutting pen never missed a beat, and he was still out the door every morning at 5 a.m, just out of habit. What Cutter loved the most, was when his daughter pulled some of the biggest moves he'd ever seen a girl do and when his son had his horse rock the pen like a pro, owning every square inch of it. That was pleasing to him.

During lunch, Raylee kept looking at Colton's empty seat at the table and she wondered how he was going. It was Dakota who pulled her attention back.

"Mom, can Avery come over for dinner tomorrow night?" she asked, and the rest of the table fell silent.

Raylee looked at Cutter. He didn't respond one way or the other. "Sure. How is she?" Raylee asked, curious for an update.

"She's good. But I think her mom and dad are suffocating her and she just wants to get out of the house."

Cutter still hadn't called their friends. Johnny had made it quite clear that he was putting a distance between them to let things calm down, and now that some time had passed, Cutter was not making the first call and neither was Johnny.

"Maybe I'll call Emma and they can all come over," Raylee suggested.

"No," Cutter said abruptly. "Not yet. If everything was fine, they'd have called by now."

"Or maybe you could call first," Raylee said lightly to prompt him.

"Or maybe we need to give them some more time?" he threw back quickly.

It was the first disagreement in the house since Colton had left and Raylee could see that Cutter was still unforgiving. If he couldn't let go of what happened in Nashville and with his father's truck when Johnny wasn't personally involved in either event, then how was he ever going to get his head around what his son had done?

Though he did feel sorry for what had happened to Avery, but as Raylee had pointed out, she was half to blame and it wasn't fair that their son had to take the fall for the both of them.

When Colton stood outside the barn and watched Jesse and Aimee drive away to go to a show for the week, he was pissed at both of them for leaving him behind. Three days into the week, he was enjoying the time spent at the barn without them. It was helping that Georgie was there from dawn to dusk and was very good company. Sharing the time, sharing a laugh, and sharing a drink at the end of each day.

He still didn't wander down to the barn until after lunch when he dragged himself out of bed. Although that was mostly due to him lying awake half the night watching movies, still feeling sorry for himself, something that was slowly easing as the days passed by.

"Why don't you time me?" Georgie said, offering to get Colton involved.

They set up the barrels and began playing around with techniques, looking for ways to cut down her best times. He was full of ideas for both her and the horse, and was pushing her along like a professional trainer.

When Georgie handed her horse over for Colton to ride, he began to feel nervous. It was one thing to make suggestions while standing in the sand, now he had to get on and prove that he actually knew what he was talking about. What if he couldn't get a faster time than a girl? Yet, just like the beers they were sharing every afternoon in the feed room, he wasn't about to say no. He wasn't about to give up and lie down, and let her think that he wasn't good enough to take up the challenge.

He gave it his best run. Colton had done barrels before to help his sister when she was practicing for an event, and had even been involved in the training process. That was a few years ago now, and he hadn't been on a horse at all over the last two months. Now she had thrown him in the deep end and he had to perform on the spot or lose credibility.

His time wasn't far off hers and she looked more impressed than smug.

"Well it looks like you know what you're doing," Georgie said when Colton handed the horse back, and they led it back to the barn. "So, what else are you good at?" she asked, flashing her smile and capturing his pride. He was interpreting her question, trying to figure her out. She was a woman, and he was out of his depth. A cowgirl, who was willing to play with him like a toy, making it fun and carrying on beyond the line of friendship.

"I'm good at lots of things," he said, playing along and keeping her interested. She followed him into the tack room, expecting to be shown rather than told. Instead, he leaned close to her, reaching out his arm and he grabbed a bridle. "You want me to show you?" he asked.

He turned around and took a cutting saddle off the rack. It was his mother's, and he'd used it many times over the years. They went back out to the stallion yard where the colt was grazing. He was still in his training years and Colton knew he wouldn't show him at his best, except that Jesse had taken the three aged horses with him to the show, leaving the broodmares and young ones behind.

They saddled him up and led him into the arena and when Colton got on, it gave him an instant buzz. He hadn't been on a cutting horse for some time and especially not one this young. It felt good and it surprised him just how much he'd missed it. He gave the colt some warm up time, riding around in circles, talking to Georgie when he rode close by. She sat on the top rail by the mechanical cow and waited for him to be ready, admiring the way he looked when he sat on a horse.

He was a natural and seemed like the complete package, giving her a rundown on what he was doing. He set the program. "You have to understand, this horse is still in training and has a long way to go," he told her, so it would lower her expectations. He followed the cow as it zipped up the wire and made the horse stop with it. "He knows what he has to do. He just has to wanna do it, and he'll be good."

Georgie didn't take her eyes off him. "Do you do this at home?" she asked.

"No ma'am. Not lately. Mostly I just work on the ranch with the cattle and I only help my dad with the horses when he needs me," he explained, not taking his eyes off the cow.

She was impressed considering he didn't do this often. There was something about the way he rode, the way he talked and the way he looked that she wished he was ten years older. Yet that didn't stop her letting the idea cross her mind.

"And lately I've been bull riding," he added, to give her a quick insight into his all round cowboy skills.

Now she was knocked over. "So that must make you popular with the girls back home?"

He laughed it off, not giving her a reply, as he pushed the colt into a sharp turn that was by far his best move yet.

With Jesse away at the show, it was good for the colt to have a run on the cow. Colton could feel that Jesse might have been underestimating him and giving up on him too soon would be a big mistake. He may still have a long way to go, but that didn't mean he wouldn't be ready for his debut. Only time and persistence was needed, and Colton thought that if it was up to him, he'd give the colt both.

They walked him back to the barn together and headed for the tack room. Georgie helped unsaddle him before they took him to the wash bay for a quick scrub. Just as he had helped her, she was returning the favor.

When all the horses were fed for the night and the feed room was tidied, Georgie grabbed a couple of beers and handed Colton one. He sat on the bales and repositioned his hat, then downed that bottle quickly. He was thirsty from all that riding and was almost sorry it was over.

"You want another one?" she asked, and she left the room to get him another beer.

It was getting dark inside the barn even though the sun was still hanging low in the sky. She turned the lights on and took up a seat on a bale next to him. They talked over the second beer about his family, while she was intrigued to hear all about his bull riding over the third. By the end of the fourth beer, he was just about gone.

"So why are you here?" Georgie asked, and Colton knew that she really had no idea of the reasons he was there visiting.

He decided to be honest about it, just in case she found out some other way and he summed it up quickly. "My girlfriend's father went a little crazy," he said, making her laugh at the sound of it.

"Are you in hiding?" she asked, curious of what he had done that was so wrong.

"Yes ma'am. You could say that. He was about ready to take my head off," he stated.

Georgie was beginning to sound more interested and provoked him. "You must have done something really bad if you've had to move to the other side of the world?"

Colton looked at her and his heartbeat went up instantly. She was moving closer into his space. Closer and closer, until their arms touched slightly and he felt hot.

"Well that depends if you're asking me or asking her dad," he said, then he locked his eyes onto hers.

Colton had been relaxed while spending time together, until Georgie decided to make a move on him. He had been slow on the uptake and she couldn't wait any longer for his invitation, planting a gentle kiss on the side of his mouth, making him close his eyes. Intimidated by her age and taken aback by her forwardness, he still couldn't turn her down. Instead, he held onto her face to lock their lips together. It was enough to send her all the right signals. There was no time to take it steady in case he changed his mind, and she made sure they were moving forward in the right direction. Fast.

She stood up and looked at him. This is crazy, was the last thought to go through his mind before he had a mental picture about what he wanted to do with her next.

Colton was leaning back on the bales of hay, feeling loose from the beers, watching her kick off her boots and strip her jeans to the ground. Her skin looked tanned against her pale blue knickers that covered very little, and when she unbuttoned her shirt, he had to restrain his hands while his eyes covered every curve on her shapely body. He felt a surge of urgency. A need to be with her. He didn't take his eyes off her and was admiring everything he could see and everything he couldn't. When she sat over him and teased him with a warm wet kiss, he released his buckle and kicked back his heels, digging his spurs into the bale of hay to hold on for the ride. The last thing on his mind now, was anyone or anything to do with Texas.

Raylee was fussing around in the kitchen, getting everything ready to make it a nice evening for everyone, including Avery. She had already given Cutter his instructions not to say anything that would draw attention to Colton or the accident, as she didn't want any tension during dinner.

When the training was finished and the sun was going down, Cutter and Westyn came up to the house, ready to have a shower, while Dakota helped set table. Raylee kept it very simple, making Marnie's special fried chicken from a recipe that she found buried deep among her recipe books, along with her mother's favorite Australian tossed salad smothered with her secret dressing that turned out to be not so secret and not too difficult to make, but a real winner among everyone.

"Is she here?" Cutter asked, when Raylee met him upstairs in the bedroom. He was standing in front of the mirror getting dressed and his hair was still wet.

"She shouldn't be long," Raylee said, and she quickly changed too. "Just remember, they're only kids and Colton really does love her."

They hadn't seen the O'Briens since the accident and tonight was going to be the first time they would see Avery with all her injuries. Dakota was desperate to spend some time with her best friend, even though they had talked on the phone every day since she was released from the hospital, while the two ranches were still at a standoff.

They heard her pull up out the front of the house and Raylee pulled the curtain back to see Avery getting out of the car slowly, with Dakota helping her. They walked up the steps and went out of sight.

Raylee raced back down to meet her. "Look at you," she said smiling, letting Avery know that she had been missed and she gave her a kiss. "How are you feeling?"

"A lot better," Avery replied. "I'm not sure when I get this neck brace off but hopefully it will be before Colton gets home," she added, and Raylee was thrown off guard with the first statement having her son's name mentioned. "When does he get back?" Avery asked, and Raylee was still unsure of what to say. She had made up her mind not to mention Colton's name with her and yet these were the very first words to fly out of Avery's mouth. It seemed that the love Colton had for her was returned.

"We're not sure," Cutter said. He had just walked into the kitchen and intercepted the question. "How're you doing?" he asked, genuinely concerned for her.

"I'm okay. I guess it could have been worse," Avery said, admitting that she got off lightly compared to how it could have turned out.

Cutter touched her on the arm for fear of hugging her with that awkward looking piece of plastic around her neck. It looked uncomfortable. He looked into her face. There were still a few cuts that were taking longer to heal, while others were clearing up without a trace. Except for the deep gash she had across her hairline, where the skin was still stitched together and an infection had set in.

He felt sorry for her. Their son had walked away with a small scratch to his hand while Avery had taken the full impact of the windscreen. It made him feel sick when he thought about it. Still, he believed that the only reason Avery was allowed over for dinner was so they could see what their son had done to her. It would be Johnny's way of reminding them that Colton was responsible.

Over dinner they kept it simple, talking about jobs and careers. The only advice Cutter gave the three kids, was to follow what they were passionate about. Westyn said very little, as he always did, although he did happen to mention that he wasn't going to college, which didn't surprise either of his parents. He had always made it very clear that he was going to follow in his father's footsteps and become a rancher and professional cutting horse trainer as soon as he was old enough, and if it was up to him, he'd quit school and start straight away.

Both Cutter and Raylee looked at the kids. They had seen them all grow up around that table and now they were talking about going off to study, looking at careers and making a life somewhere else, away from family and home.

"Don't worry, Mom," Westyn said to ease Raylee's mind. "I'm not going anywhere," he stated, as if he had no intention of ever leaving the ranch, and she laughed, knowing that one day he would move on too. He just couldn't see it yet.

"I'm sorry about your dad's truck, Cutter," Avery said when there was a quiet moment. The table fell silent again and everyone looked at him.

He sat at the end of the table in the same seat he'd always taken up, not speaking, but just thinking. It was the same place at the table where Macca had sat for all of Cutter's growing up years, and while it had taken him a long time to claim it, once he did, he never sat anywhere else.

"I saw it out the front and I didn't know it was that bad until tonight," she admitted, still wanting her apology to be heard.

He thought back to the day they had picked up the new truck. He remembered how excited he was, not only for Macca to be picking up his new set of wheels, but because he was given the keys to the old Ford truck and could finally drop off his rusty relic to the scrap yard. They'd travelled everywhere in that truck, gone to every show together, side by side. Later on it had become his, and he'd upgraded to the driver's seat while Raylee looked good on the passenger side. As the years passed by, the kids, one by one, started to fill the backseat and the blue metallic truck had taken the family everywhere.

"Dad?" Dakota cut in. "Did you hear what Avery said?" It was enough to bring him out of his deep thought.

Avery looked at him. Waiting. He still wasn't committing to any kind of response as the sight of his father's smashed up truck had cut him worse than any piece of glass that had sliced her face. He returned the look. She had been a big part of their family and was almost like one of their own kids. Everyone was waiting for him to answer.

"As long as you're alright," Cutter said kindly, and deep down he meant it. He'd never wish the truck back at the expense of someone being seriously hurt or even worse.

After they had dessert, Avery decided to push her luck, since she had always been very comfortable around the family. "Do you think it would be okay if I called Colton before I went home? I haven't talked to him since the day of the accident and my mom and dad won't let me."

It caught everyone by surprise. Everyone, except for Dakota, who seemed to know the question was coming their way. Raylee looked at Cutter. They always tried to read each other's mind and this time they didn't need to. They were already thinking the same thing.

"I don't think it's a good idea," Raylee said.

Cutter backed her up. "If your parents wanted you to call him, they'd have let you by now," he said firmly.

"But they don't have to know," Dakota pleaded, touching her father on the arm to soften him.

"I'm not sneaking around behind Johnny's back like that. That's what got us into this mess in the first place." Cutter was annoyed that they had asked and he let them know it.

"Please, Dad..." Only a daughter with those soft green eyes, just like her mother's, could convince him otherwise. Yet this time he was standing firm and wasn't falling for them.

"Don't look at me like that," he stated, and that was enough to let them both know they could win him over with a little more persistence.

"I really need to talk to him. I just want to make sure he's okay," Avery pleaded again. "Only for two minutes. I promise," she said. "After that, I'll wait for him to come home."

Cutter didn't speak.

"I really miss him," Avery kept on, and she let a tear fall down her face.

He looked at Raylee. She was not one way or the other.

"Please..."

Avery was now getting to him.

"And I know he'll be missing me too," she continued. "Please. I won't ask you again. But if you just let me..."

"Alright," Cutter said to silence her. "But you've got two minutes. No more. And if this ever leaves this house, then it will be the last time I listen to either of you again," he said severely.

Dakota and Avery both looked happy.

"Use the phone in the office," Raylee said, and the two girls left the table immediately and went to the office and closed the door.

"Hey, don't look at me. I'd never let them get around me like that," Westyn said. "Those tears do it to you every time." He stood up and picked up his plate. "Thanks for dinner, Mom. I'm going to my room to do my homework."

Raylee laughed when he left them sitting at the table on their own, wondering how their three children were so different from one another. It was Westyn who was more like his father and Raylee knew it. "He's so much like you," she said, admiring their likeness.

"Which means you must have been a real handful for your parents," he replied, referring to their other two children.

Dakota let Avery sit in her father's office chair. She stared at the phone for the longest while, wondering what to say so that she would get the most out of her two minutes.

"Hurry up," Dakota encouraged, looking at her watch. "They won't let you stay in here all night."

Avery picked up the phone and dialled Colton's number. She knew it off by heart and it took a while for the call to go through internationally. When it began to ring, it made her heart race.

On the other side of the world, Colton was lying in bed. For the first time since he'd arrived at the vineyard, he had been up early and was down at the barn helping Georgie with the morning feeds and some training on the barrels. He thought it may have been awkward to see her the next morning after their eventful frolic in the barn the night before, except that she gave him a good morning kiss that was so fulfilling, it almost replaced his breakfast.

When she convinced him to sneak her back to the house, it was easier than he thought, with Allan at work and Evelyn gone to town for some shopping. She was tucked up in his bed alongside him with the curtains closed and the air conditioning on, asking him exactly what he wanted.

He'd never been asked that before. He'd only been with a few girls who were slightly younger than him or around the same age, and since he was Avery's first, they were still finding their way. Yet here he was with a woman, who had a decade more experience than him, wanting to please him and show him a move or two.

It was the ringtone on his phone that startled him the most. He was already on edge, knowing that he was doing everything wrong in his grandparents' house and to his girlfriend who he loved. Still, who was ever going to find out?

He picked it up and looked at the number.

"Who is it?" Georgie asked, while sitting over him, admiring his boyish shoulders and arms, then leaning down to kiss him on his chest.

"It's only home." Colton downplayed the call, as if it was no big deal. "It's probably my mom. I can call her back later." He declined the call and switched it off, giving Georgie all his attention. She liked that he put her first, and now it was Colton's time to learn a thing or two when she changed her mind and whispered in his ear all the things she wanted him to do to her...

"Did you get him?" Raylee asked, when the girls came out of the office a few minutes later as promised.

"No ma'am. He didn't answer," Avery said with a dejected heart. She had one opportunity to talk to Colton and had missed it.

"Well, he's probably working hard," Cutter said to brighten her up. "He'll be doing whatever he can to keep busy while he's away."

"Maybe," Avery agreed, trying to convince herself. "I should be going now. Thanks for dinner," she said, and they all went out onto the porch to see her off. She stopped at the top step and with the neck brace so stiff, she had to turn her entire body so that she could look at Cutter. "Are you going to call my dad?" she asked, before she made for her car.

It gave Cutter a lump in his throat at the thought of it. He couldn't deny that it was his call to make first, except that he wasn't sure if enough time had passed. "I'm still thinking about it," he replied, then he gave her a fatherly kiss on the cheek.

It was good timing for Cutter that it was now dark outside, as seeing Macca's truck and Avery at the same time would have been enough to raise the annoyance in him all over again, something that he had been trying his best to bury. Although it just wasn't deep enough yet.

They watched her leave and went back into the kitchen to clean up. The girls did the dishes while Cutter grabbed two cups down and started to make the coffee. It had been a nice dinner and it was good to see Avery. They had missed her, although not as much as they had missed her parents. Johnny and

Emma were their closest friends and their time apart was very noticeable. Everybody was feeling it.

When Raylee came out and sat on the swing next to Cutter, she had no idea what was going through his mind. Only his silence told her that he was thinking. Perhaps even making another big decision without her. She touched his leg to alert him to her presence.

"What is it?" she asked, wondering where his head was at.

He was calm. Very at ease, and Raylee thought that the dinner with Avery had done more good than she expected.

Cutter looked at her. "Do you think it's time he came home?" It was clear that he had been thinking of his son, wondering if it was too soon or not long enough to bring Colton home.

"Why don't you call him. You haven't said one word to him since the hospital," she pointed out.

"I said goodbye at the airport. I can't help it if he didn't say it back."

Colton had left his father at the airport without having the need to even look at him, let alone say goodbye. It didn't bother Cutter so much. He was only doing what any father would do.

"Why don't you try him now," Raylee suggested, pushing him ever so slightly to make the call.

He finished his coffee and went into the office. Raylee sat in the quietness of the porch and swayed, with only good thoughts going through her head. Only a minute later, he was back.

"His phone is switched off," Cutter said, and Raylee could tell that he was disappointed.

"You can always try again tomorrow. One more day won't hurt," she said, to give him a lift.

Colton had left his phone off for the rest of the afternoon. He was so consumed with Georgie, that he forgot about it altogether and had left it in the room on the bedside table. They had to sneak back out before his grandmother came home. Before they were caught. Georgie sat close behind him on the quad bike and held on tight when he raced through the gullies and around the sharp bends, laughing all the way back to the barn. He took the long way back, wanting the afternoon to last.

"I think I'll give the colt another run," he said, when they parked outside the barn and went into the tack room to get a saddle.

"I was thinking the same thing," she flirted, and he fell for it.

Touching her butt, he pulled her in close for another kiss. "Well this colt is in recovery," he said when he pulled away.

They went into the arena for the afternoon and gave the colt another run on the mechanical cow. Colton was enjoying himself. He hadn't been this happy for a very long time. There was Georgie, who was keeping him entertained in the barn and between the sheets. There was the colt, who was giving him the time back in the saddle and in front of the cow, and then there were his grandparents, who were there to wash his clothes and feed him, without telling him how to run his life or to let him know that he was a complete screw up.

For the first time since he'd arrived at the vineyard, Colton was feeling good again and was not thinking about going home.

Chapter Six

A few weeks spent in the cutting pen for Dakota was very noticeable. While her brother was at school during the day, she was helping her father on the ranch with the cattle and riding the horses in the pen. They had never spent so much time together, just the two of them, and Cutter liked that she hadn't rushed off to start college when she'd finished school. He enjoyed having her around.

She was constantly under his wing. Since Nashville, with Colton having been sent to Australia, she had time to rethink her future. Dakota didn't want to be one of those girls who would bed any cowboy who looked in her direction. She didn't really like the party-life after the rodeo, and she craved the attention from someone who could see that she was smart and not just a pretty face. More than anything, she didn't want anyone from the cutting world who just wanted to end up being a son-in-law to Cutter Jones.

It would have been nice to go out on a date with a boy who wanted to get to know her for who she was. He had to be a cowboy. Strong. Good looking. Funny, but smart. Most of all, he had to have a gentle soul, just like her father. Unfortunately in this town, the choices were few and her priority list of requirements was long. There would be a line-up of boys at the front gate if she allowed it, but the elimination process would be over and done in less than two minutes, especially if her father was looking over her shoulder and had any say in the matter at all.

In the meantime, she was focusing on cutting, pulling a cow out of a small mob and putting her hand down. She was loving it. She only rode the well trained horses and that gave her the best advantage. Every day was an improvement on the last and after school of an afternoon, Westyn would join them and they'd all ride into the evenings together.

In the few days that Colton had been up early and gone to the barn, it didn't take long for Evelyn to see that her grandson was back. He was up and out the door soon after daybreak and retreated to his room after dinner each evening, looking exhausted. She was more than pleased for him now that he had settled in.

When he closed the bedroom door and flicked the light on, he saw Georgie lying in his bed and it frightened him.

"Damn it, Georgie. You scared me," Colton stated, then laughed at himself. "What're you doing here so early?" he asked, even though it was obvious, with her clothes spread across the floor and the covers pulled up not quite far enough to purposely reveal her bare shoulder.

She was lying on her side, swirling her hand over the sheets where she was asking him to join her. It was the third night in a row that she had snuck into the house. Each night Colton made sure he'd left the porch door unlocked and after his shower, he'd lie down and wait in the dark, hearing the door slide open and Georgie tiptoeing to his bed.

Sometimes they wouldn't speak, finding no words necessary and making no noise. The only sounds were of them kissing until things heated up. That was when Colton would panic and cover her mouth, for fear of alerting his grandparents to his late night visitor. A quick talk at the end while she was throwing her clothes back on was the only time they engaged in any conversation. It was more about the passion. Nothing about the friendship.

Yet tonight she had caught him out. She was early and was prepared to talk first. "I'm early because I have to leave early," she said, to let him know that time was not on her side.

He unbuttoned his shirt and stripped it off, throwing it aside. "What? You've got somewhere else more important to be?" he asked, hoping she would be impressed with his suntanned bare chest and want to stay there longer. He looked at her and was desperate to dive right in next to her.

When he leaned into her, he took his hat off and placed it on her head and the fun had just begun. "Stay here. I need to take a shower first," he said, then he kissed her.

Her leg was outside the sheets and when she pulled the covers across, she revealed his invitation to stay. "You're not going anywhere."

Each night was better than the last. Every time they were together there was something new. Just when Colton thought he'd done it all, Georgie pushed him to new discoveries. He couldn't say no to her and was sure he'd just crossed the line into manhood. He was more than impressed with himself.

As she stood at the side of the bed and dressed, he watched her. He was kicking back, wrapped up in the tangled sheets after their playful romp had turned wild and adventurous.

"It's only early. Are you sure you've gotta go?" he asked, hoping she would change her mind. The night was still young and Colton wanted to do it all over again, after a little recovery time.

"Yes," she said with certainty. "My boyfriend's been working away all week and he's coming home later tonight."

There was a sudden chill in the air. "Your boyfriend... Did you just say your boyfriend?" he asked, as if he hadn't heard her correctly and he immediately sat up on his elbows.

She laughed at him. "Yes."

There was a long pause while the thought process was taking place. "Okay, I'm dead," he said to himself, taking in her announcement.

"Why are you so surprised?"

"Because I had no idea and I thought..."

"You thought that you were the only one?"

"Well I didn't think that I was sharing you with someone else," he said.

She leaned down and kissed him and put his hat back on his head. He was blinded by her. It was an unexpected twist that he didn't see coming. All their time together, he never imagined that she had someone else to go home to. As far as he was concerned, he had her exclusively.

"It's no big deal," she said.

"Are you kidding me? It's a huge deal," he disagreed, making her see that he was disappointed.

"Look, I've got a boyfriend and you've got a girlfriend. There's no difference," she pointed out.

He couldn't dispute that.

"Except that she's not here," he said in his own defense of his reckless actions.

"It's still no different. And one day you'll figure that out." Georgie was showing no regrets and had loved every minute of their fun together.

"So what happens to us now? What's gonna happen tomorrow when I see you?"

"Nothing happens to us." She sat on the side of the bed and touched his chest. His skin was warm and his heartbeat was steady. "I'll be at the barn in the morning at the same time. And if your door is open early enough tomorrow night, then I've got one more trick I want to show you," she teased, letting him know that there were still more good times coming his way. She reached down and kissed him and he held her face with both hands, soaking up every last second before she left.

Closing his eyes, Colton rubbed his face, trying to get his head around it. Georgie having a boyfriend was no different to him having a girlfriend, and he knew it. It played on his mind. What was he thinking? More to the point, what was he going to do about it now that he knew?

He stared at the ceiling, finding the patch that covered the bullet hole and could only imagine that this scandal was far worse than what his parents had done, except that they'd got caught and he hadn't. He was playing with fire and the last thing he wanted was to get himself burnt. Only, he didn't know if he would be strong enough to resist her advances if she put it on him again, and he was willing to go to the barn tomorrow morning to find out.

Fidgeting with his shirt and realigning his hat was a sign that Colton was nervous when he walked into the barn. It was still early and he went straight for the feed room, expecting to see Georgie. He'd laid awake half the night, restless and confused, questioning himself and his better judgement. Wanting to make a decision about her and stick to it, and get it clear in his head. He still walked into the feed room without a clue about what he was going to say or do, hoping that her reaction would give him the answer.

"Good morning," he said cheerfully, when he stuck his head around the door.

"Good morning to you too. Don't you sound on top of the world?"

Colton was shocked. "Uncle Jesse. What're you doing here?"

"I work here. What do you think?" Jesse said, as if it was obvious.

Colton was thrown offtrack. "I didn't know you were back," he said, backing out of his happy mood.

"It's been a week. You got lost on the days or something?" Jesse asked.

"Yeah. To be honest, I don't even know what day it is," Colton admitted, and he looked around. "Where's Georgie?" he asked, trying not to look overly desperate to see her.

Jesse pointed to the arena. "She's warming up for some barrels. Anyway, what're you doing here so early?" Jesse asked, and Colton thought that he sounded suspicious.

"I've been riding the colt, and I think he's got a lot of potential." It was the first thing that came to his mind even though it was the truth.

"Oh really? I was just about to get him out, so why don't you get him ready and we'll go into the pen."

Just great, Colton thought. Now he was stuck with a job and was having trouble thinking of a way out of it. Finding his mother's saddle in the tack room, he grabbed everything he needed and went into the colt's stall.

There was something about this horse that Colton could relate to. While the colt was only partially trained, he was quite talented for such a young horse. He looked good and had moves that were promising, only needing more experience in front of the cow and someone to believe in him. Just like Colton, the last thing the colt needed was for everyone to give up on him.

He took to the saddle and made his way to the arena, with Jesse following him out on another young horse. Georgie had done a couple of runs and was taking a break. Colton could feel that eyes were on him from all directions and he began to sweat, although it was mostly in his imagination. When he opened the gate to go through, he purposely didn't speak to her.

"So you've met Georgie?" Jesse asked from behind.

Colton looked at her. "Yeah, we've met," he said. "Morning," he added to be polite. His acknowledgement towards her was quick and straight to the point, although she wouldn't allow him to get away with it.

"Morning back to you. Nice to see you up and out of bed so early," she said with a very over the top friendly tone. "Colton's been helping me on the barrels," she said to Jesse, to let him know that their meetings had been more than just in passing.

"She's pretty good, isn't she?" Jesse said as a compliment.

"Yes sir, she sure is," he admitted, while his eyes locked onto hers and his thoughts drifted back to the night before. "She's smooth and fast. Makes for a really good time." Colton found a little confusion even in his own words, and he hoped that Jesse didn't take his comments the wrong way.

Georgie immediately returned the compliment. "And you should see him in training," she said to Jesse. "He's been getting better and better every day. He's got moves that are downright impressive." She couldn't have praised him any more if she tried, although Colton wasn't sure if she was referring to the cutting pen or the bedroom.

Jesse was impressed by everything he'd heard. "Well then, let's see them."

They went through a few exercises, riding in large circles. Georgie took her horse back to the barn and came out with the third young horse ready to ride. She joined in and began the chase, following Colton closely and admiring him from behind. There were no words spoken as they all just got on with the job.

When Jesse slowed down, he turned the circle around and went in the opposite direction. Now it was Colton chasing Georgie, and everything she had taught him so far was going through his mind at that very moment. She was a big distraction for him, and he had to get his head right before he took to the cow.

The program was set and the colt was ready. All that was needed now, was for Colton to pull out some of those big impressive moves that Georgie had been bragging about earlier. But he didn't. He couldn't get that horse to do anything spectacular as he had done this last week, and he just went through the routine as if it was a standard procedure without so much as a spark of hidden talent.

That disappointed him.

"Hey. He wasn't all that bad, but you see what I mean? I really don't think he'll be ready for the show in time." Jesse let Colton know that he was still thinking of quitting him.

"He just needs more time," Colton pleaded, feeling that he still had something to give.

"Well he's got until the end of the week. Then I'm making a decision."

Between the three of them, they went through the other two horses. Jesse rode them all and Colton watched silently, noticing that Jesse had his father's traits. The way he positioned himself and the way he lined the horse up, was Cutter Jones style all over and Colton could tell that he had been trained by his father. Not only in the cutting pen and in the barn, but the way Jesse went about his work. His expectations were exactly the same.

When Georgie took the horses into the wash bay, Colton helped her. It was a good chance to get away on their own, since there was no way Jesse would be around to help with a job like that when there were other horses that needed riding.

"Do you think he knows?" Colton asked quietly, while they were hosing down the horse.

"If you act like you've done something wrong, then it will show on your face. Just look cool and he won't suspect a thing," she said.

"But what if he finds out?"

"Are you going to tell him? Because I'm not. So how is he going to find out?"

Georgie was right. He wasn't about to blab about his private life to his uncle. It was none of Jesse's business and what he did with Georgie had nothing to do with him. Nothing.

At lunch time, Aimee brought down some sandwiches for the four of them. They all sat down together around a table and kicked back, enjoying the rest. Aimee filled them in on their week away. Colton was so consumed with hiding his own secrets that he'd forgot to ask about the show.

"A win and two thirds," Aimee said proudly. "Not to mention a good score on the mare," she added.

"It wasn't a good score," Jesse corrected her.

"What? The cattle were tough and a two twenty was the highest all week," she said, to let them both know he'd had a successful week away.

They talked some more. Aimee was asking too many questions about the past week at the vineyard with some awkward silent moments that was sure to spell out guilt.

Colton thought to change the subject. "So, how do you know each other?" he asked, to get an understanding of how everyone fit together.

"Oh, Georgie's going to marry Jesse's cousin," Aimee stated quickly.

That threw Colton into a spin that he just couldn't get his head around it, or show anyone what he was really thinking. "What? You're getting married?" he blurted out.

"Well, not exactly," Georgie said, backing away from the commitment.

"But they will be. Once he asks her, and we all know that's going to happen sooner or later." Aimee was fully confident of their situation. "Very soon, Georgie will be part of the family."

Colton looked at Georgie. "You never said anything about getting married," he said, as if it was just the two of them having a private conversation. "Why would you do that?" he asked.

"Because I'm not. Well, not yet anyway," she replied, keeping it cool as if she was well practiced.

"Well it sounds to me like you are and everyone else thinks that you are so you must be." Colton was rambling on, giving Georgie a lecture when he had only known her for a week.

Jesse broke into their conversation. "Why does it bother you?" he asked.

Colton looked at them all. He was under the spotlight and Georgie had to come quickly to his rescue. "Look, he hasn't asked me yet so I think that everyone's getting a little ahead of themselves."

Her distraction didn't work and Jesse was still processing Colton's reaction. "But I'm curious," he said, as he leaned forward and rested his elbows on the table. "I wanna know why it bothers you so much? You'll be going home soon and Georgie will be getting engaged and married. You'll probably never see each other again."

"It doesn't bother me," Colton replied sharply. "Not one little bit." With a face that told a different story, he stood up to let them all know that lunch was now officially over.

"Do you want me to drop you off at the diner?" Cutter asked Dakota, when she was getting her uniform ready for her shift. "Your mother's going into town later and can pick you up when you're finished."

"Sure. That would be great," she agreed.

In the last month, Dakota had been picking up a couple of shifts each week, mostly over the lunch time rush. It was good experience and she added the money to her allowance from the ranch and was saving for college. It was just what she needed, to get away from the ranch and not be a cowgirl for a few hours, and meet new people from all different walks of life.

She traded in her jeans, boots and hat for her little white dress and apron, and she pulled her hair up high to keep it out of the way. If Cutter didn't know any better, she looked like she was going to a fancy dress party, not going to work.

Cutter was going to town anyway. He had to pick up some horse feed and was looking at some new tires for his truck, as it was well on its way to doing the miles, just as Macca's had.

When he dropped Dakota off at the diner, he went to the tire workshop and looked at his options. They had them in stock and could fit them if he didn't mind waiting. There was nothing that was urgent that he had to get back to the ranch for, and he wandered up the street, filling in the time. He was about to walk into the shop to put his order in for the horse feed when he bumped shoulders with Jake O'Brien who was on his way out.

It was one of those moments that could have gone either way.

"Cutter," Jake said, and he was more than happy to see him. "How you doing?"

"Hey, Jake. I'm good. What about you?"

There was nothing to suggest that their running into each other had any kind of awkwardness about it, especially since they didn't mention Johnny, Nashville or the accident. They caught up quickly before Cutter put it out there. "I'm going to the diner for some lunch while I wait on my truck. You wanna join me?" he offered.

Jake was in town for supplies too, but could spare half an hour. "Sure. That sounds good."

Cutter always had a close connection to Jake from the day he was born. When Emma had gone into labor in the middle of a storm, Johnny had been caught in town, leaving Cutter and Raylee her only hope of delivering her baby safely. Cutter had been there when Jake made his entrance into the world, when he'd ridden his first horse and when he'd started school. Practically every birthday or special event, Cutter had been there for Jake and was closer to him than to his own son at times.

They took a seat in the corner and when Dakota came out of the kitchen, she was surprised to see them both there. She couldn't ask the obvious questions, although it ran through her mind how they came to be sitting in the diner together on her shift.

"Now, what can I get for you?" she asked, ready to write down their order.

Neither Cutter nor Jake needed to read the menu, as everyone in town knew it from back to front. There had been no variations added and the specials board only had three options. They both ordered their usual, and the only reason Dakota needed to write it down, was for the purpose of telling the cook.

She wandered back to the kitchen and Jake watched her until she went out of sight. Cutter noticed and he was quick to jump on it. "You like Kotie?" he asked.

"Yes sir. Like a sister," Jake replied without hesitation, wanting to keep it simple.

Cutter disagreed. "Well I don't look at my sister that way," he said lightly.

"I don't know. With everything that's happened between our two families, I don't think it's a good idea," he said. "And besides. I'm the last person Dakota would ever look at."

"Well I don't know about that. Maybe you should ask her out on a date. I know she's always complaining that there's no one to go out with around here."

"And you'd let me take her out?" Jake asked cautiously.

There was not another boy in town that Cutter would trust with his daughter. Jake O'Brien could do no wrong as far as he was concerned and he would be more than happy if their friendship grew over time.

"I can't believe we're having this conversation. If only Colton gave your father the same respect, then we wouldn't be in this mess," Cutter stated.

"He misses you," Jake said, and it made Cutter feel a little relieved to hear it. "He hasn't said it, but I can just tell. It's not the same at home."

"Well he knows where I live and he knows my number."

While they waited on lunch, they talked some more. Cutter was getting an update on the O'Brien ranch. He hadn't been there in a long time and was genuinely interested to hear what they were all doing, while Jake was surprised to learn that Dakota was having a few lessons in the cutting pen.

"It must run in the family," Jake said. "Is she any good?"

Cutter looked at him from across the table with a subtle grin. "Like you said... it runs in the family."

The kitchen doors swung open and Dakota was making her way to the table holding two plates.

"Ask her," Cutter said under his breath.

"What? No," Jake replied, feeling a sudden surge of nerves that hit him in the gut and made him instantly lose his appetite.

She placed each plate in front of them with a smile, just as Cutter kicked Jake under the table to prompt him.

He was quick to respond before he had time to back out. "Hey, Dakota. You wanna catch a movie tomorrow night?" he asked, still feeling where her father's boot had landed on his knee.

"Sure. Why not. It beats sitting at home on a Saturday night." She gave them another smile and made her way towards the other customers.

Jake looked dejected as he watched her walk away. "I told you," he said. "She doesn't look at me the same way and I'm not sure if she felt more sorry for me or herself."

"Hey, I don't think she meant it that way." Cutter tried to turn it around. "Just go out and have a good time," he said. "But not too much of a good time, if you know what I mean."

"I don't think you need to worry about that," Jake said, believing that Dakota had no interest in him and was only going out with a good friend to break the boredom of sitting at home all weekend.

When Colton quit the barn early, Jesse felt that he was in a bad mood. Colton's reaction to Georgie made him suspicious. They'd only been away for a week and nothing was adding up in Jesse's head whichever way he looked at it. While there were still a couple of hours left of work to do around the complex, Jesse gave Georgie the afternoon off and thanked her for the help while he was away. She wouldn't be back again until the next time he had a show on, and she had to get back to her studies and work.

It left Jesse alone at the barn to finish feeding the horses and to put everything away. While he was cleaning up, he found the empty beer bottles in the trash and it raised another red flag for him. It fired him up and got him thinking some more. Could it be possible? Nah. Never. That would never happen and besides, how would he find out?

During dinner, Allan and Evelyn tried to involve their grandson in their conversation. He was unresponsive to any questions that were thrown his way, and they presumed that he was tired more than anything else. With his shoulders hunched, Colton went for a shower and came out of the bathroom looking at the empty bed. He was annoyed. Frustrated. Felt used. He looked at the time. It was Georgie time as far as he was concerned and before he went to bed, he unlocked the door to the porch, just in case.

Settling into the sheets, he took the photo of Avery out of the top drawer. He'd hidden it away so that Georgie wouldn't see it, and so that it would lessen his own guilt. How could Georgie do that to him? It was something he'd never be able to understand even though he was doing exactly the same thing. Avery's eyes caught his attention. If he hadn't been missing her before, then he was really missing her now. All he wanted to do was put Georgie behind him and think of how he was going to make things right with Avery. Unless she turned up for one last fling. That might have been enough to change his mind.

Colton put the photo down and turned out the light, after staring at the patch on the ceiling and thinking about home. He lay on his back in the dark with a thousand thoughts swirling around in his head, most of which were of the week that had been. Listening for the door, it remained silent, and he came to the conclusion that he was on his own tonight and he settled into a restful state.

Drifting slightly, Georgie's world was colliding with Avery's, and he had the two so close together that he couldn't separate them, until he thought he heard the door slide open. He opened his eyes even though it was dark. She was there. Just as she had promised, she had turned up for the last time. His heart gave a rush and when he heard the door close behind her, he settled back, pretending to be asleep.

Tiptoeing to the bed, he could hear her. She was close, and he wanted to start their last night together with a playful game so he remained still. Quiet. Expecting her to touch him, the next thing he felt was a hand over his mouth, pushing his head back into the pillow, and something sharp against his throat. He opened his eyes wide. Panicked. He was in a vulnerable position and one wrong move would spell blood. His blood. Face to face with someone only inches apart in the darkness, he had no idea who had broken into his room and was ready to kill him.

His breath was caught and it made him panic even more, while his heart was pumping so fast that he thought he may have keeled over from fright. I'm dead, was his only thought, when he felt the blade push harder against his smooth baby skin on his neck.

"You piece of shit," Jesse said, and he held the pressure on him and wouldn't let him go, not even to take a quick breath. "I leave you for one week and you couldn't keep it in your pants, could you? What the hell Colton! Did you think that I wouldn't find out? Did you think you'd get away with it?"

Jesse was throwing questions at Colton who could do nothing to answer. His mouth was covered and any sign of resistance at that point would be a mistake.

"What do you think you're doing screwing around with my cousin's girlfriend?"

Jesse pushed Colton's head down one last time before he let go of his mouth. He held the pressure to his throat with the sharp blade that began to feel wet. His skin was cut.

"I didn't know," Colton said. He was far from calm and had fear in his eyes.

"Well when you cross those lines, it's your job to know."

"What're you gonna do?" he asked, curious to know his position.

"What I should be doing is letting my cousin know. What I should be doing is sending you home."

"I promise. I won't go near her again. I'll go home and I won't come back," he pleaded.

Jesse wouldn't have it. "And somehow, I think that's gonna be the easy way out for you, isn't it?" Jesse was angry and was showing all the signs of what he was feeling. "And what about Avery? How could you do that to her?"

Colton began to answer, until Jesse cut him off. "Don't worry. I know how you did that to her. You've got no heart, no balls and no brains. You're just scum."

That cut Colton more than the blade. He wasn't all those things Jesse had said, although his actions would suggest otherwise.

"Send me home," Colton said, as a request to cover up yet another one of his screw ups.

Jesse got off him and folded the blade back inside the knife. "And that would really fix all your problems, wouldn't it?"

"What're you gonna do?" he asked again, wondering what his fate was going to be.

It took a walk around the room quickly while Jesse was fuming to figure this mess out. He put his hands behind his head and paced. He gathered his thoughts and gave it to Colton straight. "I'll tell you what I'm gonna do. I'm gonna be at work in the morning and so will you. You'll have all the stalls cleaned out by the time I arrive at five thirty."

There was an unexpected protest from Colton. "I'm not cleaning out stalls at five in the morning," he stated, as if he had a say in the matter. "I'm not cleaning out stalls at any time of the day."

"Oh yes you are," Jesse snapped at him. "And if you don't, then I'll make sure that the surveillance footage from the barn which has got your face all over it, finds its way to all the right people." Jesse was letting him know that he had the upper hand. "I'm sure there'd be some people who wouldn't mind knowing what's been going on down at the barn this last week," he added, spelling it out clearly for him. "Your grandfather has security cameras set up all over this property, and it doesn't take much to guess what your late night visitor was doing sneaking into your room every night."

Colton knew he was in deep deep shit. Jesse had seen all the evidence for himself. He had been caught on camera and with that kind of proof, there was no denying it. Jesse had him over a barrel and was willing to use it against him.

"What about Georgie?" he asked.

"You don't have to worry about her. She's gone home and you're still here. That's all you need to worry about for tonight." Jesse made for the door. "Get some sleep. Five a.m. will be here before you know it."

All of Colton's fears had come to him in the space of just a few minutes. He was left in the room with a cut to his neck and his pride broken in half. The room was still dark and he felt alone. Rolling onto his side, he broke down and cried like a baby. He was a mess. He was a complete screw up and for the first time, he actually knew it.

Chapter Seven

"He's here," Cutter called out when he saw Jake pull up in Johnny's truck just outside the house. He was standing at the window, peering out.

Raylee made a fuss over her daughter when she came downstairs. "You look so nice," she said, giving her a compliment.

Both parents looked at her with a big smile.

"What?" Dakota asked. "Don't look at me like that. It's only Jake and we're only going to dinner and the movies," she said, as if their overreaction was completely unnecessary.

Cutter opened the door for Jake when he walked up the front steps. "Hey, Jake," he said. "She's nearly ready."

Dakota pushed past him to the porch. "What are you talking about? I am ready," she said, and she gave them both a frown. "What's got into you two?"

"What time will you be home?" Cutter asked Jake.

"What?" Dakota interrupted loudly, showing her disapproval. "You want me to give you a time? I've never had to give you a time before."

"How about eleven?" Jake suggested.

"Alright. Sounds good. Eleven it is." Cutter was a little nervous for his daughter who had no concept that she was actually going out on a date. As far as Dakota was concerned, she was going to dinner and the movies with her neighbor. Her friend. Her best friend's brother. Someone she had grown up with. There was nothing more to it than that.

"I'm sorry about them," she said when she climbed into the truck. "I don't know what's got into them. They've been acting weird all afternoon." Dakota apologized for her parents' strange behavior although she couldn't find an excuse for them.

"I think after what happened between your brother and my sister, it's got everyone on the lookout," he said, and Dakota laughed at the sound of it, even though he didn't. He turned the truck around and gave Cutter and Raylee a wave out the window, then drove up the long driveway.

"You think they're on the lookout for you and me?" she asked, still amused by the thought of it.

Jake didn't give her an answer. In his mind, it wasn't an unrealistic possibility like it was for Dakota.

"Well let's give them something to worry about then," she said for some fun. "Let's skip the movie. Go parking. Find someone to marry us and on the way home, past eleven o'clock, and let's see what I can do to you in the front seat so that we roll your dad's truck over. That will make our fathers even. Then they'll know they should have looked out for us."

Just the idea of it made her laugh. Her giggle was infectious and he couldn't help but see the funny side. Mostly, he was laughing at her laugh. It was no secret to anyone what Colton and Avery were doing in the front seat of Macca's truck when they crashed it, giving Jake a nervous feeling deep in the pit of his stomach at her suggestion of it.

After parking the truck, they went into the diner for a quick bite to eat. There weren't too many places in town that you could have dinner on a Saturday night, and the diner was as good as any other, as it was usually filled with a younger crowd rather than their parents. When they walked in, they seemed to know everyone there, and would follow them on to the one screen cinema, all having the same idea.

They took a table and sat opposite each other. Dakota didn't need to look at the menu either. She knew it inside and out and from back to front, just like everyone else in town, and she rarely ate there for no other reason than it was her place of work.

"Have you heard from your brother?" Jake asked, genuinely wanting to know how Colton was going.

"My mom's talked to him a few times, but I haven't for a couple of weeks," she replied.

"Do you know if he's coming home soon?" he asked, being just as curious as everyone else.

She was quick to jump on him. "Are you a spy?" she asked, and he laughed at how that could have easily been mistaken for someone just wanting an inside advantage.

"No ma'am," he said to put her mind at ease. "I'm just wanting to know when to pack my bags and leave town. I don't wanna be around when those fireworks go off."

"Then I'm coming with you. Where should we go?"

Jake thought about it. "Well, I always liked the sound of Montana. Beautiful mountains, crystal clear waters and you can get lost in your own backyard and would never have to see another person ever again."

"If your dad hears that Colt's coming home, then Montana might be too close. What about South Mexico? We'd never be found there."

"But we don't speak Spanish," he pointed out. "And I'm not sure I could live on tacos for the rest of my life," he added. "We could get on a plane and go to England. So many people live there and that would be good place to get lost. No one from our family would ever look for us there."

"England? You can't be serious. You can't be a cowboy and hide in England. We'd stand out a mile away. They'd only have to ask at the border and everyone would know where we were hiding."

"Then it's settled. Let's just set up home in New Zealand. It's close enough to your grandparents and far enough away from everyone else we know."

She laughed with him. "Now that sounds like a plan. You could raise a few goats and I could... Actually, I'm not real sure what people do in New Zealand."

"Well I guess they do what everyone else in the world does," he said, as if he actually knew.

"And what's that?"

"Skip the movies and go parking. Get hitched and fool around in the front seat of the truck."

Dakota laughed some more. "But if we were hitched, as you so nicely put it, then we wouldn't have to fool around in the truck, would we? I'm sure you'd have me live in a huge castle with a moat and my white horse all saddled up, ready for me to ride."

"Yes ma'am. Nothing's too much for my princess," he teased.

"And our thirteen kids," she added, just in case he forgot about them.

"The more kids, the more help I'll have herding my goats."

Dakota was having a surprisingly good time. She hadn't laughed this much for quite a while, since Colton and Avery had really put a dark cloud over the two ranches lately. She'd always liked spending time with Jake, yet this was the first time that it was just the two of them alone. They had never been out without everyone else tagging along. There was something nice about spending time together that made her feel safe. He was a good friend, and he wasn't there to take advantage of her like other boys she knew.

It had been a long night at home for Cutter and Raylee, wondering how the night was going for their daughter. They had a quiet dinner with Westyn, although without his need to speak, they might as well have sat at the table on their own. Cutter kept looking at the clock on the wall, watching the minutes turn into five. Turn into ten. Turn into thirty. The hands took a long time to wind around and with an hour still to go, Cutter was doing all he could to fill in the wait. He went to the barn to check on the horses and kept looking up the driveway for lights.

"Why don't you go to bed?" Raylee suggested, when he sat next to her on the swing. She had been sitting on the porch, wrapped in a blanket, enjoying the peace and quiet and she was about ready to turn in herself.

He looked at the time for the hundredth time that night. "They should be here soon. It's nearly eleven now," he said.

"But that doesn't mean you need to stay up and wait for them," she pointed out.

"So why are you still up?"

Raylee had no excuse and she knew it. "Let me make you a coffee," she offered, to change the subject and she got up and went inside the house, leaving him on the porch.

Cutter still couldn't believe that Dakota was out on a date. When he'd seen her in Nashville on the dance floor, he was ashamed of her, embarrassed and disgusted all rolled into one. There was no reasonable excuse for her outrageous behavior, since she had not grown up in that world and he'd wondered where she had learnt those moves.

It was a heartbreaking moment for a father and since then, he had only hoped that someone would come along who would ground her. Someone who would be responsible and lead her away from that scene. A boy with the same interests who would be good for her. Someone like Jake.

Raylee came out with two cups, just as the lights turned down the driveway.

"They're here," she said, getting his attention immediately.

"Quick. Sit down," Cutter said, to act cool and not look as if they had been pacing all night. She did, and they both sat back looking like they were having a nice time, enjoying the starry night and relaxing.

Cutter waited for the swing to stop before taking a sip. The coffee was hot and was warming him from the inside out. Jake pulled up at the house and they waited anxiously for them. It was another few minutes before Dakota stepped out of the truck and headed up the steps, only turning around to give him a wave as he drove away.

She wandered over towards the swing.

"Right on time," Cutter said, to let her know that he was impressed.

"Are you seriously keeping the time? I thought you'd be in bed already," Dakota said, knowing that her parents had purposely waited up for her unnecessarily.

"How was your night?" Raylee asked.

"Actually, it was really good," she replied, and it pleased them both to hear it. "In fact, we're getting married," she announced.

Cutter spluttered and spat his hot coffee everywhere, spilling it all over his shirt and it burnt him. "What?" he asked, wondering if he'd heard right.

"Yes," she said. "And we're having a brood of kids and raising some goats." She turned and walked away. Before she got to the door, she turned around again. "Oh, and did I tell you that we're moving to a castle in New Zealand?" She laughed, watching her father clean up the spill and shake his shirt off. "You're so lame, Dad. We just had a nice night."

She walked back over and gave them both a kiss on the cheek. "I love you. Goodnight," she added, and she went inside the house.

Cutter and Raylee sat there stunned. He looked at her for reassurance. "I'm not lame, am I?" he asked.

Raylee touched him on the leg and gave him a funny smile. "Well... not all the time."

Colton had his alarm set. He hadn't slept very well anyway, and when it rang in his ear at some unearthly hour, he immediately got up and headed to the bathroom. It was dark and the light blinded him. He turned the shower on and waited for it to heat up while he stood at the basin and looked into the mirror, inspecting his neckline. He had a cut across his throat. It wasn't so much deep as it was long, and it was his reminder of the night before. A reminder not to be late.

When he arrived at the barn, it was all closed up and in complete darkness. Finding the lights, he brought the stables to life. Taking each horse out and getting to work cleaning out their stalls, Colton was fuming. He hadn't done this in years. It was not his job. This was not what he was there for. Except that Jesse had a noose around his neck and it was going to be up to Colton whether he hung himself or not.

His mood was mixed. Angry at his father. Betrayed by Georgie. Hurt by Jesse. He was feeling alone and thought about Avery. She wouldn't want to see him going through this mess. He'd caused himself this mess and he couldn't tell her that either, without openly admitting what he'd done.

As the sun was coming up, there was still no sign of Jesse. He took a hose and washed down the breezeway, looking for something else to do. In the feed room, he mixed up the individual buckets and he went around to all the horses and fed them out. He gave extra time to the colt, just for the company, as there was still no sign of anyone coming down to help.

He liked it better that way. Jesse was the last person he wanted to see and he would rather have been on his own with the horses for the entire day, though he knew that wasn't going to happen with the show coming up, as the training would be a priority from here on in.

The barn was still quiet and now clean, and a breeze came flowing in one end and out the other, making him feel at ease. He gave a yawn from the late night, restless sleep and the early morning. By six o'clock, he was really feeling it.

He took his mother's cutting saddle out and gave it an oil, admiring the detail and how little it had worn over the years. His father had bought it for her one year when they spent Christmas at the vineyard. Colton had been quite young but remembered it well and it made him think back to how great his childhood was. Those years when he loved to ride and loved to cut.

It had become a chore over the years growing up. Doing the same thing day in and day out. Going through the same routine and going to the same shows, and the buckles that his father had won, were all the same to him. Every year was the same and the only thing that ever changed, were the horses coming through. Before Colton made it his world, he'd felt burnt out from it and that's when he decided to try something else. He wanted to find a passion for anything other than cutting. He wanted to be good at something else, and he found out soon enough that it wasn't going to be bull riding.

After he'd finished oiling the saddle, he brought the colt in and threw it on, then took him out for a ride. Instead of going into the arena and riding around in circles, he decided to go for a ride over the property. Everywhere he had ridden the quad, he rode the horse. Into the gullies and around the creek bed, following it as it weaved around the property among the trees and fence lines.

He eventually made his way back to the house where he tied the colt up and went inside for some breakfast.

"I thought you were still in bed," Allan said, as he was finishing his morning coffee and was putting his plate into the sink. He looked ready for work and was straightening his tie.

Colton took a bowl and filled it with cereal. The milk was already on the table and he sat down with his grandmother. "I couldn't sleep, and Jesse needs the help with the show coming up."

They both looked impressed. Perhaps things had turned around for their grandson and they were beginning to see that he was on the right track. The right track to head home.

Evelyn looked closely at him. "What happened to your neck?" she asked, and she leaned in to get a closer look.

He put his hand over it to cover it up. "It was dark this morning and I cut myself shaving." It was the only excuse he could think of and it seemed to satisfy his grandmother who just reminded him to be careful next time.

His fifteen minute call into the house was now over and he went outside and got back into the saddle. Riding out the back of the property around the creek, he came across a mob of cattle that were lazing in the shade. He walked through them, raising some interest from the colt who was warmed up and feeling strong. It was quite sandy and he decided to pull one out from the rest and give the colt a run.

The colt had never been away from the training pen and when Colton put his hand down, the reins fell loose and the colt took over. He blocked that cow when it tried to return to the mob. It was steady, quite relaxed, and made for a good controlled ride.

Taking every turn and every run like he was trained to do, he was accurate. There were a few moves where Colton felt something spectacular and for the first time, he was enjoying being out on his own. He was on a horse that he liked, with no one watching and no one telling him what to do. There were no professional trainers looking over his shoulder and no advice being thrown at him. He was having a good ride and was doing what he wanted. His way.

The ride back to the barn was satisfying and when he neared, he could hear Jesse in the arena. Right now, Colton thought as much of Jesse as he did about his father. He would rather avoid him. Not see him. Wished him gone. Yet he rode over and opened the gate to show his uncle that he wasn't intimidated by his threats. The last thing Colton was going to do was hide.

"Where have you been?" Jesse asked, when Colton rode over to the mechanical cow.

He was quick to reply. "Well why don't you check your cameras and find out if you're so worried?" he said, as if he had no intention of letting Jesse know. "All you said, was that I had to be here before you, to clean out the stalls. And I was."

Jesse could have taken him to the ground and cut out his tongue for speaking to him like that. Though he remained calm and ignored Colton's comments, thinking that he needed to work with him, not against him. "Well you did a good job," Jesse said, to give him some kind of praise.

"It's not rocket science. It's shovelling shit, and it's not that hard," Colton replied. "You should try it sometime."

Jesse controlled his need to boil over and took a deep breath. "You wanna help me with some training then?" he offered, looking at the colt.

"He's already done," Colton said. "He's already had a run on a few cows this morning."

"How did he go?"

"Like I said. I think it would be a mistake if you quit him." Colton didn't go into any kind of detail but let Jesse know that he was impressed, without going overboard.

They rode back to the barn and took their saddles off. Jesse threw his saddle on another horse then instructed Colton to take the two horses into the wash bay. While it was his first instinct to argue, he didn't. Colton didn't muck out stalls or wash horses. That was a job for girls. He only wanted to ride, though if it meant riding with Jesse, then he was prepared to shovel shit and wash horses all day long. Taking the colt in first, he gave him a good wash, checking him all over and giving him particular attention. While he was tied up out the front of the barn in the sun to dry, he took the other horse in and gave him a sudsy wash.

For the rest of the day, Colton tried to keep busy, just to stay out of his uncle's way. Jesse was doing his best to include him at different times, with very little success. Colton had gone home for lunch and when he returned, he found jobs to do in the barn to stay clear of the arena, and by the end of the day when it was time to feed up, Jesse came into the room to help.

The tension was still lingering and Colton didn't speak, keeping his head down and ignoring Jesse altogether. When he looked around to find something to cut the twine on the bales of hay, Jesse noticed.

"Here," Jesse said.

Colton turned around to look at him and as he did, Jesse was throwing something his way. He put his hands out quickly and caught it, then looked down to see what it was. His throat tightened up again. It was Jesse's pocket knife. When he looked at him, Jesse had already turned around and was making up a couple of mixes. He flicked the blade out and stared at it. There was a smear of dried blood that took the shine away and gave him a chill, before the heat in him rose.

This was the knife that Jesse had pressed against his neck last night. This was the blade that had cut him. He was still staring at it when Jesse turned back around.

"You need me to show you how to use it too?" Jesse asked.

It snapped Colton back immediately and he cut the twine on the bales and pulled them apart. He folded the blade away and put his head down, working silently into the afternoon.

Sundays were always the slowest days of the week at the ranch, unless they were at a show. It was the day when Cutter slept in until six o'clock, the day when Raylee cooked up a storm for breakfast, and the day they quite often went to the stream behind the house for a family picnic.

It had been a tradition for Cutter growing up, and he always wanted to share that same time with his own family. It was important to him. He never really cared what day of the week they went to the stream for the picnic, until the kids started school and Sunday became the only day that worked.

"How was your movie?" Cutter asked Dakota, when she wandered downstairs late that morning. Her hair was messed up and she was still in her pajamas.

"Oh. We didn't watch the movie," she said, leaving her father to wonder what they were doing at the cinema that didn't allow them to see it. "We didn't go," she informed him.

Cutter was curious and had to ask. "Well why not?"

"Because we went to the diner for something to eat and then we decided that we didn't really want to see the movie that was showing."

His curiosity turned to suspicion and he was now all over her. "But the diner closes at nine thirty."

"Dad. I work there," she was quick to point out. "I had the keys to lock up when we were finished."

"Finished what?" he asked, treading lightly around her.

Dakota laughed at him. "Talking. I had the keys to lock up when we were finished talking. Then he drove me home. That's all."

Cutter felt a little relieved, although while they were still talking about it, he just had to ask one more question. "So, he didn't try to kiss you when you were in the diner all alone?"

"No," she said firmly. She looked at her father closely and could see the worry in him. She thought that this was the right time to set him up. She put her elbows on the table and leaned towards him and spoke softly. "But he gave me one in the front seat of the truck," she said to tease him.

"What?" he asked loudly. "One what?"

She laughed at him again. "A kiss… on the cheek. Outside this house when he dropped me off and you were waiting up for me. Spying on me. He gave me a kiss on the cheek. We are good friends, you know." She stood up from the table and walked towards the stairs. "Mom, tell him," she said to her mother.

Raylee had been standing in the kitchen keeping out of it. She looked at Cutter and finally found the right moment to join in. "You're having one of those lame moments again," she said, to let him know that he was not cool.

"I am so not ready for this," Cutter said, although it was more to himself.

Raylee heard him and laughed. She came over and sat with him at the table. "And now you know how my father felt all those years ago."

"But this is different," he said, quickly defending himself.

"Different how?"

"Because it's my daughter. And I know what was going through my mind all those years ago."

"But you didn't mind that it was Jake who asked her out."

"But I didn't ask him to spend the night locked up in the diner alone with her, or kiss her when he dropped her off."

"On the cheek," Raylee added.

"It doesn't matter. I know what he was thinking when he did."

Raylee was always more realistic when it came to the kids. "Well, from what I saw in Nashville, I'd say that Dakota's the one thinking about it, and Jake's the one you should be worried for."

Cutter couldn't dispute that. "And I thought that girls would have been easier to raise. Now I'm not so sure." He sat there thinking about his three children. "Have you talked to Colt?"

"Not for a while. Everything's gone a little quiet... Why don't you give him a call?"

Cutter had not talked to his son since he'd left for Australia, and he was slowly coming around to the idea that Colton should come home soon. Every day he was feeling less disappointed and less stressed over what happened, until he looked at Macca's truck still sitting in the yard. He had to work hard to bury those feelings, knowing that his son had made a big mistake and there was nothing he could do to change it.

Cutter looked at the time. "It's still early. When I come in later I'll give him a call."

Raylee was satisfied with that. She knew that she had to be the link to pull the family back together again. As far as the O'Briens were concerned, she wasn't sure if it was going to be that simple.

When Dakota came back down ready for work, she looked no different than the day before. There was no extra spring in her step and no extra sparkle in her eyes. She was beautiful just the way she was and Cutter often wondered, how any boy would be able to resist her. Dakota encouraged her father to get up from the table and they left the house and headed to the barn. Raylee watched them until they went out of sight. She loved that they were so close and she often wished that Cutter and Colton had the same connection.

When they walked into the barn, it was noticeably quiet and her horse was missing. "Where's my horse?" she asked her father.

"I don't know. Maybe West has her in the sand yard," he said, only as a suggestion.

Westyn was working in the sand yard and he wasn't there alone. When they neared, they could see Dakota's horse was tied to the rail with her saddle on. Jake was with him and they were going through the cattle like a couple of professionals.

Dakota smiled, then broke into a laugh.

"What's so funny?" Cutter asked, wanting in on the joke.

"Nothing," she said, knowing that her father wouldn't see it the same way. "It's just... my white horse," she added, without explaining how she came to that conclusion when her horse was bay. "All saddled up and ready to ride."

When the boys saw them, they rode over.

"Good morning," Jake said, when he pulled up at the gate. He gave her a broad smile and Cutter saw it, thinking that it was more than friendly.

"Are you coming in?" Westyn asked.

Cutter went back into the barn and saddled the mare, then joined them in the yard. They spent the morning on the cows, all taking a turn and having a great time. Westyn's horse was coming along nicely. It was from their own Renegade lines and had a similar look to the blue roan mare. She had produced many foals over the years and this filly especially, Westyn took a liking to. Cutter was pleased that they had invested the money to buy her all those years ago.

The filly was moving smoothly and her timing was good. She had an eye for the cow and had some strikingly similar moves to the mare. Westyn had her in training every morning before school, and she was only getting smarter and faster, without the need for his father to be involved.

It was not easy for Cutter to sit in the corner and watch his son make some mistakes that could easily be avoided, yet he zipped it and let him learn from them, to make him all the better for it. Just like when Cutter was learning to train horses, Westyn had to make mistakes to know what not to do.

After everyone had a ride, Cutter and Westyn let the cattle out and settled them into the holding yard. When they were done, they went back to the barn where Jake was taking off Dakota's saddle for her.

"Let her do it," Cutter said. "You're not here to make it easy for her."

"Dad," she cut in. "He's only trying to help."

"It's okay, Cutter. I don't mind," Jake replied defensively, wanting to take care of her.

They unsaddled the mare together and took her into the wash bay. Jake let Dakota know that he was impressed with how much she'd picked up in the cutting pen over the last few weeks, and she let him.

After a longer than usual session in the pen, Cutter felt a rumble in his stomach and knew that lunch was overdue. He left the barn and headed for the house, stopping by the office first to make the phone call. Colton would be out of bed now and Cutter had to pump himself up before he dialled his number. He had to be careful of what to say, so that it wouldn't strike a nerve and end up in a full blown argument.

Sitting down in the old leather office chair, he spun around to look at the wall of photos. They had been added to over the years, mostly of his children growing up. The photo that caught his eye was of Colton. A blue eyed, blonde-haired and kind-hearted little boy who was always into mischief. Never behind their back though, as he always had the front to find trouble in plain sight. He was never cheeky or destructive, but if there was something he had to stay clear of, you could bet that Colton would end up in the middle of it.

He spun back around and took his phone out of his pocket, scrolling through his contact list and just as he found Colton's name, Raylee came into the office.

"You ready for lunch?" she asked.

"Yes ma'am. I'll just make this call and then I'll be out," he replied.

"Are the kids coming up?"

"Plus one," he said. "Jake's here as well so you may wanna double up. You know he eats like a horse."

It surprised Raylee that Jake was at the barn with them and she went back to the kitchen to fill the basket with more food. It was true that he could eat well, although you'd never know it. Jake was tall and skinny, and hadn't filled out like a man yet. There was not an ounce of fat on him as his work on the ranch had taken care of that.

Jake O'Brien was the last person on Cutter's mind when Raylee closed the door behind her. He was only thinking of his son, when the phone rang in his hand and startled him. It was Colton. His son was calling him and it gave him a nervy feeling. He'd just beaten him to it.

"Hey," Cutter said when he answered the call.

"Hey, Dad," Colton replied. "How's it going there?"

Cutter was surprised to hear his voice. Not to actually hear it, but to hear his tone. "Everything's good," his father replied. He wondered if he should let Colton know that the ranch was great and that everything was running along just fine without him. That the cattle were doing well and the horses were up to speed. His brother had been doing a good job in the cutting pen and his sister had been giving it a go, impressing eveyone. That the ranch was going great without Colton Jones there to pull it down and screw it all up. He could have given him the full update, but he decided against it.

"That's great," Colton said. "Do you have a minute to talk?"

Cutter didn't need to go into all those details, especially when he felt that his son was wanting to talk about something else. Something other than the ranch. "I've got all the time you need. What's up?" he asked.

Colton gave his father a quick rundown on the colt. He started at the beginning. How old he was, how much training he'd already had on the mechanical cow and in the pen, and what Jesse thought of him. Giving his father a mental picture of the horse, he was wanting some advice on what to do with him next, since he didn't want to see the colt quit so easily.

It put Cutter and Colton on the same side for the first time in a long while. He could hear it in his son's voice that he was interested in something else, other than running amok and causing trouble. It gave Cutter an insight that perhaps Colton was finally getting his head together and he jumped right onboard with him, giving him some tips to look out for and some advice to follow should Jesse quit the horse or not.

Little else was talked about, other than to tell Colton's grandparents hello, returned with Cutter having to give Raylee a kiss for him.

When he walked out to the kitchen, Cutter put his arms around Raylee's waist and snuggled her from behind. He kissed her on the neck and she squirmed.

"What was that for?" she asked, rubbing her neck where he had just made her skin prickle.

"That was from Colton," he said.

She laughed. "He doesn't kiss me like that. That's how you kiss me."

"No. This is how I kiss you," he flirted, and he turned her around and pulled her in close. He held her face in his hands and kissed her in a way that made him want to skip lunch and go upstairs.

"Dad," Dakota yelled loudly. "We have a visitor."

They both looked up to see that the kids had arrived for lunch. Jake was standing by the door, feeling as if he was intruding, while Westyn was unfazed by their open display of affection. But it was Raylee who looked embarrassed.

"Don't you knock?" Cutter asked.

"Dad, it's the kitchen," Dakota pointed out. She turned both the boys around and shunted them out the door, leaving her parents to sort themselves out before they all went to the stream for the picnic. "You should get yourselves a room," she added severely, and Cutter thought that was a great idea.

Chapter Eight

Colton was on a mission. He wanted to work with the colt for the next few days to give Jesse no excuse to send him home. Of a morning, he would be at the barn early and had the stalls cleaned out, just as he was expected to do. He'd make up the individual mixes and feed them out, and tidy everything up before taking the colt out for a ride.

His father had told him of the trails up in the National Park, and he made sure he was out the front gate and had disappeared before Jesse came down to the barn, ready for work.

It was a good ride for both the rider and the horse. The steepness of the climb was sometimes challenging for the colt, as he had not done any work other than in the arena or occasionally being taken out the back to bring the cattle in. It was making him sweat.

The height was overwhelming when Colton pulled up on the highest peak and looked back down. He could see the vineyard in the distance below and when he took a look over the edge, it gave him an instant sickly feeling when he saw the drop. He backed away from the edge and gave the colt his time.

Talking to him, Colton was pouring out his thoughts. Touching him, he was feeling his strength. Lifting up each leg, he was checking him all over. The colt was in good shape and if Colton could only get inside his head, he would know exactly what this horse needed to succeed.

He sat down on a rock and held onto the reins. The colt stayed close and put his nose down near Colton's hat. Colton didn't look at him, but put his arm around the colt's head and rubbed his ears while he watched the sun peek over the mountain and light up his world.

Of everything that had happened in the last three months, he never expected that he would end up where he was. He'd never thought of the consequences before. From the night of the rodeo to crashing Macca's truck. From arriving in Australia to his crazy wild flings with another man's girlfriend. Nothing was too much for him and he dared himself to go those extra miles when he should have listened to his own better judgement. He had been taught better than that.

He had screwed up three times and three times he'd been caught. He'd suffered the consequences three times and if he didn't learn from them, then he was sure to screw up all over again. People were hurt because of him and he knew it. He was responsible for their pain and he didn't like that. Nothing he did now would change the outcome, and the only way he could make things right, would be to change the way he was. To make the right decisions and listen to his head. He needed to swallow his ego and get over himself to become a better man.

Today was the day he was drawing a line in the sand and on the way back down the mountain, he began to feel as if he was already on his way to becoming a someone.

When he arrived back at the barn, Jesse was already in the arena. Before he went in, he tied up the colt and sat on a chair outside the barn, letting the sun penetrate its warmth through his jeans to his legs. He relaxed, and dialled his father's number.

Cutter was surprised to hear from Colton again so soon. It should have been a good reason to worry, except that they talked about the colt and the show, and about his ride up the mountain. It took Cutter back to his first visit to the property, and he could only sit on his porch in Texas and close his eyes to see himself riding up those same trails so long ago.

They didn't talk about anything else, and Cutter could sense that his son had a need to see this through. While he wished he was there to help him, he knew it was something that Colton had to do on his own.

"Who was that?" Raylee asked, when she came out of the house and sat next to him.

"Colt's working with a horse," he stated, almost disbelieving it himself. "He just wanted to ask me a few things."

Raylee was surprised. "You know, I didn't believe it at first, but I think that it was the best decision to send him to my family. It sounds like they really know how to reach him."

"And he's not asked once to come home."

"Speaking of which... What do you think? Should we ask him if he's ready?" Raylee was more than ready for Colton to come home. "We haven't even talked to Johnny and Emma yet, so they wouldn't know if he was home or not."

"Give him some more time. He really wants to get this horse trained and ready for the show," Cutter said, pleased that Colton was giving it a go and was making the most of his time there. "After that, it's up to him."

"As long as he doesn't meet a nice girl and want to stay there," Raylee said, half teasing and half serious.

Cutter put his arm around her and pulled her in close. "Well that's not entirely out of the question, is it?" he said. "There's some really nice Aussie sheilas Down Under," he added, in an Australian accent that was so bad, that Raylee let him know it.

"That was terrible. You shouldn't talk like that. It's insulting to my country."

They laughed for a while before Dakota came up for a drink. "Oh, just so that you know, I'm going out on a date tonight," she informed them.

It pleased both her parents and since Cutter had relaxed about it, he extended her curfew time. "Twelve, no later," he said, which pleased her even more.

The afternoon was spent riding over the ranch, checking the cattle and moving them between different pastures. They brought another small herd in and placed them in the yards, ready for the next morning. Dakota excused herself early that afternoon, so she could go in and get herself ready for her big night out.

She washed and styled her hair, and applied extra makeup, which made her look five years older. Her favorite skinny jeans were showing off her figure a little too much, and her height was added to when she pulled on her high heeled boots.

When she saw the car pull up outside the house, she rushed downstairs before her date got a full drilling from her father. He knocked on the door and Cutter called him in while he looked at his daughter, then commented that he thought her outfit was a little over the top, even though he knew that Jake had the utmost respect for her and wouldn't cross those lines for fear of striking another feud between the two families.

Except that it wasn't Jake standing in the kitchen. There was an instant sense of confusion as Dakota rushed over to her date and held onto his arm, ready to introduce him.

"This is Daniel," she said politely. "And Daniel, this is my mom and dad, Raylee and Cutter Jones."

Cutter was floored. He wasn't expecting this at all. As far as he was concerned, his daughter was going out on a date with Jake O'Brien, and he tried to replay the afternoon conversation in his head to remember the finer details that he may have missed.

"Nice to meet you," Daniel said, and he stepped forward and held out his hand.

Cutter looked at it and paused. Daniel was tall and built like a mountain, and Cutter felt as if he was casting a shadow over him. He was huge.

"Dad," Dakota said to prompt him along.

He shook Daniel's hand and felt his strength. "I want her home by ten," Cutter said.

Dakota protested. "Dad, you said twelve."

"I meant ten," he said shortly, giving her a disapproving look.

"Mom, you deal with him," she said, and they walked out of the house and down the steps with Dakota apologizing the whole way to his car.

"What just happened here?" Cutter asked Raylee, as they stood at the window and watched them drive away. "Did you know about this?" he asked.

"No. Not at all. I'm just as surprised as you," she said in return.

"Do you know him?"

"I've never seen him before."

"Well who the hell is he?" Cutter asked furiously, completely annoyed that some stranger just waltzed into his house and had taken his daughter out. He was unsure how that had just happened.

It was Westyn who piped up from his position at the table. "He's the quarterback on the school football team," he said.

"What?" they said together, and they both turned around and looked at their son for more information.

"I don't know him. I just know that he goes to my school and has all the girls lining up to go out with him. I don't think he's taken the same girl out twice." They could both tell that Westyn didn't think very much of him. "I don't even think he plays football that well. If you ask me, he's very overrated."

How he played football was beside the point. Their daughter was out on a date with Daniel the quarterback with no last name, and it was going to be a very long night. Cutter and Raylee would spend their Saturday night pacing the house on edge… Again.

Looking at her date across the table, Dakota couldn't take her eyes off him. Daniel was by far the best looking boy in school and was the star player on the team. He was the same age as Dakota, although he'd repeated an earlier year, since he wasn't the brightest star in the sky. Nevertheless, what he lacked in brains he picked up in good looks.

The night was off to a good start, when he led her by the hand and found a table at the diner that was private. When they walked in together, they had every head turn to look at them. Dakota was sure that the girls were all looking at her, jealous of her hot date, while the boys who stared were looking at her new and sexy grown-up look. It was without a doubt, they looked good together.

Once they ordered, they talked, mostly about football, which was okay to begin with until it became repetitive and boring. Dakota didn't care much for the sport, as her life had always been around horses, cattle and cowboys. The school was divided. She'd hung out with kids from her own world, while he had his own groupies that placed football as the only important thing in their otherwise dull and uninteresting lives in town.

Daniel had crossed that division when he'd asked her out last year, only to be turned down when Dakota thought that her father wouldn't agree and she used her school exams as an excuse to save the embarrassment. It wasn't until an afternoon shift at the diner, when the coach and every player turned up to celebrate a winning game, that she'd caught his eye once again.

Why not, she thought. She was eighteen now and had finished school, and needed to start going out socially with friends that she liked being around. She hadn't spent enough time with him yet to know if he was good for her or not, but so far it was going well and she liked being around him.

During dinner they talked and laughed about their favorite and least favorite teachers at school, their best and worst subjects, and the kids they hung around with. It didn't take long before their discussion turned back to football. Dakota was out of her league as far as that was concerned, and Daniel could sense that he was talking a little too much about it.

"I'm sorry. You don't know much about football, do you?" he asked.

"Not much," she admitted. "It's just that I've grown up around horses and cows."

"Well it's not your fault," he said, deflating her smile. "You should come and watch me play sometime."

"That would be great," she lied. Dakota couldn't think of anything worse than going to watch a football game. "And you should come to our ranch and watch me cut."

The look on his face said it all.

"Cut cows," she said for clarification. It didn't help. "You know... cutting..."

His face was blank as if there was not another thought in his empty head other than football.

"Anyway," he said, shaking it off. "What are you doing about college?" he asked.

Finally, a question about her was thrown her way. Maybe he was beginning to find her interesting. "Well, I still haven't decided yet what I want to do. That's why I'm taking some time out to think about it, and I'm working on the ranch with my dad while I decide."

"I'm hoping to get a football scholarship. I don't really care where, as long as I get to play."

That was enough for Dakota to know that they were definitely not compatible. Her date was so self absorbed that by the end of dinner, she asked if he could take her home.

She kept it friendly on the way back to the ranch, since she didn't want to be rude and have her night totally ruined. Would she ever go out with him again? Probably not. They were from two different worlds and she could never fall for someone who loved himself more than anything else in this world other than a little funnily-shaped brown ball.

It was dark on the road and the drive was still friendly enough. Daniel was doing most of the talking, as he seemed not to be short of something to say. As long as it was about football, Dakota thought that he would talk in his sleep. She looked over at him while he drove. Disappointment had set in, as she found him to be quite a catch to the eye without the personality to back it up. Her nine thirty drop off was spelling out failure. Daniel looked at the time also, noticing that it was still early and he didn't need to have her home for another half hour. When he came to a crossroad, he pulled the car over to where there was a cleared grassed area that was sheltered by a few trees. It was dark and deserted, and they were still at least eight miles from the ranch.

"What're you doing? Is something wrong?" she asked, looking at the dashboard for any kind of indication there was a problem with his car.

He turned the engine off and sat in the dark. "Nah, there's nothing wrong with the car. I just thought you might wanna get together before you go home."

When he stretched his arm across the top of the seat, he touched her hair. She was drawn into his charm and she leaned across to get a little closer. He met her halfway and reached out to kiss her, and she felt attracted to him again now that he had stopped talking. He was a good kisser, and he seemed to know it.

With limited time, there was no holding him back and he went straight for the buttons on her shirt, popping them open and sliding his hand inside. He was touching her and she wanted him to stop, grabbing his hand away. When he put his hand on the inside of her leg, that was enough for her to pull up and back out, deciding that she wasn't going to do that with him.

"What's the matter?" he asked, still keeping his hand on her.

"I've got to get home. It's nearly ten o'clock," she said, as if it was the only reason she wouldn't go the distance with him.

He looked at the time. "It's alright. It doesn't take that long," he insisted, as if there was plenty of time to fulfil all her dreams and still get her home before her unreasonable curfew. He reached down to kiss her again and she pushed him away. "Am I your first?" he asked.

She looked at him with a fury in her eyes. "My first? Are you kidding? You're not my first anything," she said, and she buttoned up her shirt, opened the door and got out. Wanting to get away from him, she started walking.

She heard the car start and it pulled up beside her while she walked. "Come on, Dakota. Get in and I'll take you home," he said. "I'll have you home before your dad comes looking for us and I won't tell anyone at school."

That was the end of her patience. She stopped to look at him through the open window, feeling a flush of anger going straight to her cheeks.

"You won't tell anyone what?" she asked, curious as to what was otherwise going to make good headlines at school on Monday morning.

"I won't tell anyone that you turned me down."

She laughed at him, then followed with a mouthful at full volume of what was really on her mind. "I don't care if you tell everyone at school that I turned you down. In fact, I hope you do tell everyone that you couldn't get lucky with Dakota Jones. That way, everyone will know that you're not the hero you think you are, and that I've got more class than to give myself to someone who thinks they're God's gift to women and football." She strutted off down the road.

The car followed her slowly, making her feel as if she was now being stalked.

"Leave me alone," she said, not looking at him.

"I'm sorry. Look, it's still a long way and I'll give you a ride."

"Thanks, but I'd rather walk than get in with a loser like you."

"Come on, Dakota. Just because you're not a women yet, doesn't mean you have to act like a little girl."

That was the wrong thing to say and she let him know it. "If you don't get out of here now, then I'm calling my dad." She pulled her phone out of her bag and began to look for his number.

"Alright. Suit yourself," he said, and he turned the car around and drove away.

Walking up the road, she looked back to make sure she could see the tail-lights heading towards town. It was eerie all of a sudden and without much of a moon, it was difficult to see. Eight miles. Eight long miles in those boots, and with every step closer to Double J Ranch, her feet were aching.

She walked for half a mile and stopped, feeling the numbness in her toes. Her choice of footwear for the evening would be her biggest regret. It wasn't her date or turning down his advances, it was her decision to wear those heels that made her wish she'd stayed in for the night.

The sound of a car approaching had her on high alert. When it came close, it brightened up the road ahead and slowed down, pulling up alongside her. She looked at it from the corner of her eye.

"You wanna lift?" the drunken man in the backseat called out through the open window.

"No thanks," she replied, and she kept walking.

The car rolled slowly next to her, with the front passenger now encouraging her. "Come on, get in the car. We'll take you anywhere you wanna go."

Dakota could smell a strong scent of whiskey coming from the car and their laughter was drunken and twisted. Their taunting was their entertainment and now Dakota panicked. She should have let Daniel drop her at home or at least at the front gate, although it was too late now.

It was when the car came close and she felt a hand touch her from behind, that Dakota flipped out and poured out a tirade of words. "Leave me alone," she yelled forcefully. "I'm calling the cops."

She pulled out her phone again and it was enough to send them on their way. Their game was over, but not before an empty can was thrown at her and she put her arm up to block it. Sitting on the side of the road in the dark, she was shaking, feeling just how close that was. She could have easily disappeared and found herself in the worst of situations, making her break down and cry. Letting her tears go, she felt it had been the worst night of her life and it wasn't over yet. Somehow, she still had to get home.

Should she call her father? Flicking through the numbers, she hesitated. It might be the last date she would be allowed to go on if her father had to pick her up off the side of the road, and she was devastated that this was happening to her.

When she put the phone to her ear, she waited for it to answer. "Come on, pick up," she said desperately.

It was ringing and ringing and ringing. It nearly rang out when it finally answered.

"Dakota?"

"Jake. I need you," she cried out, thankful he'd picked up the phone. "I'm on the side of the road and I need you. I need you to pick me up and I can't get home and I don't need you to call my dad…" She was becoming hysterical.

"Where are you? I'm on my way."

"Don't hang up. I'm scared and I need you to stay with me on the phone," she pleaded.

Explaining exactly where she was, he instructed her to stay put, not to move, and to hide if she heard another car coming.

He talked to her to keep her calm, and to pass the time. "What are you doing?" she asked, curious with the background noises.

"Dakota. I was in bed. I'm pulling my jeans on," he explained. She could hear him stepping into his boots then rush down the stairs of the house and grabbing the jingling keys.

Emma was locking up the house for the night so he gave his mother a quick don't worry explanation on the run, and ran down the front steps to his father's truck. Dakota could hear it start and it eased her anxiety. He was on his way.

"Keep talking," she said. "I need to hear your voice."

He kept talking about anything that came to mind. "Do you know how boring my night was?" he said. "Well, it was boring until I was an hour into my sleep…"

Six miles from the O'Brien ranch felt like twenty. Every mile closer was a comfort that she couldn't explain. They talked like friends and when she saw the headlights coming, she let him know where she was. Jake hung up the phone and turned the truck around. He pulled up next to her, opened his door and got out. Dakota flung herself into his arms and burst into tears.

Standing on the side of the road in the dark, she finally felt safe, comforted by his presence. With her brother in Australia, there was no one else she would have called to come to her rescue. No one else that she could have trusted to drop everything and rush to help her without asking questions first. Jake would keep her disastrous night a secret, and it showed just how close they were. He was more than happy to have his night disturbed, save the day and cover the truth for her, if it meant holding her in his arms like that.

The drive back to the ranch went too quickly. As they turned down the long driveway, Dakota looked at Jake for an opinion. "How do I look?" she asked, straightening herself up and wiping her eyes to hide her emotional state.

"You look perfect," he answered, speaking the honest truth.

"I hope my mom and dad have gone to bed," she said, ignoring his compliment. She looked at the time. "Oh damn it. It's nearly eleven," she said, now fearful that she had gone past her curfew. "I was supposed to be home an hour ago."

"Don't worry. Your dad won't care if you're with me. I'll come in with you."

With justified reason, Cutter and Raylee had stayed up. They had a long night and were sitting on the swing, watching the time tick by, waiting for Dakota and her date. Cutter's anger turned to surprise when it was Jake who was delivering his daughter home.

"What's going on?" Cutter asked, totally confused when they walked up the front steps and headed towards the swing.

"Hey, Cutter. Guess who I ran into? I was on my way home and I offered Dakota a lift," Jake said, taking control over the questioning and looking at her. "It's my fault we're late."

Cutter and Raylee were both relieved.

"Where's your date?" Raylee asked.

"Oh, he was boring me with his football talk, so I ditched him." Dakota was doing her best not to lie, weaving her answers in and around their questions to hide what had been a disappointing night out.

Raylee felt that their tense night at home had been all for nothing. "I told you we had nothing to worry about," she said to Cutter, as if going to bed two hours ago would have been a better option than waiting up unnecessarily.

"Did you have a good night?" Cutter asked.

Dakota looked at Jake. "It got better as the night went on," she said.

Cutter didn't mention the curfew and since his daughter was now home and in safe hands, they said goodnight and went inside the house.

They waited silently on the porch until they heard the footsteps go up the stairs before they spoke. "Thank you. You really saved me tonight and I'll never forget it," Dakota said, meaning every word.

"Of course I wouldn't leave you on the side of the road in the middle of the night. But what were you doing with a jerk like him anyway?" Jake asked.

"I didn't know just how much of a jerk he was until tonight. I'll never make that same mistake again," she said firmly.

"Next time, be careful. I'd like to think I was there for you every time you needed me, but what if I wasn't?"

"I don't know what I would have done if you hadn't picked me up. I owe you."

"Owe me what?" he asked, putting her on the spot.

She threw her arms around him and gave him a squeeze. He hesitated, and slowly put his arms around her, returning the gesture. The feeling of having her body so close to his gave him a warm feeling. Holding her like that was something he'd only ever dreamed of. It was the kiss on the cheek that gave his heart a sudden blast and when he looked for her eyes, they were closed. Her lips touched him again, this time closer to his mouth.

Before he got lost in the moment, he pulled away. "Well, I'd better get going. I don't want Cutter thinking that it's me he's gotta watch out for... Goodnight."

"Goodnight," she replied, although not agreeing with him.

He turned around and headed back to the truck. Jake left the ranch drowned in deep thoughts, as it had turned out to be a not so boring night after all.

The house was deadly quiet when Dakota went to bed that night. She had sore feet and a crushed spirit. She had high hopes of actually finding a boyfriend in her home town that ticked all her requirements. Instead, she had struck Daniel the airhead quarterback off her list and she was back to square one.

At least she had Jake O'Brien as her friend. If nothing else, she had someone she could trust, someone she could rely on and someone she could be herself with. She didn't have to impress him or get to know him. Jake was always there for her and liked her for who she was.

Even though she was exhausted, when she closed her eyes, her mind was wandering.

Chapter Nine

There were no more long sleepless nights for Colton, after his early morning routine and long days had him worn out. His five o'clock start time gave Jesse a little more time at home before he'd come to the barn, as there was no need to have them both there cleaning out stalls and feeding horses at the crack of dawn.

It also gave Aimee a break, and she only dropped down for lunches or if they needed another rider in the corner while using the cows in the pen. Colton liked it that way. He was still reeling at the way Jesse was threatening him, and had every name he could think of still floating around in his head every time his uncle gave him another job to do. He was back to basics. Doing all the boring, mundane and cleaning jobs that a person would start out with when they were new to horses. For him, it was insulting, yet he didn't have a leg to stand on with Jesse bribing him in that way. If he didn't value his own life so much, then he may well have told Jesse to shove it and show the tapes to everyone. But he did value his life and the thought of Avery finding out made him feel sick.

The colt was waiting every morning for his ride. He was beginning to know Colton and was responding to him. Every spare minute on the property, Colton was giving it to that horse and they were forming a connection. The trail rides up in the National Park was adding to his training regime, and Colton needed that time to reflect on his life back at the ranch and to think about the mistakes he had made lately.

If he was ever going to make it as a cowboy, then this was his greatest chance. He would have to give it everything he had in him, so that he could go home a changed man. Not only did he need to make things right between both ranches, he also wanted to show everyone that there was more to Colton Jones in and out of the cutting pen.

The colt could be his ticket. If he could help get him ready in time, then Jesse would ride him at the show and make a good name for him. Colton was sure of it.

When he rode home and found Jesse in the pen, he took the colt in. They talked for a while, mostly about the other horses and the plan for the day. Then they talked about the colt. Today was the day that sealed the colt's fate and when Jesse put him in front of a cow, he was impressed enough to know that he had improved, just not enough to think it would make a difference.

"Look, Colton. I've got enough on my schedule at the moment and you'll be going home soon anyway. I'm sticking by what I said before. I gave him a chance, but I don't think he'll be ready in time." Jesse tried to break it to Colton gently. "But someone else might have the time and I'm sure he'll make a really good cutting horse one day."

Colton was gutted. He didn't expect it. There was no use in candy wrapping it for him, Jesse was quitting the colt and was sending him home. It didn't make any difference that he'd spent all that time with him in the barn and out riding, that Jesse had seen an improvement, or that he thought the colt had future potential. It just wasn't on his agenda to take the colt any further.

"Let me train him out," Colton said, pushing himself into the picture.

"You... train him out?" Jesse almost smiled when he said it. "I thought you were busting your ass to go home? I didn't think you had that kind of commitment in you."

"I wanna do it," he said, sure of himself.

"Do you know what it takes? And then what?"

"I don't know. Then I'll ride him at the show... In the Non Pro."

Now Jesse thought that was laughable. Not because Colton couldn't do it, but because it was still two months away and that meant another two months in Australia before he was going home.

"I don't think I can put up with you for that long," Jesse taunted.

"Please, Uncle Jesse. I need this. I need to show everyone that I can do it. That I've got what it takes without my dad getting all the credit."

That made Jesse think. "So you believe that people will give your father the credit for any horse that you do well on?"

"Yes sir. That's why I never took it on any further. Every time I got a decent score, it was because my dad had trained me the best horses. It was never because I could do it. You don't know what that's like."

"Is that why you tried rodeo?"

"If I could ride a bull, then no one could say that it was my dad who got me to the full eight seconds."

The picture was unfolding and everything was beginning to make sense. "Why didn't you say this when you arrived?" Jesse asked. "You could have told me how it was back home and I could have helped you."

Colton never thought about telling Jesse how things got so bad. As far as he was concerned, his father had sent him to Australia to get him out of Johnny's reach. The reasons behind his rebellious behavior didn't matter, but now, he wanted to set the record straight. He had done everything he could to get away from cutting and follow another path and admittedly, he had got himself lost and found trouble along the way.

They walked back to the barn and took their saddles off. "You wanna drink?" Jesse asked when they were done.

Colton thought this was a test and Jesse may have been setting him up. He took a seat on a bale of hay and rested. Since it was quite warm and the need for something to wet his thirst was appealing, he agreed. "That would be great."

Jesse came in with two bottles of water and Colton was relieved. He sat down opposite him and they talked.

"I'll tell you what," Jesse began. "I'm gonna quit him. I've already made up my mind."

After all that time and hard work, after Colton had high hopes for that horse, he suddenly felt deflated and his eyes fell to the floor.

"But," Jesse continued. "when I call the owner to let him know, I'll ask him to give you a shot at it. And if he agrees, then he's yours to train."

Colton immediately looked up and couldn't believe what Jesse was offering. There was nothing more he could have asked for. It was the best thing he'd heard in months. He was ecstatic on the inside and although he tried to hide it, Jesse could see how much it meant to him.

"I'm not promising you anything," Jesse said, to let Colton know that it was not yet a done deal. "But I'll do my best," he added.

"Can you call him now?" Colton requested, wanting immediately to know his fate.

"I make all my calls of an evening. And I'll let you know tomorrow."

"Thank you, Uncle Jesse." It was as much as Colton could say, since there was still a chance that the colt would be going home.

It was the first time since Colton had arrived at the property that Jesse found they had something in common. They were still sitting in the feed room and there was a calm between them.

"Can I ask you something?" Jesse pried.

Colton only looked at him, ready for the question to be fired his way. As long as it didn't have anything to do with what happened with Georgie, then he was okay with it.

"What's gonna happen when you go home?" he asked.

It was a fair question, although Colton needed him to be more specific. "Meaning?"

"Meaning, what's gonna happen with Avery? And your father, and the ranch? What're you gonna do with your life?"

It was something that Colton needed to think about and he could only answer truthfully. "I've not thought about it to be honest."

"Well the way I see it. You've got this one chance to turn everything around. This one shot at training a good horse and a good opportunity to go home with a fresh new start. It will be up to you if you fall back into that same place again. No one wants to see that. I know your parents don't wanna go through all that again."

"Have you been talking to them?" Colton asked, wanting to know how Jesse knew all of this.

"No. I haven't talked to them for a while. I just know it because I know them so well."

"I just don't know if I can ever live up to their expectations," Colton said, feeling their weight. "Especially my dad."

"Colton. Your parents have no higher expectations than any other parent. All they want is for you to grow into a decent man and live a good life. It's up to you if you do that."

"I'm not sure if being Cutter Jones' son has been a benefit or a curse."

"It's a challenge," Jesse said, to make him see that he was looking at it the wrong way. "There'll be times when it's an advantage, and times when you'll wish that no one knew who you were. But you are his son and you can't change that. You just have to work through those challenges and make decisions that are good for you, even if you don't like it."

"You mean like with Georgie?" he asked. Colton knew that bringing up her name was touchy, but they were talking openly and honestly, and for the first time, they were having one of those no hold back conversations.

"Exactly. You might have thought she was good for you, but you got off lucky."

That was the opening of a whole new discussion. They were talking man to man about women, while Jesse was talking as a husband as well as a father of two girls, letting his nephew know all the rights and wrongs of dating, sex and marriage. In that order.

It gave him so much to think about, and when they went into the arena for the afternoon, it was the first time they worked well together. Colton was keen to be involved and could learn a lot from Jesse in the training process. Watching his techniques, his timing, his corrections. Everything he did with the other young horses, Colton took onboard and made mental notes.

When Colton took the colt into the mob, Jesse was impressed with how much he had been watching and studying his methods. It wasn't beyond impossible, but it would be up to the owner if the colt stayed or departed from the property.

The warm shower that night was soothing to Colton's weary body. He looked at the bed when he came out of the bathroom and he stared at it. After talking to Jesse earlier that day about being a decent man, it made him cringe when he thought about Georgie sharing his bed with him. He absolutely didn't love her and there was nothing respectful about what they were doing.

He slid between the sheets and picked up the photo of Avery, wondering if she would still feel the same about him when he got home. He put it down and turned out the light, knowing that Jesse had his future in his hands and he had to wait until the morning to find out.

It made drifting off to sleep a little drawn out. His head was overfilled and bursting with everything that had happened over the last while, but it eventually shut down and he lay still in the quietness of the dark room.

It was barely daybreak when Westyn was dressed and ready to head out the door. Raylee had decided many years ago that he should be the one to move into Marnie's room downstairs, to avoid disturbing the rest of the family with his early morning routine. Every day was the same, and he'd often beat everyone to the upright position by at least a couple of hours. Everyone, except for his father. Getting that five a.m alarm clock out of Cutter's system proved to be difficult, although he was slowly turning up later and later as the weeks went on, since he'd quit training and didn't have the need to begin his day in total darkness.

Raylee would only see Westyn for a quick breakfast before he went off to school, and slightly longer if it was the weekend. Today, he tiptoed up the stairs to wake his sister.

"Get up," he said, giving her a shake.

"Go away, West. It's the middle of the night," she growled, still with her eyes closed.

He leaned down and whispered, "Come for a ride."

"Get lost," she replied, in the kindest of ways.

Westyn didn't get lost or give up. "Jake's coming too," he said.

Her eyes opened and she rolled over to look at him. "So?" she asked, playing it down.

"I know what happened the other night on your date and I know why Jake brought you home."

Westyn had baited her successfully and she sat up on her elbows, giving him her attention. "Did he tell you? You can't say anything to Dad or he'll never let me go out with anyone else again."

"I didn't hear it from Jake. I heard it at school that your date didn't go so well. It wasn't that hard to figure the rest out."

Dakota was annoyed that her date disaster was now public knowledge, even though she was still relieved that she had Jake there to save her butt.

"Come on," he said, encouraging her. "If you don't, then I might have to tell Dad everything." He turned and looked towards the door. "Dad?" he said, in a deep low voice.

"Shhh," she said to shut him up. "You little shit. You're gonna pay for this," she said, laughing at him.

Throwing on a pair of jeans and a shirt, and spending ten more minutes in the bathroom, was not what Westyn had in mind when he said let's go now. He waited downstairs and when Dakota wandered down after him, she was all glammed up and ready to go.

"I said Jake was coming for a ride. I didn't say you had to impress him," Westyn teased.

They walked to the barn and opened it up, taking out their horses and getting them ready. The morning was fresh and Dakota came alive with the coolness around her face. They rode out of the barn and headed for the gate.

"I thought we were going into the pen," Dakota said, and she looked around. "And where's Jake? I thought you said he was coming for a ride."

"He is."

As they rode up the first rolling hill, Cutter stood on the porch and could see his kids reach the peak, before they disappeared over the other side. He had no idea where they were going and wasn't bothered by their sudden need to up and leave. Since they were now gone, it gave Cutter a great idea.

He went into the kitchen and put the kettle on. The house was deadly quiet and they were now alone, just the two of them. Finding a tray buried deep inside the cupboards, he pulled it out and set it nicely for his wife. He made her a simple breakfast and took the tray upstairs to their room, where Raylee was hiding under the covers.

She had already stretched out into the middle of the bed and had made herself very comfortable, knowing that she had it all to herself until her need to rise. Although her senses knew that good morning wake up call, as her nose was alerted to the smell of fresh hot coffee that was now so close, that she could almost taste it. She rolled over and looked at Cutter.

"What're you doing?" she asked.

"Good morning," he said, placing the tray across her lap when she sat up.

"What's this for?" she asked, trying to recall what the date was, thinking she may have missed an important day in their lives.

"Do I have to give you a reason? Can't you just accept that I love you and need to spoil you sometimes?"

"Sometimes? The first time you bring me breakfast in bed in twenty years is not sometimes," she said, and that was enough to make her laugh. She apologized. "Oh. I'm sorry. I didn't mean to laugh, it's really not funny."

"I'm insulted," he said, moving close and he started touching her on the leg. "I'm spoiling you now, aren't I?"

"Of course you are, and I love it."

She took a sip of her coffee and he took it out of her hand, sharing it while she bit into a piece of warm toast. He put it down on the tray and leaned in to kiss her.

"It's not my birthday," she reminded him, in case he had the wrong day.

He kissed her again.

"And it's not our anniversary," she said, thinking hard.

He kept his eyes open and kissed her again, looking closely at her.

"And I know it's not your birthday, because you don't like celebrating birthdays."

He kissed her around the neck and up to her ear, making her shiver.

She gave up. "So what are we celebrating?"

He didn't stop kissing her while he explained. "We are celebrating an empty nest... We are all alone. The kids are out riding and won't be back for hours," he said, to let her know she could relax and be herself without the need to be discreet.

Cutter put the tray on the side table and locked the door. He stripped off his shirt then climbed into bed next to her, picking up those kisses again. It was her name that he had branded on his arm that she loved the most, and he was as much in love with Raylee as he was twenty years ago and nothing had changed. Nothing. Making every time together special.

"I'm hungry," Dakota said, as they were making their way towards the eastern boundary. "I would have had breakfast if I'd known we were going this far."

Westyn didn't speak, having no reason to answer her complaints.

"Why did you have to get me out of bed to do this? Couldn't you do it on your own? Couldn't it wait until after breakfast?" she asked, making it be known that she had food on her mind. "I would have brought something to eat with me... It's alright for you. You probably..."

"Dakota... will you shut up," Westyn said, when they arrived at the gate that joined their ranch to the O'Briens.

She looked up and could see Jake and Avery in the distance, riding towards them and she smiled, giving them a wave. "What're they doing?" she asked.

"We're having breakfast together. What did you think?"

They opened the gate and met up, finding a lush grassy area to lay out their early morning picnic. After tying up the horses, the two girls gave each other a hug, happy to see each other again.

"Look at you. When did you get it off?" Dakota asked Avery, who was now free from the restrictions of the neck brace.

"Yesterday. It's so much better, but I've got to be careful. My dad would kill me if he knew I was out on a horse," Avery explained.

"He doesn't know you're here?"

"No. They left early this morning for the sale yards, so we didn't even need to sneak out."

Jake was a little standoffish, wanting Dakota to make the first move. She did, to break that first awkward moment since he'd rescued her from the side of the road, giving him a hug also and a quick kiss on the cheek before she pulled away. It wasn't clear what sort of hidden message was behind that kiss, but the feeling from one side was more than an attraction.

The four of them sat around and watched the morning sun rise, breaking out onto their picnic breakfast. Avery had packed the food, while Jake had to carry the basket, balancing it on the front of his saddle. It was nice to spend time together as friends, and Dakota was now thankful that her brother had made her come.

It was time well spent and they all lay back, sharing the latest updates, most of which were about Dakota's date and her near miss with a car full of drunken men.

"That must have been scary?" Avery asked.

"Oh, you have no idea. I thought I was dead," she agreed.

"And you won't be doing that again. Will you?" Jake asked.

"Absolutely not. I don't know what I would have done if you hadn't picked me up."

Avery cut in. "Wait a minute... You picked her up?" she asked her brother.

It was clear that Jake had not talked about it with anyone at their home.

"Jake really saved me," Dakota said, and she gave him a smile. Avery caught sight of it and kept silent, wanting to get her best friend alone for more details.

"Now, for the real reason we're here," Westyn interrupted, as if his sister's unfortunate choice in boys was trivial, and their meeting had a purpose other than just being a social event.

"Yes," Jake agreed, although he would have been more than happy to listen to Dakota praise him all over again. "We need to work out this mess between our parents. How are we gonna get them talking again?"

There were many suggestions thrown around between them, none of which were likely to work or look like they hadn't been completely set up.

"Hey, I've already told my dad we're getting married," Dakota said to Jake for a laugh. "That would definitely bring both our families together."

"Yes ma'am, it would. Except that they would know it was a set up for sure," he pointed out, although he liked the sound of it.

"Let's tell Johnny that Colton's home," Westyn said. "This is all his fault anyway. If he thought that Colt was back, then it wouldn't take long for your dad to turn up on our doorstep."

Avery was not very impressed. "I want to see him alive again, not dead," she said, and she flashed Westyn her look of disapproval.

"Surely your dad is slowly getting over it?" Dakota asked.

"I'm not so sure about that," Avery said. "This has really got him fired up. I'm not even allowed to take my phone into my room in case I sneak a message through to him."

"Wow. Your dad's really got it in bad for him," Westyn said, without siding one way or the other. He was sitting on the fence on this one.

With Colton gone for some time now, Dakota thought that things may have settled down at the O'Brien ranch. Although it seemed that Johnny was still reeling over everything that had happened and was still wanting to settle the score. From everything Dakota had heard, she wasn't so sure it was repairable, even with more time. There was not going to be a quick fix and they all came to the same conclusion... There was nothing they could do.

After breakfast, it was time to pack up and go their separate ways.

"Hey. You should come over for a ride," Dakota offered Jake.

"Thanks," he said. "But with my dad away for the day, I've got a list of chores to do that will keep me going 'til dark."

Dakota looked disappointed.

"Maybe some other time," he added, hoping the offer would stand for another day.

"Sure. Anytime. You know where I live."

Although Westyn should have gone straight home to get ready for school, he went and checked the heifers in the far back pasture instead, to save his father the ride later. Just like his father, Westyn was thorough when he made it his business to oversee the cattle and check on their progress. On the way back home, he kept looking at the time.

"Are you going to be late for school?" Dakota asked.

"No ma'am," he said politely. "Not if I race you home," he added, making a contest out of it.

As experienced as Westyn was on a horse, Dakota had been riding the ranch every day with her father and she was fast from her days of barrel racing. They were level most of the way home, taking their sibling rivalry one step further than they should, jumping over fallen limbs and taking the shortcut through the tree studded pasture, without following the trail. Finding the most challenging way home, they were making it fun. Dakota laughed at her brother when she pulled up at the last gate just ahead of him, rubbing it in that she had just beaten him.

The kitchen was in full swing when Dakota and Westyn finished at the barn and made for the house. He took the steps in two leaps and was at the door, barging his way in. He was going to be late. It didn't bother him to see his mom and dad standing by the stove cooking a more filling breakfast, without the need to hide their love from their kids. They were still touchy feely from their eventful morning and were standing there locked together, cooking the bacon and eggs.

"Morning," Westyn said, ignoring them as he raced to his room to get changed.

Dakota followed him in the door. "Oh please. I've told you before. Not in the kitchen," she said, embarrassed by her parents' closeness. "And no breakfast for me. I'm not hungry," she added, and she raced up the stairs.

Cutter looked over Raylee's shoulder at the breakfast sizzling away. "I hope you worked up an appetite?" he said, noticing there was enough to feed a small army.

She laughed at him. "Well I know that you certainly did," she said, teasing him back.

The kids came back into the kitchen when Cutter and Raylee were sitting at the table, ready to start eating. Westyn was ready for school and looked at the time. He'd just missed the bus.

"I'll take you," Dakota offered. "I don't start work for another hour, but I'll drop you off."

While they had a minute, they joined their parents at the table. Dakota thought of ways to encourage her father to call their neighbors, although there was only one way to say it. Straight up front.

"When are you going to call Johnny and Emma?" she asked, not taking her eyes off her father, making him feel under pressure.

Cutter wasn't expecting it. "I don't know. I haven't thought too much about it," he replied, downplaying his need to call his best friend.

"Well what happens if you run into them? Wouldn't it be better if you made things right before that happens?"

Dakota was right. It would be awkward to just run into each other in town or when he was out fixing a fence. They were bound to come across each other sooner or later, somewhere in their travels.

Cutter sat there thinking.

"Dad, we really miss them. All of them," she said, to let her father know that their feud was impacting on everyone in the family.

He didn't say anything.

"You know you could pick up the phone and fix this," she added, giving him those daddy daughter eyes. "It would be so easy."

He took a sip of his hot coffee and eyed Raylee. Reading her mind, he knew that she was thinking the same thing.

"You know you can't not talk forever," Dakota persisted.

He then looked back to her.

"And if you..."

"Alright," Cutter said to silence her. "I'm hearing you. Just give me some time and I'll do it," he agreed.

"Today?"

"Yes, alright. Today. Are you happy?" he asked. "Now don't you two have to get to town?"

Dakota stood up from the table and gave her father a kiss on the cheek, then headed for the door with her brother only two paces behind her.

Raylee sat the table and smiled at him.

"What?" he said, suspicious of that look she was giving him.

"You're such a pushover," Raylee said. "She has got you wrapped around her little finger."

Cutter agreed. "That girl is enough to drive any boy crazy," he stated, and Raylee knew that he was right.

Chapter Ten

With a house full of kids and a barn full of horses to train, the ranch was not very often quiet. It was rare that everyone was away, either in town, at school or upstairs cleaning the house. It left Cutter sitting at the kitchen table on his own, reading the newspaper. His phone sat on the table and he kept looking at it.

He knew that he had to make the first call. He knew that he just had to dial the number and call his best friend. That was the easy part. Nothing had ever come between him and Johnny before this, which made the standoff so much bigger than it should have been. He kept reading.

The phone caught his eye again. It distracted him from the article he was reading as he was unable to concentrate on it. It had been months since the kids had crashed his dad's truck. Surely everything had settled down since then.

Reading through the classifieds, he hoped that the small advertisements were enough to keep him entertained. They weren't. He couldn't stop looking at his phone, now feeling guilty. He picked it up and dialled Johnny's number.

It rang, and it struck him that he hadn't even thought about what he was going to say. He'd never needed to rehearse a conversation with Johnny before. Yet he was now unsure of what to say and how to break the strain between them. It rang. It kept ringing. It rang out.

Johnny didn't answer.

Had his call been ignored? Did Johnny miss it? Was he doing something else that he just couldn't pick it up? Cutter decided that he'd been the bigger man and had made the first call and now it was up to Johnny to return it.

He picked up the paper again and kept reading, only taking a glimpse at his phone in between reading the ads.

It was the longest night of Colton's life. If Jesse had some good news for him when he arrived at the barn that morning, then he would get straight into a training program that was suitable to the colt and where he was already up to.

If the news was all bad and the colt was going home, then Colton felt that he could go home too. There was nothing else to hold him to the vineyard and he'd get straight on a plane and get out of there as soon as he could.

He thought about going to Dallas to live with his other grandparents, Pete and Beth, and pick up a job in the city. While it was the last thing he wanted to do, it would be more in order to stay out of the way of Johnny O'Brien.

After a quick shower, he pulled on his jeans and shirt and went out to the kitchen. It was still dark, and he grabbed a bowl of cereal and threw it down before he headed to the barn. If all his hopes were heading his way, then there would be no time to stop for breakfast later.

The barn was in darkness too but Colton soon brought it to life with a hit of the lights, and he went about his business as if he was actually enjoying it. He made sure that every stall was cleaned out thoroughly before he mixed up the feeds and fed them out. He could hear Jesse's truck, stopping to open the gates on his way in and it gave him a mixed feeling of nerves and hopefulness. His fate was already sealed. He just didn't know which way it was going to go.

When he heard the truck door close, he rushed to meet Jesse outside. The sun was making an appearance and the stillness in the yards was coming alive with the sounds of horses and birds, and the distant sound of traffic was picking up as it went by the front gate.

"Morning," Colton said, very happy to see him.

"How'd you sleep?" Jesse asked, knowing it would have been a long night.

"Not real good to be honest."

"I suppose you're wondering how things went last night?"

"Please tell me you have some good news."

Jesse could see that Colton wanted this badly. There was a desperation in his voice that matched his eagerness in the barn that morning. Nothing would make Colton happier than Jesse telling him exactly what he wanted to hear, although Jesse walked into the barn and Colton followed, hanging onto his next words.

They went into the feed room and sat down.

"Did you call the owner?" Colton asked.

"I did," Jesse replied, making Colton feel that it didn't go the way he wanted.

"And?"

"And I've got some good news and some bad news."

That was enough to leave all his hopes hanging in the balance.

"So give me the good news first," Colton requested.

Jesse didn't hesitate. "Well, we talked about the colt and I told him exactly what I thought of him at this stage of his training. I gave him my honest opinion and I let him know that I wasn't gonna continue on with him."

"And what did he say?"

"He tried to talk me out of it. He wanted me to give him some more time. But I told him that I'd already made up my mind."

"So did you tell him about me?"

"I did. And after a lot of convincing, we agreed that he would stay and that you would finish him off."

"Wooo. Yes... Thank you, Uncle Jesse," Colton said on his feet, pleased with the outcome. He couldn't hold back just how happy he was and he couldn't keep still while he was pacing around the feed room, thinking and planning out the colt's next move.

"But," Jesse said. "Now for the bad news."

That brought Colton back down to reality and he settled on a bale of hay to listen to the rest of their arrangement. "That doesn't sound good," Colton said reluctantly, unsure of what was coming next.

"The only way I could get him to agree, was if I watched over your training," he said, to let his nephew know that he didn't have unlimited freedom to do whatever he wanted with the horse.

"I can handle that," Colton agreed.

"And..." There was more. "You cut the training fees in half. He'll only pay you half of what I was charging him."

"Wait... I'm getting paid?" he asked, surprised by this announcement. Colton had never thought about getting paid to train a horse. He would never have asked for payment and as far as he was concerned, he would have done it for free.

"Only half," Jesse confirmed. "But he will pay for your entry fees at the show if you have him ready in time, and you'll be riding with the pros."

If that was the bad news, then Colton was well on his way to accepting the deal. He couldn't have been more pleased with the arrangement and it was enough to let Jesse know that he appreciated what he'd done for him.

The rest of the morning was spent in the arena. Colton took the colt in while Jesse rode the others, both taking turns on the mechanical cow. When he listened to Jesse talk, he could tell that his experience was worth listening to. Giving him some sound advice, Jesse made sure that he would stand by his word and watch over Colton's training.

Their time together in the pen was a time for learning and a time for looking forward. The past was in the past and Jesse no longer held it against his nephew for messing up with Georgie. What had come to light over the last while, was that Colton was still a kid, a kid who was growing up fast and finding his way, making stupid mistakes on his journey to becoming a man. It was nothing to hold against him, and he needed all the support and encouragement he could get. Jesse knew that with focus and dedication, Colton could turn out to be a champion cutter. A champion, just like his father.

Every day was a repeat of the day before with all the horses noticeably improving. Colton spent most of the day with the colt, either riding up in the National Park on trails or in the arena on the mechanical cow. When they brought the cattle in, they worked together on their moves. He'd often ride over the property and call into the house for his breakfast and lunch, tying the colt up at the side of the house in the shade before going in for a quick bite to eat. On his way out the door, he'd grab an apple and would share the remains with the colt as a treat, before they'd head back to the barn and get back to work.

With everything the colt was learning, Colton was learning something too. His five o'clock start times were not a struggle anymore, as he was keen to get to the barn and start the day. The sooner he'd have the stalls cleaned out, the sooner he was saddled up and out riding.

There was daily improvement, and every couple of days Colton called his father to ask questions or to get an opinion. Mostly it was to hear his voice. He was really starting to miss his dad and it was starting to sink in just how much he'd let him down.

"I'm sorry," Colton said, after they had discussed the training. "I'm sorry about your truck. I know how much it meant to you."

Cutter swallowed the lump that was building in his throat. "I'm sorry too," he replied. "I shouldn't have fired up at you like that."

"Yes you should have," Colton disagreed. "I needed that. I needed you to be hard on me."

Deep down, Colton knew that his father's reaction to everything that had happened between Nashville and Macca's truck was justified. He had done some stupid things and had caused a lot of problems within the family and beyond.

"Have you talked to Johnny?" Colton asked.

"Not yet," he replied, and Colton could hear it in his father's voice that he didn't want to talk about it anymore.

"You know, I'd love to buy this horse and bring him home," Colton said, being more hopeful than realistic.

They talked some more about the breeding and training, when the show was on and how Jesse was going with the other horses. They were talking like friends. Like a father and son should, and when he hung up the phone, Cutter sat on the swing and looked over to the barn.

"What did he say?" Raylee asked, when she came out of the house and sat next to him.

"He wants to buy that horse he's training," Cutter said, while he sat there thinking.

"I saw that horse when I was in Australia and I know he won't come cheap."

"I'm sure he won't," he agreed. "And that's not where it ends. Then you have to pay to get him home."

"He must be really attached to him?"

"I know the feeling," Cutter admitted. "There are some horses that you train and you never wanna see them go. And then there's others that you have no connection with and you don't care if you never see them again. Every trainer goes through that. It's something that Colt's gonna have to figure out on his own. He can't keep every horse he works with."

When Dakota came out onto the porch, she was a little overdressed for the ranch.

"Where're you going?" Cutter asked.

"I'm going to town to meet up with Jake," she said casually.

"Aren't you supposed to ask us first?"

She looked at them sitting on the swing. "Dad," she said cautiously, with an undermining tone as she walked towards them. "Do you think it would be okay if I go to town with my friend Jake? Who I am not on a date with, and he's only my friend... If we do decide to go out on a date, then you will be the first to know but other than that, we are just going to have lunch. And he won't try to kiss me and I won't try to kiss him, because it's not a date and he's only my friend. Not my boyfriend."

Raylee was silently amused. Dakota was poking fun at her father while making it quite clear that there was nothing going on between them except for a friends' day out and he had nothing to worry about.

"And what time will you be home?" he asked.

"Dad," she said severely, "you're doing it again."

"Alright. Have a good time and be careful," he said, and she gave them both a kiss and headed for her car. "I'm so not good at this," Cutter said to Raylee, and he stood up and leaned on the rail. As he watched Dakota leave, he knew that one day she would be leaving him for good, and watching her drive up the driveway, it was almost enough to bring him undone.

Raylee kissed him on the shoulder and went inside the house, leaving Cutter on the porch alone. He took out his phone again and stared at it. He hadn't heard back from Johnny and he was determined that he wasn't going to call again. He thought of his son. Stuck in Australia against his will and now training a horse. Cutter couldn't have been more pleased for him and while he wished he was there to help, he also knew that it was the last thing Colton needed.

"What do you think about going home to Australia and watching Colt ride at the show?" Cutter asked Raylee when he went inside.

She sounded very interested. "When is it?"

"A few more weeks," he said, without definite dates. "If we go, then we can watch him ride and see what this horse is like that he so desperately wants. We can catch up with the family and then we'll bring him home."

"If he's ready... It sounds to me like it's you who's ready for Colt to come home?"

"Yes ma'am, I am," he agreed. "And I wanna be the one to bring him back."

There was a little more to Dakota's lunch with Jake than she told her parents. It was not a date, just like she had said, but he did ask her to go out with him and help buy his mother's birthday present, which afterwards resulted in them having lunch together and a good time. Just the two of them.

Their friendship was strong. Every time they were together, the night of her disastrous date came up. Dakota thanked Jake again for coming to her rescue the night she was stranded and left walking on the side of the road, and he was never tired of hearing it. If only she thought more of him than just a friend to rely on. He'd never push that onto her, for fear of being rejected by the girl that secretly consumed him.

"My dad is really suspicious of you and me," she said, sitting opposite each other in the bakery in town.

Jake nearly choked on his lunch. "What, why? I've done nothing wrong," he stated.

Dakota laughed at him, as if she backed up that crazy idea also. "I know. I don't know what he's thinking."

In Jake's mind, Dakota was reassuring him that there was never going to be any kind of spark between them, so he laughed along with her while he was drowning in his own misery.

"Imagine if my dad was after you, just like your dad is after Colton." Dakota was still giggling, leaving Jake to wonder if there was any kind of suggestion in her remarks. He didn't need to imagine it; it was always on his mind.

"Nah," he said. "Your dad would be happy for us. I know he would."

"I suppose," she agreed. "You are like another son to him."

"And you know how much my mom loves you," he added. "Which is why she will love what you picked out for her birthday." The silver bracelet had stood out in the shop window and when Dakota saw it, she picked it out immediately. She tried it on and Jake admired how good it looked on her wrist. It was then placed in a box, wrapped in pale pink paper and had a sparkly bow on top. Jake would have easily bought it for Dakota, if they were a couple, and for an experimental moment, Dakota secretly pretended that he was buying it for her, just to see how it made her feel.

Both Dakota and Jake were dancing around the idea of being together, with neither of them openly suggesting it. They left the bakery and headed back to her car which was parked next to the old work truck.

Jake leaned on her car door. "Thanks for the help."

"Like you said, I owed you one," she said, then gave him a fun smile. "Well, I'd better get going before my dad sends out a search party."

Jake went to move away from her door when she put her hands on his shoulders and kissed him with a closed mouth. She didn't pull away quickly like a friendly kiss, but when she did, she looked closely into his eyes. He was stunned and didn't speak, wondering how to read that kiss. It was an awkward moment and Dakota covered up her forwardness. "You're the best," she said in a very friendly way. "And thank you for lunch." They said their goodbyes on the side of the road.

As Dakota drove away and headed home, Jake stood at the side of his truck and watched until she went out of sight. He was confused about that kiss. He so desperately wanted to read more into it. It was going to play on his mind for the rest of the day and before he completely forgot about the horse feed, he gave himself a pep-talk. "Will you pull yourself together," he said to himself, then he headed towards the shop to place his order.

The drive home was a good way for Dakota to replay the day. She was more uncertain now than ever before. When she arrived home, she could see her father at the barn and she went into the house, looking for her mom. She found her in the sitting room, reading.

"How was your date?" her mother asked, with a huge hint of prying.

"Very funny," Dakota said. She was up and down. Up that she had a good friend in Jake, and down that she didn't know what to do about it. "It was nice. But I'm so confused," she admitted.

"Sit down," Raylee offered, and Dakota sat at the opposite end of the couch facing each other. "What's up, you don't look happy?"

"Every time I'm with Jake we have a really good time," she said.

"So what's the problem?"

"The problem is that he's my friend. I've grown up with him and he's my best friend's brother."

"So?"

"So, he's nothing like any of the boys that I like. He doesn't rodeo or cut. He's so skinny and he wears his hat all wrong that makes me want to get hold of the front of it and sharpen it up for him."

"And?"

"And they're all the reasons why I shouldn't want him as my boyfriend."

Raylee was starting to see where her daughter was going with her confusing dance around the subject. "So Jake doesn't fit the ideal boyfriend model, and somehow you still find him nice to be around?"

"Is that normal?"

"I don't know," Raylee admitted. She'd always had her sights set on a boy in boots, and when Cutter came along, she fell for him boots and all. "But what I do know, is that Jake doesn't need to rodeo or go cutting to be a cowboy. He already is one. And he might be skinny now, but he won't always be, and his hat? Well, you can easily fix that for him."

"I guess... But here's the problem," Dakota said, ready to lay it all out on the line. "When I kissed him, he didn't kiss me back, and now I don't know if I pushed that onto him and he's freaked out about me being so forward."

"Wait... You kissed him?" Raylee sat up a little straighter.

"Only to say thank you for lunch. And don't tell Dad because he'll only make a huge deal out of it."

Raylee was deep in thought. She was never one to date lots of boys when she was younger, so she was a little inexperienced in that area. "You know what I think?" she said.

Dakota listened, hoping for some good advice.

"Before you get yourself all worked up over it, or throw yourself in deep and end up with a broken heart, take a step back. Don't be so forward and see what happens. If you spend some time apart, then you'll soon know if it's in your head or in your heart."

"I don't know, do you think that will work?"

"Well, if you don't spend so much time together, you'll soon work out if you like him or love him."

The word love gave Dakota a funny feeling in her chest, making her certain that it was her heart that was falling for Jake O'Brien, not her head.

They sat together for a while longer and talked about everything that was on her mind. It was rare to get her mother on her own, and Dakota loved that she could openly ask her anything. Unlike her father, who would overreact, over dramatize and over analyze everything.

"You know, you're right. If Jake is the one for me, then some time apart won't make any difference. Right? It should only make it better."

"Make what better?" Cutter asked. He stood at the door of the sitting room and looked at his wife and daughter sitting together having a meaningful conversation, wondering why he was left out.

Raylee got up and walked over to him. "Time," she said, then walked past him to the kitchen.

Dakota gave him a kiss on the cheek. "It makes everything better," she added, and she followed her mother out of the room, leaving Cutter to stand in the doorway trying to figure out what on earth they were talking about.

With her need to keep busy, Dakota was spending more time with Westyn in the cutting pen. She was offered more work at the diner, though with her brother still away and her father needing the help on the ranch, she only took on one extra shift and gave the other three shifts to Avery. She had been looking for a job and it suited her that they could drive into town together for at least two of those days.

They loved to spend time together, as the last few months had created a distance between them that was not at all intentional. Taking turns to drive to work, they passed the time by talking about Colton.

It seemed that Avery was still hung up on Colton and couldn't wait for him to come home. With her being house bound since the accident, it made for a very lonely time and she spent her days thinking of him and wishing him back. Dakota loved that her brother and best friend were together. She couldn't think of anyone else taking her place.

When it was thrown back at her, she felt a little uncomfortable about Avery's suggestion. "And if you marry my brother, then we'd really be keeping it in the family," she said.

"What makes you think that me and Jake are right for each other?" Dakota asked, looking for a reason why she should, or a reason why she shouldn't.

"Because I know he really thinks a lot of you. He really likes you," Avery said, then changed her mind. "Actually, I think he loves you."

It gave Dakota a hot flush when Avery said it. "He does not. We're just good friends," she defended. "That's all."

"Oh yeah? Well good friends or not, I think he's got it bad for you. You're just blind if you don't see it."

They arrived at work in just enough time to end their conversation, much to the relief of Dakota, who wanted to hear that a boy had fallen head over boots for her. She just wasn't sure if she wanted that boy to be Jake O'Brien. It wasn't that she thought she could do better. In fact, she was certain that he would make a great boyfriend. She just didn't know if he was already too close.

The girls made work fun. Before the start of every shift, they bet each other a coffee after work who could earn the most in tips, making them go about their work with the most positive attitude and going that extra mile to make the customers happy. It made the shift go faster, and they'd often compare halfway through to push them along towards the end of their five hours.

When they finished and cleaned up, they added up their tips and decided on who's turn it was to buy the coffee for the trip home. After Dakota handed over the money at the bakery, they took their cappuccinos and left, making their way to the car.

"Hey, there's your dad," Avery said, when she saw Cutter picking up some fencing supplies, throwing the wire into the back of his truck. They both stood by the car and watched him.

Dakota tapped Avery on the arm and pointed. "And there's your dad," she said, letting her know that Johnny was in town also.

The two girls watched their fathers. They were on opposite sides of the street, and when Johnny climbed into his truck and started it up, Cutter did the same and pulled out into the flow of traffic. There was no acknowledgement from either side and it left the girls' expectations flattened by their fathers ignoring each other.

"Maybe they didn't see each other," Avery said.

"Maybe... But I know that my dad called your dad and he didn't pick up," Dakota added, to let her friend know that her father had at least made the first call.

"And if it's not sorted out soon, then it certainly won't be when Colton comes home."

Avery was spot on with her statement. Every day was another day closer to Colton coming back to Double J Ranch, and yet the tension between the two ranches was still as strong as it had been after Nashville.

Chapter Eleven

The Tremayne vineyard and complex was running along smoothly. As the show was closing in, the training was taking up all of their time. Jesse was pleased with the way Colton was working with the colt, and did very little to interfere with his methods, only when he was asked or thought it was in both their best interests.

Leading up to the show, they went to a couple of pre-works to get the young horses used to the routine of travel and showing. They were regularly shod and the boys made sure they were in good condition, adapting their diet closer to the time.

The rides up in the National Park were a daily routine for the colt, and his strength was noticeable compared to the other young horses. Jesse almost wished now that he had gone on those rides with Colton, as part of his training.

"It's official," Jesse said. "You're entered to ride him at the show. All the paperwork came through today."

Colton was excited as much as he was nervous. They were all sitting around the dinner table, as Evelyn had invited the family over for a barbecue. The two boys were getting along better, since Jesse had a clear understanding of what Colton had been feeling and he wanted to help him. He needed to work with him, to give his nephew the best chance possible at going to the show with a good opportunity to make a name for himself, and to go home to his family a changed man. He just wasn't sure if Colton was ready to go home and face Johnny.

Aimee always brought life to the party, wanting to make an announcement that she thought was going to be pleasing to everyone. "Did Jesse tell you?" she asked Colton.

"Tell me what?" he answered.

She looked to Jesse. "You didn't tell him?"

Jesse tried to shut it down and make it go away. "It's not important. Colton doesn't care," he replied, playing down her good news.

Colton looked curious now, wanting to know what was so important that she just had to tell him. He looked to Aimee, expecting her to spill like she always did.

"Forget about it," Jesse cut in. "Just let it go."

Everyone was now waiting to hear what was at the center of their debate.

Aimee overruled his request to let it slide, taking her role of sharing good news very personally. "Georgie's finally joining the family," she announced with over the top excitement. "They're engaged. He asked her last night and she said yes."

There was no immediate response from anyone. Colton looked to his uncle, wondering why he hadn't said anything earlier. Jesse gave him a look back, as if to say get over it... and he did. "That's great," Colton said, hiding what he was really feeling, and he expressed his support. "I'm really happy for her."

"Anyway, we're here to discuss the show. Not what our family is doing," Jesse said, to get everyone focussed on the Futurity.

They made plans and talked through the details of the week they would be away. Colton had been to every big show with his father, even turning back in the corners when he was old enough, though this show was taking on a whole new aspect for him and he needed to get his head right. Not be distracted by Georgie, Avery, or anyone else for that matter.

Allan conceded that he was too old now to get on a horse and help out, with the added persuasion of Evelyn, who was convinced that his cowboy days were over, dead and buried. "You thought that twenty years ago on our first visit to Texas and look at what happened," he said, to remind his wife that she was wrong back then and maybe she was underestimating him now.

Evelyn laughed. "I must admit, I didn't see you getting back on a horse, let alone riding at the rodeo."

"Wait a minute," Colton interrupted. "You rode at a rodeo?"

Allan was still proud, and remembering that night always made him feel as if he could conquer anything. "Sure did. In the team roping with your dad."

"Well how did you go?" he asked.

"Pretty damn good if you asked me... In more ways than one." Allan looked to Evelyn, knowing that the rodeo was what ultimately got them back together.

"Did you know any of this?" Colton asked his cousins, who had been sitting silently at the table all night.

"We've heard it a hundred times," Paige said, and from the sound of her reaction, they actually had.

"And don't get them started on Dad's ride," Lucy added.

Colton was now wanting to hear more.

"Jesse won the saddle bronc and the team roping with Johnny," Aimee said, still impressed by his achievements that night. "And that was my first rodeo," she added.

"And her last. I never rode in another one again." Jesse let Colton know that he was committed to cutting, even though he would have made a good bronc rider.

Colton still couldn't believe that he'd never heard this story. When Johnny got a mention, it made him uneasy. Just the thought of going home and facing that man was enough to make him want to stay in Australia and hide.

"And let me guess. My dad must have won something there?" Colton asked.

"Of course he did." Allan had always sung the praises of his son-in-law. "Your father is good at everything he does and you wanna know why?"

"Why?"

"Because he loves what he does and he gives it everything he's got." Allan knew that Cutter was a cowboy from the inside out. "And you could be the same. You've got the talent. You've got the backing. You just need the heart."

Colton took it as a compliment as well as encouragement. He needed to hear it and it made him feel as if he was already halfway there. He did have the talent, spending most of his childhood in the cutting pen and riding over the ranch. He undoubtably had the backing, riding the best horses trained by the best trainer. It was now up to Colton if he found the heart.

When Colton went to bed that night, he thought about what his grandfather had said. The words replayed over and over in his head. Cutter Jones was well known in the rodeo arena and a household name in the cutting pen. There was no question about that. His work on the ranch was his life and he gave it everything he had in him, making the ranch work around the family, and the family work around the ranch.

He picked up the photo of Avery and he immediately thought of Georgie. She had taught him so much in their short time together, and while he would never be thankful to her for that, he was at least going home to Avery with a better understanding of women.

He put the photo down on the side table and turned out the light.

"I can't believe we're going," Raylee said, as she was neatly folding and packing her clothes into her bag.

"Do you really need to take so much?" Cutter asked, looking at the size difference between their two bags. "We're only going for a week," he stated, as if she didn't know.

"Do you think it's too much?"

"Yes ma'am. I think you're not gonna wear half of that."

They were upstairs in their room, getting everything organized for their trip. Raylee was more excited about going home this time as Cutter was going with her. Going together, she could have stayed longer, if it wasn't for her leaving their other two children behind.

Without Johnny there to oversee the ranch, there was no choice but for Dakota to stay at home to watch over everything, and for Westyn to help out before and after school each day. All the cattle work was up to date and the horses only needed feeding morning and night. As far as any training, the two kids would fit that into their schedule when time allowed.

It left Dakota having to give up her shifts at the diner for the week with Avery taking on a couple extra and the rest being shared around among the other girls.

"Does Colt know that you're going over?" Dakota asked her parents at dinner.

"No. So don't say a word," Cutter said, in case they happened to talk. "I don't want him to know."

"Well you know what happened the last time you surprised him," Westyn said, to remind his father about Nashville, and it made Dakota want to hide under the table when he mentioned it.

"How did this kid get so smart?" Cutter asked Raylee.

"He gets it from you," she threw back without any thought.

Westyn looked at his parents and disagreed. "Nah. I get my riding from Dad and my good looks from you, Mom," he said, to let her know that she had contributed something special towards him, even though Raylee always thought he looked exactly like his father. "And I'm just naturally smart."

"And what have I given you?" Dakota asked, not wanting to be left out.

Westyn looked at his sister and thought for a moment. "From you, I learnt patience... and a lot of it," he said.

After they teased and laughed at each other, it was time to get down to some serious instructions about the week they would be away.

Cutter gave them both a rundown on the dos and don'ts, and who to call for each situation. They had enough feed, enough money and enough food at the house to last for an entire month. If they were flooded in while their parents were away, they would survive.

"We're leaving early in the morning but before you go to school, I need you to go to the eastern boundary and repair the fence. It was too late on my way back home tonight. And you'll need to take Kotie with you." Cutter explained where he had seen the fence down and with cattle grazing, he wanted it fixed before they made their way through to the O'Brien ranch and started eating up their feed. The last thing they needed, was another reason for Johnny to blow up.

"Wake up," Westyn said, shaking his sister. "I'm not your alarm clock, you know."

She rolled over in bed, adjusting her eyes. "What do you want?"

"It's time to get up. Mom and Dad have left, and I've gotta go out and repair the fence before school," he explained. "Hurry up."

"Do you really need me to come and hold your hand?" Dakota rolled back over and pulled the covers up, disgusted at the untimely suggestion to start work.

Westyn wouldn't give up so easily. He pulled the covers off her and dragged them with him as he ran for the door, flicking the light on when he left. She gave a scream, followed by a tirade of words that was most unpleasant for that time of morning.

She was now up. Up and awake without a choice. Dakota made for the bathroom and changed into her jeans, grumbling under her breath while she washed her face and brushed her teeth. Since it was still early, she pulled her hair back roughly and tied it into a bunch.

"I'm so going to kill you," Dakota said, when she arrived downstairs. She grabbed a bowl down from the cupboard, having no intention of leaving the house just yet.

Westyn looked at her. "What're you doing?"

"I'm having breakfast," she said, as if he should have known. "Now, if I'm holding you up, then you can go to the barn and saddle my horse. But I'm eating now whether you like it or not."

It was a compromise. Westyn left the kitchen and headed to the barn, pulled out their horses and started to get them ready. He was never one to start the day with breakfast, as he always found it was too early. He'd much rather get his chores out of the way, then eat on the run while getting ready for school.

"Have you got everything?" Dakota asked, when she arrived at the barn ten minutes later.

He could only look at her as if to say who made you boss? Of course he had everything. He was on the job and she was just coming along for the ride. Just in case he needed her.

As they rode out the gate, it was becoming light. The sun was slow to rise yet it was starting to warm up. Dakota looked at the time. Their parents would soon be boarding the plane, leaving them behind. She was happy for them both, and even more pleased that her brother would finally be home next week. She had really missed him.

Checking the fence lines all the way to the eastern boundary, Westyn was being thorough in his work, making sure everything was secure. He checked that the cattle were in the right pastures with sufficient water and he did a quick head count. Dakota admired how her brother loved the ranch and did a good job. Her father couldn't have left it in better hands.

"Have you decided what you're doing about college?" Westyn asked.

They were riding side by side like they had done many times before.

"Not yet. I'm still looking at my options."

"You know that no one wants you to leave." Westyn couldn't look at her when he said it and she picked up on his sincerity.

"Are you going to miss me?"

"Me? I meant everyone else. I won't have to saddle your horse for you or listen to all your complaining," he said, playing with her.

"And you won't have anyone to ride with at this ridiculous time of morning."

"Exactly... Now, when are you leaving?" he asked.

They came to the right pasture and followed the fence.

"There," Westyn said, when they rode along the fence line that joined the two ranches, a hundred yards past the gate, just as their father had said.

Riding up towards the broken line, they could see that it had worsened overnight, as the wire was gone completely and the cattle had busted through onto the O'Brien's side. They had to decide whether to repair the fence first or get the cattle onto the right side before the neighbors found out.

"Open the gate and we'll push them through. There's only a dozen." Westyn spoke just like his father, taking control of the situation, leaving Dakota to follow his instructions.

It was easy to move them, with Dakota rounding them up on one side and Westyn coming from behind steadily. When they were all through the gate, they made sure they pushed them deep into the pasture to keep them out of the way while they made the repairs.

They tied their horses up to a nearby tree and made their way through the long grass to the broken line, to assess the damage. It was not as easy as Westyn anticipated, and he decided that he would tighten it up as best as he could, and repair it like new after school when he came back with all the right tools and some new wire.

They worked well together. Dakota was following everything her brother was telling her, getting the job done fast. She had her head down, leaning over to pull the bottom wire tight when a voice came from behind.

"It looks like you've beaten me to it," Jake said, giving them both a fright. He was riding out to repair the fence and found Westyn and Dakota with the job nearly done.

It gave Dakota a funny feeling. She had been avoiding Jake intentionally to see how she felt about him. Seeing him now made her more confused than ever, since she was unsure if she was pleased to see him because he could help repair the fence, or if she had missed their closeness of late.

"Well it's not done yet," she said, although it was more to invite him into the teamwork.

Jake gave her a good morning smile and when she stepped back, he leaned down and helped Westyn pull the wire tight.

"Just grab me my tool bag," Jake instructed Dakota, and she walked back through the long grass to the horses, where he had a small bag attached to his saddle.

When she neared, the horses spooked suddenly and her effort to calm them was not helping. Pulling against the tree, her horse reared up and Dakota put her hand up to steady her. It didn't help.

"Wooo," she said. "What's wrong?"

The horses were all fearful, pulling and kicking. It caught the boys attention and Jake stood up to see what was going on. Dakota had her arms up high to settle the horses when her loud scream alerted the boys that something was wrong. She fell to the ground in the long grass and disappeared.

"Jake," she called out with every bit of unbearable pain she felt.

He ran for her with Westyn following behind. "What is it?" Jake called out, before he reached her.

She couldn't answer, although her screams for help let him know that she was in trouble. When he reached her, she was down on the ground, holding her leg and rolling in agony.

"Dakota, what is it?"

Her cries were uncontrollable and she couldn't answer. Westyn went for the horses to settle them and when he did, they remained on edge.

Jake couldn't get any sense out of Dakota and was panicked, while she still had a firm hold on her leg, lying on her side. "Take that saddle pad off and give it to me," he said to Westyn, and he did, while Jake picked her up off the ground and moved her towards the tree.

He lay her down and knelt in front of her, then pulled her jeans up above her boot.

"What is it?" Westyn asked, looking over Jake's shoulder.

Jake didn't need to guess anymore. "Snake," he said quickly. He turned to look at Westyn, ignoring Dakota's screams. "Get my dad. Tell him to bring the truck."

Without answering, Westyn untied his horse quickly and rode away towards the O'Brien homestead. He was fast and with good reason. He knew the seriousness of that bite and time was not something he could afford to waste.

Jake looked at her lying against the tree. Tears, panic and pain. She had it all going on and he had to think straight. He took off her boots and unbuttoned her jeans then pulled them down to inspect the wound. There were two puncture holes that had gone through her lightweight jeans into her leg, just below her knee, and it was now clear that she had taken the full impact of the bite. He had to ignore what she was going through and remain calm so he could focus on giving her the right treatment.

"You need to sit up" he said, although she barely heard his voice over her cries for help and she ignored his suggestion.

The intensity of the pain was traumatizing her, at the same time as he was trying to help, with her screams only making the situation worse. He had to take control.

"Dakota. Look at me," Jake said, pulling her to an upright position and making her look at him. "You're gonna be alright," he said. "You're tough, Dakota. It will take more than a snake to bring you down."

"Am I going to die?" she asked, and it gave him a gut wrenching feeling.

"No ma'am. I won't let that happen," he assured her. "I've got you."

He sat behind her and comforted her with his arms wrapped tightly around her. She rested her head on his shoulder and began to settle when he talked. He was talking quietly and reassuringly into her ear, keeping her calm. There was nothing more he could do now, except to sit there under the tree in the morning sun and wait.

She began to feel another burst of fear coming on and she started to cry again. Without asking for her permission, Jake put his hand on the inside of her shirt and rested it gently on her heartbeat. He needed her to stay calm and her heart rate needed to slow down.

"Do you remember when we were kids?" he asked.

She thought back to when they were young.

"You were always so accident prone," he said in a quiet tone to make her concentrate and listen hard. "Every time we played together my mom would always say, 'Watch out for Dakota. Make sure you look after her.' And I always did."

Her cries stopped and he looked at her face and wiped the tears away. Her heart was beginning to slow down. He repositioned his hand to add more pressure to her already hot skin.

"Do you remember when I pushed you on the tree swing and you fell off and scraped your knees and broke your arm?" he asked. "Your mom said it wasn't my fault but I thought that it was, and I cried all night."

She gave a slight laugh when she thought of it, remembering that day clearly. She put her arms around his knees for support, trying to relax. "I thought you pushed me too high to make me fall off," she said. "I thought you did it on purpose."

"Why would you think that? I'd never do that to you. Not back then and definitely not now."

"What about when we rode your horse bareback and you went too fast and I fell off the back," she said. He'd forgotten about that and it made him laugh too. "You didn't even come back for me."

"That's because it was so funny and I couldn't stop laughing. But I knew that you were okay."

While he kept her talking, it was passing the time and easing the pain in her mind. She lay back in his arms while they reminisced about the past and it kept her heartbeat steady. She stopped talking, then she closed her eyes and tilted her face in towards his neck.

"Dakota," he said severely. "You've gotta stay awake." He touched her face then rubbed the top of her leg to waken her.

"What?" she said, very sleepily.

He couldn't let her drift off, needing her to stay with him. "Do you really think we should move to New Zealand?" he asked.

"I've been wanting to talk to you about that. I think that it might be too far from home," she admitted. "And I really don't want thirteen kids. Maybe two. Three at the most."

"And just so that you know, I'm not really good with goats. But I do know a lot about horses and cattle."

"And I like my bay horse. Not white. But I'll still let you saddle her for me anytime you like."

"I can't promise you the castle, but I know this great little place not far from here. It would be a great place to live and raise our two or three kids with horses and cattle and everything you'll ever want."

"That sounds perfect," she said, and Jake silently agreed.

Jake was not keeping an eye on the time and only that he was enjoying their closeness and fantasy conversation, he didn't notice the sound of his father's truck pulling up at the gate. Johnny and Westyn ran for the tree and crouched down in front of them.

"So, what's going on here?" Johnny asked, keeping calm. Although he knew exactly what the situation was and how desperate it was to get her to the hospital.

"Apparently I'm tough," she said looking at him, and it made Johnny smile.

"You're just like your mom," he said fondly, and he scooped her up in his arms and headed for his truck.

Jake sat in the backseat and Dakota leaned on him, while Westyn untied the horses and rode back to the O'Brien barn. It was a little bumpy on the way back, through the pastures, around the trees, following the trail. Riding over the ranch was always an untimed event, yet today it was straight to the house without closing gates behind them. It wasn't a concern if the cattle wandered and were mixed up, over the need to get Dakota to the hospital as fast as they could.

When Westyn had ridden to the barn earlier to get help, he couldn't find Johnny anywhere. He'd run into the house and when he burst into the kitchen uninvited, he got the immediate attention of both Johnny and Emma with his hysterical words. Johnny had dropped his breakfast and grabbed the keys to his truck, leaving Emma to call for an ambulance. She thought that would speed up the treatment that Dakota needed.

The ambulance was waiting with the doors open and flashing lights when Johnny pulled his truck up next to it. The medical team were there to take over and put Dakota into the back, securing her to the stretcher.

"Can I come with you?" Jake asked the officer.

"Of course," he said, and he went to the front of the ambulance and picked up his radio to let the hospital know they were on their way.

Emma was ready to go and was anxiously waiting on Westyn. "We'll follow you in soon," she told Jake.

It left Johnny and Emma standing outside their house, watching the ambulance drive away. Johnny looked up and saw Westyn coming through the last gate with the horses and he went to the barn to help him unsaddle them. It was another ten minutes before they made their way into town.

Westyn sat in the backseat of Johnny's truck. It was a long drive into town and the silence was adding to the exceptionally long miles. He pulled out his phone and called his father. It rang...

Cutter and Raylee were sitting on the plane, waiting for takeoff. When the call came through, it alerted everyone onboard that he still had his phone turned on. He looked at it.

"It's West," Cutter said to Raylee quietly, while he tried to silence it.

"Excuse me, sir. We're ready for takeoff and all devices need to be switched off immediately," the flight attendant told him politely, and she wouldn't leave until he did.

Cutter looked at it and declined the call. "He probably just wants to give me an update on the fence before he goes to school," Cutter said.

"They know what they're doing. There'll be nothing they can't handle," Raylee said for reassurance. She was confident of her kids' ability. "That's because you've taught them well."

Chapter Twelve

When Jake was asked to stay outside in the waiting room at the hospital, he was beside himself. There was nothing he could do for Dakota now, while she was taken into a room where the doctor was expecting her. He paced around the room, took a seat, checked the time and stood up again, just to give himself something to do. He was a wreck, hoping that Dakota was going to be alright and knowing that she wasn't out of danger yet.

Every tick of the clock was slow. His heart was running faster than the time and his head was filled with concern. How could this happen, he asked himself a thousand times more than was necessary.

When the front doors of the hospital opened, Westyn came in followed by Johnny and Emma.

"Where is she?" Westyn asked.

"The doctor is seeing her now," Jake answered, and he could see the panic written all over her brother's face.

"This is all my fault. I shouldn't have asked her to come with me." Westyn was feeling guilty, that he should have left his sister tucked up in bed where she wanted to stay.

"It's not your fault. It's nobody's fault," Johnny said, and he put his hand on Westyn's shoulder, like a father.

They all took a seat in the waiting room. The four of them sat in silence, trying to be patient, though anxious to hear from anyone with an update.

"Where's your mom and dad?" Emma thought to ask, after looking at her family there instead of Dakota's.

"They're on a plane to Australia," Westyn said, as if it was no big deal.

Johnny leaned forward on his chair. "What for?" he asked, to confirm what he was already thinking.

"They're bringing Colton home," Westyn said, looking at Johnny for his initial reaction.

Johnny remained calm and didn't reply.

"My dad tried to call you to discuss it, but you didn't answer him or call him back, so he figured that you didn't care anymore. But he wants Colton back home. He's been away long enough."

Westyn's explanation was more or less telling Johnny that it was time to suck it up and get over it.

When Emma looked to Johnny with a look of confusion, it was clear that he hadn't told her about the missed phone call. It wasn't the right time to discuss it, and neither of them brought it up again in front of the two boys. There were more important things to worry about.

Jake looked at the doors of the treatment room. They remained closed. Not knowing anything was making him think the worst. What could be taking so long? If anything happened to her, then he wasn't sure how he would cope. He'd taken care of her most of their childhood and today her life was on the line, hanging in the balance. Dakota would be very sick if she made it through, and just the thought of her being unwell made him want to trade places with her.

When the door flew open and a nurse came out, it brought Jake to his feet, although the nurse went in another direction and didn't look at them at all. He sat back down.

He thought back to the last words he'd said before they wheeled her into the room. "I'll saddle your horse for you every time, as long as you want me to." Did he really say that? Couldn't he have just told her that he loved her? No. Instead, he wouldn't let her know exactly how he felt and now he was regretting it.

Everyone kept looking at the time. It was dragging on. Just a quick update, that's all they wanted. Just to know if she was alright.

The nurse went back into the room for the third time without looking at anyone and she closed the door behind her, again.

It was another hour or so before the doctor came out. They all stood up at the same time and swarmed around him for some news. "She'll be okay," the doctor announced. "She's very lucky. It looks like you boys saved her life."

Emma looked at her son. He didn't accept the compliment from the doctor although he did ask to see her. "Can we go in now?"

"Very quickly," he said. "And only two at a time."

Without asking who was going in first, the two boys made for the door, leaving Johnny and Emma to wait their turn.

"You didn't tell me that Cutter called you," Emma said when they were left alone. The tone in her voice was not happy.

"Because I didn't speak to him, so there was nothing to tell," he defended.

"You should have told me that he called, and you should have called him back."

"I wasn't ready."

"Well I am. I can't keep doing this. It's months ago now and it's time to put everything behind us and move on," she said. "Especially if Colton's coming home."

Johnny looked at her with a stern face. "That's all the more reason not to call," he said abruptly, letting her know that he was far from ready.

In the room, Dakota was laid out on the bed wearing a hospital gown. She was connected to a drip and her leg was bandaged. The boys sat on opposite sides of the bed and Jake picked up her hand and held it. She was resting and was unaware of her company.

"You saved her," Westyn stated, impressed with Jake's quick response to the situation.

"And you helped me," Jake added, to let Westyn know that he couldn't have done it on his own. He needed Westyn to ride for help and they were both responsible for getting Dakota the treatment she required.

She was heavily medicated for the pain and didn't wake up to see them. Half an hour passed and they were asked to leave, much to their protests.

"You can come back later today when she wakes up." The nurse was firm with them and any argument would see them on the losing side.

Both the boys left the room reluctantly.

"I'll help you repair the fence and then we'll come back in this afternoon," Jake said. He was looking for something to do to fill in the long day ahead, and since Westyn had missed school, they would make the fence a priority.

The time spent driving back to the ranch was filled in by the two boys retelling the morning events, how they'd all come to be together repairing the fence, and how the horses had been spooked by something in the long grass. Jake explained how he'd kept Dakota upright and calm, to stop the venom travelling through her body. He admitted to everyone just how scared he was, even though he wouldn't show it to Dakota. She needed him to be strong... and he was.

Sneaking into Sydney unannounced made Raylee feel as if they were on a romantic getaway. A well deserved break. A second honeymoon. If they weren't going to a cutting event, then it could have easily passed as a holiday.

The show had already started and the first go-round was over and done by the time they were driving into the vineyard. They couldn't wait to turn up on the doorstep and give Allan and Evelyn a nice surprise.

Except that the surprise was on them, when they arrived at the house and no one was home.

"Where do you think they are?" Cutter asked.

"I don't know," Raylee said, while she was looking through the windows. "Everything is locked up. Maybe they've gone to the show too."

"Maybe. But how do we get in?" he asked.

Raylee knew where the spare key was hidden and she knew the updated security code from her previous visit.

Entering the house gave Cutter a walk down memory lane. He remembered the first time Raylee invited him inside, instructing him to leave his boots at the door as if he was some rough and ready cowboy who needed house training. The couch was still the same and he commented on it, recalling all their talks over a late night coffee when they had the house all to themselves for an entire month. Cutter felt very much at home when he was at the vineyard and since no one was around, he went straight for the guest bedroom door. Raylee was on his heels when he burst into the room.

"What're you doing?" she asked curiously.

"Do you remember when you showed me to my room?" he asked, looking around. It hadn't changed a great deal and he wandered around looking at everything.

"And you said you'd be happy to sleep in the barn," she reminded him.

"Yes ma'am," he agreed. "But it was a good thing that I didn't." He touched the bed end. "And this is where it all started," he said, giving her those come on baby eyes.

Raylee laughed. "And this is where my father was going to kill you."

"Lucky for me he wasn't a very good shot." Cutter pulled her towards the bed and sat on it, making her sit over him. He reached up to kiss her. "I wanted you so bad that day... And every day since."

She took his hat off and threw it to the end of the bed and ran her hands through his hair, kissing him back. They had never stayed in the guest room since that day and she was up for it if he was.

"We might get caught again," she said, forewarning him that her father might not be too far away.

"I don't care. As long as there's no guns involved," he said, then he pulled her over onto the mountains of pillows while she giggled playfully.

There were no surprise interruptions from Allan Tremayne this time and Cutter lay under the covers looking up to the ceiling. He had his arm around Raylee and she rested her head on his chest, snuggled up close. The patch on the ceiling caught his eye and it made him smile. There was nothing on his mind right then and he closed his eyes, feeling very relaxed and ready for either a big sleep or a big feed. He was still undecided which.

"I wonder how the kids are going," Raylee said. She was obviously thinking of home.

Cutter was less than worried. "I should give them a call later. But I don't want them to think that I don't trust them to look after everything."

"Then maybe leave it a couple of days," she suggested, and Cutter agreed. He was confident that the ranch would run as normal and if there was any kind of problem, then the kids would call them.

Raylee threw the covers back and sat up.

"Where're you going?" he asked.

"I don't know. But we can't stay in here for the rest of the day," she said.

Cutter disagreed. He wrestled her back to the pillow and pinned her down. "Say's who?"

Colton took the colt into the wash bay. He didn't have anyone to take care of his horse like the other trainers had and he was more than happy to do it for himself anyway. The water was lukewarm and the colt stood still, enjoying his reward.

For such a big lineup of professional trainers and well bred horses, Colton was pleased with the colt's first performance and the way he showed him. He was in the big league now, having to compete with the best of riders and horses, including Jesse, who had a good run on both his fillies.

When the colt was back in his stall, Colton wandered up to the stands where he found his grandmother and cousins watching the other riders. They were impressed with his ride and had his score in the safe zone for the first go-round. If he could raise another decent score, then it would almost guarantee him a place in the final. A lesser result might see him out.

It was Lucy who shifted his focus. "Those girls over there can't stop looking at you," she said, giving her cousin a jab in the ribs.

He looked. "Who, those girls?" he asked.

"They keep looking over here and I don't think they're looking at me," she said to make fun of him.

Colton looked over at them again. They were young. Possibly still at school. The last thing he needed right now was girl trouble. He'd had enough to last him a lifetime. He looked back to Lucy. "Maybe they like your hat," he said to make her laugh.

"Or maybe they like the way you ride."

"Or maybe they're jealous of you sitting with me."

"Or maybe they like the funny way you talk."

He caught another sneaky look. There were three girls all trying to catch a glimpse of him, although he had already decided that he was done with women. He was still in love with Avery and wouldn't look sideways at anyone else now. To send them the right message, he put his arm around Lucy and pulled her close.

"What're you doing?" Lucy asked, almost freaking out.

"You're saving me from having to break hearts."

It was her burst of laughter that was insulting, yet it seemed to work, as the three girls all looked away.

"You see. Now all you have to do is act like my girlfriend for the rest of the week and they'll leave me alone," he said.

She jabbed him some more. "I can't tell you how sick that makes me feel," she said. "So it's probably going to cost you."

"Cost me what?"

"Well, there's a nice pair of boots I saw in the shops today," she said, thinking she was pushing her luck.

"You got it, kiddo," he agreed. "As long as you keep me out of trouble for the rest of the show, then you can consider them yours."

Lucy was more than happy to play along, if it meant scoring a new pair of boots for putting her acting skills to good use, and because it was for her cousin, it was no trouble at all.

The knock on the door was only to announce that Jake was coming into the room. He was at the hospital to pick Dakota up and take her home, as her brother was too young to drive. Westyn stayed back at the ranch, going into the cutting pen to keep his horse sharp before going for a ride to check on everything while he waited for them to arrive home.

"They tell me you're ready to go," Jake said, happy to see her.

She was sitting on the side of the bed, waiting, and she brightened up immediately. "I can't wait to get out of here," she said. "I've been ready for hours."

"Well I don't know what the hurry is. By the looks of you, you won't be doing anything for a long time," he noted. Her leg was still bandaged and she looked washed out. She just wanted to get back to her own house and back to her own bed. She just wanted to be at home.

A nurse came in with her clearance papers and medication, and helped her into the wheelchair. Jake pushed her up the corridor and out the front doors. When he opened the truck door, he leaned down to her.

"Put your arms around my neck," he instructed, and he picked her up and sat her in the front seat.

The drive home was steady. Jake took his time since there was no need to rush. There would be no welcome home party waiting for them. They talked about the snake and Dakota let him know just how painful it was. He didn't need to hear it from her. He was there. Her screams and cries of distress had been enough to let him know how much it hurt.

When they arrived at the ranch, Jake parked his truck as close as he could to the front steps. He helped her out with his arm around her waist while she had a firm hold around his shoulder. They hobbled up the steps and went inside. Westyn had done a good job of cleaning up. He knew that his sister would be in no fit state to take care of him, and that he needed to rise to the challenge to help take care of her.

It was a little slower going up the stairs to her room, and once she was settled on the bed, Jake ran around and got her comfortable. Placing pillows behind her back, pulling the curtain across to stop the glare of the sun and putting all her comforts within arm's reach.

When he was done, she asked him to sit with her. "Thank you," she said, looking at him.

He felt closer to her than ever before. "Well with your parents away, Westyn wasn't about to drive into town to pick you up," he said.

"I mean about taking care of me... West might be fast on a horse, but he couldn't have looked after me the way you did. I'm really thankful that you stayed with me."

All Jake wanted to do was lean over and kiss her. It was on his mind, thinking of how close he was to losing her, how he should have told her how he felt, and how close he wanted to be to her right now. He'd never been in her bedroom before, and here they were, sitting on her bed with no one home. It seemed like the perfect timing.

"Dakota?" he said hesitantly.

"Yes?" she answered, expecting he would tell her what she wanted to hear.

"I think your brother is home," he said, and he looked at her bedroom door.

Westyn was taking the stairs two at a time and on a count to six, he was standing in her doorway. "Hope I didn't interrupt anything," he said, actually wondering if he had.

"Come in," Jake invited, and he stood up quickly. "I've gotta get home and now that you're back..."

"You're leaving?" Dakota asked. The look on her face said disappointment, and both the boys could see it.

Westyn agreed and came to his sister's defense. "Yeah, please don't leave me alone with her. I've got homework to do and a ranch to look after and I can't deal with all her whinging and whining while I'm trying to work. And I've got to get back to school tomorrow. And the horses need..."

"Alright," Jake said, to pull him up. "You can stop with your excuses. I've gotta go home and pick up a few things but I'll come over later."

With Cutter and Raylee away for the week, it was now up to the three of them to take care of each other as well as the ranch.

"I'll be back in a while," Jake promised, and he stood in the doorway and looked at Dakota lying on her pillows.

"Don't be long," Westyn pleaded. "I've still got horses to feed and a sister that desperately needs you."

She leaned over to punch her brother on the arm but he was too quick. He jumped to his feet, out of the way.

When Jake went home to take a shower and get some clothes together, Emma asked what he was doing. "Why do you need to be there? Can't Westyn take care of her?" she asked.

"Mom. He's got school and he needs to take care of the ranch and the horses," he explained, sharing Westyn's excuses with his mother.

"So why do you need to sleep there? Can't you just go over in the morning?"

He looked at her and began to see her concern. "Mom, you've got nothing to worry about," he assured her. "We're just good friends and she needs me. Dad's alright here and I'm only a phone call away. Besides, even if I liked Dakota that way, she doesn't look at me the same."

"Just don't forget what happened with your sister," Emma said, to remind him of how bad things are between both ranches over the entanglement of Colton and Avery's reckless antics.

"You don't need to remind me. It's in our face every day and just so that you know, no one's happy about it so it had better get sorted out soon. Especially with Colton coming home."

Emma was with him on that. "I'm hearing you," she said. "I don't know what's going to happen when your father sees him again."

After Jake packed a small bag, he gave his mother a kiss on the cheek and headed back to the truck.

"Wait," she called out, and she ran after him with her hands full.

"What's this?" Jake asked.

"It's something for dinner." Emma handed him the dish. "You make sure you look after her," she added, before he climbed into the truck and started it up.

Emma stood on the porch and watched him drive away. She cared deeply for their friends and neighbors, especially their children, and it had broken her heart that things had turned out the way they had.

When Jake pulled up at the house, Westyn was stepping into his boots. Jake walked up the steps with his bag over his shoulder and dinner ready to serve.

"Where're you going?" he asked.

"She's driving me crazy. She's got me doing the most ridiculous things for her, so I'm going to the barn," Westyn explained, then he left Jake standing on the porch.

He went in and put the dish down on the kitchen counter before going upstairs. Dakota was in her room resting. She looked peaceful and he couldn't see her driving anyone crazy. Well, not in that way.

Wondering where to put his bag, he went across the hall to Colton's room. It had been cleaned and was fresh, ready for his return. Jake threw his bag up onto the bed and unpacked a few things, making himself at home. Here he was, across the hall from Dakota in the opposite room, and he felt so close. He sat on the side of the bed and stretched out, lying back, looking at the ceiling.

He wondered if Colton had snuck Avery into this room or into this bed. He immediately put this to the back of his mind when he decided that he really didn't want to know the answer to that question. Especially if he had.

It was still early and it was going to be a long night.

"Jake?" Dakota called out. "Are you up here?"

He sat up on his elbows. "Yes ma'am," he called back, staring at the door.

"Can you come here?" she asked.

Dakota needed him. Just not in the way he wanted. He wandered across the hall and stood in her doorway.

"I thought I could hear you. What're you doing?" she asked.

"I was just putting my bag in Colton's room. I hope that's okay?" he said. She didn't answer and he walked into the room and sat on the bed. "Do you want something to eat? My mom sent over something for dinner," he offered.

"That would be great. Then we'll watch a movie."

"You want me to watch a movie with you?"

"Well not unless you've got a better idea on how to spend the rest of the night."

Of course he had a better idea. He just wasn't going to suggest it.

"Dinner and a movie? That sounds like a date," he said lightly. "And you don't even have to get dressed up."

"And you don't have to pick me up or drop me home." Dakota was more than happy to reel him in.

"And you don't have a curfew."

"And my dad won't be there to ask me a million questions after you leave." She laughed at the thought of her father when she said it.

"Seriously... What does he ask you?" Jake was now all of a sudden wanting to know more after she had opened up a conversation that would have been better left alone.

"Well, he asks me if I had a good night."

"And, what do you tell him?"

"I tell him yes. And then he asks me where we went."

"And, what do you say?"

"I tell him where we had dinner. And then he asks me if..." She stopped before she took it too far.

"What? What does he ask you?"

"He asks me if I was kissed."

"And what do you say?"

"I tell him the truth... That you like to kiss me on the cheek like a good friend," she said. "And that you are very respectful when we are together."

Jake would love nothing more than to be disrespectful and kiss her on the mouth. If he had the courage, then he'd have done it right then and there. Except with Dakota lying on the bed in her shorts with her bare legs stretched out in front of him, he wasn't so sure where it would stop. For his own sake and without putting their friendship at risk, he knew it was better not to and he resisted the temptation.

"And that's why he trusts me to take you out," Jake said, to finish their friendly game. "I'll get the dinner. You choose the movie." He stood up and left the room, before she really did drive him crazy... again.

Dakota watched him leave. She was disappointed that he wouldn't take their game just that one step further, leaving her to wonder if he would ever like her more than just a friend.

He needed the time away from her, just to get his head straightened out and he went down to the kitchen. Finding everything he needed, he only had to reheat the dish and it was ready. He left a note for Westyn on the kitchen counter to say his dinner was in the microwave. When he returned to her room, Dakota was already sitting up, waiting. He placed the tray on her lap and she handed him the movie to put on. She used the remote control to turn everything on and he put the disc in the player to start it.

She moved over on the bed to let him sit next to her and shared the tray while they ate dinner together. It was nice. Friendly and nice, and when they finished eating, Jake put the tray on the floor near the door. He relaxed back on the bed and she rested her head on his shoulder.

While the movie was not the best he had ever seen, he was having a good time just being together, and even though they were not speaking, their closeness was growing. It passed the time and as they headed into the night, the movie came to an end.

"I'm going downstairs to clean up," he said. "You look really tired. You should probably get some sleep now."

"I'm okay," she said, although by the time the word tired had registered in her head, she began to yawn.

"You really do need to sleep," he insisted. "The doctor said it will take you a while to fully recover."

"But I'm so bored," she said, then yawned again.

"It sounds to me like you need all the rest you can get if you're planning on watching movies all week. Avery will be here tomorrow to see you, and she'll help you into the shower."

Dakota hadn't even thought about needing help to get showered and dressed, but Jake had it all under control. She could never ask her brother and Jake was definitely off limits as far as that was concerned. When he unexpectedly leaned down towards her, it was only to turn off the side lamp and the room fell dark.

"Goodnight, Dakota," he whispered.

"Goodnight," she whispered back.

Chapter Thirteen

Riding in circles with the other riders was getting Colton in the mood. He needed a good result if he wanted to make the final and this was his last chance. Unlike everything else he'd done recently, he couldn't afford to screw this up.

He didn't want anything as badly as what he wanted out of this ride. Just to qualify for the final would be an achievement in its own right and would prove to himself and everyone else that he could do it. His good night's sleep and the early morning freshness kept him alert during the build up. The pressure was mounting and instead of coming down with a bad case of nerves, he was finding things to think about that would fire him up. He was determined to give this ride everything…

The vineyard was looking hazy during the morning, as the sun was trying to break through the mist that seemed to settle around the house and the surrounding vines. When Cutter stood at the window and took his last gulp of warm coffee, he was in deep thought. They had been at the house for a couple of days now and decided to wait and see if their son qualified before they drove to see him.

Cutter didn't want to add unnecessary pressure onto Colton by turning up to watch him ride and announce that he was going home. Colton needed to be focused on his ride and his parents thought it was best if they stayed away. For now.

"I've got it," Raylee called out, still looking at the computer screen. She had found a laptop in the office and set it up on the kitchen table, finding the show on a live streaming site. It was coming in clear.

"How close is he?" he asked.

"It looks like he's up in two more."

Cutter began to pace around the room. "Come on, Colt," he said to himself. He was anxious, although not as much as what Colton was…

When he finished doing laps, Colton pulled the horse over to where Aimee was waiting with his chaps, ready to put on. He had gone from feeling confident and ready to ride, to instantly feeling sick, with a gut full of fear. His full of confidence, pumped up, self-belief, turned upside down and he was now feeling doubtful and ready to puke.

"Whatever happens out there, Jesse and I are very proud of you," she said, adding to his already over the top nerves.

"Thanks, Aimee." It was all Colton could say, since he was dry in the mouth and she handed him a bottle of water.

"Just go out there and have a good time. This is only the beginning. You've got a long career ahead of you if you want it." Aimee was doing her best to keep him calm and fully focused, letting him know that he'd already done an impressive job on the colt and he had nothing left to prove.

Although in Colton's mind, he had everything to prove and he wanted a good result.

He got back in the saddle and began to ride around, making the colt respond. As the cowboy left the pen, another team took his place, leaving Colton in the prep lane behind the judges stand to get himself together…

"One more to go," Raylee said, making Cutter's stomach turn over too. He'd never been this nervous before, not even on his own ride and he couldn't keep still.

They watched the rider in the pen, pulling out a cow and lowering his hand. He was in control and both the horse and cowboy were having a good ride. They knew their son was riding with the big guns now, taking on professional riders who had been cutting for years. The scores were high and so were the stakes, as the cut-off for the final was creeping up with each rider.

"No," Raylee said severely, halfway through the cowboy's ride, and she immediately got Cutter's attention.

"What is it?" he asked, and he stopped pacing to look over her shoulder at the screen.

"The battery is going flat."

"Where's the lead? Find the lead and plug it in," he said, to hurry her along.

Cutter sat down in her seat and watched the screen. The battery symbol had gone into the red and was flashing at them. "Quick, Raylee. Hurry up," he added.

She ran into the office, looking everywhere and couldn't find it. She pulled out drawers and rummaged through them. There was no lead. Opening up every cupboard, there was no sign of it.

"I can't find it," she said in a panic.

"It must be there somewhere," he said, as if that was enough to make it magically appear.

She kept looking, with no luck.

"He's coming on," Cutter called out, and Raylee ran out of the office and back into the kitchen just as Colton rode past the time line. She squeezed Cutter on the shoulders. Not as a comfort, but for her own feeling of tense anticipation for her son.

Colton looked good and the announcer gave him a very simple introduction. Nothing was mentioned of his family background and the horse's breeding was kept to a minimum. That would only help Colton, that he didn't have that extra pressure put on him. Or perhaps the announcer hadn't put it all together yet and didn't know exactly who he was.

"Look. There's Jesse," Raylee said with excitement, when the camera zoomed in and they saw Colton ride past him in the corner.

"He's a nice looking horse," Cutter commented, when Colton took a deep cut into the mob and pushed them forward. The colt had a presence about him that was clearly seen, even on the small screen. "I can see why he likes him," he agreed. "And there's Aimee." They could see Aimee in the opposite corner, keeping the herd together. "Makes me wanna be there now."

"He's better without us there to distract him," Raylee said, trying to be positive. Although with the battery power running low, she now wished she was at the show to see him ride in person.

When Colton was left with one cow, he put his hand down and braced himself. The cow was steady, making short tight turns in the middle of the pen with the colt sinking low and blocking its escape. Raylee squeezed Cutter's shoulders a little too hard and it made him flinch, and he knew that she was hanging on for Colton and the colt. He too was gripping his fist tight, wanting to see no mistakes and some thrilling moves.

The cow was now desperate to get around this dynamic pair and picked up the speed to try and slip past. Colton had the colt do everything right. Not only was he successful in blocking its attempts, but he was looking good and was in control.

"He's having a good ride," Cutter said. "Ooh, that was close," he added, when the cow darted quickly and Cutter saw some daylight between them. Colton picked up the pace again and was all over the cow.

"I don't know if I can watch much more," Raylee stated, wanting it to be over.

"Well I don't think this battery is gonna last, so you might get your wish."

"It will. He's halfway there. It's got to last."

Colton picked up the reins and went back to Aimee's corner. She was pointing out another cow for him to bring forward. He'd already had a good first cow and another that he could work with would give him some valuable points on the board.

"It can't be this bad when I'm riding?" Cutter asked.

"Are you kidding? It's always this bad, especially at these shows. Half the time I can't even watch."

Cutter was now understanding how it was to be sitting on the rails watching. If the first half of Colton's run wasn't terrifying enough for his parents, then the next cut into the herd really had them on edge. Colton lowered the reins and was focused on the cow, but not as much as the colt. He turned it on for the crowd and the judges, and wooed them with his impressive reflexes, keeping up to every stop and turn. The way he reeled that cow back to the center was not something that every horse could do, yet he had it in the middle of the pen and hustled it with every bit of eagerness he had in him.

"Is that our son?" Cutter asked. "I can't believe he's getting that horse to do that."

"It's impressive," she agreed. The sounds of the crowd was coming through the speakers and they could tell that they were loving the performance Colton was putting on for them. "This has to be better than the first go-round," she added, confident that he was doing enough.

With twenty five seconds left on the clock, the screen blacked out.

"No," Cutter yelled, and he stood up in complete disbelief. "No, that did not just happen," he added, then he looked at Raylee.

"I can't believe it." She sat there stunned, still frozen to the screen and put her hands to her face.

Cutter paced around the room with his hands behind his head, thinking. "Now what?" he asked. "What do we do now?"

"Damn computer." Raylee was full of frustration. "Trust my dad to have no battery and no lead."

"I wonder what he scored? He was having a great run." Cutter was as fired up over the battery as he was over not knowing the end result.

Raylee sat back down again and laughed. "I can't believe how well he's riding. I think it was a great idea to send him here."

Cutter backed her up. "He really needed this."

All they could do now, was sit back and go over those impressive moves again, and hope that the closing seconds of his ride were just as good as what they had seen. It left them wondering where the judges had him on the leader board.

"Let's call him and find out." Raylee was keen to know if he had done enough to make it through. She was willing to pick up the phone and dial anyone.

"Or maybe we should wait until he calls us first. He won't know anything until everyone's had their ride, and if he's got some good news, then he'll want to let us know."

Raylee packed up the laptop. They had to wait most of the day for the rest of the second go-round, and it was going to be torturous. "Let's go for a ride," she suggested, just to pass the time.

Cutter thought that was a great idea. "Baby, you can always read my mind."

On her way to work for an afternoon shift, Avery called in to see Dakota and helped her into the shower. She had been busy, picking up the extra work at the diner and was still expected to help her father while Jake was taking up residence at the Jones' ranch. She'd hardly had the time to visit and was excited to spend some time with her best friend, even if it was only for half an hour.

"I've been asked out on a date," Avery announced, while she was picking out some clothes for Dakota to wear.

"What? By who?" she asked.

"Not by who, but by how many, I hear you ask," she said playfully, making fun of the situation.

Dakota tried to sound happy for her, even though she wasn't. "You've been asked out more than once?"

"Yes ma'am. Three times in fact, by three different boys," Avery stated. "It seems that working at the diner has everyone noticing that I actually exist. It's always been you they're all chasing, not me. So it's nice to be noticed for a change."

Avery had always felt that she existed in Dakota's shadow. She was much shier at school and the boys always noticed her best friend first.

"What about Colton?" Dakota asked curiously, wanting to know where her brother stood.

"Is he ever coming back?"

"You know my parents are over there now and are planning for him to come home."

"I know. But what if he doesn't love me anymore? What if he doesn't feel the same way about me when he gets back? Or worse still... what if he's found someone else? I haven't talked to him since he left."

"So, have you been out on any dates yet?" Dakota asked, ignoring all of Avery's what if questions.

"No. But I'm keeping my options open. I'll see what happens when Colt gets home first."

From their quick talk, Dakota couldn't tell if Avery still had the hots for her brother or if the time apart had mellowed the feeling. She felt in the middle and couldn't decide whether to be supportive or disapproving, choosing to leave it alone for now.

After Avery had left to go to work, Dakota was lying on her bed all fresh and ready for some action. "I'm bored," she said to Jake, who had gone to the barn when his sister arrived, to give them both some privacy.

"I've heard that so many times already and it's only the third day. By the end of the week, you're gonna be a big pain in my butt," he said, making her smile.

"So you have to think of ways to entertain me then," she said, and she gave him some suggestive eyes that could have easily been read differently, depending on who was receiving them.

He looked at her and didn't reply. It made him think of all the possibilities.

"I've got an idea. Wait here," he said.

Jake ran downstairs. Dakota didn't know where he was going or what he was doing. She sat up on her bed, fixed her hair and put her lip gloss on, just in case it was going to involve something up close and personal. She gave a light spray of her favorite perfume, thinking it may have been the encouragement that Jake needed to make a move.

She could hear him coming back up the stairs and she tried to look relaxed as if she was waiting patiently.

"Where did you go?" she asked.

"I've got a surprise for you." He helped her off the bed to make their way downstairs. Her leg was feeling slightly better, although she wouldn't let him know it. She put her arm around his neck and he held her up, as they hobbled one step at a time. When they got to the bottom, he picked her up.

Dakota laughed. "What're you doing?" she asked, and she locked her hands behind his neck, holding on tight.

"What do you think? I'm entertaining you," he said. "Door please."

She pushed on the door and they went out onto the porch. The fresh air was nice on her face, although she wasn't looking at anything else when he walked down the steps. She was looking at him, still smiling.

"Let's go for a ride," he said, and she looked up to see her horse tied to the rail.

"I can't go for a ride."

"Yes ma'am, you can... and I'm coming with you." Jake had brought her horse out of the barn but left the saddle behind. He helped her throw her good leg over and she grabbed hold of the reins. He threw himself up and over and sat in close behind her. There was nowhere else to put his hands so he rested them on her hips, then kicked the horse along. Her bare feet dangled just in front of his boots.

"We can't go too far in those ridiculously short shorts you're wearing, but let's go up and check the mailbox," he said, only as a suggestion to give them something to do.

As they rode up the driveway, Millie barked and started to follow. They were talking, reminiscing and laughing at how it was better this time that he was sitting on the back and not her.

"I'm not gonna fall off... unless you push me," he said.

"What, so that you break your leg? Then who's going to look after me?"

"You won't need me in a few more days. Your mom and dad will be back and they'll take care of you," he said, to let her know that they only had a short time together before their alone time was seriously interrupted.

"Well, we could always keep riding," she said, when they reached the mailbox at the front gate.

"And how far do you think we'd get?" he asked, looking up and down the road. There were no cars around and it was quiet.

"When Colton gets home, no one will even realize I'm gone."

"I wouldn't bet on that. I'd know if you weren't here," he said, to let her know that she would be missed.

"And that's why you'd be coming with me."

"But I can't miss you if I'm with you."

Jake slid off the back of the horse and walked over to check the mailbox. There were only a couple of letters and he tucked them into the back of his jeans before he tried to get back on. Dakota put her arm down and he grabbed it to pull himself up. This time, he put his arms around her and took the reins. She leaned on him, feeling the sun on her face when she put her head back and closed her eyes.

Her flirting and faint smell of perfume was enough to send him all the right signals, though he wasn't about to ruin what was turning out to be the perfect afternoon. When they arrived back at the house, Millie settled straight back onto the porch, panting heavily, while Dakota wanted to keep riding. There were not too many places they could ride that wouldn't see them out over the ranch or in the cutting pen, so they headed behind the house towards the stream.

It had been maintained well over the years and was always a place the family had shared with the O'Briens, making it a place that they both knew well. Jake tied the horse up to a tree and helped Dakota down. Without her boots, he had to carry her over to the stream and sat her on a rock, letting her dip her feet into the running water, not letting her leg get wet any higher than the bandage, just below her knee. It was cool and soothing.

"What do you think your dad will say when he finds out that Colt's coming home?" she asked.

"He already knows," Jake replied, to let her know that there were no surprises coming his way.

"And what did he say?"

"I don't really know. But I don't suppose he's too happy about it."

"Do you think he's right?" she asked. "It wasn't all Colton's fault. Avery was there too," she pointed out.

"I don't think that was the problem... It was all their sneaking around. Colton should have come to my dad and been up front. Then none of this would have come as a shock to anyone." Jake looked at her sitting on the rock. Her hair was pulled to one side and her face was glowing from the sun's reflection on the water. "But you weren't surprised, were you?"

Dakota couldn't deny it. Avery was her best friend and only for the two of them sharing every last secret, she'd found out sooner than anyone else. "So in other words, you don't believe in sneaking around?"

He laughed, thinking how to respond to her question. "Well that's half the fun, isn't it?" He made her laugh too. "Except that Colton and Avery aren't having much fun now, so I guess it really wasn't worth it. They'd have been better off coming clean with everyone."

She could see his point. The best part about sneaking around is the fun. The not so fun part is getting caught, and that always seems to happen.

When the sun went behind a heavy cloud, the temperature began to drop. Neither of them were wanting their private moment to end, but it was Jake who decided it was time to head back to the house.

"I'd better get you inside, before something bites you on the other leg." He lifted her back onto the horse and he climbed on behind her. They rode back to the house and he helped her inside. Standing in the kitchen together, she leaned close into him and he instantly felt hot, uncertain of what she was going to do. She didn't break eye contact when she reach around and took the mail from the back of his jeans, and she threw the letters onto the counter.

"I had a nice time. Thank you," she said. "I needed that more than you know."

"Yes ma'am, so did I," he agreed, before he left her in the kitchen to take the horse back to the barn. Really, he needed to be back outside in the fresh air again.

It was a long day at the vineyard. Cutter and Raylee had gone for a ride over every part of the property and were now back at the house, waiting patiently for Colton's call. The most crazy thoughts were going through both their minds as to why he hadn't contacted them. Did he screw up the last cow? Had something happened that they'd missed? Did he get a score on the board at all? The more Cutter was pacing around the house, the more anxious he was becoming.

"Why don't you go for a walk?" Raylee suggested to calm him down.

With time to waste, he took a walk back to the complex to check on the horses. He fully expected that his son would be calling soon and he had the phone in his back pocket, ready. The horses were all out in the yards and all the gates were closed. There was no sign of anyone and he sat on the top rail, looking into the arena, remembering when he'd ridden Midnight there so long ago.

They were so young back then, and now it was their children who were growing up and going through those years of discovering who they are, what they want out of their lives, and who they want to share their lives with. As parents, it was something that was out of their control, just like his parents had never forced anything or anyone onto him. They were always supportive in every decision in his life and that was part of the reason why he became so successful.

When the phone rang, he nearly jumped off the rail to pull it out of his pocket. It was the call he was expecting. It was Colton.

"Hey," Cutter said very casually, even though his heart rate was going into overdrive.

"Hey, Dad. Sorry, I know it's late over there and I hope I didn't wake you up, but I couldn't wait to tell you," he said, and Cutter could hear the excitement in his voice.

"Tell me what?"

"Dad, I made it to the final. I had two good rides on the colt and I got him in."

"That's great." Cutter was genuinely surprised, as they still hadn't followed up the results after they lost the battery power to the laptop, only for wanting to hear it from Colton himself. "I'm really pleased for you," he added.

They discussed the colt, the first and second go-rounds and the scores. The cattle were a little tough, although the working side of the ranch had its benefits and clearly gave him an advantage. Colton was on a high and it was nice to hear. While he had no expectations of going out there and winning the final, he was just happy that he had done a good job for the owner and had shown everyone that he could do it.

Jesse was impressed too. He qualified one of his fillies, while the other missed out by quite a few points and Colton was quick to remind him that he'd quit the wrong horse.

"It would be so great if you could come and watch me ride in the final," Colton said, hoping there was a slight chance that it was a possibility.

"It sounds like you don't need me there," Cutter said, navigating his way around the suggestion of it.

"I'll always need you. Anyway, what're you doing?" Colton asked.

Cutter was not one to lie. He didn't do it very well and this time, he didn't have to. "I couldn't sleep, so I'm just out wandering around," he said truthfully.

"Can you let Mom know in the morning?"

There was a difference in the way Colton spoke. There was an honesty in his voice and a need. A need that hadn't been fulfilled yet. A fire. A burning for something more.

They talked more about the colt and Cutter was beginning to see that there was more to him than just a liking.

"If you could just see him, you'd wanna buy him too," Colton said.

"You don't even know if he's for sale," his father pointed out. "Not everything's for sale, Colton. Just remember that."

That was true. But even if he was, Colton was sure that it would be at a price tag that he couldn't afford. When he hung up the phone, Cutter was pleased. He walked back to the house feeling uplifted and he couldn't wait to tell Raylee.

When Jake tucked Dakota into bed, he'd already made her dinner and they had watched two movies together. It was late, and by the end of the second one, she was struggling to stay awake in the closing scenes. He was over it too and now they both needed to sleep. She was still weak and was only slowly getting better each day. Their ride on the horse had washed her out and all that fresh air added to her feeling sleepy and content.

For Jake, there should have been no difficultly falling to sleep at the end of the day, but thoughts of Dakota were driving him crazy, and his body could shut down but his head couldn't.

It was well into the night when Jake rolled over and thought he could hear voices. The house was very still and Dakota's voice started to get louder and more desperate. She was calling out. "No... No... Get away from me."

He sat up on his elbows to listen.

"Help me. Get my horse... Please help."

He couldn't work out what she was talking about and he sat up on the side of the bed, only half awake. Her next scream captured his attention. It filled the house and echoed in his ears, like a piercing of his ear drum and he ran for her room.

"Dakota?" he asked, quite panicked.

She didn't answer.

He stood at the door and looked at her, and she became restless. "It's a snake. Get it away from me," she called out, and her legs began to kick at the sheets.

Jake was quick to reach her, lying on the bed and holding her, trying to calm her down. "I'm here," he said, holding her tight. She was extremely hot and only woke up when she felt his arms and heard his voice. "It's alright. You're only dreaming. I'm here with you."

"Jake. There was a snake and I couldn't get away from it," she said, still breathing heavily while recalling her dream.

"There is no snake. You're in your room and I've got you," he assured her.

She didn't speak anymore. He was snuggled in behind her, holding her close, then she held his hand and placed it on her heartbeat. It was pumping fast and Jake knew that she was a wreck.

He didn't know what else to say, just feeling her skin and rocking her to soothe her mind. It was the most unplanned, unexpected twist in all their close encounters so far, as he lay behind her, thinking that this would be the perfect chance with no parents and a desperate need. Except that right now, she needed him in other ways.

His comfort calmed her down and her heartbeat slowed back to a regular rhythm, then he slid his hand out from her shirt and rested it on the bed in front of her. She pulled it back and held her close. "Don't leave me," she whispered.

He was more than happy to stay for a while, only under the circumstances. "I'm not going anywhere," he said, letting her know that he had no intention of leaving anytime soon. The most outrageous thoughts went through his head for the rest of the night as he drifted in and out of a broken sleep, while Dakota slept soundly with the added warmth from his touch.

When the sun came filtering through the window, Dakota woke up, still feeling Jake close behind her. She vaguely remembered her dream and she knew that he had comforted her. What she didn't realize, until she opened her eyes, was that he stayed for the rest of the night.

She tickled his arm and he woke with a fright. "Oh, damn it," he exclaimed, now aware that it was daylight and that he shouldn't have stayed as long as he had. He sat up to get away from her before she felt his obvious need.

Dakota rolled over and looked at him. He was rubbing his face and sitting on the side of the bed, facing the door. "Good morning," she said.

"Well you're more chirpy than you were last night," he said, not looking at her, trying to relax.

"I had a really bad dream." Dakota was trying to remember it in full, but it was still quite hazy.

"I know," he said, and he stood up and headed out of the room.

"Where're you going?"

To get away from you, was what he was really thinking, so that she didn't know that he was bursting out of his boxer shorts to be with her. "I need to take a shower, then I'll get you some breakfast." His departure from the room was sudden.

Dakota lay back, looking at the ceiling, wondering what the urgency to eat was. She was more than content to wake up together and spend the morning leisurely around her room. She was now awake and decided to get up too. Hobbling around her room, she found some clothes and gathered them up and made her way to the bathroom, ready to take a shower. She didn't need Avery's help today, although it would take her a little extra time. Then again, she had all day to do nothing.

Supporting herself against the wall, she walked as best as she could to the bathroom. She was steady on her feet, just taking her time. When she looked up, Jake was coming out of the bathroom, dressed ready to go. His hair was still wet and his shirt had the water drips coming through as if he was in a hurry. They met at the door.

"Hey, you shouldn't be up walking around without me," he said, and he grabbed her around the waist to take the weight off her leg. The scent of men's body-wash lingered and his aftershave was masculine. His damp hair made him look fresh and she didn't want to let him go.

"Thank you."

He helped her into the bathroom. "Do you need me to do anything for you?" he asked. She looked at him and her face told him the answer. That was a stupid question to ask. There was nothing he could do to help and he started to back out of the room. "Right... So I'll just leave you here and go downstairs and get you some breakfast. I'll be back for you in ten minutes." He closed the door behind him and stood in the hallway, then thumped his head with his hand.

He went down to the kitchen and began making something light to eat. Instead of bringing breakfast back to the bedroom, Jake thought it would be nice to bring Dakota downstairs, since she needed to move about and it would help to break the boredom. He also needed to be away from the privacy of her room.

After they had eaten and Jake did a quick clean up of the dishes, they went out and sat on the porch. Westyn had already gone to school and Dakota hadn't seen him since yesterday morning. Everything looked in order at the barn. The horses had all been fed and had their heads down, picking at the remains.

"Have you thought about what you're doing about college?" Jake asked, curious about her plans.

"I really don't know," she admitted. "Everyone keeps asking me, but sometimes I think that I don't want to go. Sometimes I think that I'd be happy to stay here, around my family."

"But nobody's pressuring you to go?"

"No. It's my decision, totally. My mom and dad didn't go to college, so they have no expectations that I have to. And I don't want to waste my time on a degree that I'll never use."

"So you'll just live on the ranch for the rest of your days then?"

"With my mom and dad? Hell no. One day I'll have my own," she said confidently.

"With two or three kids and some horses and cattle?"

She laughed. "That's the dream."

Jake left her on the swing and leaned against the rail. He was trying not to get roped into that discussion again, as it always left him tied up in knots. Dakota looked at him. For the first time, she saw a man standing there. He was thinking and looking out at the view. She stood up and leaned on the rail next to him.

"Can I ask you something?" she said.

He found her eyes. "Yes ma'am," he replied, not knowing what she had in mind.

"Can I fix your hat for you?"

He wasn't sure what the reason was behind her need to fix his hat, but he tilted his head forward. She took it off and held it up, looking at what it needed to sharpen it into the right shape. Pinching the corners at the front, she held it up again and was satisfied.

"That's better," she said, and he stood up straight while she carefully lined him up and put it back on his head, pulling the front down into position.

"Something tells me you've been dying to do that for quite some time," he said. They were standing so close now and Jake thought this was as good a time as any, although he resisted.

"I have," she openly admitted. "And that's not all I've been dying to do," she added, and she reached up and pulled his face into hers and kissed him on the mouth.

It caught him by surprise. The timing was perfect. She looked beautiful, standing there in her shorts and bare feet, with her long blonde hair still messed up from the night before. He was in heaven. Dakota Jones was kissing him, and all his time spent imagining what that first kiss would be like, was nothing compared to the real thing.

He pulled her in close and she leaned back on the rail while he went from her lips to her neck and back to her lips again. She wasn't driving him crazy anymore. He was crazy. Crazily in love with her and now she was driving him insane.

Picking her up, they went inside the house. The empty house. Westyn was at school. No neighbors were going to stop by for a friendly visit and her parents were on the other side of the world. There was no stopping what could possibly tip him over the edge.

In her room, Jake lay her down on the bed and threw his hat aside. He was quick to lay over her, kissing her, feeling her skin and wanting her. She pulled off his shirt to get closer, kissing him back and wanting him more. He stopped and looked at her. She was breathing heavily. He tried to read her eyes, as there were no words that could say what they both wanted. It seemed that she was wanting him just as much as he had been wanting her all these months. All their silly flirting games on their friendly dates and their closeness in her room, had led them to this intense moment.

There was very little that would come between them now. Dakota ran her hands through his hair then down his back, feeling his skin. She could barely control herself and she went for his jeans, touching him where it felt so damn good. She went to undo them when he pulled away and sat up on the side of the bed. He put his head down in his hands. "I can't do it," he said. "I'm sorry, Dakota, but I just can't."

"What? Why not?" she asked, as if there was a precautionary measure they were missing.

"I can't do this to you. To your family. In this house," he said, and he stood up and walked around the room, thinking.

"What're you talking about? I was about to give myself to you. You were going to be my first," she said. "I want you to be my first."

He looked at her lying back on her elbows. There was nothing more in this world he would rather be doing right now than to be her first love. Their first kiss was not going to stop at a kiss and he knew it. She was willing to go all the way with him. It was everything he wanted. Everything he'd dreamed about.

"Don't you want me?" she asked.

He sat back down on the side of the bed and leaned over her. "Yes ma'am. More than anything, I want you."

"So why did you stop?"

"I stopped because I know how this will end and it's not what I want."

"You're not making any sense."

"Look. This is no different to what Colton and Avery were doing and we all know how that turned out. I want you, Dakota, but I want you the right way. I have a lot of respect for you and your family and I wanna make sure there's no sneaking around." It was the best and worst of timing. "Do you really want me to be your first?" he asked.

She did. "Isn't it obvious?"

"Well I do too. But I also have this need to be your one and only, and rushing into this could be a big mistake. To give us the best chance, we have to do this the right way."

There was some untimely logic in this very heated moment, and it seemed that Dakota was as frustrated as he was. She sat up and pulled him in.

"But you still want to kiss me, don't you?" she asked, and she closed her eyes when he couldn't resist her in that way.

After all this time, it was difficult to pull himself away. "You know, loving you has been torturous," he said.

"Wait... You love me?" she asked.

"Yes ma'am. I've always loved you. There's not a time I can remember not loving you," he admitted. "But now, I'm in love with you."

"Wait... You're in love with me?"

He laughed as to why that would surprise her. "Yes ma'am. More than you'll ever know," he said, and he leaned into her and kissed her again.

Chapter Fourteen

Cutter was undecided. Should they go to the show and watch Colton ride in the final, or should they keep away and let him be fully focused. He had to put his own selfish needs aside and work out what was going to be best for his son.

"We could go and just hide out amongst the crowd. He wouldn't know we were there," Raylee suggested as an option, although he had thought of it a hundred times already.

Cutter pointed out the obvious. "But if anyone finds out, then it could backfire. I don't want that to happen."

"But I really want to watch him ride," Raylee said, not wanting to miss anything. "What happens if he wins and we weren't there to see it?"

"I doubt that's gonna happen. But any kind of good result would be a shame to miss. And I'd love to look at this horse he keeps raving about."

It had been a relaxing time at the vineyard on their own. When they thought about it, they hadn't been on their own for more than a day in the past twenty years and both Cutter and Raylee were certainly making up for lost time. While at first it seemed strange to use her parents' house for a second honeymoon, they were quick to get over that when they realized that Allan and Evelyn were away for the entire week and they settled into the house, making themselves very comfortable.

They still had two more days until the final to make that decision. In the meantime, Cutter and Raylee would go to the complex and take a couple of horses out for a trail ride. They'd have a few runs on the mechanical cow, eaten out at the restaurant and taken a drive around the other vineyards, catching up on some lazy time. It was time out for them both and they needed it.

As they headed into the weekend, a decision had to be made. Cutter sat next to the pool and watched the sun sink low towards the mountains. There were so many reason why they should go and support their son, but when he weighed them up against all the reasons they shouldn't go, he was back to being undecided.

He made use of Evelyn's fancy new sun lounge and closed his eyes. What would Macca do? He'd know exactly what to do and yet he couldn't ask him. That's what he missed the most about his dad. That he wasn't there in his life when he had to make those hard decisions. He now had Raylee to bounce his ideas off, and she was as stuck on this one as he was.

It was the ringtone on his phone that made him jump. He picked it up off the side table and answered it. "Hey," he said.

"Hey, Dad. I just needed to hear your voice again," Colton said.

That pleased Cutter more than anything he'd ever heard his son say. "How's the show going?" he asked.

"It's going okay. But I'm starting to get nervous," Colton admitted. Cutter could tell by the sound of his voice that the pressure was starting to get to him and he knew that feeling well.

"You'll be alright. You've got Jesse and Aimee there and you've got nothing to prove to anyone," he said for reassurance. "You've done this all on your own."

"But it's not the same without you."

"So what difference would it make if I was there or not?"

"Well, I'd have you in my corner for a start. And you'd be picking me up on any little things that you see. Things that I'm doing wrong," he said.

"Jesse can do all that for you," Cutter was quick to add.

"But it's not the same. Jesse has done a good job for me, but it's not like having you here."

That was enough for Cutter to make up his mind. Before he ended the call, they exchanged some competition cutting talk and discussed the colt some more. Cutter wandered back into the house and found Raylee sitting in the office going through some old photo albums, laughing to herself.

"You can pack your bags. We're going to the show," Cutter announced.

Raylee put the album down and was curious. "What changed your mind?"

"Our son."

After Jake had a shower, he found comfort on Dakota's bed, waiting for her, and he was feeling on top of the world. They had progressed from friends to almost lovers, back to somewhere in between, all in the space of a few short days.

She came into the room, still hobbling around but managing a lot better. Before she put the movie on, she lay on the bed too and looked up at him.

"What?" he asked.

She didn't speak, but reached up and kissed him. He closed his eyes and thought he was the luckiest guy in the world. When she sat up and threw her good leg over him, his thoughts changed. I'm the luckiest dead guy in the world if we get caught doing this. She was hard to resist but he let it go on.

When she ran her hands up the inside of his shirt, his heart raced and it gave him a burning feeling deep in his gut. His need for her again was instant. No one would know. One time was not going to hurt. How this was happening was beyond his belief, and when she teased him with a kiss, she placed his hands on her. He was getting carried away, so he grabbed her hands and stopped her, helping her to get off.

"What's wrong?" she asked.

"I told you. I can't do this," he replied. "You are seriously blowing my mind and I'm sure you're doing it on purpose."

"So it's working then?" she asked with a giggle.

"Hell yes. Can't you tell how badly I want you?"

"So, who's going to know?"

"We'll know," Jake said firmly. "And when I can't look your dad in the eye, he'll know too."

She leaned into him and kissed around his cheek, down his neck and back to his mouth while her hands started to wander again, finding the button on his jeans.

"Stop it," he said. "Dakota, it's not funny," he added, when she began to laugh more. He looked at her. "I don't know how to be together with you and not be with you. I think I'll have to go to the other room."

Eventually she stopped playing with him. His threat to leave and go across the hall for the rest of the night was enough for Dakota to quit her games. Although she was seriously wanting him, he was more serious when he threatened to say goodnight.

They watched another movie like two good friends and at the end, he gave her a soft kiss on the lips and went into Colton's room. As he lay in bed, he couldn't help but be overwhelmed with Dakota and her want to be with him. He wasn't sure how this had happened so quickly and he wasn't sure where it was going next. How long would he be able to resist her? There were no other thoughts, other than her, dancing around in his head. Her long blonde hair, her little bare feet and those sweet kisses that made him want to cross every line that was ever put in front of him. They were all swirling around, making him smile. His longer than usual drift off to sleep and his restless night were all because of her.

He didn't hear her hobbling across to his room, or know that she pulled the quilt back, but he did feel her body when she slipped into bed behind him and cuddled up, burying her face into his back.

"Are you alright?" he asked quietly, feeling how hot she was.

"I am now. I was having another dream."

He pulled her arm in close to him and they both drifted back into a healthy deep sleep.

It was still dark and the house was quiet when the door flew open. The light in the hall and the crash of the door hitting the wardrobe was enough to wake them up suddenly.

There was a panic. Mostly from Jake, who had no idea where he was until he heard Westyn's voice. "Dakota," he said severely. "What're you doing in here?"

She rolled over and looked at him while Jake sat up, feeling that the very questionable sight needed a very good explanation. Although no matter what excuse he came up with, Jake knew it would not sound convincing.

"Westyn, what're you doing? Get out," she said abruptly.

"This is so not what it looks like," Jake defended, as these were the only words that came into his head in that split second.

Westyn looked at them together in the bed, wondering what else it could be. "Yeah right. That's what they all say."

"What do you want? It's four o'clock in the morning," Dakota said, after she looked at the bedside clock.

"Actually, it's ten past. And I've got a mare down who's about to have a foal. I thought you might wanna see it," he announced. "But hey... if you're too busy?"

They threw the covers back and scrambled for some clothes. Westyn ran back to the barn while Jake and Dakota were a little slower making their way down. It was dark, though she knew the way even with her eyes closed and she jumped on Jake's back from the bottom of the steps.

There was a dim light on inside the barn and they huddled around the stall, looking in. Westyn was kneeling beside the mare, rubbing her all over.

"How long has she been down?" Jake asked.

"Not too long. It must be close now." Westyn was confident of his hands-on skills during the foaling process. He'd done this quite a few times with his father and he knew the procedure well. Dakota watched him with interest. He was a natural and was doing everything right.

"When is she due?" she asked.

"She's a bit early. But she looked like she was getting close a few days ago," he said, as he had been keeping a close eye on her this past week.

"So how did you know that tonight was the night?" she asked.

Westyn gave her a strange look. "Dakota. I've been sleeping in the barn. Where did you think I've been all this time?" he asked.

She had no idea that her brother wasn't sleeping in the house. She hadn't noticed that he wasn't even there. When she looked over at the bales of hay, she saw that Westyn had his bed laid out and had been camping there each night. It was only because Dakota and Jake had been so involved with each other, that neither of them had noticed. As far as they were concerned, Westyn was up at five and in bed by nine and during the day he was at school.

It didn't take long before the mare was ready. Westyn sat in the straw with her and kept a watchful eye. When the foal's nose was exposed, Dakota was excited to see it. The mare was pushing the foal out slowly, breaking the sack. The markings on its face was exactly like the mare and it blinked at the feel of the fresh air on its face.

It gave Dakota that warm fuzzy feeling to see a new foal come to life in their barn. She put her arm around Jake's waist and gave him a squeeze while he put his arm around her shoulder and squeezed her back.

"It's a filly," Westyn announced, after she was out.

"Dad's going to be happy. I can't believe he missed it," Dakota said, pleased that everything had gone so well.

The next twenty minutes was spent watching the mare take to her foal as they were edging closer to each other. They were lying in the straw, bonding. When the foal stood up, it was a good sign. She was all legs and while her front legs were fully extended, her back legs were wobbly and there was little control. Stumbling up and down, she was shaky.

"Hey, that looks like you on that leg of yours," Jake said to Dakota to tease her.

They waited for the mare to get up and once the foal began to suck, Dakota and Jake left Westyn at the barn and made their way back to the house. He carried her up the steps and in through the door, only because it was quicker.

"You want some breakfast while we're here?" he asked, to avoid going back up to bed and getting himself into a situation that he couldn't get out of.

"That would be great," she said, and she took a seat at the table and put her leg up on a chair in front of her. "Did you know West was sleeping in the barn?"

"No ma'am, I didn't. And come to think of it, I haven't seen him for a couple of days," he admitted. "But I knew he was here when I saw the dirty dishes in the sink and the milk disappear." He came over to her and put one hand on the back of her chair and the other on the table, leaning into her. "Now, what would you like for breakfast?" he asked.

She reached up and touched his face. "Do you really need to ask?"

Driving to the show, Raylee laid her seat back and put her feet up.

"You look comfortable," Cutter said, as they drove up the steep mountain ranges.

"I was just thinking of the kids at home. Wondering what they've been doing all week," she said.

In between the vineyard and the show, Cutter had at times been wondering the same, although without hearing from either of them, he presumed that everything was running smoothly.

Cutter knew the routine. "Well, I'd say West would be riding over the ranch and training the horses, then dragging himself off to school and Kotie... well she'd be bossing him around and telling him what to do and how to do it."

"I wonder if Jake's been around?"

Cutter instantly became suspicious and he couldn't help but ask. "Why would he?"

"I don't know... Maybe because they've been seeing each other a fair bit lately."

"But they're just good friends."

"Except that I'm not so sure it's going to stay that way," Raylee said, only as a suggestion.

Cutter took his eyes off the road briefly to look at her. "Raylee," he said in a very deep and questionable tone. "What aren't you telling me?"

"Nothing. Honestly. It's just that after the couple of times they've been out together, she's not sure if she likes him more than just a friend."

"And you wait until after we've left her alone to tell me this?"

"Well first of all, she's not alone. And secondly, she's not entirely sure he feels the same way and thirdly, we're only away for the week. What could possibly happen in that time?"

Cutter was reluctant to admit it. "On that second point," he said cautiously.

"What about that second point?"

"Well... it's just that Jake does like her more than a friend. He more or less told me," he finally confessed.

Raylee was piecing it all together. "So Jake likes Dakota, and Dakota likes Jake... and we just left them alone for a week to work it out?"

Cutter didn't take his eyes off the road while he was contemplating the situation. "Oh great," he said, once he realized that they'd walked away from the ranch leaving their daughter in a very compromising situation. "Let's just hope they don't work it out before we get home," he said, thinking that they both had ranches to run, which left very little time for socializing. "You think she really likes him?"

"That's what she told me."

"Wait... She told you and not me?"

Raylee laughed. "You're her father. She's not going to tell you everything. Especially when it comes to boys. She thinks you'll only freak out and lock her away in her room if there's a slight chance that she might be in love with him."

"Wait. Stop... She's in love with him?" he questioned, almost freaking out at the thought of it.

"Like I said. She knows you so well." Raylee was less stressed about it, since nothing had happened yet. "I can't believe you didn't tell me," she stated.

"And I can't believe you didn't tell me," he replied. "Well it's a good thing she doesn't know exactly when we're coming home. That will really keep her on her toes," he said. "And with any luck, they haven't seen each other all week."

They drove to the edge of town and Cutter remembered the equine center well. He'd only been there the once, when he was helping the Tremayne team in the rodeo. That was when he threw good sense and his better judgment aside and rode a bull for the first time in years. What was a big mistake, turned out to be the turning point for him and Raylee, and their love affair began after that very night.

"Lucky there's no bulls here this weekend," she said, when they pulled into the car park.

"I don't know. It might be better if there was... I can't tell you how nervous I am right now," he admitted.

Cutter was no stranger to competition. He'd been at the top of his game, out of it altogether, then back on top. He was well known in the industry for his results as well as producing some of the best horses in the country.

Now, he was feeling the pressure for his son.

Walking into the arena brought back memories for them both. Cutter held onto Raylee's hand and they made their way around the top level, catching some of the action in the pen when they stopped to watch a couple of runs.

"I wonder where they are?" Raylee asked, looking around at everyone.

"Stay here and I'll find out," he said, and he found a quiet corner and pulled out his phone, returning a short time later. "Let's go." He was quick to pick up her hand again and headed to the cafeteria, where Jesse and Colton were catching a quick lunch.

"Can I ask you something?" Colton asked Jesse, who was downing a burger.

"Sure. What's up?" Jesse replied, thinking that Colton wanted to go over the game plan for tomorrow's final.

"Well... It's just that I don't know what to do when I get home," he said, sounding a little uncertain.

"About training?"

"No sir. I know all about that and I'm gonna pick it up as soon as I get back. And I couldn't have done this without you." Colton was getting personal with Jesse while he had the chance. "I mean about Johnny... What should I say to him?"

Jesse found Colton's question to be a sign that he was wanting to turn things around. He didn't rush into an answer. He thought about it first, wanting to give Colton the right advice. "Well, why don't you ask your father?" he said.

"I can't. I need to sort out this mess and I have to do it without my dad. To show him that I know that I screwed up and that I'm sorry for it."

"So maybe you should tell him," Jesse said, as if it was that simple.

"I will... When I go home. I know I've got a lot to make up for, to my dad and to Johnny. But I don't know where to start," he said. "Especially with Avery," he added.

"Or... you could just tell him now." Jesse's eyes left Colton and looked past him. It made Colton turn around.

Standing behind him, were his parents.

"Mom. Dad. What're you doing here?" Colton asked, when he stood up. Raylee threw her arms around him and his surprise was real. The last time Colton had seen his father was at the airport, being sent away for an unknown time and he was bitter. Now, Colton was more than happy to see him and he let him know it, giving him a longer than usual firm hug while his eyes turned to water.

Colton turned to Jesse. "Did you know?" he asked.

"Only two minutes ago," he replied, and he stood up also and gave Cutter the bro-hug.

"Where's Aims and the girls?" Cutter asked, wanting to see his sister.

"Where do you think?" Jesse said, leaving Cutter with no real idea. He presumed he was talking about the stables. That's where Raylee would have been. "The shops," Jesse informed them. "I swear that girl doesn't know when to stop."

They all sat around the table and Colton gave them a day by day rundown on the last week. Colton couldn't speak highly enough of the colt and gave his parents an impressive recap of his last ride a few days ago.

"Where's my mom and dad?" Raylee asked, expecting them to be not too far away.

"Don't you know? Aimee always takes Allan shopping," Jesse said, and that didn't surprise anyone.

Colton couldn't wait to take his father to the stables to look at the horse. When he led him out of the stall, he could tell that his father was impressed, even though he didn't openly say it.

"You wanna ride him?" Colton asked, offering his father to take him out into the sand yard.

It was more than tempting, although Cutter turned him down. "Nah," he said. "I trust you. And I don't wanna interfere with your program."

"Dad. You're not just anyone. You're the best trainer in the world and I want you to ride him. I wanna know what you think." Colton didn't let up. He was so pleased to see his father and was desperate for him to ride the colt, that he kept at him until he gave in.

Cutter reluctantly agreed, just to satisfy Colton's need. "Alright. But just a quick ride."

Colton picked up the saddle and threw it on. "Nice saddle," Raylee commented.

"It's my lucky charm," Colton told his mom of her saddle. "So don't think you're getting it back before the end of the show."

Cutter took to the saddle and rode around in one of the open yards. He then rode the horse to the practice pen and waited for a slot. A few whispers around the arena spread fast and before too long, there was a crowd gathered to watch the best trainer ride this unknown horse.

Neither were put to shame, as the horse was responsive to the cow as it zipped up and down the wire, following it attentively. The moves were sharp and the crowd was growing behind him. Everyone was impressed and when the buzzer sounded to end the run, Cutter pulled the colt up and turned around, not knowing he had such a large audience.

He handed the colt back over. "You've done a good job with him," Cutter said, giving his son a compliment.

"What do you think? Can we buy him?" Colton blurted out.

"Wooo, I don't know about that. He might not be for sale and he won't be the last horse you train that you wanna keep."

"But Dad. He's something special. I know it."

"And his owner might think so too."

"So let's ask him?"

There was less of a commitment from Cutter. "See what you think after the final. You don't need to worry about that now. You just need to be focused on your ride."

"And you and Mom will be in my corner, won't you?" he asked.

Cutter looked at Raylee. "Do we have a choice?"

It was something that Cutter and Raylee wanted to do, yet they would never push in and expect it. They were pleased that the team was getting back together. Just like old times.

When Jesse called Aimee to meet him upstairs, she was beside herself, not letting her brother go. It had been a couple of years since they'd seen each other last and she couldn't contain herself. Aimee was just as surprised as Allan and

Evelyn were, especially since they had no idea that someone had been living in their house for the last week.

As they headed into the evening, everyone met for dinner at the restaurant. Raylee looked around the table. She loved that they were all together again and had missed those times. She especially missed Jesse and Aimee, and watching the two girls grow up.

It was getting late when Allan and Evelyn excused themselves to go back to the room, taking the girls with them. It left the two sister-in-laws at the bar and the three boys to sit at the table and talk about cutting. It was going to be a big day of finals and now that Cutter was there, he was feeling it for both of them.

While they talked about the horses, it was Colton who got offtrack and wanted to talk about something else. "Am I going home with you?" he asked his father.

"That's why we're here," Cutter said. "We thought that it was time."

"Have you talked to Johnny?"

"Not yet."

"Dad, it's been three months."

"I know," he agreed. "But the timing hasn't been right."

"I'll fix this. For you and Mom. I have to make this right."

"And what about Avery?" Cutter asked.

Colton looked at Jesse. He knew that he'd screwed that up too. "I guess I'll have to see how she feels when I see her."

Jesse had been listening and couldn't remain silent any longer. "And you know what you have to do?"

"I think so," he said, although Colton wasn't exactly sure which part Jesse was referring to.

"You can only fix this if you own up and face this like a man. No hiding behind your father. You need to go and see Johnny alone," Jesse said, to make him see that if he really wanted to repair the damage, then he was going to have to man up. "And then you need to be honest about everything with Avery," he added.

"But she'll never understand," Colton said, leaving Cutter to wonder what on earth had happened while he was in Australia.

"That will be her choice. She can't make a good decision if she doesn't know all the facts," Jesse said.

"Do I need to know something?" Cutter interrupted.

"Nothing that's gonna change anything," Jesse replied, keeping their secret between the two of them.

At the bar, the girls sat and talked while they ordered coffees for the boys, just to keep them away longer.

"What's wrong?" Raylee asked, looking at Aimee's saddened eyes. She could tell that Aimee was a little flat, especially when she looked over to where her brother was sitting.

"I really miss him," she said.

"Who, Cutter?"

"Yes ma'am. And all of you. I really miss everyone."

"This happens every time we see you. You always get this way and you always say the same thing."

"Not this time... Raylee, I think I'm ready to go home. I just don't know if Jesse is ready yet."

They looked back over to the boys at the table. "Have you asked him?"

"A couple of times. But he always says just one more season... I think he would go too, but he doesn't want to let your dad down. Allan can't deal with the complex on his own and he'd have to find a replacement trainer if Jesse left. And that's not going to be easy."

"But that's not your worry. My dad can deal with anything thrown at him... In fact, he should be thinking of slowing down or retiring. Maybe I'll have a talk to him about it."

"Would you? Because it might be better if it comes from you."

"I'll talk to him before we leave," Raylee agreed, to put Aimee's mind at rest. "Anyway, how's Colt been going? I hope he hasn't given you or Jesse too much grief like he gave his father."

Aimee didn't know anything about Colton and Jesse's run in over Georgie, so she could only answer honestly. "He's been alright. I think it's been good for the both of them. Jesse included."

"What would you like to do today?"

It was the one question that Dakota wanted to hear. She had been restricted to the house and her bedroom long enough, and the few times she went to the barn or rode her horse with Jake, was her only taste of fresh air in almost a week. She was starting to feel better and because Jake was offering, she knew exactly what she wanted to do.

"You can take me out to lunch," she said.

Jake hadn't considered leaving the ranch, and thinking that it sounded like a good idea, he agreed. "Now I won't argue with that," he said. "Where should we go?"

Spending so much time together alone was getting too intense for them both. Without any interruptions, there had been some heated moments in the house, and they were beginning to get too close to the point of no return.

Jake had fallen asleep during one late night movie and woke up the next morning to find them both cuddled up together. Luckily for him, Dakota was under the covers and he was lying on top. They were getting very cosy very quickly, so a public outing would see them both on their best behaviour. They needed that.

They changed and headed out the door. Jake helped her down the front steps and into the old work truck that he had kept close to the house and they drove to town. It was nice to be away from the ranch. While they were enjoying the time behind closed doors, it was becoming more difficult to keep their hands off each other.

They took a seat at the diner. When Avery came out from the kitchen, she was surprised to see them there.

"How's my bestie?" Avery asked, when she sat down next to Dakota.

"I'm good now," Dakota said. "I've been really well looked after," she added, then flashed a quick look at Jake.

Avery noticed. "Have I missed something?" she asked.

"No. Not a thing," Jake said to cover up any suspicion.

"You know," Avery continued, not letting her moment go unheard, "this is exactly how me and Colton started, and look how that turned out... If we could do it all over again, we'd have just come out and told our parents. We should have let everyone know. Then there'd have been no sneaking around and getting caught."

"Well thanks for the advice. But as you can see, we're not sneaking around. We're not doing anything other than I'm looking after her." Jake wouldn't even confide in his sister and even though the girls were best friends, he hoped that Dakota wouldn't either.

When the cook gave Avery a frown, she took their order and delivered it to the kitchen.

"It raises a good point," Dakota said.

"A good point about what?"

"Well, in a way we are sneaking around. It's just that my parents are away and don't know you're taking care of me, and your parents know but don't think there's anything going on," she said.

"So what's wrong with that? We're not sneaking around. We're here in front of everyone."

"Yes we are. But there is something going on and you know it. Or... maybe you don't think we're official yet?" she questioned him.

"Look, I'm just waiting until your dad comes home, then I promise you, I will talk to him."

"Are you scared of my dad?" she asked.

"Yes ma'am," he replied quickly. "Your dad is so intimidating... But I'm not scared of him in the way that you think. If anything, I'm scared he'll send me away."

Dakota reached over the table and held his hand. She loved that he would go about things the right way and a few more days until her father was home was not going to change the way she felt. The only change was that Jake would be leaving the ranch and going home. They had been so close this last week, and soon they would be miles apart again.

"What're you going to say to him?" she asked, curious as to how he would approach it.

He thought about it first. "I'm not sure. Maybe I should ask him if I could take you out on a real date?" he suggested.

"Isn't this a real date?"

"Nah... This is just a practice run."

He always made her laugh and Dakota thought it was nice to not be out on a real date. Every time they talked, it was only reconfirming there was a strong connection between them. They were expanding their already tight friendship, and Dakota was torn between wanting to see her parents come home and knowing that Jake would be leaving when they did.

"Or maybe I'll just cut through all the bullshit and family drama and ask him if I can marry you," he teased.

She giggled some more. "And tell him if he says no, then we're eloping."

They had a nice lunch and when Avery found a quiet moment, she sat down with them again.

"So, have you been out with any of your admirers?" Dakota asked.

"No," she said, almost depressingly. "I thought I'd be able to, but every time I think about Colton, I just can't do it. Do you think he's coming home this week?"

"That's what my parents have gone for."

"I really hope so. I need to see him."

Avery was doubtful that her father would let her anywhere near Colton, let alone pick up where they left off.

"Well, you should point out, that if your father doesn't let you see him, then he's only setting you both up to go behind his back again." It was the wrong advice for Dakota to be giving, yet Avery jumped all over it.

"You're right. He's damned if he does and damned if he doesn't. And I'm going to let him know it."

Avery left them to wind up their lunch date when the cook rang the bell to pull her away from their table. Jake paid for lunch and helped Dakota out of the diner and back into the truck. When he closed her door and ran around the front to climb in, she had already slid over and was quick to land a kiss on him. He accepted her show of love by holding her face.

"What was that for?" he asked.

"That was to say thank you for taking me out... but not on a date," she said, then kissed him again.

When Emma walked out of the bakery, she saw the old work truck parked across the street. She was about to walk over when she saw Jake and Dakota in the front seat, passionately sharing a moment that was unsuitable for their prime parking position and the time of day. It stopped her in her tracks. She didn't know what to do.

They were not taking a breath and Emma pulled her phone out of her bag and dialled Jake's number. Jake didn't stop kissing her, even when he reached for his phone out of his back pocket. He quickly looked at the number and declined the call.

"I love you," Dakota said. It was the first time she had said those words and he loved to hear it.

"You do?"

"Yes. I do."

"Say it again," he requested.

"I love you I love you I love you," she said playfully.

"Then I guess that means we're official now," Jake confirmed. "And I love you too, Dakota Jones."

Chapter Fifteen

When they arrived at the equine center, the rumor mill had gone into overdrive and everyone was on the lookout for the best cutter in the world to make an appearance. It was exactly what Cutter didn't want to happen. He wanted to be there to support Colton, and wasn't interested being in the spotlight.

It didn't make any difference if he was up in the stands ordering a coffee, looking in the shops at all the tack, or down in the stables helping out, all eyes were on him and he could hear the whispers from people as he walked past. He mostly kept his head down to detract from all the attention.

He was approached by a journalist to give an interview on his career and family connections in Australia, and to talk about his son's impressive rides in the two go-rounds, but he politely turned down the request until after the show, just to keep everyone grounded. They were a long way from home and a long way from where they were three months ago, and nothing or no one was going to come between Cutter, Colton and the colt. It was all about this next ride.

Raylee and Aimee took the horses into the loping area to get them ready, leaving the three boys to sit in the stands and watch the other riders and cattle. They had both drawn the second herd and both had one chance to show well.

"After the final, can I meet the owner?" Colton asked Jesse.

"He'd be disappointed if you didn't," Jesse said. "I know he flew in this morning to watch you."

"I just hope I do this horse some justice."

"You've already done that," Jesse said to encourage him. "And I hear that he wants you to take him into his Derby year."

That gave Colton the boost that he needed. Not that he had any intention of staying, but that the owner thought enough of him and his training, to want him to continue for next season.

They were sitting in the first row, watching the cattle huddled together on the back wall. Only a few riders had bad luck or near misses, leaving the score board top heavy with some great trainers already returning some excellent results. A two twenty-four was the score to beat going into the second herd, and while that almost seemed unreachable for Colton with the extra weight of the world he was carrying, it wasn't impossible.

Cutter and Colton sat close together, discussing the cattle and each rider. Cutter was giving him some last minute tips to give him extra confidence before he went down to the horse.

"Whatever happens out there, I want you to know that I'm proud of you," Cutter said.

Colton hadn't heard those words in years, and he knew that his father would never say it unless he meant it. "Thanks, Dad. I just hope I don't let you down."

"You're not gonna let me down," Cutter said. "You could go out there and run a royal wreck and you wouldn't be letting me down. All you have to do is give your best and give it everything you've got. Whatever happens in the pen is just part of your training. Part of your career path. We all have our good days and bad, and you can't win them all."

"But you do," Colton was quick to remind him.

"Not all the time. And don't forget how long I've done this for. I've got a lifetime of experience. You're just at the beginning. So whatever happens out there, take it onboard and learn from it."

Jesse stood up when it was time for them to go. "Thanks for the pep-talk," he said, to let them know that he was there also.

As they were walking towards the loping area, Colton walked between his father and his uncle, feeling as if this was where he belonged. He was in the big time now, and he liked knowing that he had got there on his own. He also felt that he was being followed.

"Please tell me I don't have three little hotties following me," Colton said to Jesse quietly.

Jesse turned around for a quick glance. "Well I don't think they're following your dad," he said.

It raised Cutter's interest. "Who said they're not following me?" he asked, thinking that he wasn't past it just yet.

"Bro. They're like, fourteen," Jesse said. "I don't know about Texas but in Australia, that's highly illegal."

Cutter turned around to sneak a look also. "You're right. They're all yours son," he said, as he grabbed Colton on the shoulder.

"I know how to fix this." Colton pulled his phone out of his pocket and dialled his cousin. "Hey, Lucy. I need you right now," he said, stressing the urgency, then hung up and put his phone back in his pocket.

"What was that all about?" Jesse asked.

"You'll see," he replied, knowing that he had it all under control.

As they kept walking, Lucy came out of nowhere, throwing her arm around her cousin while he put his arm across her shoulder. They kept walking, not missing a beat.

"You mind explaining to me what this is all about?" Jesse said, curious about their sudden closeness.

"Don't talk to me, Dad. This is my first paid acting role and I need to make it look believable," she said to her father.

It seemed to work, as the girls not only stopped following, but they also disappeared.

"You're the best," Colton said to Lucy.

She gave him a kiss on the cheek. "Hey, good luck for the final."

Saying that was enough to raise Colton's nerves all over again and now he had to pull himself together and fast.

"And what about your old man?" Jesse asked, expecting a bit of good luck to be thrown his way also.

"Don't screw this up, Dad," she said, then she wandered back to her seat to sit with Evelyn and her sister.

When the girls pulled the horses over to the side, they met up with Allan, who was waiting for them. Colton and Jesse put their chaps on while standing on the sand, while Cutter went to get on a horse.

Colton stopped him. "Take the colt. Give him a run," he said.

Cutter looked at him. "If you were anyone else at any other show, I would. But you can do this without me. I'll be there for you in your corner," he said, to give his son the support and confidence that he needed. He took to the turn back horse and the team did the same.

To get himself ready, Jesse rode out into the prep lane and gave the filly a tune up. Raylee felt silently anguished for him, as this could well be his very last ride in Australia if Aimee got her way. He just didn't know it. At the sound of the buzzer, the team made their way out to the corners. The announcer gave Jesse a strong introduction, recapping his career highlights and giving the filly's long list of breeding. It had surprised Cutter and Raylee, as they had lost track over the years of just how much Jesse had won and how greatly he was respected as a trainer.

It had been a long time since Cutter had sat in the corner at a show, and it would be something that he would be getting used to a lot more now that he had given up competition. "Might as well get used to this view," he said quietly to himself.

When the bell rang to start the countdown, Jesse rode towards Cutter, who had his eye on the mob. He was well prepared and confident, and the filly was looking good. She had been consistent through her go-rounds and had pulled out some big moves that had pleased the crowd and impressed the judges.

Cutter pointed out a good option for him, and when he pushed the cow forward, Jesse dropped his hand when it was left standing alone in the middle of the pen. The music blasted through the speakers and Jesse was high on anticipation. It was time to cut.

The filly provoked an immediate response and had the cow on the move from the very beginning. Darting from left to right, it was setting the filly up for a faultless run. She had the skills and the training to respond to the cow's quick accelerated sprints across the pen, and blocked every bid to get past.

Colton was watching from the loping area. He was riding around in circles, keeping one eye focused on the colt, and the other on Jesse, who had the crowd behind him as he swooped down low and rocked the arena floor. Nothing was slowing the run down, and when the cow had one last burst, the filly felt a spur in her side and was equally as fast, wearing it down and making it shy away.

Jesse picked up the reins and turned around. If the reaction from the crowd was in line with how the judges saw this run, then he was sure to score well.

He had enough time on the clock to take a breather, and he went to the back wall again and found the cow that Cutter had pointed out. Moving it forward with the mob, Jesse was looking to get it clear and when he did, he loosened the reins and lowered himself into position.

That was enough to get the crowd wooing him again. The filly was on edge and was anxious for the next move, swishing her tail in the sand and laying her ears back. Together they were putting on a good show. The filly was coming on strong. She was aggressive and was driving that cow into a panic, making it determined to return to the mob, although she wouldn't allow it, intercepting every attempt to find a way around.

Cutter couldn't help but be impressed. The way Jesse pushed the filly into the turns and the way she pulled him out of the deep sand, it was clear that he had trained her well. If only Colton could pull off a ride like this.

As the seconds were coming down off the clock, the filly was stealing the spotlight, giving the crowd every reason to make some noise and think that this could be the winning ride. The team were pleased. Aimee knew what winning this event would mean, and if it was to be Jesse's last season, then he would go out with a bang.

When he pulled up the reins and turned around, he had just enough time to pull a cow off the top and drive it out, placing his hand down and finishing with a little boogie in the middle of the pen. The sound of the buzzer had everyone in his corners pleased that it was over, as Jesse couldn't have done any more.

He turned and looked for his team. Aimee was riding over to him, giving him that winning smile. "You did it," she stated.

"Now you don't know that," he replied, although he liked to think that he had.

"Well if you ask me, it looked pretty damn good." Cutter had just joined them in the middle of the arena floor and the three of them walked out together.

The announcer was filling in the time while he waited on the score to come in. "What a great ride from Jesse McCallister," he said enthusiastically. "And if you didn't notice, that was the number one trainer in the world sitting in his corner. Put your hands together for Cutter Jones…"

When Cutter heard his name, he was given an applause from the crowd and he acknowledged them with half a wave then put his head down, wanting to get out of there as soon as he could. He was hoping that he would go unnoticed, at least until after Colton had his ride. Now everyone in the arena knew he was there and the expectations on Colton were going to add more pressure on him.

When the applause died down, the announcer gave a burst over the loud speaker. "A two twenty-six," he called out, putting Jesse on top of the leader board with five riders still to go.

It gave the team a reason to celebrate. It also gave Colton a higher score to chase. He was still riding in the loping area when the team returned and he didn't look at Jesse or speak, remaining fully determined to give his ride everything he had in him. He made his way into the prep lane and Cutter couldn't blame him, leaving him alone to get his head right.

As the team rode back out into the corners, the announcer had finally put the connection together and gave Colton an introduction that drew attention to the already tense moment. Everyone in the stands was watching the arena floor intently, wanting to catch another look at the legendary Cutter Jones. He sat in the corner and looked again at the cattle, ignoring the hype that he was trying to avoid.

He looked up and watched his son prepare himself. Colton was fidgeting with his hat and was delaying the start, when the official gave him the hurry up.

"Come on, Colt... You've got nothing to lose," Cutter said to himself.

When he gave the horse another few short runs, Cutter knew that he was nervous. He stopped and straightened out his shirt and the official gave him no more time.

"Come on, Colton. Do this for you," Cutter said, not taking his eyes off him.

Colton held the reins high and started the walk towards the time line. What was going through his mind was a mystery to everyone, although Cutter could only imagine. He'd been there before and would have been happy to take the ride for him. Except that it didn't matter now if he won or screwed it up, he had made the final and was well on his way to becoming a good trainer. He just needed the experience in competition and no one else could do that for him.

When he met his father in the corner, Cutter kept it professional, pointing to a cow that had not already been cut. Colton looked at it and agreed, then moved it forward in the mob.

He was looking smooth and calm, and when Jesse and Aimee did their job and pressured the cattle back to the herd, he finally had it singled out on its own and he put his hand down, and waited.

It was late when Westyn locked down the barn for the evening. He had been there all day with the horses and now he was there again doing a last minute check and tidy-up before he went to bed. He wanted everything in order before his parents came home, although Dakota was sure he was wanting to spend more time with the new foal.

Every time she looked at her brother, she could see her father. They had the same passion for the horses and the same love for the ranch. Westyn was a cowboy in every sense of the word.

When he came back to the house, he walked to the end of the porch and took a seat under the office window while Dakota and Jake sat on the swing. She had her bandaged leg across his knee and Jake was swirling his fingers on her bare skin to soothe the pain away.

"Have you heard from Mom and Dad?" Westyn asked.

"No. Have you?" she asked in return.

"No. They're either having a really good time or they don't care about what's happening here." Westyn didn't mind though. He had everything under control.

"Or maybe they trust us?"

Westyn looked at them both. "Do you think they would trust you if they knew what was really going on here while they're away?"

"There's nothing going on," she insisted. "Well, not yet anyway."

He stood up. "Just promise me that as soon as they get home, you tell them everything. I don't want them sending you to Australia next." He walked towards the door and turned around before he went in. "Besides, who else is gonna drive me to school when I miss the bus?"

They watched him go inside the house.

"He would really miss you," Jake said, knowing it was Westyn's way of letting her know that he cared.

"Oh really? I don't think so," she said for certain. "But I hope you would."

"I'm not gonna miss you because you're not going to Australia. I would rather break it off and let you stay here, than be together with you from the other side of the world. At least I'd know you were safe and with your family."

"So you don't care if I'm happy or not?"

"Why would you be unhappy?" he asked.

"Because I wouldn't be with you."

He leaned over and kissed her, as he had done every five minutes since their first kiss only a few days ago. The quietness of the front porch was what she craved. Their time alone looking out at the stars, wrapped in a blanket to take the night chill away, and her boyfriend touching her on the leg while kissing her softly. There was nowhere else she wanted to be.

Dakota didn't know how many more days they had before her parents would return. She was torn between wanting them to come home so that their secret relationship would be out in the open and they could start moving forward, and knowing that their alone time would come to a sudden stop. She could only imagine fast forwarding the clock five years from now and could see them sitting on their own porch, looking at the same stars and feeling the same way with all the blessings from both their parents. Wouldn't life just be so perfect.

When Dakota grabbed his hand and made it wander, it was too much for Jake. He tried to get away from her and he stood up. She still had hold of his hand and pulled him back down and he knelt on the floorboards in front of the swing. She sat up, leaning in to kiss him again. The nights were the most dangerous time of day to be kissing each other, as it was the easiest time to get carried away. Every feeling that went through him, was hidden in the dark. The look in her eyes when she stared at him, was hidden in the dark. There was not another thought in both their minds as they wished to be together.

"When it finally happens, you'll know that I couldn't resist you for one more minute," he said, to let her know that he was planning on it.

"And when it does, you'll know that I've been doing my best to wear you down," she said, to let him know that she was planning on it too, sooner rather than later.

The colt was on high anticipation. His ears were twitching and the lightness of his footwork in the sand had him ready to pounce in either direction. When the cow made a run, the colt was almost ahead of it, stopping with a powerful force that had the cow retreat across the pen to get away. It couldn't, as the colt was covering every step at an equal pace. It was fast.

Whatever nerves Colton felt before he put his hand down, had now turned to adrenalin. They were in the middle of the pen, getting low in the sand and battling it out with the cow. The colt was consistent with his extraordinary ability to read the cow's intended moves and every attempt to get past was only provoked by his captivating eyes and his intimidating presence, nose to nose. He had complete dominance over it and had that cow rattled.

Raylee was on edge, hoping that Colton wouldn't pull out any risky moves to impress the judges that could threaten his superb performance. At least he wasn't riding a bull. She could at least watch every part of his ride even though she held her breath and her heart was racing fast, just like Cutter, who was feeling every sprint and every stop as if he was riding the colt himself.

When the cow finally gave in and turned away, Colton pulled up the reins, giving the colt a much needed rest and they headed back to the mob. When he looked to his father, he gave Colton no sign of what he was really thinking, making no big deal out of it and was keeping focussed. After all, Colton was only halfway there.

Another cow like that was what he was looking for when he drove the mob forward. Taking his time, he didn't want to rush this. He was smooth and steady with his reins held high while he gripped the horn on the saddle with the other.

The girls moved in to add weight to the mob, pressuring them to find their way back to the herd. They backed off when Colton was left with four, and they let him peel them away one at a time until he was down to one. His heart gave an explosion when he dropped his hand and the colt sunk in the sand, ready for this make or break showdown.

Crushing the cow's attempt to get past, the colt gunned it and shut down any chance of it finding a gap, keeping it at bay. Every run was electric and every stop was severe. Every turn was powerful and it was during their little cut and kick-ass dance in the middle of the pen, that Colton tuned into the crowd who were raising the roof with their shouts and applause.

When the cow made a desperate run, the colt pulled himself out of the deep sand and undermined it at the turn. It became frantic and charged at the colt, ready to fight its way through, only to be convincingly denied a clear run back to the mob. It was shut out.

Colton and the colt were closing all doors on the cow, leaving it nowhere to go, except back and forth across the middle of the arena floor. When it paused in the sand, the colt's weight was shifting from side to side, anticipating the cow's next move, while Colton was on edge as to which way it was going to run next. A mad dash to the left saw him hotfoot it and block it at the turn, and its return sprint to the right had the sand fly high from his hooves as he was strikingly fast in his reflexes.

It put fear into the cow and with no more heart, it finally gave in and looked away. It was exciting to the crowd who were now on the edge of their seats, wanting the last fifteen seconds to be as equally accurate and entertaining as his first two cows, and he went back to the mob and took a cow from the side.

Raylee kept looking at the clock, wanting it to be over. She wasn't enjoying the thrill ride at all, and was tense for her son. For Raylee, it was worse than watching Cutter and Jesse in the pen and she closed her eyes and looked up momentarily before an "ahh" from the crowd brought her attention back to the pen.

This cow was slick and tricky, and found a lucky break, leaving the colt buried deep. His strength from his daily riding in the National Park saw him dig his way out fast and chase that cow down, matching it in the turn. He lured it to the center of the pen where he struck back in the dying seconds with his nose down, giving the cow a full dose of his aggression while his tail swept the sand arrogantly. He was showing off and making up for that miss.

The crowd were giving him the countdown, from five seconds down to one and when the buzzer sounded to finalize the end of his run, Colton pulled up the reins and breathed. He sat quietly in the middle of the pen, taking in that ride and listening to the crowd. He let the colt know just how pleased he was when he put his hand down and rubbed him low on his neck, feeling the heat. They were both pumped.

"Good ride," he heard his father say when he rode over to him.

"He's gonna make it. Isn't he?" Colton said, to let his father know that he was right about the colt all along, that he had a good future ahead of him.

"Well he's got what it takes," Cutter admitted. "And so do you. That was a great ride," he said, and all Colton could do was smile.

As they rode out of the pen alongside Jesse, the announcer was giving the crowd the fill-in spiel, waiting on the score to come through. He was letting everyone in the stands know that they had just witnessed one of the greatest and most successful cutting horse families, all in the one pen at the same time.

"What do you think?" Colton asked his father of the score.

"I don't know. But to me, who cares about the score. Sometimes it's more about the ride."

Colton tied up the colt while Raylee was trying to throw her arms around him and give him a congratulatory hug with Aimee coming in from the other side. "Mom. Aimee," he said as he wriggled to get away. "Stop it, you're embarrassing me," he said, although not really meaning it.

Raylee didn't care. She was proud of him and couldn't help herself, while Aimee thought it was funny, making sure that she went overboard to make him squirm.

When the announcer came back on with the score, Colton held his breath. He knew he'd given it his all, and one miss might well have been enough to put him far down the leader board where he didn't want to be.

"It's a two twenty-two," the announcer said, still hyped up from the Jones atmosphere in the pen.

That still left Jesse on top with two riders to go.

"For your first time in the big time, that was a good shot." Jesse was silently pleased that Colton had not beaten him in his first ever pro event. He was now sorry that he had quit the colt, and happy he was sitting on top with the leading score on the filly. More than anything, he was pleased that Colton had come through to make the final and had performed well. Jesse knew that Colton was on his way.

The next two cowboys had everyone on edge. With two good riders and two well bred horses, the next few minutes and end result were in the judges' hands and Jesse didn't want to watch. He stayed with Aimee and the horses, waiting and listening for the crowd to tell him how they were going in the pen.

Their reaction told him it was going to be close, as the noise filled the arena for the full length of the run. Jesse looked up when he heard the buzzer, and looked back down again when the result came in. A score of a two twenty-four kept Jesse on top and pushed Colton down another place. The next two and a half minutes were out of his control, and Jesse got back in the saddle and kept busy in the loping area, walking the filly around. He only caught a few glimpses, when the excitement from the crowd had him a little nervous. He was so close to the winning buckle, yet still another minute away.

As the seconds were coming down, the tension was rising. Never before was it going to be this close and it could come down to the wire, with the judges splitting points. Both this cowboy and Jesse had won there before and both were popular among the crowd. It was keeping everyone anxious and taking sides. When the buzzer sounded, the cowboy pulled up the reins and knew he'd had a good ride.

While the announcer was waiting on the judges to deliver their verdict, he wound up the crowd and recapped the entire week, with his spectacular voice that blasted over the speakers and filled the arena.

Jesse wanted to hear it, and didn't want to hear it. While ever it was unknown, he was still sitting on top. But a two twenty-seven was enough to steal the victory and push Jesse down to second place and now it was over.

Done. Finished. There was nothing more he could do except to give his congratulations to the winner and wait for the presentation.

It didn't wipe the smile off Colton's face. He had finished the final in the top five and was more than happy after recognizing that he was up against a very long list of professional and talented trainers. They were all experienced and successful, and had been competing for years and for Colton, he was just at the very beginning.

Chapter Sixteen

When they took the horses back to the stables, Colton was stopped many times and was congratulated for doing a great job in the pen. He met some horse owners who were wanting to discuss his training schedule for next season. He didn't make any kind of commitment to them, because in his head, he was already leaving.

After the colt had been to the wash bay, Colton led him back through the breezeway to his stall. Raylee had cleaned it out and he tied him up to the rail out the front. He was preparing him for the trip home when Jesse came up from behind.

"Hey, Colton," Jesse said, making him turn around. "I want you to meet Tony."

Colton shook his hand. "Nice to meet you, Tony," he said, then kept working on the colt.

"That was a great ride," Tony commented, wanting to engage in a conversation.

"Thanks." It was all the time that Colton had, since he was busy with the horse.

Jesse wasn't there just to fill in the silent gaps. "Hey, Colt," he said. "Tony wants to talk to you about next season."

Colton didn't stop working but looked up. "I'm not interested... Thanks anyway, but I'm going home after the show."

Jesse and Tony looked at each other. "So you're not interested in training another horse for me next season?" Tony asked.

"Wait... Do you own the colt?" he asked, and all of a sudden he was wanting to talk.

"Well I did," Tony said. "But after his ride today, I was offered more money than I thought he was worth... so I sold him. But I've got some others coming through that you might want to look at."

Colton stood up straight. "You sold him?" Colton was angry that he had missed the opportunity. He knew he couldn't afford to buy the colt, but he would've liked to have been given the chance.

"Thanks to you I had a couple of decent offers." Tony was very thankful that Colton had done a good job with him. So good, that he was willing to send another horse his way. "I think it helped having your family name behind him."

"I can't believe you sold him without asking me." Colton stood by the horse and felt that his high had just hit another low point. There was nothing he could do now, except to get him ready to go home before he'd be picked up by the new owner, and he was hoping that would all take place after he left Australia.

He tried to remain professional as they stood around and talked some more about the final. Colton was trying to get his head around the fact that the colt had slipped through his fingers, without letting the owner know that he was deeply gutted. If he was ever going to make it as a professional trainer, then this was one of those challenges that he had to overcome.

"It was nice to meet you," Colton said to Tony. "And thank you for the opportunity to train your horse. But you'll have to excuse me now. I've got a promise I have to keep," he said, and he walked away.

"Hey, where're you going?" Jesse called out, curious about his sudden need to leave.

"I'll be back. Don't leave without me."

Jesse could only apologize to Tony for his nephew's need to up and leave so quickly, and to save face, he called Cutter over and introduced them.

It was another show over. Another tiring week finished, and the pack-up was done mostly by the two girls who had everything away in the truck by the time the boys offered to help.

The drive back to the vineyard went quickly. Raylee gave up her front seat position so that Colton could sit next to his father and the two of them talked about the final several times during the drive home.

Disappointment had already set in when they drove into the vineyard, and Cutter was doing his best to let Colton see that the colt was only one horse, that there will be many, and he needed to let it go and move onto the next phase of his training. He needed to keep up the pace and start working with a new young horse as soon as he arrived home, to take his mind off the colt and to focus on a new beginning. He needed to go to as many shows as he could, to gain more experience and prove to everyone that he wasn't a fluke, that he was in it for the long road.

Cutter was telling him everything that he already knew, everything that Colton was already planning on doing.

It was like turning back the clock when the following day was spent down at the complex. What should have been a day off for Jesse, turned out to be a full blown family cutting event in the arena. Since Colton was disappointed at how things had turned out with the colt, he was more than ready to leave and today was his last day in Australia.

They all had a turn of cutting cows, including Lucy and Paige, who were still learning. They were more than happy to take some pointers from Cutter instead of their father, as he was a novelty and they had underestimated just how successful their uncle was until they had gone to the show.

Allan was loving it. He sat on a horse in the corner and was enjoying being in the saddle again among the action, surrounded by his family. They only took a break when Evelyn brought down lunch for everyone and they all sat around the barn and shared the fancy sandwiches that Evelyn had prepared. Everyone, except for Colton. He was spending his last hours with the colt, still wondering how he missed the chance to make an offer.

It was when Raylee gave Cutter the nod, that he noticed Colton's absence and he left everyone sitting around and walked over to him.

"You've trained him well," Cutter commented. "And he's brought out the best in you," he added, giving both Colton and the colt some well deserved praise.

Colton couldn't deny it. "He's taught me more than you know. And now he's gonna teach me how to say goodbye and walk away."

Cutter knew the feeling very well. He had no choice but to sell his champion colt to pay for Macca's treatment when he fell sick all those years ago, and he knew the heartbreak. He knew what his son was going through and all he could do was grab him on the shoulder.

"There'll be others," Cutter said, to give him a reason to look forward.

"I know. But it doesn't make it any easier."

"That's true... So when does he go to his new owner?"

"I'm not sure," Colton said. "I didn't ask. But I'm pleased I won't be here to see it."

"So, are you ready to come home?"

Colton was. "I can't wait... As much as I love it here, it's not the ranch and I can't wait to see everyone."

"And everyone can't wait to see you," Cutter said. "Well... almost everyone."

Colton didn't need an explanation. He was certain that he was the last person Johnny was wanting to lay eyes on.

The laughter from the other end of the barn was telling them that it was time to go back and join in on what was so funny. The family was always laughing at something or someone, and when they rounded the corner, it was Lucy who was sporting her new boots and explaining to everyone how she came to be wearing a five hundred dollar pair of exotic skinned cowgirl boots, much to the surprise of her mother, that they didn't come from Allan. Colton came up to Lucy from behind and put his arm around her neck, holding her in a friendly headlock.

"She really saved me this week," he said, then he let her go.

"You're such a heartbreaker," Lucy teased, giving her cousin a fun smile. "Those girls only wanted to talk to you. They didn't want to get on the plane with you tomorrow," she said, making him see that maybe he'd overreacted.

She moved over and he pulled up a seat next to her on the bale and he began to relax with the family. "Let me tell you something, Lucy," he said seriously. "Talking is where it all begins."

Colton loved everyone there, even Jesse, and while they didn't hit it off from the beginning, after he'd hit rock bottom, their run-in was the start of Colton getting his life back on track. He needed the ass kick that Jesse had given him and if Jesse hadn't, then he would never have found himself on the right path and training the colt. He would never have ridden at the show.

If he could pick up everyone and take them home with him, then he'd be more than happy. He looked at Lucy. Although there was an age difference, she was starting to grow up and they had really started to bond over the last few weeks. If she was back home, Colton would look after her like a big brother.

He thought of Dakota and their trip to Nashville. What was he thinking in taking his sister to a place like that and putting her into that situation? It was irresponsible of him and luckily for her, their parents came at exactly the right time. He could only imagine that she would be off the rails by now and it would have been all his fault. He didn't want that. He didn't want that for his sister, knowing that she deserved better.

The afternoon was spent back in the cutting pen and everyone had a run on the cows before taking the horses one at a time into the wash bay. Colton had taken pride in the barn and when they were winding down for the evening, he couldn't help but clean up after everyone, just to keep on top of it. He threw a rug over the colt and led him back to his stall. His new owner would be coming any day now to pick him up and Colton wanted to have him ready. He was not spiteful in any way, just disheartened.

"You really like him?" Raylee asked. She was leading a horse to go out into a yard for the night and stopped by the stall.

"He's special," Colton agreed.

"He reminds me of you." Cutter had joined them and was leaning over Raylee's shoulder. "He's young and smart, but he still has a lot to learn... And I have no doubt he'll be a champion one day and so will you."

His son or not, Cutter knew that Colton was a cowboy who would one day make it, but only if he wanted it badly enough.

"What time do we have to leave tomorrow?" Colton asked.

"No later than seven," Raylee said, knowing that he was wanting to go for one last ride in the morning before he left.

The rest of the night was spent at the house with the family getting every last minute they could out of each other. Aimee didn't leave her brother's side and as the hours ticked away, she was becoming more clingy. She had already decided not to see them in the morning, as she was never good at saying goodbye. It left Raylee in a quiet corner with her father, letting him know that it was time to hang up the hat and retire. It had crossed his mind a few times over the years, although he was not prepared to close the doors on Jesse while ever he wanted to keep training.

Raylee suggested that they needed to discuss it together, and hinted that the only reason they were still operating, was because neither of them wanted to let the other one down. Jesse was extremely loyal to Allan, and in return, Allan gave him free rein to work the complex and breeding program as he liked. He had no intention of selling up or closing down while Jesse was still wanting to be in it.

Whatever they decided to do about the vineyard, Raylee would give them her full support. The vineyard and complex had been a huge success, but if

Jesse was thinking about packing up the family and moving back to Texas, then Allan wasn't sure if he wanted someone else to come in and take over.

More than anything, Raylee was thankful that her parents had taken good care of her son over the last three months and she let her father know it.

"Maybe I'll keep it going for Colton," Allan suggested. "He might come back and take over from Jesse one day."

"Absolutely no way," Raylee said, jumping all over him. "Colton's coming home and staying there. And don't you dare mention it to him."

Allan gave his daughter a warm fatherly smile. "And now you know how I felt all those years ago."

When Cutter threw his bag up onto the bed, it was to pack the last of his things. They'd had a very late night and Jesse, in the end, had to drag Aimee away in an emotional state when they said goodbye. After little sleep, it was now early in the morning and Raylee walked out of the bathroom, dressed for the long flight.

They wandered into the kitchen, expecting to see Colton with his bag ready by the door.

"Maybe he doesn't want to leave," Evelyn said. "He's been a very good house guest," she added, unaware that her grandson had behaved so badly in her home.

"He must be at the barn," Cutter said. "I'll go down and get him. We have to leave soon," he added, and he went for the door.

"I'll go," Allan said to pull him up. "You stay and have some breakfast and I'll go down and bring him back."

That suited Cutter just fine. He took a seat at the table and Evelyn fussed over him for one last time.

The lights were on at the complex, as Colton couldn't sleep and he had been down there before daybreak. He'd already been out for an early morning ride and had the colt washed, rugged and fed and was putting him back into his stall, ready for the handover.

"What is it that you like about him?" Allan asked, standing by the gate.

Colton thought that he was on his own until he heard his grandfather's voice. Thinking that he now had to hold it together when he said goodbye, he wasn't so sure if he was that strong.

"Well, he's really smart and switched on, and I could tell straight away when I took him away from the arena and put him in front of a cow, that he wanted to please me."

"It looks like he did that. You had a great ride in that final and the next time you come back, I expect you'll be taking home a buckle."

"Yes sir, I'd like to think so. And I'm going home to start training... As soon as I find a decent horse to work with." Colton wasn't sure exactly how he was going to make that happen, but he was determined. "But what I love the most about this horse, is that he saved me."

Allan knew that it was the colt who had given him that fire. That need to win. The colt was the one horse that gave him a new direction.

"You deserved the chance to buy him," Allan said, although he knew it was out of reach for Colton to even consider it. "So I'm sorry that I beat you to it."

It took a few seconds for his grandfather's comments to register in his head. "Wait... What're you saying?" he asked, looking up and looking hopeful.

"I'm sorry... I couldn't help it. When I knew that you wanted him, I bought him for you out of your trust fund."

If Colton hadn't been leaning against the stall, then he may have fallen over in the breezeway. "My what?" he asked. "You actually bought me this horse?"

"It was your money. I just spent it for you. I hope you don't mind."

"Are you kidding? Of course I don't mind." Colton couldn't contain himself and he threw himself at his grandfather, hugging him tight and that was when he started laughing and crying at the same time.

"What did Mom and Dad say?" he asked when he pulled away.

"I didn't tell them. They don't know. This is between you and me. They don't even know that you have a trust fund. And don't tell your brother and sister either... Their time hasn't come yet."

Colton could only laugh. He loved his grandfather and he loved that he would do that for him. He turned around and gave all his attention to the colt. "Now all I have to do is get you home," he said to him quietly.

Allan was already on it. "Leave that to me. I'll make all the arrangements."

"How can I ever make this up to you?" Colton asked.

"Well, you could promise me one thing."

"Of course. Anything," he committed straight away.

"When you get home, I want you to give it everything you have in you. Make it your life. You've got a chance to make it and make it big. So don't blow it. And listen to your dad. He's got a lot to say and he's been there and done it better than anyone else. You could learn a lot from him."

"Did you really try to shoot my dad?" Colton asked again, just because he really couldn't believe it.

Allan laughed. "Yes. But it would have been the biggest regret of my life if I hadn't missed."

"And mine," Colton agreed.

Chapter Seventeen

"Welcome home," Cutter said to Colton when they left the road and drove through the entrance of Double J Ranch.

It had been a long time away for Colton and he was happy to finally be home. He didn't realize just how much he'd missed the ranch until they drove towards the barn. All he wanted to do was see his sister and brother, and find a way to see Avery when there was a chance.

When Cutter pulled the truck up at the barn, they saw that Jake was parked near the house. It was dark, and the only lights on inside the house were in the kitchen and Dakota's room upstairs.

"What's he doing here at this time of night?" Cutter asked suspiciously, as the three of them climbed out and made for the house, leaving their bags behind. Millie knew Colton, even in the dark, and she let him know that he was missed, running in circles and whipping her tail against his legs.

Raylee felt a panic coming on. Dakota had shared her feelings about Jake with her and with their week away, she wondered if those feelings had been brought out into the open. Why else would Jake be there? "I don't know," she said honestly. "But whatever you find, just keep calm," she warned him before they went inside.

The kitchen was empty. There was no sign of anyone and the only sounds they could hear, were the footsteps upstairs in Dakota's room. Cutter was feeling the heat rise in his chest. "Stay here," he said quietly to Raylee and Colton, who remained in the kitchen and were expecting the worst. This was not what either of them wanted to come home to.

Cutter was silent when he took one step at a time on the stairs, treading lightly so as not to make a noise.

"Don't you start without me." Cutter heard Dakota's voice as she walked across the hall towards the bathroom. "I won't be long," she called out.

"I"m not gonna start without you," Jake's voice called back. "I need you to turn this thing on for me," he said.

Start what without her? Turn what on? Cutter stood halfway up the stairs in the dark, wondering what was going on inside his house.

Dakota came out of the bathroom and he heard her footsteps walk back across the hall towards her room. "Okay, you can put it on now. I'm ready for it," she said, loudly enough to be heard. Her voice was uplifted and their conversation raised immediate suspicion.

Put what on? Ready for what? Cutter took another two steps towards the top, just to hear more.

"Are you sure you wanna do this?" he asked. "Maybe I should fix you up first."

"Why do we have to do it now?"

"Because we didn't do it this morning and I might not be in the mood later. Besides, you might be too tired."

"Alright," she agreed. "But only because you insist. I don't ever want to hear you say that you never get your own way with me."

Fix what up? Too tired to do what? Cutter listened intently, finding every reason to burst in on their fun, but he waited, choosing the right moment. There was a silence.

"How does it look?" she asked.

"It's looking really good," Jake replied a little too keen. "You are one very lucky girl, Dakota Jones."

"I'm only lucky because I have you here with me," she praised him. There was a silence again and Cutter waited. Waiting for them to speak.

"Are you ready for this? It's gonna be a little uncomfortable but you know I can't help it," Jake said, pre-warning her.

"I'm ready," she replied. "But be careful. You really hurt me yesterday."

"Just lay back and close your eyes. Try to relax... Are you ready?"

"I think so."

There was a pause. A long pause.

"Ahh," she called out. "That really hurts... Ahh. Jake, stop."

"I told you it would hurt... I'm trying to be as gentle as I can but if I do it quickly, then it will be over before you know it."

"Ahh, Jake, you're hurting me."

"Just keep your eyes closed and don't look at what I'm doing," he said. "I'm nearly done." There was another stretch of silence and Cutter crept to the top step so that he could be ready. "There. I think you've had enough for one night... How does that feel?"

She hesitated. "That feels good now that it's over. I never knew that could hurt so much. Although I must admit, it didn't hurt as much as the first time."

That was it. It was game over. Cutter stood up straight and took a deep breath, then burst into Dakota's room to catch them out. "What the hell are you doing to my daughter?" he asked abruptly.

"Dad," she called out. "You're home."

"Yes I'm home. But what're you doing to her?" he asked Jake aggressively, who was sitting on the bed with her bare legs all over him.

"Cutter," Jake said, feeling guilty for being in his daughter's bedroom. Cutter looked at the scene. It wasn't what he was expecting to see although he wasn't sure exactly what they were doing. "I was just cleaning around this wound on her leg," he half explained.

"What?" Cutter asked. "What wound?" He came further into the room and gave his daughter a kiss on the head before he looked at what Jake was doing to her leg.

Jake was nervous, even though he had no reason to be. He had done a good job of cleaning around the outside of the infected area and was ready to wrap it up again. "A snake bit her," he defended.

"What? When?" Cutter all of a sudden became frantic.

"It's alright, Dad. It was last week and Jake's been looking after me," she said, then she gave Jake a warm smile.

"Why didn't you let us know?" Cutter asked.

"Because I didn't want to worry you and ruin your trip." The last thing Dakota wanted, was for her parents to turn around and come straight back home again when she was already receiving the best of care.

Cutter went to the door and called out downstairs. "It's alright. You can come up now."

They both looked at him as to why he thought it wasn't safe to come up earlier. "We didn't know what you were doing," he explained. "And by the way, what exactly were you starting up and turning on?" he asked, just for some extra peace of mind.

"Dad," Dakota growled. "We were going to watch a movie," she said severely, waving the disc in one hand and the remote control in the other.

Jake was wrapping Dakota's leg back up, trying to keep his laughter under control when Raylee and Colton stood in the doorway, needing an explanation as to what they were looking at. Everyone was excited to see each other and none more than Dakota and Colton. They had really missed one another.

Raylee made a fuss over Dakota and couldn't thank Jake enough for taking care of her. They all sat on the bed and went over the events of last week, the snake bite and Dakota being rushed to hospital, and Colton's ride in the final.

"Westyn rode down to get my dad," Jake said, hoping that would strike a need for both sides to put the past behind them.

"And Emma has been cooking us dinner and sending it over," Dakota added, to let them know that their neighbors were still their friends.

It left Colton silent. He knew that he had to fix the mess he'd made.

"Hey, where's Westyn?" Raylee thought to ask.

"He's probably gone to bed. He's been sleeping in the barn and gets up in the middle of the night, you know," Dakota explained, as if 5 a.m was something she strongly detested.

"In the barn?" Cutter asked, surprised that his son had not only taken up residence with the horses, but that it also left his daughter and Jake in the house alone.

"He's been on foal watch. But he's back in the house now," she explained. "And we have a new filly."

This was exciting news to everyone who expected the mare was still a few weeks away.

"Well I hope he's been sharing the load and taking care of you too," her mother said.

"He's been doing a great job here on the ranch and with the horses, and he only missed one day of school," she said in his defense, of the day she was taken to hospital. "You really should think about putting him on full time here."

"Are you giving my job away?" Colton cut in. "Because I only just got home and I need my job back."

"Well from what I hear, you'll be a professional trainer soon," she said, giving her brother all the encouragement he needed.

It had been weighing on Colton's mind and he was desperate to ask. "How's Avery?"

The room fell silent.

Dakota and Jake looked at each other, knowing that Avery had been considering going out with other boys. They didn't want to be the bearer of bad news. "She's good," Jake confirmed, and that was all they needed to say at that time.

He looked at Colton. "Well, it looks like I've lost my room, so I should be going home now," he added.

Cutter thought better of it. "I thought you were watching a movie?"

"Yeah, and I'll sleep in the barn tonight," Colton offered. He was more than happy to take his bag up to the loft and set up for the night.

Jake started backtracking. "Thanks, Colton. But you don't have to do that."

"Oh yes I do... I don't wanna be here running around after Dakota for the rest of the night," he said, taunting his sister. "I'll bet she's been driving you crazy," he said for fun.

"She sure has," Jake agreed, in more ways than anyone could imagine.

They all left Dakota's bedroom and headed off in their own directions. Raylee was wanting to take a shower and needed to crash into bed, and Colton went downstairs to the barn, taking his bag up to Jesse's old room in the loft.

"Can you turn this on for me?" Jake asked Dakota of the dvd player. "I still don't know how it works," he added, while he was uselessly studying the remote control.

With the bedroom door left open, Cutter heard the rest of their open conversation before the movie began, and he had a quiet laugh to himself. He was happy to have all his family back home together again.

When Westyn slid the barn door open, he wasn't expecting to see that his brother had already cleaned out the stalls and had a horse saddled, ready to ride in the pen.

"What're you doing here?" Westyn asked, surprised to see Colton.

"Nice to see you too, bro. Didn't you see the truck out the front?" Colton asked.

"Yeah. I mean, what're you doing at the barn? It's not eleven o'clock yet."

"It's work time," Colton said smartly. "You wanna come for a ride?"

Westyn saddled his horse while they caught up on the last few months. When he was ready, Colton looked at the time. "Where's Dad? Isn't he coming?" he asked.

"He doesn't get down here until after six," Westyn explained. "Although lately it's been closer to seven."

"What? Why? That's not like him."

They were standing in the breezeway, ready to go. "Didn't he tell you?" Westyn asked.

"Tell me what?"

Westyn didn't know if he should be the one to tell his brother, so he tried to squash it. "Maybe you should ask him yourself."

"Now you've got me worried," Colton said. "Should I be worried?"

"Not unless you think that quitting his training and competition is something to worry about?"

"What?" Colton said loudly, not quite believing him. "He's quitting? Why would he do that? He can't quit."

"He can and he has. He says he's doing it for us so that he can work for us and give us all the help we need."

"He didn't tell me he was quitting." Colton was genuinely shocked that his father had given up everything that he loved and hadn't told him. "I can't believe he's not gonna cut anymore. That he would just throw it all away. Maybe we need to talk to him. Try and turn him around."

"Mom's already tried... He won't change his mind."

Colton knew that if his mom couldn't change his father's mind, then no one would be able to. It was now daybreak and the boys rode out of the barn. Macca's truck caught Colton's eye. It was the first time he had seen it and it raised the memory and guilt of the day he was responsible for crashing it. It was still sitting along the fence, out of the way, as Cutter was still undecided about what to do with it. Colton knew that his father had to look at it every day while he was away, and it would be a reminder of what he had done and what it used to be.

They rode out the gate, taking a ride over the ranch before Westyn had to go to school. It had been many months since Colton last rode the ranch and he had a new outlook as he stopped to look back at everything he had missed. At everything he loved.

Cutter was now up and stood on the porch, watching the boys as they disappeared over the first rolling hill. Nothing made him more proud than to see his boys taking on the workload. It had been something that he'd only dreamed would happen, his two sons working alongside one another. One day, they would take over the ranch completely, although with the way Dakota had been working with him over the last while, their bossy sister may want to call the shots.

With the colt coming over from Australia in the next few weeks, they needed to think about building another yard for him away from the other horses. Cutter wondered if he should leave that up to Colton, to see what ideas he came up with. It was his horse, his investment, and Colton needed to stand up and take on the responsibility.

His thoughts were interrupted. "Raylee asked me to give you this," Jake said, when he came out onto the porch and handed Cutter his morning caffeine fix. "She said she's jet lagged and couldn't sleep."

"Thanks," he said, graciously accepting it. "You going home?"

"I think my dad's gonna start advertising my job if I don't get back to work," Jake said. They were both leaning on the rail looking out towards the barn.

"Thanks for taking care of Kotie while we were away," Cutter said. "It sounds like she was in good hands."

"About that…" Jake thought that if he delayed asking Cutter the big question, then he may have opted out altogether. "While you were away," he began to say, and it instantly raised a suspicion in Cutter that he had already buried last night. "Dakota and I have spent a lot of time together this week."

"And?"

"And we've done a lot of talking about us," he said.

"Wait," Cutter interrupted. He looked at Jake and was stringing some thoughts together in his head. "Have you and Kotie already… I mean, did you and she while we were gone… Have you and her…" Cutter wasn't sure how to put the question. He couldn't find the right words to avoid giving Jake any ideas in case he was on the wrong path.

"No sir. I swear, we haven't crossed any lines," he said in defense to the messed up question that Cutter couldn't get out of his mouth.

That was a relief.

"But I would like to take her out," Jake said.

"Sure. Anytime. You know that," he said in total support.

"No. I mean, I would like to take her out… all the time."

That should have blown Cutter's mind, except that he knew they already liked each other and he was half expecting it. Jake was asking for his permission to date his daughter permanently and Cutter was torn between a forced acceptance of their relationship and denial.

He tried to remain calm. Cutter looked back out to the barn and took a long sip of his hot coffee. "And if I said no, would you walk away or fight for her?"

Jake didn't need to think hard for his answer, he just wanted to make sure he gave Cutter the one he was wanting to hear. He was testing him.

"I'd fight for her," he said truthfully.

"And if I said yes, would you take care of her?"

"Yes sir. I promise you, I'd take better care of her than anyone else... I've already done that this week," he said.

"And do you promise to man up and not rush into anything too soon?"

Now that was pushing all the boundaries of where this conversation should be going, although Jake would be open and honest. "You know, spending time with her already drives me crazy," he said, letting Cutter know that the thought had already crossed his mind.

"Well, if you put her first and take good care of her, and you let her drive you crazy some more, then I don't see anything wrong with you taking her out. As long as you do everything right by her."

"Can I go and tell her now?" he asked.

"Jake. She's still in bed," he said. "Why don't you come back for dinner. I'm sure she can wait until then."

Cutter watched Jake climb into his truck and drive up the driveway and out the front gate. He couldn't believe that he'd just had that conversation with him. About his daughter. This was the little baby that he held in his arms all those years ago, then watched him grow up, having him follow in his shadow whenever he was around. This was the little boy that had grown into a man before his eyes, and Cutter looked on him like his own.

He found an instant comfort in being home, and with the added warmth of the coffee, he was feeling very at ease. His two boys were out riding the ranch together. His daughter was dating the only boy that he would ever approve of, and the family were finally back together. They had only been home for one night and everything seemed to be falling into place. Everything, except for his conflict with Johnny O'Brien. Somehow, he had to sort it out. He just didn't know how. He went inside when he could smell breakfast cooking and sat at the table.

"Jake gone home?" Raylee asked, standing over the stove, feeling wide awake as she was still on Australian time.

"He'll be back," Cutter replied. "I think we'll be seeing a lot more of Jake in the future."

"Why?" Raylee asked, although she figured she already knew the reason. She just wanted it confirmed.

"Because it seems the friendship did grow while we were away," Cutter said. "And I'm guessing he'll have a permanent place set at the table after tonight," he added, thinking that Jake was going to be around more often than not.

It was still early when the boys were making their way back home, thoroughly checking every fence line and each mob of cattle. Westyn was explaining what stage each of the different herds were at and which ones had already been through the cutting pen. When they reached the gate that joined their ranch to the O'Brien's, Westyn showed his brother where the snake had attacked Dakota, then he explained how Jake stayed with her while he raced to get Johnny's help.

Colton looked over the fence to the other side. It was playing on his mind how he was going to make things right. He knew the O'Brien ranch as well as their own and he decided that if Westyn was alright to ride home, then he'd brave it and go and find Johnny, to face him like a man.

All the way to the O'Brien barn, Colton prepared himself for what he would say. The excuses, the reasons, the justification for his actions. Nothing seemed to be acceptable although he had no other way around it. He rehearsed his apology, trying to make it sound genuine and honest, deciding that it sounded too well practiced and not at all like it was something he would say. It wasn't sounding believable.

When the homestead came into view, he could see Johnny's truck parked just outside the barn and he rode through the last gate and looked around, assessing everything around him, looking for his quickest escape if things got out of hand.

He tied the horse up and wandered around, before he heard someone working on the other side of the barn. When he neared, he felt a sudden rush of nerves and guilt coming over him again, feeling as if he could easily turn around and go home. Hide and not face up to what he had done. Man up or coward out. One was easier than the other yet both would define him forever in different ways.

The sound of wood chopping didn't register over the other thoughts swirling around in his head, until he'd already turned the corner and saw Johnny swinging his axe, splitting some firewood. Although the days were warming up, the nights still had a slight chill and Johnny was finishing up the last of the pile.

When Johnny looked up, he was as much surprised as Colton was, who was now feeling that the option to coward out would at least see him still alive.

"What're you doing here?" Johnny asked, then took another swing of his axe at the block of wood. It split in two equal pieces, both falling to the ground.

"I've come to apologize," Colton said. "You have every right to not wanna hear it, or to take a swing at me with that axe... But I'm here to say sorry. Sorry for everything that happened with Avery and with my father."

Johnny didn't answer. He was already hot and now he was fired up, splitting each block of wood without even thinking about it. He had his axe taking the full brunt of his anger.

"I don't know how I'm gonna make it up to you or my father, but I need you to give me a chance."

That threw Johnny into a rage. He stopped chopping and held each end of the axe handle as he approached Colton, pushing him up against the barn. He held the handle across Colton's chest, pinning him against the wall. "If you think that you're getting another chance with my daughter, then you've got rocks in your head. Now what is it that you really want? Why are you here?"

"I wanna make things right. Between you and my dad. Between our two families."

"It's gonna take more than you asking to do that."

"I'll do whatever it takes... I'll come and work for you. To prove that I'm sorry. I'll work every day for free. I'll clean out your barn, wash your horses or train them. Whatever you want, I'll do it." Colton was pleading for Johnny to give him any job that would even the score. "I screwed up and I know it. But you and my dad don't need to fight over my mistakes."

"I don't know if you can fix this one," Johnny said, then he released Colton from the barn wall.

When Johnny turned back to his chopping block, Colton gave his chest a rub where the axe was pushed hard against it.

"I'm starting to train horses now. I had a good show in Australia and I've got a colt coming home that I'm gonna start breeding from." He looked to Johnny for a response, but he kept chopping the wood. "I'm straightening out my life. I'll prove to you that you can trust me again."

"I told you, Avery's out of bounds."

"Give me some time. I'll change your mind," Colton said, although Johnny was not convinced. "And I really need your help," he added.

Johnny stopped again. What sort of hide did this kid have to be asking for his help? He couldn't believe that Colton had actually asked for a favor. Something for nothing.

"I need your help and you're the only one who can do it for me," Colton said.

Johnny was prepared to listen. After all, he was more curious than interested as to what Colton was asking. It didn't take long for Johnny to give him an answer, except that it was only on one condition. A compromise. Johnny would help Colton, if Colton would help Johnny. There was no other way it was going to work.

Johnny kept splitting the wood with one eye as he watched Colton walk to the house with his shortened stride and sunken shoulders. He walked up the steps and knocked on the door, taking a step back when Emma answered it. Johnny couldn't hear them speak, although he did see them both look in his direction. Emma went inside and a few minutes later, Avery came out.

From his view at the barn, Johnny could see Colton stepping back further and put his hands up, just to be out of arms' reach. They stood at a distance and their discussion was short and to the point. An argument. An outburst. It was when Avery launched herself at him and punched him with both fists on his chest, that he knew Colton had broke it off. Avery ran inside the house, slamming the door and Colton wandered back to his horse without even looking at him.

"So, about our arrangement?" Johnny called out.

Colton didn't look up. "We'll start next week," he said, then he left on his horse in a hurry.

Raylee had the table set for six. She gave everyone the five minute call to bring them all to the table together, although Cutter had to go to the barn and pull the boys away from the horses. He didn't mind though, as their dedication to the barn and the training was pleasing to him.

When they all sat down, they began to pass the dishes of food around. Jake had sat at their table many times before, yet for some reason, it was a little awkward, since he was now sitting there as Dakota's boyfriend. She could sense it and was doing her best to fill in the silent gaps. Nothing was helping and the conversation didn't flow easily. Dakota decided that enough was enough and she would strike up a good reason for everyone to start talking.

"So, I hear that Granddad nearly shot you the first time you met him?" she said openly to her father.

Cutter nearly choked on his potatoes. "What?" he spluttered out, looking at Colton who had a smug look on his face. Before he could catch his breath, Dakota continued on.

"You remember... When he caught you and Mom in bed together," she said, as if he needed reminding.

Raylee tried her best to hide her smile, but she started to giggle. It had caught her out too. As far as she was concerned, recalling that day always made her laugh and the table had just come alive.

Westyn looked to his mom and dad, wondering if it was true.

"You remember, don't you?" Dakota asked her father again, as he still hadn't responded. "It was after you rode the bull at the rodeo and Mom took you home from the hospital and you ended up together in the..."

"Yes, I remember. Thank you," Cutter said to pull her up. "And you don't need to remind me. I was there," he added sternly.

"Well if you remember it so well, then why haven't we heard about it before now?" she asked.

"Dakota, we have company," Raylee interrupted, not knowing what else to say. She really didn't want their sex life discussed at the dinner table in front of their guest, but it was too late now.

"It's alright, Mom. It's only Jake, and we all want to hear your side of the story. This is your chance to set the record straight." Dakota was making fun of her parents at the same time as she was wanting them to confirm Colton's story of events.

Cutter looked at Raylee who returned the look back to him. "I really don't think it's open for discussion right now," he said to shut it down.

His head-strong daughter wouldn't allow it. "But I heard that he shot a hole in the ceiling when Uncle Jesse took the rifle out of his hands and then you had to sleep in the barn," she said, filling in the missing pieces and provoking her parents' reaction.

"That's enough," Cutter said severely. Westyn was looking at both his sister and his father as they spoke. "Nobody wants to hear about it."

"I wanna hear about it," Westyn said, making everyone surprised at his sudden interest. "What happened next?" he asked.

That was enough to lighten Cutter's mood and he joined in on some family fun. "What happened next, was that I had to go and face your Granddad and apologize for behaving inappropriately with your mother in his house. Can you imagine how difficult that was?"

The kids all laughed, since they knew that wouldn't have been easy for anyone to do.

"So it seems that you and Mom broke all the rules too," Dakota stated in her brother's defense as well as her own, even though she hadn't broken them yet.

"Now don't you go getting any ideas. It was wrong and I admit it," Cutter said, looking at the kids, including Jake.

"But you got to make your own mistakes... Why can't we?" Dakota asked.

Dakota was right and they all knew it. There was no disputing that everyone has the right to learn from their own decisions. The good and the bad. Everyone has a right to choose and to learn.

When the fun had died down, Westyn got up from the table and took his plate to the sink. "I've got a friend coming over at the weekend for a ride," he announced, before he ducked away to do his homework.

When they weren't away at a competition, Westyn would use his Saturday mornings to ride over the ranch and train his horses in the sand yard. He'd be there before daybreak and would work until after dark, so it was good that he had a friend to spend the day with. It wouldn't stop Colton going about his training, as he'd picked up the two young horses that Cutter handed over to him. They were from their own lines and had been coming along nicely, although they were now needing more time riding over the ranch and in front of cattle. There was no doubt that Jake would be hanging around as much as he could with his new position at the table now set in stone, and that was sure to keep Dakota entertained as she was still moving around slowly, hobbling on her leg.

After a quick clean-up, everyone went their separate ways, leaving Cutter and Raylee to go outside and sit on the swing in the quiet of the early night.

"Can you believe that our kids are nearly grown up?" she said, almost disappointingly.

"Where did that time go?" he asked, feeling the same way. He put his arm around her. "Maybe we should have another baby?" he teased.

Raylee burst out laughing. "A baby? Not a chance. I love them all and I hate to see them all grow up, but a baby is not going to happen. No way," she rambled on. "Never and not on your life."

"Well then, we could always go upstairs and just pretend," he said, making her laugh some more. "You know I like to keep well practiced."

Raylee knew that he was more than serious. "How much practice can one cowboy have?"

"Well, the way I look at it, it's just like cutting," he said. "The more you practice, the better you get."

"And just like cutting, when you've had enough, you quit," she said, stirring him along.

"Baby, I ain't ever quitting you." Cutter kissed her suggestively, letting her know that after more than twenty years together, the spark was still burning and his need for her was still as strong.

Raylee wanted to know more about Cutter's talk with Jake that morning. "What did you say to him?" she asked.

"Just to let Kotie drive him crazy. That it won't kill him if she does."

"This is Dakota you're talking about and you know it's not going to stop at that just because you said so."

"Yes ma'am, I know," he agreed. "But I was hoping to scare the shit out of him to make it last a bit longer."

"You? Scare the shit out of someone? No one is scared of you," she said, then changed her mind. "Except for Colt. I think after what happened to your dad's truck, it was the first time he saw that look in your eyes."

They looked over to the truck. It was dark, yet they knew where it was parked with the moonlight hitting the hood and making it shine brightly.

"What're we going to do about it?" Raylee asked. "It can't stay there forever. We don't need it there to be a constant reminder."

Cutter rubbed his face as he always did when he was thinking. "I don't know, Raylee," he answered truthfully. "I'm not ready to send it away just yet." It had been on his mind every day and he knew that he had to deal with it. If he sent it to the scrap yard, then it would be gone forever and if he kept it, then it would only be in the way and would always weigh heavily on him. He was more than happy to be undecided.

Raylee understood. She also knew that it was the dark cloud hanging over the family and their neighbors, and it had to be dealt with soon.

When Dakota and Jake came out onto the porch, it was so he could say goodbye and go home.

"Thanks for dinner, Raylee," Jake said, standing at the top of the steps. He turned and looked at his new girlfriend, unsure if he should kiss her in front of her parents. They were standing close and were whispering, wondering how to deal with the situation, given that they had a tough audience.

"You're right," Jake said quietly. "Your dad does scare me. Especially since he's watching us right now."

Dakota looked at them sitting on the swing and gave them both a silent growl. It sent the right message. Cutter and Raylee got up from the swing and went inside. "Goodnight," they both said.

They were now alone. "But right now, I think your parents are scared of you," Jake said.

She laughed. "So I'll see you tomorrow?"

"You won't be able to keep me away." Jake leaned down and gave her a kiss goodnight before he drove away in his truck.

When the lights disappeared up the road, Dakota went inside where her parents were waiting for her. "What?" she asked, looking at their expressions.

"We need to talk to you," Raylee said, making it sound serious.

"I haven't done anything wrong if that's what you're implying," she said in defense.

"We didn't say that you had."

"And if it's about dinner. I'm sorry. But you should have told us how things were in the beginning with you two," Dakota said. "I was only playing with you," she added, still finding it quite funny.

"It's not that," Cutter said. "Well, not entirely."

Dakota was confused. Were they annoyed or pleased that their little secret was now out in the open, or did they disapprove that it was shared beyond their own family boundaries? Were they worried or regretting their decision to allow her to date Jake O'Brien? Perhaps their closeness was making her parents feel uncomfortable? Whatever was on their mind, it certainly had everything to do with Dakota. She stood in the kitchen and felt as if she was on trial.

"It's about you and Jake," Raylee said, taking the guesswork out of the family meeting.

"What about me and Jake?" she asked defensively, and there was a sudden apprehension from both her parents. "Well," she said, prompting them along. "What is it?"

"It's just that…" Cutter began, then stopped.

"What?"

He couldn't find the right words. It was clear that he wasn't good at dealing with the situation they were in.

"Your father and I are going away to a show next weekend with the boys," Raylee said on his behalf.

"And?" she asked, before she knew exactly where they were going with it. "And you're worried about me staying here on my own. Or not on my own."

"Yes," he confirmed. "It's not that we don't trust you. And I know you can look after the ranch for two days without any help. But…"

"But you don't want to leave me alone with Jake, is that it?" she asked.

Cutter didn't need to answer. He paced around the room, not looking at her. "We can't all go and your mom is prepared to stay at home with you," he said.

"Dad, I don't need a babysitter. What do you think's going to happen?" Dakota stood her ground. "It might be too late anyway, so you may be worrying for no good reason," she added to bait him. "We've already spent the last week here alone."

"What? Nooo," Cutter said with absolute surprise, and he stopped pacing and she had his full attention. Had they missed something and this was her way of telling them? "Dad. Nothing happened," she confirmed, and he instantly looked relieved. "But it could have, and only that Jake thinks too much of our family that it didn't. I wanted to, but he stopped it."

"Dakota!" Raylee said loudly to pull herself back into their conversation.

"Mom. I'm not going to apologize for it, and you and Dad can't talk. Look what happened with you," she said. "Now, do you want me to sneak around like Colton and Avery, or do it in the barn or in the backseat of his truck? Because I don't. Now I'm not asking for your permission and I'm not going to announce it to you when it does happen, but you can't look over my shoulder at everything I do, or lock me up and throw away the key forever."

"But..." Raylee tried to say, before she was quickly cut off.

"And one day soon I will be ready even if you're not, and there's nothing you can do about it. So stop worrying because it's not going to change anything."

Without going further into a heated argument, Dakota went back upstairs, leaving her parents to wonder how they had lost control of the discussion.

"That went well," Cutter said, leaning on the kitchen counter with his arms crossed.

Raylee looked at him. "What happened to you and the big talk you were going to give her?" she asked.

"I'm not real sure. But I do know one thing... I'm not ready for it, just like she said. But if she is, then there's nothing I can do about it. Raylee, what're we gonna do?" he asked.

There was no right answer. They were in a situation and knew they couldn't control what she did outside the house.

"I don't want her sneaking around. And I don't want them having to go to the barn or the truck. Or worse still, out over the ranch somewhere," Raylee said in defense of her daughter.

"Now there's nothing wrong with the tack room," he said, flirting with her again. He pulled her in close, locking his hands behind her back, reminding her of the more interesting places they had been together. "Or in the backseat of the truck."

"No there's not," she agreed. "But not for your first time."

Cutter couldn't agree more. "I don't know. Raising boys or girls, it's all the same. They're no different. Maybe we're just out of touch."

"Well at least she's open and honest. You can be thankful about that. And she will talk to us about it if we listen to her. I don't want her to think that she can't talk to us."

"Except the way I see it, Kotie is doing all the talking."

"And you know we've got to go through this all again, one more time," Raylee pointed out.

"With West? Are you joking? That kid is nothing like the other two."

Chapter Eighteen

Raylee always loved the weekend. If they weren't going to a show, then they were all together on the ranch and she would have an extra long lie in on a Saturday morning before cooking up a storm for everyone to kickstart two days of family time. It wouldn't slow down the two boys, who would ride over the ranch at daybreak and come back to the house for breakfast, before filling in the rest of the day in the cutting pen.

During breakfast, Westyn was looking relaxed even though he kept checking the time.

"When's your friend coming over?" Raylee asked, when they sat down at the table all together.

"Anytime now," he said, and he scoffed his bacon and eggs down fast so that he could go back to the yard. He more or less raced out the door.

Colton followed quickly, leaving Dakota at the table with her parents. Before a second go-round, she stood up and started to clear the plates.

It was when a truck and horse float pulled up outside the barn, that Raylee questioned it. "Who's that?" she asked.

"I don't know," Cutter said, and he left the table also.

They stood on the porch and watched from a distance. Westyn met the people at the back of the float and pulled down the ramp to unload the horse.

"Is that the friend?" Raylee asked.

"Well if his friend is a girl, then I'd say yes."

They watched Westyn lead the horse towards the barn with the young girl following closely. Her mother left them and made her way to the house. "Good morning," she said, when she reached the bottom of the steps. "You must be Cutter and Raylee? I'm Sandra. I'm Chelsea's mom."

After their introductions, they all went inside the house. It was news to Cutter and Raylee that Westyn had a friend who just happened to be a girl. They'd never heard him talk about Chelsea. Then again, Westyn was not big on words or personal information and was not one to draw attention to himself or what he was up to, leaving his parents with a lot of unanswered questions.

While Raylee made everyone a coffee and they settled around the table, Westyn and Chelsea saddled their horses and went into the sand yard. They went through some warm up exercises and chased one another around in large circles. To keep out of the way, Colton found little jobs to do in the barn that he needed to catch up on, letting his brother have the time alone with his friend.

When the horses were hot, Westyn called Chelsea over to the side and they began to talk about cutting. She was an accomplished rider, although he was explaining the basics of cutting a cow. He set a program on the mechanical cow and set up his horse in front of it, talking as it zipped up and down the wire, explaining everything he was doing.

Cutter, Raylee, and Sandra all wandered down to the yard to watch.

"She's ridden her whole life," Sandra explained. "But when we moved here last year, she met Westyn at school and she wanted to learn to cut. Her father trained the horse and sent it over for her. She just needed someone to teach her how it's done."

"What about her father... If he trained the horse, wouldn't he teach her?" Cutter asked.

"Her father and I were a mistake from the beginning," Sandra openly admitted. "She barely knows him. He has another family now and he sent the horse over for her birthday. But I think it was more out of his own guilt."

Raylee's thoughts were saddened, that this young girl didn't know her father. It was like Cutter and Pete all over again. "Well she's found the right one to help her," Raylee said, giving her own son a compliment. "And she's got a good friend in him too," she added.

"You mean boyfriend." Sandra saw a confused look in their eyes. "Didn't you know? I'm sorry, I thought you knew. Chelsea hasn't stopped talking about Westyn for the last five months."

Cutter and Raylee didn't know, and wouldn't make a big deal out of it in front of their guest. They stood by the fence and watched Westyn throw his leg over Chelsea's horse. When he put it in front of the mechanical cow, something out of this world happened. The horse sunk low in the sand and was switched on to that cow, following every move it made, leaving a lasting impression on everyone.

"Wow. I'm not sure which part of that was the horse and which part was West," Cutter said.

Sandra was impressed too. "Your son is very talented," she commented. "But when I researched the bloodlines of the horse, she goes a long way back to your stallion."

Hearing that won Cutter over immediately. He was always proud of Midnight and impressed with his progeny, even though this mare was a long way down the line and didn't look much like him. Her moves, however, were strikingly similar.

Westyn and Chelsea tied up the horses in the yard and walked over to their parents, holding hands and laughing between themselves. He introduced them. "Mom and Dad, this is Chelsea," he said. "And this is Cutter and Raylee," he said to Chelsea, keeping it simple.

All Chelsea could do was smile. She was as cute as a button and Cutter knew immediately what his son could see in her. She was petite, with dark hair and the kindest of eyes. "Hello," she said politely.

"Nice to meet you," Cutter said. "Looks like you've got yourself a red hot horse there," he commented.

"My dad trained her. He's one of the best trainers around," she informed him. "But not as good as you," she added, to let Cutter know he was still the best in her eyes. "I think you might know him."

"Maybe. Who's your father?"

"Tommy," she said proudly. "Tommy Parker."

Her announcement got Cutter's attention. It blew his mind. Of course he knew Tommy Parker. They had a history that was borderline friends and enemies, depending on his mood.

"He's a great trainer," Cutter said honestly, thinking what else could he say. He wasn't about to dog her father out. Whatever happened in the past with Tommy was between them. Though he did feel sorry for Chelsea, that Tommy had moved on with another family and had given her very little. A horse might well have been a nice gift, but it wasn't like being there as a father every day of her life.

"Westyn's going to teach me how to cut and then I'm going into competition," she announced.

"So you'll be competing against each other?" Cutter asked.

"Dad, it's not me she wants to go up against," Westyn said, as if there was another reason she was wanting to learn.

Sandra explained that Tommy's other children didn't recognize Chelsea as their sister and wanted nothing to do with her. She had a brother and a sister, who just like Colton and Westyn, had been riding all their life. They were younger, and Cutter had seen them at different shows. Talent ran through the Parker children and Westyn wanted to bring the best out in Chelsea before she went up against them at a show.

"I just want to show them who I am and what I can do," Chelsea said.

"Well you've got yourself a good horse." Cutter let her know that Tommy had done a good job in training her a decent cutting horse. "And you've got an even better teacher," he said of his son. "But it's not gonna come easy and you'll need to give it some time. Cutting's one of the hardest disciplines to get right. Anything can happen on the day."

"That's okay. I really don't mind." It was obvious that Chelsea wanted to spend time with Westyn and she was happy for it to take as long as was needed.

When they headed back into the cutting pen, Cutter went into the barn and saddled his horse, ready to ride. He looked around for Colton, but he was gone. He went into the pen and the three of them began working out a cutting program. Since Chelsea was a confident rider, and now had a good cutting horse underneath her, she picked up the moves quite easily. A real cow would be the next level, but with practice and patience, Cutter was sure she could do it.

While Cutter was genuinely surprised that he'd been kept in the dark about Westyn's girlfriend, he admired how his son respected her and talked to her with the utmost care and consideration. It was also returned, as Chelsea spoke to Westyn as if he was her hero, praising everything he did right and encouraging him through his mistakes, even though there were few. They were like an old married couple already.

Raylee and Sandra seemed to hit it off too, as their run-ins with Tommy over the years had left them with a lot in common. She had not talked to Emma in months, so it was nice to spend some time with another mom and their kids' friendship added to their interest. Raylee secretly hoped that Aimee would be coming home soon, but since they had not heard from her since they got back, she was sure that Jesse just might have got his way. At least for one more season.

Dakota came down to the barn and was introduced to Sandra. Although Raylee couldn't openly explain Westyn and Chelsea's relationship status, it didn't take long for Dakota to piece together the situation. She flashed her questionable eyes at Raylee as if to say who's been sneaking around now?before excusing herself to head over to the O'Brien ranch for the afternoon.

"Have you seen Colton?" Cutter asked, when they were finally done with the session and had the horse back on the float. He'd walked into the kitchen and interrupted the girls' second cup of coffee.

"I thought he was at the barn with you," Raylee said, surprised that he wasn't.

Both Cutter and Raylee were thinking the same thing, and hoped that he hadn't gone out to secretly meet up with Avery.

"He'll be around here somewhere, I'm sure." Cutter was only trying to put his own mind at ease, although it was taking some convincing. He let Sandra know that the horse was loaded and they all walked back to the barn.

"It was nice to meet you. And I'm sure we'll see you more often now," Raylee said.

Chelsea couldn't have been more thankful to everyone. She was sweet, and Cutter couldn't help but think that Tommy was missing out more than she was. He watched with one eye when Westyn helped Chelsea into the truck. Westyn touched her on the arm and kissed her on the cheek, making Cutter feel as if he should have turned away. He was soft with her and Cutter admired that.

"So… When were you going to tell us you had a girlfriend?" Raylee asked, while they stood together, waving after the truck as it made its way up the driveway.

"As soon as you asked," Westyn answered, and he walked back into the barn.

They both stood there and watched him. "We really need to talk to him more," Cutter said, and Raylee could only agree.

He put his arm around her as they made their way back to the house.

"Where do you think Colt is?" she asked.

Cutter was thinking the worst. "I have no idea. But wherever he is, I hope he's alright…"

Colton was alright, in one way. He'd asked for Johnny's help and today was the first day that they would work side by side. At first it was a little strained, but while ever they talked about the task and not about Avery, they were fine.

"When's your colt coming home?" Johnny asked, trying to sound interested.

"A couple more weeks," Colton replied. "And I can't wait. He's a great horse. Wait 'til you see him, you'll think the same."

They began talking like old friends again.

"You never said. How did you go in Australia?"

Colton was more than happy to talk about the show. "I made the final in the pros and finished in the top five, and Jesse is the reserve champion. He's riding pretty good, you know."

"I wouldn't expect anything less." Johnny kept working and was looking down. "He had the best teacher in the business," he admitted.

"Are you and my dad ever gonna get back to where you were?"

"To be honest... I hope so. I just don't know if that's what he wants."

"It's what I want. I want you and my dad to get through this, and this is the only way I know how to make it right between everyone."

They kept working, digging holes. It started to get a little too personal and Johnny pulled it up before he felt the need to forgive Colton. He liked it better the way it was. For now.

The sun was burning. What should have been a good job for early mornings or late afternoons, was only hindered by the training and work around the barn, and Colton's need to keep their meeting a secret. Johnny had brought the fence posts and rails in the back of his truck and together they unloaded a few, placing them into position. It didn't take long to see the project taking form. They worked well together for a few hours and were starting to find some common ground. It would still take every spare hour they had, with only limited time, and they hoped to have it finished by the end of the following week.

Johnny was lining up the next post, crouching down with one eye closed and looking down the fence line. "When I asked you to break it off with Avery, I didn't ask you to come up with some bullshit story about bedding another girl," he said.

Colton looked at him and his chest tightened up when he thought about Georgie. They caught each other by the eye and there was a deathly silence. Johnny only presumed that Colton had come up with that lame story to make the breakup easy and quick. When Colton didn't respond, it was clear that perhaps he was wrong.

"I see... It's not bullshit, is it?" Johnny asked.

"No sir, it's not," Colton admitted. "And I came home to make up for all my mistakes, and that was one of them. Except I don't think Avery will ever forgive me for that."

"Then why'd you tell her? You didn't have to and no one would ever have known," Johnny said, curious about Colton's sudden honesty.

"Because I wanted her to know that she could trust me."

His statement was contradictory and it threw Johnny.

"I didn't have to tell her and it was only me that had to live with it. By telling her, it showed her that I was honest," Colton explained. "A complete screw up. But honest."

"I think your dad was right to send you to Australia," Johnny said in support of Cutter's decision. "It was good for you, I can tell."

Colton was grateful to hear Johnny say it. He never thought he'd ever hear him say those words. "And maybe one day you'll let me take Avery out on a date?"

"Don't push it," Johnny was quick to respond. "I said it was good for you. I didn't say you were good for Avery."

"I'll change your mind," Colton said with a smile.

It was friendly enough while working alongside one another, and when they'd both had enough, they stood back and admired their work.

"Your dad's gonna be surprised," Johnny said.

Colton agreed. "Same time tomorrow?"

"Same time," Johnny confirmed. "And soon, we'll be able to put everything to rest, once and for all."

They packed up and said their goodbyes. Colton untied his horse and rode home, checking everything on the way back. He was feeling more uplifted riding through the pastures and looking over the cattle, taking on the responsibilities of the ranch and finding a way to make it up to his father and Johnny. They were starting to put the past behind them and look forward, although the road back to Avery was looking more doubtful. Johnny would make sure of that.

"Where've you been?" Cutter asked, when Colton pulled up at the barn and began to unsaddle his horse.

"Just out riding. I like to ride on my own," Colton half lied. "How did West go with his new friend?" he asked.

"Friend? Turns out she's his girlfriend," Cutter announced.

"What?"

"And that's not all. She also happens to be Tommy's daughter."

The look on Colton's face said it all.

"I know, don't say it," Cutter said to squash any further comment from his son. "It looks like keeping secrets might actually run in the family," he added.

After spending an hour in her room getting ready, Dakota came downstairs when she heard Jake pull up out the front. She was wearing a short skirt with high boots. Her hair was half up with curled ends and her earrings were so long, they nearly touched her bare shoulders.

"You can't go out looking like that," Cutter said, just as Jake was walking up the steps.

"Why not? I'm not going out to impress anyone else," she said in her own defense.

"But you don't need to tease him. Maybe you should cover up a bit more," he suggested. "Put on a pair of jeans and you really should take a jacket. It's cold out there."

"Dad. When I'm Mom's age, I'll tone it down. I promise," she said, and Raylee suddenly felt a little old. "I'm eighteen. It's what all girls my age wear."

"But it's not even summer yet."

"I think it looks great," Jake agreed. He was standing in the doorway, admiring the way she looked.

"Well you would," Cutter said harshly, putting himself back into the center of the conversation.

Dakota gave her father a kiss and grabbed a jacket before she headed out the door, just to please him. "And don't wait up for me," she said cheerfully.

"Twelve," Cutter called out after her.

"I know. I was just testing you," she called back.

"And have a good night," Raylee added.

They left the house to head into town for the night and Cutter and Raylee followed them out to the porch to watch them drive away.

"Did you see how short that skirt was?" Cutter asked.

"Yes. It reminds me of the skirt I wore when we first met."

"I know. And look at what happened to us," Cutter said, reminding her of how good she looked all those years ago.

"I'm not old, am I?" Raylee asked, curious about his thoughts.

He touched her face. "Baby, you'll never be as old as me," he said. "And you're still so damn beautiful." The way he held her and his gentle kisses told Raylee that he meant it.

The porch door flew open. "Where's Colt?" Westyn asked, intruding into their private moment. He was all dressed up in a clean pair of jeans and fresh shirt, with nowhere to go, that they knew of.

"He's around here somewhere," Cutter said, before he heard the heavy footsteps coming through the kitchen.

"You ready to go?" Colton asked his brother and without waiting for an answer, he looked to his parents. "We're going to town."

Raylee was surprised. "What for?" she asked.

"West is meeting up with Chelsea at the diner. Didn't he tell you? I'm just his taxi for the night," Colton explained, then they all looked to Westyn.

"You're full of information," his mother said. "That's two surprises in one day. It doesn't hurt to ask. Or at least let us know."

"I'm letting you know now." Westyn could not have been any more laid back about it if he tried. He couldn't see what all the fuss was about.

Since the family had arrived home from Australia, everything had settled down. The two boys were working well as a team and spending time together pleased both their parents. The wounds from the past were slowly healing.

"Dad... Can I borrow the truck?" Colton asked, trying his luck but with extreme caution.

Everyone was silent and all eyes were on Cutter. His thoughts went straight to Macca's smashed up truck, remembering how it used to be and there were so many reasons why he should have said no. "Just be careful," he agreed.

Cutter and Raylee stood leaning against the rail and watched the boys leave. They were all alone again, just like they were in Australia for the week. "It's the weekend and our kids have left us to go out for a night on the town. Now I really feel old," Raylee stated.

"Well, I have the perfect remedy for that," Cutter said, and he picked her up quickly and went back inside while she laughed all the way.

The diner was always busy on a Saturday night, although tonight it was packed. When the boys walked in, they could see Chelsea already sitting at a table, reading the menu. It was clear that she was new to town and hadn't eaten there often.

"Thanks for the lift," Westyn said. "What're you doing for the rest of the night?"

Colton looked around. Instead of going home, he decided to grab something to eat while he was there. "Don't worry. You won't even know I'm here," he assured his brother.

He pulled up a seat around the corner to be out of the way, although he did have a good view of the entire room. He picked up the menu and read it, only because he hadn't been there in months. It was going to be a long night waiting for everyone to finish enjoying themselves while he sat there and waited on his own, feeling sorry for himself. He looked around the room again. He saw Dakota and Jake sitting together and they were laughing at each other across the table, and he wondered what was so funny.

He kept looking at Westyn and Chelsea. He didn't need to know what they were talking about, as Westyn's hand signals were a dead giveaway. They were talking about horses and cutting.

He scanned the room further, looking for a waitress to take his order when he saw Avery walk in.

Wooh, Colton thought. She was all dressed up and looked downright amazing. Except that someone was holding her hand as they walked to the last available table and took a seat. This was his worst nightmare. Avery was out on a date with someone else and Colton couldn't get his head around it. There was an instant jealousy that fired him up and burned in his chest.

There was not another girl in this town who tormented him the way that she did, and while Avery had no intention of purposely making him feel that way, she did. In fact, she didn't know that he was there at first and would have gone somewhere else instead. He tried to look at the menu again and found it not as interesting as it should have been. He had just lost his appetite. Luckily for him he was not at a bar, or he may have been tempted to order a beer.

"What can I get for you?" the waitress asked, then looked up at him from her notepad. "Wait... Aren't you Colton Jones?" she asked.

"Yes ma'am, the one and only." He was just being friendly to drown out his bad mood.

"So you're Dakota's brother? Avery has told me all about you," she said.

"Well I don't know what she told you, but it's probably all true," he admitted, to hopefully scare her away.

She didn't look scared. "Really? Because I thought she must have been exaggerating."

Now he really wasn't sure what she'd heard, but this was his one chance to find out more.

"Can I ask you something... Who's that guy with Avery?"

They both looked to Avery and her date. She seemed to be having a nice time. Not overly happy, but he didn't seem to bore her either. They were getting along quite well.

"Does it really matter?" she asked. "It looks like Avery's moved on and maybe you should too."

She stood in front of him to block his view. Her name badge was in direct eye shot and he read it. "Grace, is it? Well I'll tell you what, Grace... Avery might be ready to move on but I'm not. Not yet," he said.

"Well maybe I can help you move on?"

Why did he never have any trouble attracting girls? She would have made a very good distraction if that's what he wanted, but when he weighed up the strong appeal against the unnecessary need, he turned her down. "Thanks. But I'm not sure I wanna move on right now."

"That's okay," Grace said, being nice about it. "I understand how you feel. I've been dumped before and the best way to get over it, is to go out and have some fun."

Fun was the last thing on Colton's mind. "First of all, I didn't get dumped. And secondly, I'm not about to have you throw yourself at me for my entertainment or yours." Colton was making it quite clear that he was not interested.

"Who said anything about throwing myself at you?" she asked. "You sure are full of yourself... You don't have to get into bed with someone to have fun." She looked down and began to write something on her notepad.

"I'm sorry... I didn't mean to..."

"Assume?" she answered for him. "You assumed that you're just so irresistible that I wouldn't be able to help myself and fall head over heels for those baby blue eyes and gorgeous smile... Or maybe it's your hat and those cowboy boots you think are turning me on?"

Now Colton wasn't sure if she was flirting or trying to humiliate him. He couldn't decide if he should play along or not.

"What's the matter?" she asked, handing him a note with scribble on it. He looked at it. "It's my phone number. When you're over Avery, or want to have some fun, or if you just want to drown those sad sorry baby blues of yours, I'm your girl." Now she really had him confused. "But right now I've got other customers I need to take orders from, unless you want something to eat?"

Colton had just lost his appetite altogether. He put the menu down and said goodbye to Grace and walked over to his sister's table.

"Hey, Jake... Can you give West a lift home? I'm not staying," he said.

"Pull up a seat," Jake offered, although Colton declined. He didn't want to be that unwanted third person that made the table unbalanced. They were on a date, and when he looked at them sitting at the table, he knew that it could have been Avery sitting with him, openly dating each other for all the world to see.

All he wanted to do now, was leave. Before he turned and headed for the door, he took one last look at Avery. He caught her eye and their stare was brief before he left in a hurry.

As he unlocked his father's truck, he heard his name. "Colton?"

He knew that voice. "What do you want, Avery?"

"I want to know why you did it?" she asked. Avery had left her date sitting at the table. It was her one chance to confront him.

"Shouldn't you be inside with your new boyfriend?"

"He's not my boyfriend. It's a first date. But answer me. Why did you have to cheat on me with someone else while you were away?"

"I told you I'm sorry. I don't know what else to tell you, but I am so sorry." Colton didn't have all the answers for her. "I didn't have to tell you. I could have come home and not said a word and you wouldn't have known."

"In a way, I wish you had."

They were both talking loudly and forcefully at each other and luckily for them, they were alone.

"Look, I made some big mistakes before I left and I was at my lowest point. I screwed up in so many ways and now I'm trying to turn it all around." Colton wasn't looking for sympathy. He wasn't sure what he was looking for.

"I can't forgive you," she said.

"And I don't expect you to."

Avery was now angry and raised her voice to the next level. "So what do you expect?"

"Nothing... I don't expect anything from you... I want you to give me another chance but I don't expect it."

"Grace told me that you turned her down."

Colton couldn't believe it. Everything was processing in his head quickly. "Did you set me up?"

"I had to." Avery was desperate to know and couldn't deny it. "I wanted to see what you would do."

"I told you, I'm sorry. But just because you don't wanna be with me doesn't mean that I'll bed the first girl that comes along." Colton was pissed now. He opened the door and started the truck.

"I just needed to know."

"Well now you know... I love you, Avery. And if you don't love me, then I guess we're done. But I'm not gonna hang around and wait for you to go through every other guy in town before you work it out that no one will love you the way I do."

He put the truck into reverse and backed out. Avery moved quickly out of the way and stood on the side of the road, watching him leave before she broke down and cried. Again.

Colton was throwing all his spare time and energy into training. After his father had quit his two young horses, Colton picked them up as soon as he arrived home. They were in the early stages of their program and had a long way to go, and he was learning as much as they were. All he wanted to do, was keep busy. Every day, Johnny gave him the time to fulfil their arrangement and their project was coming along well. They were slowly letting down those barriers and had started to build up the trust again.

The gentle breeze didn't help to take the heat out of the midday spring sun, as Colton had his head down and was digging.

"You're quiet today," Johnny noted.

They had not said two words outside their job, while Colton kept focused and was working harder than Johnny. Not intentionally. He was replaying the events from last night, over and over again in his head.

"I don't wanna talk about it," Colton threw at him without looking his way.

Johnny kept working too, although he would not give up. "Something happen last night? You were fine yesterday."

"It's nothing," Colton replied sharply.

"Well nothing doesn't look like that."

Colton wasn't interested in going into the details with Johnny. "Help me put the top rail on," he said, and they both went to pick up each end of the rail lying on the grass. When they put it into position, Johnny lined it up straight. He crouched down and closed one eye, looking down the fence line.

"It's not straight," Colton said critically.

Johnny looked at it again. "It looks straight to me."

"No, it's not."

"Colton, it's perfectly in line with the rest of the rails."

"It's out. I can see it."

"It's fine," Johnny tried to persuade him.

Colton ripped out the rail before it was attached and threw it to the ground.

"Hey, Colt. What're you doing? It was straight."

Colton released his anger when he walked away and let his frustrations echo through the ranch.

"You wanna talk about it?" Johnny asked, knowing there was more to his let go than the top rail being out of line.

"I just wanna make it perfect for my dad," he said.

Johnny did too. "Look, it's coming together and it looks great."

Colton took a deep breath and came back over, crouching down where they were working.

"What is it, Colton?"

He hesitated, but looked at Johnny and felt as if he could tell him. "It's you. It's my dad and it's Avery... But most of all, it's me."

"Well you sound like you've worked things out with your dad. And I'm here with you, aren't I?" Johnny said for reassurance.

"And what about Avery?"

Johnny was less forgiving about what Colton had done with his daughter. "Of everything that happened, breaking her heart was the worst that you did."

"I know. But I can't change it," Colton said, totally down on himself. "I saw her last night," he announced, and it put Johnny on high alert.

"Where?"

"At the diner. I was dropping West off, and I saw Avery there with someone else."

"And how did that make you feel?"

Colton didn't need the time to think about it. He'd thought about it all night and all morning. "Betrayed. Jealous. It's not that I've got any right to feel that way, but I couldn't help it."

"So now you know how she feels."

"Do you think she'll ever forgive me?"

"I don't honestly know," Johnny admitted. "But have you ever thought that Avery might not be the one for you. I know you can't see it yet, but maybe you need to go out with other girls to find that out."

Colton wasn't sure if Johnny was right, or if he was trying to put more distance between them. Either way, it didn't look as if Avery was going to be forgiving of him any time soon.

After finishing off for the day, they began to pack everything away in the back of Johnny's truck. Colton stood back, admiring their work. They still had more posts to put in the ground and rails to attach. The last job was to swing the gate and a few more days would see it completed.

"You've done a good job," Johnny praised him. "And your dad will think so too when he sees it."

"I hope so... Hey, it's Mary-Ann's birthday at the weekend," Colton said. "I think that Sunday should be the day."

Johnny thought so too. "I'll make sure everything's ready while you're away."

Colton rode home, checking everything on the way. He was not so uptight anymore and instead of thinking about last night with Avery, he thought of his dad. Not only how much he admired him as a rider and a cutter, but also as a father. His decision to quit everything he loved for his kids showed Colton just how much his father loved his family and how he put them first... every time.

Chapter Nineteen

By the following week, Colton had really settled into being back. He decided that he liked staying in the loft and had spent every night there since he arrived home. His needs were few, and he only brought down from his room what he could carry, leaving his old life behind and starting anew. Cutter and Raylee were not too concerned that he had moved out of the house, as he was making the barn and the ranch his life, and that was pleasing to them both.

He would, however, turn up for every meal and give his parents a daily update on the progress of the horses and the cattle. As difficult as it was, Cutter was doing his best to take a step back, letting the boys take over and learn. He would be there whenever he was needed, and gave an opinion when he was asked. It gave Cutter the time to spend with Raylee, although with their wounded patient still hobbling and hanging around, it seriously impacted their time alone.

"Why don't you come with me to the barn?" Cutter suggested to Dakota. She was bored and was looking for something to do.

"Dad. I can hardly walk," she said, as if he should know better.

"Well I didn't see you struggling to go out last Saturday night with Jake. You seemed to be walking around just fine in those high boots when he wanted to take you out for dinner." Cutter had caught her out. "Why don't you get into your jeans and I'll take you for a ride."

It seemed that Cutter was as much looking for something to do as Dakota was. He had already read the newspaper from front to back and went through it again just in case he had missed something, while he waited for her to get changed. He was only distracting himself so that he didn't think of their neighbors.

Dakota had been spending a lot of time at the O'Brien ranch over the last week, and when she came back down, she thought it was worth a mention. "Johnny was asking about you last night," she said, looking for his response.

Cutter gave it to her. He looked up and looked surprised... Almost hopeful. "He did?" he asked with a subtle smile.

She let him down gently. "No. He didn't... I just wanted to see what your reaction would be." She sat down with him at the table. His smile was gone.

"But that tells me that you really miss him. That you should go and see him. Be the first one to make a move."

"I was the first one to make a move. When I made that call," he said, to let her know that it was now up to Johnny to make his decision.

"I'm sure he misses you too," she added, trying to soften him. "Even if he didn't say it."

"Not enough to pick up the phone," Cutter threw back at her.

Dakota was fighting an uphill battle. Here she was in the middle of their standoff, spending equal amounts of time between both families and both ranches. If only there was something she could do, she thought. Actually, there was something she could do... She could go for a ride with him and take her father's mind off it.

When she pulled her boots on, she jumped on his back and he carried her to the barn. They were laughing all the way at nothing, just like they always did. Cutter helped bring her horse in and threw the saddle on for her, leaving her to buckle it up and put the bridle on.

He silently watched her when he threw his saddle on his horse. She was his little girl, all grown up and starting life as an adult. He knew that she loved him and relied on him. She had a trust that her father would never let her down and only want the best for her. But his time was coming to an end. Someone else would come along and take his place. He didn't want to think about it, but he knew that one day, she would give herself to another man and depend on someone else. In Cutter's mind, that someone else was going to be Jake O'Brien.

He thought of Johnny. He'd already gone through that with Avery. Only it was Colton who had taken that away from him and after everything that had happened, Cutter wondered how Johnny would ever get over it. Looking at Dakota, he wasn't so sure that he would be able to.

"Do you need a leg up?" Cutter asked, when they led the horses out of the barn. She did, and he helped her into the saddle, placing her foot into the stirrup.

They rode towards the gate. Cutter didn't need to check on anything as Colton was already out riding. He just wanted to be back in the saddle and was on the ride more for Dakota than himself, taking every last chance he could get to be her hero.

"I've made a decision," she said firmly, riding through the middle pasture where the cattle were grazing in the shade.

Cutter felt hot. What kind of decision needed this kind of announcement? Was she going to tell him every father's worst nightmare? That would have been Dakota's way of going about things.

"If it's about you and Jake…" he said.

"How did you know?" she quickly asked.

Now he felt as if he was burning up. "You know, Kotie. As much as you don't believe it, I remember being eighteen. It might have been a long time ago, but I remember it as if it was yesterday. You may wanna rush into things with Jake because you think you're ready, but you have your whole life ahead of you, and if Jake is to be the one, then I don't see what the hurry is."

It was Cutter's chance to lay it on the line.

"And it is all it's cracked up to be," he added. "I'm not gonna lie and pretend that it's not, just so I can talk you out of it. But you can hold him out a while longer. Let him love you in other ways first."

It wasn't Jake that needed holding out, Dakota thought to herself, but she let her father continue.

"When I met your mom, it was on my mind, and I wouldn't have listened to anyone either. There was no stopping it. But when your grandfather caught us, I didn't know what he was feeling as a father," he admitted. "Same with Johnny. I can't imagine what he was going through when he saw his daughter at the hospital all cut up, knowing that Colton was responsible."

"You see, I know you'll give yourself to Jake one day. And I know that you'll think it's great. But I can't sit here and tell you that I'm happy about it," he said, to let her know that he was also realistic.

Cutter took a slight breather and Dakota could finally get a word in. "So, will you be happy when I tell you that I'm not going to college?" she asked, after her father had been widely sidetracked by other ideas.

"Wait… This is not about you and Jake?" he asked.

"Yes it's about me and Jake. We had a talk about college and I decided that I'd rather stay here… with him, and my family," she explained. "I'm not ready to leave the ranch just yet."

"So this has nothing to do with you and him?"

"Dad. It has everything to do with us. Just not in the way you're thinking," she said. "Do you think I'd tell you that before it happens? I'd much rather see your face and listen to your complaints after it does." Dakota was making fun of her father, like she always did. It was clear that he loved her so much and wasn't good at dealing with all the issues of her growing up.

"You know, you couldn't ask for anyone better for me," she said, to try and get him on the right side. "You can at least be thankful for that."

He looked at her while they kept riding. "Don't you understand, Kotie?" he said. "No one is ever going to be good enough for my daughter."

They reached the next gate and were about to go through when they saw Colton riding home. Cutter leaned down and opened the latch and swung it open, waiting for him.

"We were just on our way out the back," Cutter said.

Colton was lucky that he hadn't got caught working with Johnny. "No need. Everything is good out there. Let's go back to the pen. You can help me put some cattle through," he said, to divert them away from where he had been working. He wanted to have a few runs on the cows in the pen before they left for the show the next day, and he had to get everything organized for when his brother got home from school. It was another day closer to the weekend, and for Cutter, that meant another day closer to leaving Dakota at the ranch on her own. He tried not to think about it.

When Raylee saw them riding home, she went to the barn and met them. Together they changed horses and changed saddles, gearing up for some family cutting time. Colton was more than impressed when Dakota had a run on a cow, since he had never seen her cut before and he wondered why she had never gone into competition. Her leg was not even a consideration when her horse laid its ears back and turned it on for everyone. Together they were showing off.

Just as he was with Westyn, Cutter remained silent when he watched Colton on the cow, letting him work through those tough mistakes and learn from them. It would have been too easy to pull him up and let him know what he was doing wrong, and it was very difficult to sit there and say nothing. He was only there to keep the cattle together and would only interfere if he was asked.

The kids loved it when their mother pulled a cow out and put her hand down. She might have been a little rusty, but they could tell that she loved every second of it. Raylee still had it in her to go to some local shows and have some fun, except that she just enjoyed spending the time in their own pen with the kids.

After her turn, Raylee settled back into the corner, expecting that Cutter would take the next run. He didn't.

"Come on, Dad. You're up next," Colton said, inviting him into the herd.

"Thanks. But you can take my run," he replied, declining the offer.

It was clear that Cutter had not only quit training and competition, but he had also quit the need to cut. At least for now. No one pressured him to have a go, and Colton and Dakota took turns while the cattle were in the yards.

"Hey. Leave some for your brother," Cutter said, as if everyone had forgotten about Westyn. He was at school and would want to ride his horse before it was loaded the following afternoon.

Back in the barn, everyone took their saddles off. Colton took charge of everything and sent the girls to the house to make lunch while he washed their horses and put them away. Cutter admired how much he had changed. He'd never spent so much time in the barn and when Cutter watched him work, there was a pride and a satisfaction that Colton had never shown before.

"I don't know what went on down in Australia to change you the way it has, but I'm pleased that you went there." Cutter had an opportunity to talk to his son while it was just the two of them and he took it.

Colton was hanging up the bridles. He didn't stop working. "I screwed up, Dad. While I was in Australia, I screwed up badly," he admitted, without going into the details. "But Uncle Jesse pulled me through. I couldn't have done it without him."

Cutter didn't want to know what had happened. It wasn't going to change anything and he'd rather not know. "Whatever happened, it was for the good. You might not think so, but I can see it's been good for you in more ways than one."

Colton looked to his father. "Do you believe in me... That I can make it?" he asked. "I'm not the rider you are, and I don't think anyone will ever come close to you in the cutting pen."

Cutter wasn't expecting such a compliment, but he turned it around. "When it comes to cutting, you've got the right bloodlines. It will be up to you how far you take it."

"Are you sure you really wanna quit? I don't like being responsible for you making that decision," Colton said, letting his father know that he was still not happy about it.

"I only quit because I have faith in you. In both of you," Cutter replied, praising both his boys. "I know you're gonna make it and I know your brother will make it too. And I'm prepared to get behind you to make that happen."

If Colton couldn't make it as a trainer with his father's full support behind him, then he would never have made it without him. He was thankful that he had everything on hand and in front of him, and the rest would take time and a lot of dedication.

"Just make sure that when you screw something up next time, it's worth the lesson," Cutter added, as they made for the house and passed Macca's truck.

The guilt had just set in again. Crashing the truck was Colton's biggest mistake and the lesson was huge. Mostly because it could never be repaired. It wasn't mentioned again, since Cutter wasn't there to rub it in his son's face. Instead, he put his hand on the back of Colton's neck as they walked past it, and he gave him a squeeze.

That's what Colton loved the most about his father. Deep down, through all the anger and regrets, the stupid mistakes and hard lessons, he knew that his father was there for him.

Dakota kept checking the time. While everyone was busy packing the truck, she stood on the porch and looked out as far as she could see, waiting for Jake to arrive.

It was Friday afternoon and knowing that Jake had now finished work, she was expecting to see him ride over the last rolling hill anytime soon. She didn't want to spend the weekend alone and now she was feeling anxious, staring at the horizon. Much to her father's open disapproval, Dakota was determined to wear Jake down, just like she had promised him.

All day, Cutter had been in a bad mood and was doing his best to stay out of her way and not look in her direction. The weekend wasn't sitting well with him. He was trying to focus on loading the horses, while silently sulking in his own fatherly misery.

While watching the boys work busily around the barn and yards, she heard the screen door and turned around to see her mother walking out, holding her bag. "Have a good weekend," Dakota said cheerfully. "And don't worry about me. I'll be fine," she said for extra reassurance.

"I know you'll be fine," Raylee said. She knew that Jake would take good care of her while they were away. Whatever else happened after that, was going to be her daughter's decision. "It's more your father I'm worried about," she added, looking at the truck.

"He hasn't talked to me all day."

"He'll be alright. He's just not coping with you having a steady boyfriend," Raylee explained. "I just hope that Jake turns up after we've left."

Out in the distance, they could see that Jake was closing the last gate before he made his way towards the barn.

"Too late now," Dakota said, and just the sight of him made her heart flutter. "You'd better get on the road. I don't want Dad to make a scene and regret saying something he shouldn't."

Raylee agreed. "I'll call you tonight when we arrive. Just to make sure that everything is okay." After the experience Dakota had with the snake, Raylee would now keep in close contact while ever they were away.

When Jake pulled up his horse at the barn, he stopped to talk to everyone before they hit the road. Everyone, except for Cutter. He kept busy and avoided him. Feeling the tension, Jake unsaddled his horse and walked to the house, just to keep out of the way. He stood close to Dakota on the step, watching the family pile into the truck and start their journey. They gave the truck a wave and in return, the two boys and Raylee gave them a wave back. Cutter didn't look in their direction and kept his eyes on the road. He was not in a good place.

"I feel sorry for the boys," Dakota said, standing behind Jake on the step above him with her arms wrapped around his shoulders.

They gave a final wave. "Why?" he asked, as if she should have been happy they were going to a show.

"Because my dad's not happy that you're staying with me... And that's going to make it a very long drive for them."

Jake turned around when the back of the truck became smaller as it went up the long driveway. "I could always go home," he said to tease her.

"Are you trying to please me or my dad?" she asked.

"Both," he replied quickly. "But now that he's gone, I'm planning on pleasing you."

"Then you know what you have to do," she flirted, taking his hat off and leaning down to kiss him. When she pulled away, she put it back on his head.

"We should at least wait until they arrive at the show," he suggested, looking back up the driveway, feeling guilty, nervous, but most of all... ready.

"Or, we should at least wait until they reach the mailbox," she said, giving him a fun smile.

The thought of being together was on both their minds. They had talked about it and had waited long enough. Jake picked her up and she wrapped her legs around him, kissing him and laughing at the same time, and he carried her inside the house and up the stairs to her room.

The weekend show was a good chance for Colton to get more experience among the pro riders. He rode a well trained gelding that his father had trained many years ago and had been riding over the ranch every other day. He was sound and he gave Colton a good solid run, building his confidence and show ability, which in return would give him great experience before he went to the bigger, more important shows that would really put him in the spotlight. Westyn, on the other hand, was still riding in the young teens. He was up against team Parker, who didn't bother him one little bit in the cutting pen, although it was Chelsea who he was fired up for. He wanted to win against them for her.

They both kickstarted the weekend with some good scores.

The two boys were working well together and were sharing the load. Each one helping the other when needed, and when Cutter looked at them, he could see that they were becoming good friends. That was pleasing to him, since he grew up without a brother and only found his sisters later in his life. It was Johnny who had been like a brother to him, although it seemed that he had slipped away altogether now.

"You're up in three more," Raylee said to Colton, who was standing by the fence putting his chaps on again. He was going out to ride the mare in another event while the rest of his family helped out in the corners. After his ride on the gelding, Colton had a lot of interest come his way, as the news of his father's retirement and the results from Australia had everyone talking about what was really going on at the Jones' ranch.

There was some talk of his training schedule for the coming season, and if he was really up for the job while still being so young. To secure his first paid client, Colton had to pull his father into the deal when he assured the horse owner, Mrs Bradshaw, that Cutter Jones would be looking over his shoulder all the way to the end. Mrs Bradshaw didn't mind though, and at a more affordable rate, she was happy to take a chance.

It gave Colton the confidence he needed when he threw his leg over the mare and took her into the prep lane for a tuning. He was looking world class. Full of himself. Determined to show off his horse and woo the judges. While everyone took up their positions in the corners, he was going through his routine. Readjusting his hat. Fidgeting with his belt. Straightening out his shirt. It was something he did without knowing, all the while he was looking at the cattle.

"Let's do it," he said quietly to the mare, and with a gentle touch of his spurs, the mare walked towards the time line just as she had done so many times before. It was his name that brought everyone to the stands to watch him ride, and he didn't disappoint. As soon as the mare found her groove in the sand, she let that cow know that she meant business.

For the full two and a half minutes, the mare put on a good show. Burning up the sand. Tearing into the turns. Leaving nowhere for the cow to go. She was Cutter Jones trained and had the skills to respond to every move the cow made. Every swivel and turn, every streak across the pen, she pressured that cow to make a desperate run and blindsided it with her presence and stance in the sand. Standing her ground, it was her territorial right that told that cow she owned the pen.

As for Colton, he was relaxed in the saddle, feeling her strength and impressed by her cow sense. Again she provoked the cow to make a run, only to show her extraordinary ability and threaten its safe return to the mob.

Colton was riding with heart. The mare was having a great run.

This is where Colton belonged. Not at a rodeo. Certainly not on a bull. He belonged in the cutting pen working with the horse against the cow.

When his second cow picked up the speed, his heart went into fifth gear as they chased it down and pressured it back to the middle of the pen. When the mare and the cow locked eyes onto each other, it was a showdown. Their quick hustle in the sand gave the crowd something to cheer about, as she got down low and threw her weight around, sending the cow into a state of madness.

Only for there being enough time left on the clock, he pulled a cow off the top and put his hand down, letting the mare give the cow a little boogie time in the last seconds before the buzzer sounded. They had rocked it. Smashed it. Cleaned up. There was nothing more he could do to impress the judges and as he rode out of the pen, it seemed that he had impressed his team also.

"Like I said. You've got the right bloodlines," his father said proudly.

"And it helps that you can train an ass kickin' good horse," Colton said, praising his father in return.

It didn't take long for Colton to get swamped with phone numbers after his score hit the top of the leader board. Mostly they were from people only enquiring, although with Cutter behind him on his team, there was going to be no stopping him now.

As it turned out, being Cutter Jones' son did have its advantages, and Colton was prepared to ride them all the way. He was a cowboy who loved what he did. He was a man who was on a mission to succeed. Colton Jones was a cowboy who was rising to the top.

Chapter Twenty

After spending all night and all day alone, Dakota had her way with Jake more than once. Not that he put up much of a fight. They had barely made it outside the front door since he arrived on Friday afternoon, only to feed the horses and have lunch in the warmth of the sun. The rest of their time was spent upstairs in her room, and Dakota had fallen more in love now than ever before.

It was early into the afternoon and their need to lie tangled up together was seriously interrupted when there was a loud knock on the door, followed by a man's voice. "Jake. Are you in here?"

It was his father. Jake opened his eyes wide and looked at Dakota. He checked the time quickly. "Oh damn it. It's past one o'clock. My dad's here already," he said, and he scrambled for his jeans and hopped into them one leg at a time. "Where's my shirt?" he asked, looking around frantically when he couldn't find it.

Dakota lay back in the bed fully naked, only covered up by the sheets and she laughed at him.

"Help me find it," he said, scanning the floor.

He checked under the bed. In the bed. Under the pillow. He couldn't find it anywhere. "You're not helping," he pointed out. He was lifting up everything and looking everywhere. His shirt was nowhere to be found. "I can't go down looking like this."

"Why not? You look really good if you ask me," she said, playing with him.

"If you don't help me find it, he could come up here and find us."

Sitting up on her elbows, Dakota was still finding it funny. But not as funny if it was her father downstairs calling out. That would have been tragic.

"Jake," she said to get his attention.

He stopped to look at her and she pointed to the bedside lamp. His shirt was hanging off the side of the lamp from when Dakota had ripped it off his back earlier and thrown it aside. Where it landed, neither of them cared.

Throwing it on, he raced out the door to stop his father wandering through the house to look for him.

"Hey, Dad," Jake said casually, when he walked into the kitchen.

Johnny was staring at the wall of photos, remembering every photograph that was ever taken. He was in quite a few with his best friend, from their childhood riding horses to the day they got their licences to drive. It reminded him of how close they used to be and he felt regretful of everything that had happened, making him want it back.

He straightened himself up and looked to his son. "Afternoon," Johnny said. "Did you just get out of bed?"

"No sir," Jake replied a little too fast, making it sound as if it was a lie. "Why would you think that?" he asked.

"Well I don't know. Maybe because your hair is all messed up and you look like shit," Johnny said. Jake ran his hand through the back of his hair, making it sit flat. "But mostly because your shirt is on inside out and your face has got guilt written all over it."

Jake looked down at his shirt, noticing that he had thrown it on without even looking at it. He had been caught out and he didn't know what to say or how to explain himself. Luckily for him, it was his father standing in the kitchen and not Dakota's.

"I shouldn't be in here," Johnny stated, feeling uncomfortable. "And knowing what you've been doing up there, you shouldn't be either. Meet me outside in five minutes. We'll get this job done so I can go."

Johnny turned around and left the house, waiting for Jake on the porch.

He ran back upstairs where Dakota was sitting up, waiting for him. "What did he say?" she asked.

"He said go up there and finish what you were doing with Dakota. You don't wanna disappoint her or keep her waiting all day," Jake teased, sounding believable.

Dakota fell for it. "Did he really?"

Jake gave her a look as if to say I can't believe you fell for that. "No ma'am. Of course he didn't," he said, and she swung the pillow at him.

He took his shirt off and turned it in the right way. "I shouldn't be long. Are you gonna be okay until I get back?"

"I'll miss you," she flirted.

He sat on the side of the bed and leaned over her. "But not as much as I'll miss you," he said. "And luckily for us, we still have one more night before your parents get home."

She reached for his hat and put it on his head, pinching the corners and making it sharp, just the way she liked it. "I'll be waiting for you."

He leaned down and gave her a soft kiss before he left the room.

With twenty seconds left on the clock, Raylee was sitting in the corner of the pen, holding the cattle together and watching her son. It was going to be close, as he was chasing the high score on the leader board and was reeling it in.

He had been having a flawless run, until the cow challenged the horse and tried to blast its way through. The pressure was now on. Westyn and his horse were experienced enough to block its assault and put it back in its place, keeping it at bay. That was close, Cutter thought, and although Westyn had the control back, it was enough to lose valuable points in the dying seconds.

When the time was up, the buzzer sounded and Westyn pulled the horse to a stop.

"Hey. Don't worry about it," Cutter assured him when he rode over. "That cow would've got past the best of them. You did well to stop it."

As far as the judges were concerned, the damage was done. Westyn still scored well, but not well enough to take a placing. His sixth place overall disappointed him, as he finished five points below Kyle Parker. That fired him up. All he wanted to do, was take a win for Chelsea, especially against her arrogant brother.

It was Sunday morning and they were all packed up and back on the road before lunch. Raylee just happened to slip a sneaky phone call through to Dakota, to let her know that they were on their way home. She didn't want any surprises for Dakota or her father, after their unexpected early draw in the second herd and their early departure from the show.

"Do you think she knows?" Jake asked, after Dakota hung up the phone.

"I don't know," she replied honestly. "I couldn't tell. But she did call to warn me."

"I think it would be a good idea if I'm not here when your dad gets home," Jake said. He had thought about it all weekend and it was playing on his mind.

Dakota was quick to agree. "Maybe you're right. As much as I don't want to hide, I don't want to make him feel any worse about it than he already does," she said. "But we still have a couple of hours," she suggested, wondering what they could possibly do to pass the time.

There was no second guessing. They had already been to the barn and fed the horses, and had a nice Sunday morning breakfast on the front porch. Now they had time to kill before Jake needed to up and disappear.

Driving down the driveway towards the barn gave Cutter an unsettling feeling. He was unsure about what he was going to be faced with when he saw his daughter. He was half expecting the worst and hoping for the best, not knowing if he would be able to tell the difference. He pulled the truck up outside the barn and everyone piled out, getting straight to work unloading the horses. Looking at the house gave him a sickly feeling.

Cutter had been through some tough times in his life and as far as he was concerned, this moment was up there with the worst of them.

Leading the gelding into the barn, he was surprised when Dakota came out with her horse, all saddled up and ready to ride. There was apprehension from both sides, until she gave him a warm smile and looked him in the eye. He couldn't read into what had happened while he was away, but he was pleased to see her.

"Where're you going?" he asked, after he gave her a kiss on the cheek.

"I'm going to the resting place. Aren't you coming?" she asked.

It was Mary-Ann's birthday and before everyone was settled in for the afternoon, Dakota thought it would be a good idea to ride there now, as a family.

"Where's Jake?" he asked. It wasn't that he really wanted to know the answer, as much as he wanted to piece together the weekend in his head.

"He's at home. Why would you think he would be here?" she asked.

"I just thought," he tried to say before he found some peace of mind. "Did you have a good weekend? You look like you have everything under control."

"Yes sir. Everything's good," she confirmed. "It was a quiet weekend... Here," she said, taking the rope, "let me saddle your horse."

Cutter watched her tie up the horses then go into the tack room looking for his ranch saddle. She gave him no sign that anything had changed while he was away and he decided that he'd rather not know anyway.

Before anyone had gone to the house, the family were riding out the gate. It was one of the worst days on Cutter's calendar, but knowing that he was surrounded by his wife and kids as they rode together to the resting place, made him feel comforted and content.

It had been a long time since he had ridden the boundary, leaving his sons to take care of everything. He had missed this. The ranch and cutting had been his life and it was not easy to step away from both and he decided that as of next week, he was getting back in the saddle to get behind the boys, on the ranch and in the cutting pen.

"What're you thinking?" Raylee asked, while they were riding close together. The kids had ridden away to walk through a lazy mob of cattle and the boys were encouraging Dakota to cut one out and put her hand down.

Cutter was thinking of many things. Mostly about his family. "I'm just thinking how lucky I am to have met you," he said, making her wonder where that had come from.

She loved to hear it, although she didn't know what had inspired him. "Why?" she asked curiously.

"Because you have given me three great kids," he said thankfully. "Look at them. Look at us. I couldn't have asked for anything more out of my life and it's all because of you."

Raylee felt the same way. She had grown up with what most people would want in life. Everything had been at her fingertips, her father made sure of that. Although money couldn't buy what she had right there in front of her. A happy family.

They looked over at their kids. They were subtly surrounding the mob, coming in steadily from all directions, keeping quiet. Dakota went straight for the middle while the boys held them together. This was not planned or rehearsed. They would do this whenever they saw an opportunity and their parents watched, admiring how it was second nature to them. They just loved to do it.

"Go, Kotie," Cutter yelled out when she had her hand down and held that cow out from the mob. "She gets that from you," he said to Raylee.

"Me? I think she gets that from you," she said in return. "Look at her go."

They kept riding, letting the kids play around before they left the mob and caught up to their parents who were now in the field of flowers. Both Cutter and Raylee were leaning down, picking a couple of bunches for the special people in their lives, the people who were responsible for shaping and guiding them into the parents they had become. Macca, Mary-Ann and Marnie. Although Raylee had never met Cutter's parents, she knew him well enough to know what they were like as parents. They shone through him every day.

The kids all got out of their saddles and messed around among the flowers. Colton tackled his brother to the ground and wrestled with him, making Dakota pounce on top to join in on the fun. They hadn't done this for years, and their laughter echoed through the ranch, capturing their parents happiness.

Everything was back to how it used to be.

Riding through, the flowers were deep, brushing Raylee's boots as she rode towards the gate. There was a peacefulness that was adding to the family's love for one another and a slight breeze that was cooling to the warm day. "What's that? Cutter asked, when the resting place came into view.

They were all stopped at the gate, looking.

No one spoke. Cutter couldn't take his eyes off it, and he unlatched the gate and spurred his horse to ride over, wanting to get a better look. When he neared, he went straight to foot and tied the horse up to the rail, not moving his eyes away. He was speechless. Taking it all in. He hadn't been to the resting place since Marnie's birthday and was now overwhelmed. How did he not know about this?

Raylee joined him, equally surprised and when everyone tied up their horses, it was Colton who stood next to his father. "I wanted to do this for you," he said, looking at him.

Cutter swallowed hard the emotion that was starting to rise up into his throat. "I can't believe you did this." Seeing Macca's truck sitting in its own purpose built yard next to the resting place pulled on his heartstrings.

"Well I didn't do it alone," Colton added, and Cutter looked to Westyn.

"Hey, don't look at me," Westyn said. "I've been going to school."

Cutter knew that it couldn't have been Dakota, so he looked back to Colton, expecting that it was Jake who was in on it too.

"Johnny helped me," Colton announced.

That completely floored him. It was as if he hadn't heard right. "Johnny?" Cutter asked. "When did you see Johnny?"

"My first day back," Colton said. "I didn't waste any time and I wanted to make things right," he explained. "When I asked for his help, he said yes. He didn't even have to think about it. He wanted to do this for you too."

All this time, Cutter presumed that Johnny had wiped him as a friend after their scuffle in Nashville and their run-in at the hospital. Little did he know that Johnny was working with his son to make this happen.

He looked down and read the sign that was leaning against the front fender. Macca's Truck. RIP.

"Do you like the sign?" Colton asked. "Avery made it for you."

He loved the sign. He loved the yard and it was the perfect place for the truck to rest alongside his father. He looked over to Macca's grave, his mom and Marnie's. They were all together now.

It was an old oilcan that sat next to the sign that caught Raylee's attention. She had been silently sobbing, not saying a word. She opened the gate and took the flowers in, placing them in the oilcan and she stood up, looking at the truck and it hit her just how much she missed it.

A gentle squeeze on the back of her neck brought it out of her, and she buried her face into Cutter's shoulder when he placed his arm around her for comfort.

Right on time, the O'Brien family were making their way through the last gate. Cutter was the last to turn around to see their neighbors and best friends riding towards the resting place. Not only had they not talked since the dramatic scene at the hospital, but they had not seen each other in months and Cutter felt anxious, happy, and strange all at the same time.

It was now even more overwhelming when the kids all stood back and watched their parents. Johnny didn't hesitate to show Cutter what he was feeling, what was going through his mind and what he really thought of him. That was the moment Raylee fell apart completely, watching Cutter fall to pieces when Johnny gave him a bro-hug and wouldn't let go. There was a forgiveness that was instant. There was no need to look back. Everything that had happened was now behind them.

"Thank you," Cutter said, looking at his father's truck.

"We had some good times in that truck. You, me and Macca," Johnny reminded him. He was remembering back to when it was brand new and they'd all pile in of a weekend and drive to the shows, before Macca fell sick and it was retired to the garage. "And it seems that our kids did too," he added, looking over at Colton and Avery, who were standing next to each other, not too close.

"And who knows," Cutter said. "You may not think so now, but maybe one day we'll laugh about that too." Cutter had already relaxed about it. He just wasn't sure where Johnny was at.

Raylee and Emma were still catching up. They were crying, talking and laughing. In that order. It pleased the kids, who were all standing around, letting their parents find the friendship that they had lost.

They looked to their kids, all standing in a line. Jake was up close behind Dakota with his arms wrapped around her shoulders. Westyn stood in the middle, shadowed by his brother who was trying to edge closer to Avery, without any success. Their children completed them. They were the future of both ranches, but most of all, they were family, just like their parents. Cutter and Johnny could only have hoped that their kids would end up as close as they were. Never did they expect that they would end up as close as they had.

"Hey, Jake," Colton said, so that only the five of them could hear. "You should go over there and tell my dad now." He figured that he knew what was going on at the ranch while they were away. He wasn't stupid.

"What? No," Jake was quick to respond.

"Go on. It'll get Avery and me off the hook," he said. "Unless he scares you?"

"I'm not scared of your dad," Jake lied. He was not scared, he was completely terrified of Cutter after the weekend he'd just had with his daughter, and he hoped that it wasn't obvious. All he had to do, was look her father in the eye and keep it together. That was all.

The kids walked over and stood by the gate and the two families gathered around the truck, admiring the yard that Colton had built with Johnny's help and the sign that Avery had made. They talked like old friends again. Like nothing had ever happened. There was no division or apprehension. No silent moments or awkwardness. It was like old times and they picked up where they ended it months ago, like no time had passed at all.

To show Avery that there were no hard feelings hanging over them, Cutter walked over and gave her a hug. "I can't tell you how sorry I am," she said, letting a couple of tears roll down her face. The only way Avery knew that she was forgiven, was when Cutter gave her a squeeze and kissed her on the top of her head.

He walked the line of kids, giving Colton an air swing at his gut, making him jump out of the way fast to be sure that he missed. Colton laughed at his playful game. "Too slow," he taunted his dad.

Westyn had been standing there watching the afternoon unfold. He had nothing to do with the truck or the dispute with their neighbors, and was only looking in as an outsider. He'd been keeping to himself all these months, like he always did. His father stood face on and looked at him, and Westyn caught a glimpse of the man he was becoming, until his father pulled his hat down low so that it covered his sight.

As Cutter edged closer, it was Jake who was feeling the guilt. The fire rose from his stomach to his chest in an instant, and he felt a burning sensation all over when Cutter gave Dakota a kiss on the cheek. This was the man that Jake admired and respected. The one person who he'd never want to let down or do wrong by. A father figure, a role model, a friend. Someone who he trusted with his life and in return, trusted him to take care of his daughter.

He just couldn't help it that he had fallen in love with her.

Keep calm, stay focussed and look him in the eye. Jake's thoughts were going through his head so fast, that he couldn't concentrate on what to say next. All he had to do, was hide the truth from him. But when Dakota stood aside, Cutter grabbed Jake on the shoulder and his eyes hit the ground. As much as Jake tried, he couldn't look at him and Cutter knew straight away.

He squeezed Jake's shoulder and kept looking at him, wanting to look deeply into his eyes for a sign of the truth, although Jake wouldn't allow it.

"She finally drove you beyond crazy… didn't she?" Cutter asked reluctantly, looking past his daughter at him.

Jake didn't answer and Cutter was silently gutted. There was nothing he could do about it now and he knew it. His little girl was all grown up and had found the man that she wanted to be with. The man who would take a higher place in her life. He'd always looked to Jake like a son and today, he had to decide if he was going to show them both what he was really feeling or bury it deep inside.

When Dakota threw herself at her father and hugged him tight, she softened him. "I still love you, Dad," she said quietly, so that no one else could hear. "And I always will."

It hit him in the heart. Whoever came into her life and stole her love from him, couldn't steal the one thing that he owned. The one thing that was his. He would always be her father. "And I'll always love you too, Kotie," he whispered back.

While Cutter still had Dakota in his arms, he extended his hand to Jake. He was standing behind her and he finally looked at him, only guessing what was going through her father's mind. He reached out and grabbed Cutter's hand and felt an extra firm grip that was almost threatening. "You remember our deal?" Cutter said firmly.

Jake did, and he renewed that promise. "I'll take good care of her," he stated, feeling an acceptance that was somewhat forced.

"Dinner is at our house," Emma announced loudly, to break up the moment that was getting way too deep and emotional, and everyone left the truck in the newly built yard and went for their horses. Untying them and getting back into the saddle, everyone was ready to ride to the O'Brien ranch for the afternoon.

Cutter was about to ride away when it struck him. "Wait," he said, then he landed back on the grass making everyone look at what he was doing. "I have one more thing I need to do before I leave," he added, holding everyone up.

He swung open the gate of the resting place and went in, kneeling down in front of his mother's grave.

It was his mother's birthday, and with everything going on with the truck and their friends, he'd nearly forgotten. He stared at the headstone and read it, like he would do every time he visited, and he wondered if his kids looked at him the same way that he looked at his mom. Admiring everything that she was, Cutter held her in a special place that could never be touched.

There was an unbreakable love that was his alone. A love that had no boundaries. Mary-Ann had led him to the life that he loved and shaped him into the man he became. A loving son. An adoring husband. A caring father. She was everything to him and when the breeze picked up and gently swirled the leaves on the ground, he closed his eyes and felt close to her.

It was a touch on the shoulder that brought his thoughts straight back. He was kneeling in Johnny's shadow. "Everyone's gone," Johnny said, to let him know that the family were on their way back to the house, leaving them to ride home together.

It was all the time Cutter needed and he stood up and closed the gate behind him. It was now a time to look ahead. A new beginning for both their families, and as they rode away, it was a time to catch up on all they had missed.

"So, Colton tells me you quit?" Johnny asked, wanting to hear it from his best friend, as if he didn't believe it from anyone else.

"Yep," Cutter confirmed. "I haven't cut a cow in months."

"Well what the hell would you do that for, bro?" he asked, showing his disapproval.

They were already back on track.

They could see their families in the distance, as they rode side by side as they had done since they were kids themselves. Riding through the gate into the field of flowers, Cutter looked back at the resting place.

It was the most perfect place for the truck to rest and rust, and he wondered why he hadn't thought of it himself. There was peace in his heart when he rode away, knowing that the ranches were back together again and everything that had torn the two families apart, was now left behind with Macca's truck.

They were still a long way behind everyone when they closed the gate.

"Hey, you wanna race home?" Johnny asked, and Cutter didn't need to be asked twice.

Acknowledgements

For those who have read the first two books in the series, The Cutter, and The Cowboy Code, and have loved them both, then this book has been written for you. There was not a time during writing that I did not think of our seven children, how different they are from each other, and how they have all challenged us through their growing years. They all inspired the characters in this book.

My thanks go out to family and friends who have been a huge support.

To Juliann, once again you have given me your tick of approval, and that means so much to me. Thank you x

Thank you to Anders for taking the time to do the cover shot. Although I had to twist your arm and talk you into it, it didn't take long to capture the image that I had inside my head. Thank you x

To Cilento Publishing and the editing team, again you have delivered. It's always such a great pleasure working with you and I learn more from you with every book.

To my mom, another manuscript has been transformed into a book. I know that you are enjoying the series as much as I have enjoyed writing them. You've always been so encouraging, thank you x

To Greg, nobody will know the hours that have gone into writing The Cutter Series, but you. You have seen the long nights of writing after work has stopped for the day. I have asked you endless questions about horses, tack, and cutting, and you have so patiently talked me through it. My dream for writing finally happened because of your encouragement. Thank you xx

For the readers who have read the books and given me your feedback, thank you. As an author, there is nothing better than to hear just how much you have enjoyed the books so far, and I'm so certain that you are going to love this one! You don't have to be a cowboy, cowgirl, ride a horse, or live in the country to hear the messages that are hidden in these stories.

Finally, to all the cutters, lopers, officials, members, spectators, family, and to everyone on the team, enjoy the ride!

Linda

Note to the reader –

Thank you for reading The Cutter Series. In the world of publishing, where millions of book titles are available online at the click of a button, it's extremely difficult to get noticed. However, the reader has the power to boost searches by giving a star rating and writing a review.

This review can make all the difference to the next potential reader. If you can take the time, please leave a review on Amazon (if you are a regular customer) and Goodreads (the reviewing website) *Visit www.goodreads.com and register *Search by title - The Cutter, The Cowboy Code or Cowboy Rising and/or The Cutter Series.

*Leave a star rating and review And lastly, tell your friends. Word of mouth is still a great way to share what you have liked.

Thank you in advance!

Linda

x

www.ingramcontent.com/pod-product-compliance
Lightning Source LLC
Chambersburg PA
CBHW022025120726
47901CB00008BA/2250